Rock Legend

Rock Legend

Nothing but Trouble, Book Two

TARA LEIGH

New York   Boston

Copyright © 2018 by Tara Thompson
Excerpt from *Rock Rebel* copyright © 2018 by Tara Thompson
Cover design by Brian Lemus. Cover images © Shutterstock and iStock.
Cover copyright © 2018 by Hachette Book Group, Inc.

Forever Yours
Hachette Book Group
1290 Avenue of the Americas, New York, NY 10104
forever-romance.com
twitter.com/foreverromance

First published as an ebook and as a print on demand: July 2018

Forever Yours is an imprint of Grand Central Publishing. The Forever Yours name and logo are trademarks of Hachette Book Group, Inc.

The publisher is not responsible for websites (or their content) that are not owned by the publisher.

The Hachette Speakers Bureau provides a wide range of authors for speaking events. To find out more, go to www.hachettespeakersbureau.com or call (866) 376-6591.

ISBNs: 978-1-5387-1281-8 (ebook), 978-1-5387-1280-1 (print on demand)

ALSO BY TARA LEIGH

The Nothing but Trouble Series

Rock King

The Billionaire Bosses Series

Penthouse Player
Deal Breaker

To my readers.
Without you, torturing my imaginary friends
wouldn't be nearly as much fun!

Acknowledgments

A huge thank-you to my agent extraordinaire, Jessica Alvarez of BookEnds Literary Agency. Your critiques and career guidance are invaluable!

Lexi Smail—you have been an absolute dream to work with and have spoiled me for all future editors. Thank you for seeing the potential in this series and inviting me to join the Forever family of authors. Many thanks also to the rest of the Forever team: the talented cover designers, the publicity team, Kallie Shimek, and everyone else who has played a role in bringing the Nothing but Trouble boys (and the women who love them) to life.

To my readers—you are EVERYTHING!!! I love reading your reviews and value your honest feedback! And all those messages/posts/tweets/e-mails you send as you're reading—they make my day! **hugs** This is my first book to release with my #TeamTL Review Team and Tara Leigh VIPs Facebook Reader Group—how did I ever write without you guys?

To all the amazing bloggers (who are always readers first)

that have championed this series—you are all rock stars! Candi Kane, you are an absolute powerhouse and beyond generous with your time and expertise. Melissa Teo (Booksmacked), I adore you for a million reasons. You are an incredible cheerleader for contemporary romance books and their authors—and the best ~~stalker~~ PA ever! Serena McDonald, thank you for always having answers to my endless questions and always pointing me in the right direction! Maria (Steamy Reads), thank you for your encouragement, gorgeous graphics, and suggesting *Rock King* to Jenny and your readers! Cristina (CristinaReads), You were the first blogger I "met" on Goodreads and were the best guide anyone could have hoped for! Amy (Obsessive Book Whore), your enthusiasm is infectious! Sarah (Musings of the Modern Belle), you come up with such creative ways to bring authors and readers together—I love it! Sue Bee, from my very first book, you have been a valuable sounding board. Thank you for all of your advice and encouragement, and especially for your unfiltered honesty. Christina Santos (Recommended Reads), I'm so glad you reached out to me—I'll Facebook "party" with you anytime! ;) Tina, Karen, Sophie, Crystal, and Vicki (Bookalicious Babes Blog), you've created one of the most supportive places for newbie authors. Thank you for being so welcoming! Jeri (Jeri's Book Addict), Eve (Between the Bookends), and Bianca (BJ's Book Blog), I love our e-mail chats! Mary (USA Today HEA), your excerpts and features are my go-to source for finding new reads, and I'm thrilled to have been included!

By the time this book goes to print, there will be many more I wish I could thank, and I'm sure I've missed people, too. Please forgive me!

There are so many authors who have been beyond generous

with their time and expertise—if I named them all, I might fill as many pages as this book! However, Alessandra Torre, your invaluable website www.alessandratorreink.com is a must for every new author, and you have built a virtual cheering section via Facebook. And Al Jackson, thank you for setting the bar when it comes to rock star romance. My In The Loop Group authors—love you ladies!

To RWA and everyone I've met through this incredible organization.

Lauren Layne and Anthony LeDonne of Last Word Designs, thank you for my gorgeous logo and website, www.taraleigh-books.com!

Jessica Hildreth, thank you for all the gorgeous teasers!

Dr. Tara Kerner, thank you for helping me figure out how to get Landon and Jake into the same rehab facility.

Amy Bernheim, thank you for explaining the type of injury that could give a drummer problems.

Jessica Estep of Inkslinger PR—you rock! Thank you for your insight and hard work. Oh the places we'll go! ;)

Deb and Drue of Buoni Amici Press—thanks for bringing this newbie up to speed and spreading the word about this book!

Moments by Andrea, thank you for the fabulous head shot.

To my aunts Jill and Joan—I love seeing all your posts of support!!

I am lucky to have a great group of girlfriends surrounding me. You know who you are—and I'm sorry for ignoring your calls when I'm writing!

My neighbor Cindy, you are a wonderful friend to me and an absolute blessing to my kids. Moving next door to you was one of the smartest decisions Stephen and I ever made! Thank you for being one of my first readers and catching even the tiniest typos!

Grandma, you left me nearly twenty years ago, and not a day goes by that I don't miss you. For any smokers reading this—put the cigarette down. Think of the people in your life who will one day watch you struggle to breathe and, when you lose that battle, will miss you desperately.

Thank you to my mom for never ripping all those "bodice-rippers" out of my hands as a teen/tween, and to my dad for showing me what it means to work hard. (Who needs weekends or vacations, anyway?)

Stephen, thank you for being a wonderful husband and supporting my dreams. I love you. Logan, Chloe, and Pierce, thank you for being so considerate of my writing time. I am blessed to be your mother.

Our lives are enriched by our sweet rescue puppy, Pixie. The wonderful organization that brought Pixie into our lives is Goofy Foot Dog Rescue, and if you would like to welcome a dog into your family or donate to their organization, please visit their website: www.goofyfootrescue.org.

And if you would like to see more pictures of Pixie (and who wouldn't?) please sign up for my newsletter at www.taraleighbooks.com—she's my writing buddy!

Rock Legend

Chapter One

Piper

I would have missed the call, but I'd just flung my purse into my car, the contents spilling out onto the passenger-side floor mat like a burst piñata. Despite the tears clouding my vision, it was impossible to ignore the flashing letters—DELANEY FRASER—vibrating from within a sea of tampons, makeup tubes, and spare change.

Unable to check the impulse, I reached for it, taking a second to wipe at my wet eyes before swiping my thumb across the screen. "Hi, Delaney."

It sounded like a frog had crawled into my throat. If I was lucky, Delaney would be too polite to mention it.

"Piper, are you sick?"

Of course I wasn't lucky. I'd never been before, why should today be any different?

But despite the cocoon of self-pity I wanted to wrap myself in, I couldn't miss the genuine concern bleeding from Delaney's voice.

Not that I deserved it.

Delaney and I had known each other since nursery school back in Bronxville, the suburb of New York City where we'd both grown up. From throwing sand in her face rather than sharing my pail and shovel, to snubbing her in favor of the mean girls clique in high school, I'd done nothing to deserve Delaney's concern, or her friendship.

The truth was, Delaney's *niceness* had always scared me. I had secrets to keep, even back then. *Especially* back then. I couldn't afford to let my guard down for a minute. And being friends with a girl like Delaney—someone who cared about more than just the labels sewn inside her clothes or her boyfriend of the month—terrified me.

Crazily enough, Delaney Fraser was now my closest friend. My only friend, actually. As a public relations assistant for one of the hottest talent managers in Hollywood, I had yet to master work-life balance. But with Delaney clear across the country finishing up her degree at NYU, my overscheduled calendar wasn't an issue for us.

Forcing a huge, fake smile on my face even though she couldn't see me, I automatically shifted into my default mode: Fake It Till You Make It. Maybe that was why I'd been so drawn to Tinseltown. Here, whether you had your SAG card or not, everyone was an actor. "Nope. I'm great. How are you?"

There was a pause. "Piper, you don't sound great."

Delaney was no one's fool, and she'd picked up on the truth. A truth I wasn't ready to admit yet. It was too new, the wound too raw. "Of course I am," I insisted, even though it was obvious

I was one step away from falling apart. "And I'm going to be late for work, so…"

"Wait."

My finger hovered over the END CALL button on my screen. As much as I wanted to, I couldn't hang up on Delaney.

"I was calling to tell you that I just booked a flight to LAX. I want to surprise Shane at his show tomorrow."

The knot in my stomach drew tighter; the warm, stuffy air inside the car choking me. If Delaney was coming to Nothing but Trouble's show tomorrow, I would need to book a car service from the airport to the venue, get her an all-access backstage pass, a hotel room—no, she would be staying with Shane, of course…

Details. My mind latched on to the expanding to-do list in my mind, anything to avoid thinking about what I'd just seen or a certain member of the band I'd have to avoid tomorrow. "What time are you getting in? Do you have an outfit to wear? I'll arrange for hair and makeup—"

"Piper." She cut me off with a laugh. "You don't have to fuss over me anymore."

That wasn't exactly true. Her relationship with Shane Hawthorne was no longer a press stunt, but as long as Shane and his multi-platinum band, Nothing but Trouble, were my boss's biggest clients, part of my job still involved fussing over Delaney.

"And how exactly would I explain leaving you to fend off the horde of paparazzi that stake out LAX to my boss?" Although Delaney wasn't a celebrity herself, after the media circus surrounding Shane had gotten ahold of her, her face was nearly as recognizable—and profitable—as her rock star boyfriend's. "Believe me," I continued, "fussing over you is a hell of a lot easier that trying to placate Travis Taggert."

"I don't know how you put up with that man," she conceded.

Right now, I was pretty sure all men were the scum of the earth, but as far as bosses went, Travis wasn't bad. And it was because of him that Delaney and I had reconnected.

When Travis had been faced with the unenviable task of informing an A-list actor that his director had hired a body double for his upcoming sex scene because his ass wasn't as finely sculpted as it had been a decade ago, Travis and I decided to strategize, or maybe just procrastinate, over drinks.

Delaney had been our waitress.

Neither Delaney nor I realized it at the time, but Travis had taken one look at her and instantly known she would be perfect for Shane.

As always, Travis's instincts had been spot on. Once Shane and Delaney became an item, I was assigned to manage her introduction to Shane's possessive fans. At the time, it had been a huge promotion, but because of our prior relationship, Travis wanted me on board.

The moment Delaney moved to New York for school, I'd asked to be taken off the Nothing but Trouble account.

Rock stars were not my thing.

Not anymore.

"He's my boss, so it kind of comes with the territory. When are you getting in?" I might not be assigned to the band anymore, but I still pitched in where Delaney was concerned. We spent the next few minutes going over her travel itinerary, and after we hung up I jotted down notes in the planner I kept with me at all times.

The knock on my window made me jump, my pen streaking across the page. I'd forgotten that I was still sitting in the parking lot right outside my building.

Adam was standing there, looking regretful and apologetic, and irritatingly pulled together. Had he taken the time to shower after I ran out his door?

I didn't even bother rolling down the window. I had nothing to say to my boyfriend.

Correction: *ex*-boyfriend, as of twenty minutes ago.

Starting the ignition with a shaking hand, I backed out of my parking spot, not caring if I ran over Adam's toes. Not caring if I ran over any part of Adam's anatomy, although there was one in particular I would have preferred.

Delaney might have found her Prince Charming, but so far I was more of a frog magnet.

Landon

I should buy stock in Trojans.

The random thought skittered across my brain as I flushed the condom down the toilet, my gut twisting as I watched it shudder and swirl before finally disappearing. I know flushing latex is bad for the plumbing and the environment, but when the condom is filled with *my* sperm—I can't go leaving that shit around.

Over the years I'd dealt with more baby-daddy scandals than I cared to think about. None of them had turned out to be valid, and I intended to keep it that way.

Forever.

Not only was I the drummer of Nothing but Trouble, the most successful band of the decade—according to the tweet that just vibrated through my phone—I was also…

Wait for it…

The Most Fuckable Rock Star on the Planet.

Apparently, I'm a legend.

Am I surprised? Fuck, no.

It's a reputation I've earned behind my drum kit *and* behind closed doors. In dark corners of dingy bars and in full view of anyone with eyes. I am nothing if not generous with my skills. Spreading the wealth and all that.

But when it came to my sperm, I knew better than to leave it unattended.

Ridiculous, really. I mean, chicks weren't exactly lining up to bring me home to meet Mom and Dad. And I would hardly fit in at a PTA meeting—not with my tattoos and piercings and penchant for illegal substances washed down with hundred-proof liquor.

Turning on the tap, I splashed water on my face, pushing rough, drumstick-callused hands through my hair. I didn't bother checking out my reflection in the mirror. I knew what I looked like, saw myself reflected in the hungry eyes of people wanting a piece of me every damn day.

I was desperate for a shower, but that would have to wait. I needed to rouse the girls in my bed and get them out first. Otherwise they were bound to wake up while I was scrubbing their scent from my skin and strip the hotel suite of everything I'd touched. Clothes, sheets, dirty glasses still sticky with the residue of whatever liquor I poured down my throat last night—given the opportunity, they'd all be up on eBay before I reached for a towel.

I'm living the dream.

Except that when I wasn't onstage or in a recording studio pounding away at my custom built drum kit, it felt more like a nightmare.

When I was playing, my chaotic thoughts suddenly made sense. I could spot patterns. Arrangements of energy to be identified and interpreted, set to a unique rhythm.

From the relentless noise inside my mind, I made music.

But when I didn't have a pair of drumsticks in my hand, I spent most of my time doing another kind of banging.

Hence, the two girls in my bed.

Because otherwise I'd be banging my head against the wall.

Maybe I should have checked into the hotel alone last night. Today, of all days, I wasn't fit company for anyone.

One day out of three hundred and sixty-five. A day spent trying to forget about what I'd done, the lives I'd destroyed, the family I'd decimated.

My family.

Lost in an oblivion where yesterday never happened and tomorrow didn't exist.

Unfortunately, I had a show tonight.

It was my own damn fault. If I'd paid more attention when Shane had thrown out potential dates for a concert benefitting the foundation he'd started in the name of a childhood friend, I could have vetoed this one.

Except, as usual, I'd been breezing through life, not sweating the details. Agreeing to everything. Caring about nothing.

Tonight's show was important to Shane, so it was important to me. Even though we were playing a venue just an hour south of L.A., our tour coordinator always booked us into a nearby hotel for the night of the show. I'd checked in early. Wouldn't be the first time I drank the day away in a hotel room. Played a perfect set even when I couldn't walk a straight line.

But I couldn't play if the guys couldn't find me, and if I stayed in L.A. I was liable to make the rounds of the seediest bars I could find and pass out somewhere I shouldn't be…and wake up, too late, with someone I didn't know. I might be a fuck-up, but when it came to our band, I didn't fuck around.

Sighing, I made my way into the bedroom. Time to get rid of the girls I'd brought with me. "All right." I rapped on the headboard. "Time to get up, I've got sound check."

The one with dark hair stirred slightly. Not enough. We'd just finished round three—no way could she be sleeping so soundly already.

I reached down to nudge her shoulder, and she countered by rolling over and trying to pull me back into bed. Normally I'd have let her. Hell, on any other morning, I'd have still been between them.

See? This day brings out the worst in me.

Instead, I wrapped my hands around her shoulders and tugged her upright. The sheet fell away from her body, exposing a pair of large breasts I loved last night but looked more like pointy flotation devices this morning.

Backing away, I stalked to the windows and yanked at the drapes. Sunlight flooded into the room, eliciting a pair of irate groans.

The blonde sat up. "C'mon, Landon, what's your rush?" Her attempt at a seductive pout was hindered by the streaks of makeup crisscrossing her cheeks.

"Sorry, ladies." I spread my hands out, gritting my teeth as I forced an easygoing attitude. "Gotta give the fans a good show tonight."

"How about we give you a good show right now?" The brunette rose onto her knees, turning to her friend, one hand plowing through the blonde's sex mussed mane, the other hand cupping her breast. She lowered her mouth, giving her lips a lick as she glanced my way. "You know you want to."

An all-too-familiar blend of lust and loathing curdled within my gut, and I rubbed a palm over my face to keep my expression neutral. Watching two gorgeous women go at it, knowing I could join in the party at any moment was tempting, despite being a frequent opportunity. But not today.

Somehow I managed to lure them out of bed and into their clothes, although not without calling our show coordinator to come to the room with two tickets and backstage passes for tonight. Lynne didn't even bat an eye at the request, or the pouting women I shoved at her. She was used to it.

Once I was finally alone, I sagged back against the door, thumping my head against it once, twice, three times.

Growing up in a working-class neighborhood at the edge of the Mojave Desert, no one would have laid odds that I'd become famous. Infamous, maybe. Notorious, probably.

But successful? Never.

Not that I could blame them. I sure hadn't believed it myself.

I didn't come into my own—if that ridiculous expression made any sense—until I arrived in Los Angeles and connected with Shane Hawthorne. We'd both had a lot to prove, although I didn't realize that he needed to succeed as badly as I did until recently.

At the time, we'd just been finding our footing, connecting with other musicians, playing in shitty venues for nothing but beer and blow jobs from groupies who would happily take care of our *equipment.*

There had been one person who believed in me though.

At least, until I fucked her over, too.

A blonde-haired, blue-eyed, sharp-tongued temptress—who

should have been too smart to fall for me. That beautiful face of hers always buried in a book, studying her ass off at UCLA. Focused on her goals, her résumé, her fucking five-year plan. I should have left her alone and walked away, contented myself with women who told me exactly what I wanted to hear. Preferably garbled moans around my cock. But I was stupid, and selfish. So fucking selfish.

I made it my mission to woo the college freshman—pursuing her as fiercely as my music career. Giving her my heart with one breath and promising the moon with the next.

Until the day I had to make a choice.

My girl or my career.

I chose music. Fame and fortune. Hollywood Hills and chemically induced thrills.

Of course, I'd spent every day since then trying to convince myself I didn't regret it.

Want to know the difference between a legend and a fairy tale?

Only one of them ends happily ever after.

Chapter Two

Piper

I spent the entire day praying for storms over the Midwest, or a glitch that would ground all cross-country flights. A mild case of food poisoning, perhaps, or a sudden head cold that prevented Delaney from flying. Anything to keep her in New York.

Anything to keep me from tonight's Nothing but Trouble concert.

By the time I faced the truth, that Delaney's flight had taken off—with her—I'd waited so long to book a ride that the company we normally used had no openings. And neither did any of the others I'd used in the past.

It was awards season in Los Angeles. I should have known.

If I drove my own car, it would mean subjecting Delaney to the mercy of the paparazzi while we spent twenty minutes walking from security to the parking lot.

Which was why, when the only livery service with an available vehicle arrived, it wasn't a basic black Lincoln. Or basic black at all. No, my ride was a silver stretch monstrosity, complete with a driver wearing a cheap tux who waved at me from across the street because he'd been afraid to navigate the tight turn into the parking lot of my apartment complex.

Beggars can't be choosers.

After I slid into the back of the pimped-out limo—literally, since I nearly skated right off the slippery pleather seats—I checked my phone again. And cursed. Not because Delaney's flight was late. Nope, it was *early*.

Of course it was.

Because even my most fervent hopes were ineffective.

You know what is effective?

Tequila.

I spotted the bottle tucked behind half a dozen others crowded into a built-in bar just as we pulled into LAX's arrival lane.

I'd never been one to enjoy drinking alone, although I was temped now. Somehow I dredged up enough willpower to leave the bottle untouched and head inside the terminal.

Once I had Delaney in the car with me, however, all bets were off. If she passed out on the bench seat, she couldn't exactly drag me into the arena, could she?

I am a terrible, terrible friend.

Even with the ball cap pulled low over her dark hair, Delaney was easy to spot. I shook my head at her outfit—head-to-toe lululemon and bright pink sneakers. "You've gone to the dark side, haven't you?"

Delaney stopped in front of me with her Tumi carry-on, pulling the zipper on her jacket to reveal a SoulCycle T-shirt. "Guilty as charged."

I groaned, throwing my arm around her shoulders. I tried to convert Delaney into a fellow yogi, but she'd never taken to it. Figures that she would go back east and become a SoulCycler. My butt hurt just thinking about it.

The only good thing about her outfit and our decidedly tacky ride was that we passed by the gang of photographers without even a whiff of suspicion.

"Please tell me there is something appropriate for tonight in your bag," I pleaded, suddenly realizing I'd shown up empty-handed. Had I been thinking straight, I would have brought dresses, shoes, and a full makeup bag.

Clearly, I was off my game. I'd been so distracted today, my professional mind-set had fallen by the wayside.

"Of course. Several actually, I'll let you pick."

I sighed in relief just as Delaney pulled up short, her eyes going wide as she took in the sight of our obnoxious limousine complete with coordinating driver. "Are we going to a concert or prom?"

I laughed it off. "Oh please, you wouldn't have been caught dead at prom."

"Kind of hard to go when no one asks you." Delaney spoke softly, but the flash of pain in her aquamarine eyes had me leaning against the door for support. Delaney and I weren't friends in high school, and I definitely hadn't gone out of my way to be nice to her. Back then, I'd been so concerned with maintaining my facade of "perfect daughter and popular cheerleader" I'd avoided anyone who didn't reinforce the image I was determined to project.

But I had heard what people called me behind my back.

Perfect Piper.

They needn't have whispered. I loved it. Hoped that if people said it often enough, it might actually come true.

I'm sorry, Delaney. The words were at the tip of my tongue, but what came out instead was, "And look at you now, you're Shane Hawthorne's girlfriend."

Caught somewhere between an apology and a compliment, my response lacked the benefits of either, falling flat on the dirty pavement at our feet.

I ducked into the back of the car and reached for the bottle I'd spotted earlier, brandishing it like a peace offering as Delaney crawled in after me. "Tequila?" Without waiting for an answer, I poured two shots and handed one to Delaney.

She frowned. "No limes?"

"No, unfortunately. I didn't plan ahead for this." Tossing my head back, I drained the glass with barely a wince, then looked expectantly at Delaney.

She was staring at hers, lips pursed, nose wrinkled. "I can't."

"Of course you can," I urged. "Open your mouth and swallow. It's easy." Grabbing the bottle, I poured another shot and downed it quickly.

Delaney looked at me strangely. "No. I mean, I'd rather not show up to the concert smelling like I've come from a Cinco de Mayo fiesta."

For a second I was confused, and then I remembered. *I'm worse than a bad friend, I'm an idiot.* Shane had given up hard alcohol years ago. Of course she wouldn't want to kiss him with tequila on her breath. "Crap, Delaney. I'm sorry." I took the shot glass she was holding, my head already buzzing.

Except there wasn't anywhere to put it, and I didn't want to open the window just as we were merging onto the highway. Lifting my shoulders in an awkward shrug, I swallowed it down, my stomach heaving in protest.

Delaney took the empty glass from my hand and slid it into its allotted space in the bar. "Are you okay, Piper?"

Her bewildered expression acted like a mirror, reflecting my odd behavior. "I am," I lied. "It's just been a long day." For a second I was tempted to blurt out what I'd walked in on yesterday morning, or reveal the reason behind my reluctance to attend tonight's concert.

But that would have been a mistake.

If I was going to get through tonight without shattering into a million pieces, I couldn't talk about either one.

I'd come to L.A., hoping things would be different here. That there would be less "faking it" and more "making it."

That hadn't happened. I still wasn't *enough*.

Shitty friend. Underwhelming girlfriend.

The least I could do was be a decent stylist. I jerked my chin at the small suitcase Delaney had refused to let the driver put in the trunk. "Let's figure out what you're going to wear, because I'm not letting you out of the car in that." I gestured at her workout gear, attempting a teasing smile.

By the time we pulled up to the arena, Delaney's spandex and sneakers had been replaced by a significantly sexier ensemble.

And my tequila buzz had been completely eradicated by a droning, unsettling agitation.

Pulling two all-access passes from my purse, I handed one to Delaney with a last, longing glance at the bottle she'd taken from me.

I really could have used another dose of liquid courage, but there was no time. The door was pulled open and Delaney practically bounced through it, a huge grin on her face. My own exit was significantly less enthusiastic.

Flashing the laminated cards hanging from our necks at each

security-staffed checkpoint, we made our way through the bowels of the building. The venue was crawling with people. Roadies, security, groupies, vendors, dealers, fans. Successful bands were like truffles—worth their weight in gold but smothered in sludge.

With each step, the music became louder, the rhythmic base vibrating forcefully through the soles of our feet.

Being under the same roof as Landon Cox filled me with a bizarre mix of exhilaration, dread, and absolute terror.

And the idea of actually setting eyes on him had every cell in my body screaming: *abort, abort!*

I tried to hang back as we neared the edge of the stage, but Delaney grabbed my hand and pulled me beside her. We'd arrived just in time for an explosion of fireworks, the kind that could be set off inside a packed arena. Streaks of color—neon blue and blazing white, vibrant green and blinding red—raced overhead like choreographed comets.

My heart slammed against my chest as I caught sight of Landon's blond head and shirtless torso rising above his drum kit, a plume of fog billowing around him. My breath caught in my throat, holding precious oxygen captive and rendering my brain cells useless.

Landon never played wearing a shirt, and tonight was no different. Most of his body was obscured by equipment, but one glance at his torso and arms and you knew the man was jacked. Every inch of him.

No man had a right to look that good.

Luckily, the fog and lights prevented me from getting a clear view of Landon's face. I didn't think I could have handled it.

Despite working closely with Delaney over the past year, I'd always had an excuse at the ready when it came to being around the band. The few times my presence had been required, I'd kept a low profile, taking care to stay in the background, as far from the guys as possible. At least, from one guy in particular—Landon.

It hadn't even been that hard. My job was public relations—I spent most of my time cultivating relationships with the media and trying to spin bad press into good. Between Shane and Delaney, there had been an explosion of bad press to work with. The roller-coaster ride they'd dragged us all on last year barely left me enough time to breathe, let alone stand still long enough to attract Landon's attention.

Besides, the man usually had a circle of groupies around him three deep, and his vision was obscured by all the silicone aimed his way.

There had been good press, too. Nothing but Trouble's Victory Tour had broken all kind of records, and the ballad Shane wrote for Delaney won the Grammy for Song of the Year. They had also won Album of the Year, Best Rock Performance of the Year and just about every category they'd been up for. But what really made them the hottest band on the planet was the highly publicized romance between Shane and Delaney.

The best part—it was genuine.

Of course, the lovebirds only made the antics of Shane's bandmates appear that much worse. Landon was rarely photographed without a gorgeous woman, or three, draped all over him.

And the only thing that had kept me from gagging at every tabloid and gossip site was believing I had someone of my own to spend my life with.

I was settled.

I was happy.

Lies. Clearly, Adam hadn't been happy. And maybe the truth was that I had simply settled, period.

With a thunderous explosion, Landon launched into their set. For the next hour and a half, I watched and listened, completely entranced.

By Landon. By Shane. By Jett and Dax. By the lights and the effects. By the music itself.

Nothing but Trouble had come to *play*.

For the first time in years, I let myself get lost inside their performance. Let myself drink in the sight of Landon in the place where he shined brightest—on stage. It felt illicit, decadent. To allow myself this guilty pleasure, this small window of time to enjoy the show as just another faceless fan among thousands and forget about who he'd once been to me.

Of course, I wasn't just another face in the crowd. I was standing stage left. And Landon knew my face well. Every moment I remained here was a risk.

For years, I'd been so careful, so cautious. Always keeping out of sight on the occasions when my job required me to be within Landon's orbit. Resisting the gravitational pull he still had on me. The pull he'd always had on me.

Maybe it was the tequila. Or maybe I was feeling reckless after Adam's recent betrayal. But I stayed for the entire set, not coming to my senses until they began wrapping up.

Signaling to Delaney that I was going to the ladies' room, I scurried off to hide.

Except that the small space was crowded with women planning which member of the band they were going to seduce. Now that Shane was very definitely taken, that only left three. Landon's name was batted around as if he were a trophy to be won.

They didn't know what I had learned the hard way—the man was no prize.

My head pounding from stress and shots, I flashed my pass at the bored-looking security guard standing in front of the first door I saw. He stepped to the side without a word and I threw myself on a battered sofa that had seen better days.

After a few minutes I glanced around the space, regretting that I hadn't asked the bouncer whose dressing room this was. Since tonight was just a one-off benefit concert for the charity Shane had set up last year in honor of his deceased childhood best friend, the room was lacking personal mementos. Technically, I had at least a seventy-five percent chance of it *not* belonging to Landon.

Groaning, I massaged my temples, trying to will my pulse down to a speed that didn't leave me feeling like my heart was about to crack through my ribs.

It was no use. I was too close to Landon for any semblance of normalcy.

Intending to head for the parking garage and send Delaney a text from the limo, I was reaching for the doorknob when it was yanked open from the other side—by the last person on earth I wanted to see.

My heartbeat stuttered for a brief second, then took off at a full gallop, racing through my veins.

Watching Landon Cox on stage from forty feet away had been bad enough. But here, now, close enough to touch, I was jolted by the power of his presence.

Still shirtless and sweating after an intense performance, my eyes danced over the rippling muscles rising from beneath the inked skin of Landon's naked torso, his broad shoulders tapering to slim hips, perfect V cuts forming an arrow pointing south.

Vitality seeping from every pore.

My gaze was drawn inexorably upward. Blond hair a damp mess, the faintest trace of stubble darkening a jawline that could have been cut from marble. A face so symmetrical, so severely beautiful, it would take even the most talented sculptor a lifetime to get right.

Landon Cox was a fantasy in the flesh.

I'd imagined this very moment dozens—no, hundreds—of times. But now that the moment was here, Landon and I, alone in a room again after all these years, I had *nothing*.

In a blink, Landon's expression wavered. His winged brows, three shades darker than the hair sweeping across his forehead, pulled together. Eyes like hot coals burning into me.

As if the sight of me caused him pain.

I tore my gaze away from his face, but it only landed on the swaths of ink covering his chest and extending over his arms. My mouth watered at the sight. I wanted to trace every tattoo with my tongue, every slash and swirl and stripe. After six years, how would Landon taste?

Like regret, I realized with a sickening thud. Because regret was all that remained of what we'd once shared.

Landon

One minute I was trying to decide which chick I'd let blow me in my dressing room and the next... The next, I was blown away.

Caught completely off guard, I could only stare.

Piper Hastings.

Shock rippled through me, my heart pounding against my ribs.

Not quite a full head shorter than me, Piper's blonde hair fell to her shoulders, like sunshine that had been spun into silk.

Those fathomless blue eyes I hadn't seen in years—except for the countless nights they'd haunted my dreams—went from surprise to horror in seconds as she took a reflexive step back, crossing her arms in front of her chest.

I fought an urge to close the distance between us, hard. Shoving my hands into my pockets, I somehow managed to resist the itch to plow them through Piper's hair, to wrap those golden strands in my fists as I plundered her lips.

"Piper...Long time, no see." Judging from the animosity clinging to her skin like a shadow, I had no doubt she would sooner bite my tongue off than kiss me back. "You enjoy the show?"

One shoulder lifted in a dismissive shrug. "Your fans seemed satisfied."

I grunted at the insinuation that Piper wasn't one of them. "We aim to please."

The perimeter of blue wrapped around her pupils brightened, flashing at me like a warning sign. "No one more than yourself, I'm sure."

Piper may as well have waved a red flag at a bull. That spark inside her—it sure as hell wasn't indifference. Proof she still felt *something* for me kindled hope inside my chest, triggering a throaty growl. "Once upon a time, I pleased *you*."

Piper took another step back. "Once upon a time? You might want to hold off on the fairy-tale comparisons. You're no Prince Charming, Landon."

She was right, of course. Gallant, I was not. Never wanted to be, either. I'd grown a thick skin early in life, and the only one who'd ever gotten under it, burrowing way down deep, was the woman in front of me.

"Actually," I said, extending my arms out in either direction. "Haven't you heard? I'm a fucking legend."

She leveled an icy glare my way. "You're a fucking asshole."

One corner of my lips quirked up. Fire and ice, my Pippa. "That, too."

Some of her anger melted away at my response. Her expression softened, easing into a sideways smile on the way to a full-fledged grin. A soft laugh escaped through her lips, light and sweet and more beautiful than any music I'd ever made.

It was contagious.

Laughter shook the air between us. Eye-watering belly laughs that sucked the tension right out of the room. And that urge, the one I'd temporarily managed to push down, came roaring back with a vengeance. I snaked my arm around Piper's narrow waist, pulling her into the well of my chest. Holding tight.

Energy from our contact raced up my arms, spreading along every vein, every nerve ending. I looked down, needing to drink in the sight of her beautiful face.

The mood shifted, until we were holding on to each other for reasons that had nothing to do with ego or anger, and everything to do with lust.

Fire and ice.

Hot and cold.

Love and hate.

Our eyes met, laughter fizzling into a wary, charged silence. Piper whimpered—a nervous, desperate sound I wanted to swallow. Swipe my tongue against the doubts rising from her skin like steam off the sea. Devour her obvious reluctance and expose the desire filling her sweet center.

Piper's spine arched away from me, as if her head was trying to tell the rest of her body to pull away but the message got lost before her feet could step back. My hands roamed down her sides, curving against her ass, fitting her tightly against me so the proof of my interest was impossible to deny.

We fit together. Perfectly.

Even after all this time.

Did Piper feel it, too?

If she didn't, I was about to show her.

I walked Piper back a few steps, until she was pressed against the arm of the couch. "I—we shouldn't," she panted.

"Yes. We should." Another growl, primal and possessive, rose up inside me as I lifted her. Long legs wrapped around my hips, nestling me exactly where I really wanted to be. "We definitely should."

Our mouths were an inch apart, her breath warm on my lips as I inhaled her scent. Sweet, but with a little kick to it. Like she'd covered up a round of pre-show shots—Fireball, or maybe tequila—with spearmint gum. Her favorite, I remembered.

Fuck, I'd missed this girl.

An explosion sounded, somewhere beyond the closed door, loud enough that Piper jumped. "It's okay," I soothed. "Just the pyro guys cleaning up."

But the moment was broken.

Piper shivered, dropping her forehead to my shoulder as she unwrapped her legs and slid down my length. My dick pulsed, trying to find a way through the zipper.

"I—I should go."

"No, don't. I shouldn't have done that, I'm sorry."

She tilted her head to that side, regarding me seriously. "No, you're not."

"No." I tossed a smirk her way. "You're right. I'm not sorry at all."

She made a strangled noise in the back of her throat, like she didn't know whether to run or pull me down for a kiss. I knew which option had my vote.

"I really should go." Not the one I was hoping for.

"We'll go together." After six years, I wasn't ready to let her go again so soon. Wherever Piper went was where I wanted to be.

She shook her head. "I don't think that's a good idea."

"Why not?"

"Why not?" she repeated, giving a slow blink. "You're really going to ask me that?"

Piper's bristling indignation should have bothered me—but it didn't. I soaked it up with a grin, loving the way she defended herself even as I hated that she felt obliged to defend herself from *me*. Not that I could blame her. "Yes. It's been a long time. We should catch up. I want to know what you've been doing the past few years." Six. Years.

And who she'd been doing it with.

Had she thought of me, dreamed of me?

Had she missed me?

Anger rose up in my gut, but it had nowhere to go. It just sat, festering, as I stared at Piper Hastings.

Because it was all directed inward. Every moment I'd missed with the woman in front of me, it was all my own damn fault.

Piper closed her eyes, a frown digging between her brows as a silent battle was waged within her mind.

Who was she fighting?

Because I wanted her to be fighting *me*. In battles there were winners and losers. Victors and vanquished. If Piper wanted to square off, I'd vault into the damned ring.

Seeing Piper again after all this time was all it took to strip away the elaborate pretense I'd fooled myself into believing— that I was doing fine without her.

I wasn't.

And on the anniversary of the day I'd lost everything, maybe I would get a second chance at something real.

A second chance at a prize that truly mattered.

I'd been too stupid to see the truth six years ago.

Too stupid, too selfish, too self-righteous.

But before I could ask for another chance, those blue orbs snapped open, the crease smoothed away. Decision made. "Landon, if you deserved to know, you already would."

Her voice was soft, an echo of all the intimate whispers that had once passed between us. Soft, but steely. Determined. Cutting through what little remained of my conscience with ease, flaying me to the core.

There was no denying that she was right. So fucking right.

Six years ago, I'd traded Piper's intimate whispers for center-stage drum solos, her dazzling smiles for the anonymous adoration of a million faceless fans.

I had a hell of a nerve asking anything from Piper.

I didn't deserve answers to my questions.

I didn't deserve access to her body, or her thoughts.

Money and fame weren't worthy tender for a woman like Piper. No matter how many *Billboard* hits I accumulated, or how many zeros I added to the bottom line of my bank account—I would never deserve her. I lost that right a long time ago, when I walked away without a backward glance, so afraid that if I turned around, even for just for a split second, I'd be incapable of leaving her at all. Ever.

And I'd been running from the regret ever since.

I didn't deserve her then and I sure as hell didn't deserve her now.

Except I couldn't take my eyes away from the curve of

her lips. There was a time they'd worn a smile meant just for me.

A ghost of that same smile had reappeared tonight, just for a moment. An apparition that was already haunting me.

Chapter Three

Piper

Landon Cox barely resembled the struggling musician who had stolen my heart. Back then, he'd been a drummer who didn't even own a complete set of drums, a man who could fit all of his belongings into one beat up duffel.

Now, he was a *rock star* for god's sake.

And a stranger.

Even so, something deep in the marrow of my bones was responding to him in a way that was all too familiar, his mere presence sending an undeniable shiver of awareness down my spine.

Feeling light-headed, I reminded myself to take slow, even breaths.

I wanted to leave.

Landon wanted to follow.

A situation that was exactly the opposite of where we'd been six years ago.

Payback was a bitch.

And right now, that's who I needed to be. A bitch who could walk away from Landon Cox with her head held high, impervious to his charms.

A bitch he wouldn't want to follow.

I mustered my haughtiest glower. "I'm leaving. Alone." I'd learned the hard way that so much of life was out of my hands. The only thing I could truly control was *me*.

And Landon couldn't have me.

Landon's features rearranged themselves into a hardened veneer I could no longer see through. A veneer I was willing to bet he didn't let *anyone* see through. His eyes swung away from my face, looking me up and down, inspecting my body with a sensual ease.

My skin prickled with awareness, nipples dragging against the lace of my bra with each shuddering inhale.

Being around Landon had apparently severed my mind-body connection. Because my mind wanted to be an imperious bitch, but my body wanted to be an irresistible vamp.

Landon noticed. "You sure that's what you want?" The pure intensity of his gaze brought back a flood of memories that had nothing to do with his ultimate betrayal.

Instead, I recalled sweet, stolen kisses and shared confessions. A baseball diamond worth of memories. Even home plate.

Especially home plate.

Landon hadn't stolen home, though. I'd given it all too willingly. Blissfully.

If I could, I'd snatch it right back.

Damn him.

Six years ago, Landon had put me on a pedestal, and the view had been beautiful. But I shouldn't have let him. Because when he took off, kicking it out from underneath me, the fall had been brutal. Hitting the ground, I hadn't just lost my breath. I'd broken bones, shattered them completely. The jagged slivers hadn't pierced skin though. Instead, they left wounds so deep they didn't even show.

Wounds so deep they'd never healed.

Landon Cox taught me what love felt like, even how it tasted.

Our love was like the first sip of celebratory champagne, the first bite of chocolate soufflé. Bubbly and decadent, so good I didn't know when to stop. Devouring it until I was sick.

Lovesick.

And I never wanted to feel that way again.

A deep-rooted instinct for self-preservation kicked in, giving me the momentum to duck beneath Landon's arm. I needed to leave. And I needed Landon to stay. Because there was only so much of the man I could resist. If I fell again, I might never get back up. "You want me to spell it out for you? I'm leaving. You're not." The finger I pushed into his chest was meant to underscore my intention. His pecs flexed beneath it, sending a surge of desire to throb between my legs.

Jesus, I was so weak.

Recoiling as if I'd been burned, I yanked at the door and propelled myself through it.

I didn't make it very far. Landon's long legs caught up with me in just a few strides, his hand grasping mine, our fingers entwining as if it was the most natural thing in the world.

I stopped in my tracks, my jaw dropping as a slew of indignant words lined up to jump off my tongue. "Take your—"

"There he is!" A blonde and a brunette came rushing up,

wearing only enough clothing to cover the essentials—barely. The dark-haired one slid between me and Landon, her hip crashing into mine with the accuracy and force of an NHL player.

But right then, I was grateful for her complete lack of subtlety, wrenching my hand from Landon's grip and stumbling toward the nearest exit.

Landon

Shaking off the brunette, I bummed a baseball cap and windbreaker from one of the security guys and caught up with Piper as she made her way to the underground parking lot. A platoon of black SUVs, town cars, and one pimped-out silver limousine waited, exhaust from the idling vehicles thick and foul inside my throat.

A driver sporting a silver tux, ostensibly to match the limo, jumped out of the front seat and darted to open the back door, grinning like a fool as Piper charged toward him.

I slid in just behind her, pulling the door closed myself. Fierce blue eyes slammed into me. "Don't you dare."

"What? Can't a guy catch a ride?"

"No. Get out."

Because I'd always been a good listener, I rapped on the roof of the car, barking, "Drive."

Back in the front seat, the driver, who looked like he'd gotten his license yesterday, blushed an uncomfortable shade of red. "Sir, I believe the lady—"

The kid had good manners, I'd give him that. He was probably working to buy his sweetheart a night at the nearby Courtyard so their first time would be a magical experience. I whipped off my hat, staring pointedly at him through the rearview mirror. His flush deepened. "Lan— I mean, Mr. Cox. I'm so sorry, I didn't recognize—"

"You'll drive now, yeah." It wasn't a question.

He still hesitated, eyes flicking to Piper. "Uh, are you sure—"

Piper flashed me a venomous look, scooting to the farthest end of the bench seat. "It's fine," she said, taking pity on the kid. "You can drop me off at my place. Mr. Cox will *not* be coming in."

I raised the privacy partition once the driver began maneuvering out of the parking garage, waiting until we had merged onto the highway before I shifted my back against the door, the borrowed jacket rustled as I angled my body toward Piper. "You don't have to run away from me."

"Like you should talk," she scoffed, folding her arms over her chest and looking pointedly out the window.

"Pippa—"

Even from my angle, I saw her wince. "You don't get to call me that. Not anymore."

I exhaled a heavy sigh, my unmet stare filled with remorse. "I had my reasons."

Her head swiveled back to me. "Reasons, huh?" Her arched brow was a silent dare to list them.

A dare I wasn't about to accept. I could barely admit my *reasons* to myself, let alone say them out loud.

An uneasy silence descended. The driver hadn't turned the radio on, so our soundtrack was wheels on asphalt and the whoosh of cars passing cars, punctuated by the occasional horn or siren. My bones ached from the tension.

I owed Piper an apology. That was why I'd followed her. But would it mean anything without an explanation?

Probably not.

The only thing I knew for sure was that I wasn't ready to leave her side.

Several minutes passed. "Who were those women?" Piper's voice was coolly indifferent, only the rigid set of her shoulders revealing that she cared about my answer.

"Who—the ones back at the arena?"

She gave a jerky nod, not saying anything.

"Just girls that follow the band."

"Groupies." Her disdain swirled in the ammonia-scented interior of the rented car, the toxic combination thick enough to choke on.

Much sooner than I expected, the car rolled to a stop across the street from a midsized apartment complex. Realizing my time was up, I reached for Piper, sweeping my thumb beneath her chin. "Look at me."

She resisted. "I think I've seen more than enough."

I played my last card. "Half an hour ago, you didn't seem to think so."

Clearly a bad one.

Knocking my arm away, Piper shoved at the door before the driver could open it. "Go fuck yourself, Landon."

I should have stayed inside the car's low-class interior. I should have let Piper be the one to walk away from me this time. A small part of me knew I owed her that.

But everything about Piper, even her anger—maybe, especially her anger—was drawing me in, an invisible cord pulling tight.

I got out of the car, following her along the sidewalk until she stopped at a door. Before her key was in the lock, I grabbed Piper's wrist, spinning her around and pulling her graceful body against me. She gasped, her cheeks pink beneath the murky outdoor lights. "And why should I do that?" I whispered, my fingers gently tracing her delicate jawline. "Not when you so clearly want to do the honor."

Thick lashes flared upward, nearly reaching the arch of Piper's brow. "You, you—"

I leaned down, swallowing her outrage with a kiss, knowing it was a desperate measure. We had unfinished business.

Maybe what I needed wasn't another chance. Maybe what I needed—what we both needed—was some goddamn closure. One night.

Because there was no way Piper could feel, no way she could fuck, as well as I remembered.

Memories of us had pushed me into bed more times, and with more women, than I could count. But no matter how many times I tried, no one had ever succeeded in erasing the memory of Piper Hastings.

Which was why my memories had to be wrong. Too good to be true.

Piper sighed into my mouth, the key in her hand falling to the ground as she wrapped her arms around my neck and slanted her face to give me more access. Access I took eagerly, pushing my fingers through a curtain of blonde silk to cradle her skull.

Her energy shuddered through me, flipping a switch I hadn't realized had been locked in the off position until now. Until seeing Piper. Touching Piper. Kissing Piper. Again.

And damn, it was every bit as good as I remembered. Better, even.

Fuck.

I wanted to taste and lick every inch of her. Hell, I wanted to devour this girl whole.

Piper's nails dug into the skin of my neck as she hiked up

onto her toes to get closer to me, her breasts pushing against my chest. I grinned against her mouth. My kitten was coming out to play. Our tongues tangled, fighting for power. She tasted so damn good. Slipping a leg between her thighs, I loosened my hold to slide my fingers down the curve of her spine as she ground against me.

"Pippa." This time she didn't object to the nickname I groaned against her lips.

It was a plea.

For this girl, only for this girl, I would beg. After what I'd done, the way I left, she deserved it.

As long as she let me have this one night. One night so I could get her out of my system and we could both move on with our lives. Not that I knew anything about her life. Maybe she'd already moved on. But from the way she was responding to me, the heat of her skin, the neediness of her kiss, I didn't think so.

"You gonna let me in?" My voice was like old gravel, gritty, with all the sharp edges worn away. I backed up just enough to grab the key that had fallen at our feet, dangling it in front of Piper's dazed eyes. Her lips were full and swollen from our kiss, and she pressed them together as she glanced at the glinting metal before looking back up at me. "Yes."

Yes. How could one word, one syllable, have the power to do me in?

Wrapping one arm around the curve of Piper's waist, I pulled her against my side and jabbed the key into the lock. The door gave easily, opening with barely a push. I picked her up and swung her over the threshold, pressing her against the nearest wall. Grabbing the backs of her knees, I hooked them over my hips. "Knew the second I laid eyes on you tonight, I had to taste you. Just didn't think you'd taste as good as I remembered."

Piper made a sound low in her throat, like an audible smile, and clung tighter, kissing deeper. I shouldn't want her this bad. This was supposed to be a way to rid me of my craving, not make it stronger.

Suddenly the lights blazed on, and we pulled apart, blinking at each other in confusion. Figuring she must have accidentally flipped a switch, I grinned at her swollen lips, pink-tipped nose, the mess I'd made of her hair. Piper was always elegantly put together, not a hair out of place. But when she let me muss her up a little—she was fucking gorgeous.

"What the hell?"

It took me a second to realize the question hadn't come from the woman in my arms.

Chapter Four

Piper

How was it possible that this day kept getting worse?

Although, since it was after midnight, maybe it couldn't be considered the same day.

Looking between Landon and Adam, I didn't have the mental capacity to concern myself with abstract details. My reality was complicated enough.

I straightened, pushing my shoulders back. As if good posture could distract from my swollen lips and lustful, panting breaths.

Posture hadn't been a priority a moment ago. Encircled within Landon's arms, my hands riding the swell of his biceps, I'd melted into him, groaning at the pull and flex of the muscles that had held me up, pushed me against the wall. The bulge between his thighs pulsing with a life all its own.

But that temporary lapse in sanity had come to an abrupt end. For me, at least.

Landon had arrogantly dismissed Adam with a glance. Turning his attention back to me, Landon's jaw was clenched, his gaze still hungry. Like I was a meal to be savored, but ultimately devoured. And he was impatient to get started.

No wonder. Until Adam's interruption, I'd been about to serve myself on a platter.

Landon could ignore Adam, but I couldn't. Forty-eight hours ago, I thought I would marry the man. At first he'd been my neighbor, then my friend, and for the past year or so, my boyfriend. We weren't engaged yet, but he'd been dropping hints. I loved him, and I loved his family. Marriage had seemed like the logical next step.

Until an overheard conversation proved I'd had my head in the clouds.

And now I was standing between the two men I'd once looked at with so much hope, so much possibility. Two men that had betrayed me. Liars, both of them.

After six years, my feelings toward Landon should have cooled. I'd been a college freshman away from home for the first time. A teenager wrapped in a naïve, hormone-fueled bubble. I should have gotten over him ages ago. But I hadn't.

Meanwhile, the sting of Adam's betrayal was only days old. I should be devastated by it, by him. But I wasn't.

If I needed proof that my feelings for Adam were a pale imitation of what I felt for Landon—a sparkler compared to a laser light show—this was it.

A fact that only made me angrier.

Because Landon and I, we had crashed and burned a long time ago.

First things first. I pointed to Adam. "You have no right to be here. Not anymore." I swung my arm toward the front door. "Get. Out."

"Piper, we need to talk. Don't throw away the last year because…" He glanced self-consciously at Landon. "Because of a—a…misunderstanding."

I didn't want to have this conversation with Landon standing here. Although, in my heart, I knew it was impossible to throw something away if it had never been there to begin with. "We will, Adam, but not tonight."

"So, you expect me to leave you here with, with"—he glanced again at Landon before turning back to me—"him?"

"He's leaving, too." The words leapt from my mouth, and I knew it was the right choice, even as Landon's jaw sagged, obviously surprised by tonight's unexpected twist.

The tiny glimpse of vulnerability had me wanting to kiss him again.

With a resolve that was seconds from crumbling, I backed up a few steps and forced a stern edge to my voice. "I mean it. Both of you—out."

And then, like a coward, I scurried into my bedroom, locking the door behind me and putting my ear to it. The heavy thud of Landon's boots was unmistakable, and when I didn't hear another pair, I wondered if his had covered the sound of Adam's footsteps.

A piercing whistle said differently. "Dude, I'm not leaving you in here."

I tried to imagine Adam's face. He probably would have left on his own, but just didn't want to walk out with Landon. I guess I couldn't blame him. The intimidation factor was pretty high when you're staring at a man whose ripped muscles are covered in ink and insolence.

Landon Cox had been so different from the boys I'd known back in Bronxville, and the not-quite-men I'd met at UCLA. From the second I laid eyes on him, I'd been lit by an unexpected urgency, a need to claim Landon as my own. Looking back, I should have known it was ridiculous. Like trying to pet a rattlesnake.

Landon was dangerous, carrying a lethal poison inside him even when he was hiding his tail, sheathing his fangs. The only surprise was that there had been no attack. No ruthless, lunging bite.

He'd simply slithered away.

Killing a part of my soul anyway, no venom required.

I ran a tentative tongue over my lips. They ached from the press of Landon's mouth, and stung from his absence.

Our kiss hadn't been nearly satisfying enough after all this time. Not nearly long or soft or hard enough to make up for the past six years without. Not nearly *enough*.

That made sense, I guess. Because, six years ago, I hadn't been *enough* for Landon.

Tonight, there had been intention in his kiss. And the power to make me forget the past, forgive him…everything. But to what end? Did I deserve nothing more than the scraps Landon was willing to toss my way?

There had been lust, too. Between the two of us, so much lust we could have powered the city.

Or burned it down.

Landon

"That yours?" The asshole who'd just interrupted what would have been, without a doubt, a fucking incredible night, sneered at the silver embarrassment that couldn't manage the turn into Piper's apartment complex.

I glared at him. "Why? You want a ride?"

"Don't need one." The smile he gave made me want to slap it off his face, but I only watched as he walked away, stopping in front of an apartment two doors down and taking hold of the knob. "Piper and I are neighbors."

Neighbors. Before I could lunge for his throat, Piper's *neighbor* slipped inside his apartment and shut the door. Which meant he could go back to her place the second I left.

How fucking convenient.

Was he Piper's fuck-buddy? Her boyfriend?

I had no idea, but either label had my blood pressure skyrocketing.

I stomped across the street and threw myself into the back of the limo. "Where to?" came the voice squeaking through a small crack in the privacy partition.

"You in any rush?" I grabbed a glass from the door panel and sloshed a mix of liquors into it, needing to feel an ache in my gut that didn't come from animosity.

Or jealousy.

Jesus.

Maybe I'd left my balls in Piper's apartment, too.

And it didn't look like I was getting them back tonight.

"Actually, I was—"

"Just sit tight for a bit, yeah. I'll tell you when you can drive me back to my hotel."

I was tempted to have him take me back to my house. The few things I'd left in my hotel room could be packed up by Lynne or one of her lackeys.

I lived less than an hour away, deep in the Hollywood Hills.

I bought the place a few years ago, well after Shane, Jett, and Dax had homes of their own. Before that, I'd been content to rent a small house not far from our favorite recording studio. I didn't need much, and it was more satisfying to bank the cash I was earning, watching zero after zero added to the trust fund I'd set up.

But then some fan had discovered where I lived and was waiting for me, naked in my bed, when I stumbled home one night. She was hot, or at least she'd looked good in the dark, so I stripped down myself.

Who fucks a stalker after they break into his house? Me.

Almost.

I would have, except that when I put the condom on, my fucking dick poked out of the tip. Not exactly sober, I figured it was a fluke.

Until the second one split apart as I pulled it on.

Turned out the crazy chick had used a pair of scissors to poke holes in the condoms in my nightstand drawer. The entire fucking box. If she'd been smart enough to use a needle, I probably wouldn't have realized it until the problem had a goddamn birth certificate with my name on it.

I bought a house of my own the next week. Surrounded by a high fence and monitored by a security system. The only people that had ever been inside were Travis, the guys, and the couple that lived in my guesthouse and took care of the main house and grounds.

To my surprise, I loved being a homeowner. It became the oasis I never knew I needed. A place I could let my guard down. The only place, actually.

Besides my housekeeper, no chick had ever crossed the threshold, although I might make an exception for Shane's girl,

Delaney, who had grown on me a little bit. I hadn't been a fan of her at first, figured she was just another fame-chasing tart, like Shane's previous "girlfriends." The same kind that chased all of us.

But Delaney had surprised me; she wasn't interested in fame. Wasn't interested in much besides Shane, actually. Except for going back to school, which she was doing clear across the country.

The guys used to come over occasionally, but now that Shane was spending most of his time in New York, it seemed strange to invite just Dax and Jett to swing by. What would we do—work on our tans by the pool? Geek out playing videogames?

Until this moment, I'd never actually realized how solitary my life had become. I was a part of one of the most famous bands in the word, surrounded my fans and staff and groupies twenty-four-fucking-seven. But here, my frustration fogging up the glass of this four-wheeled embarrassment, staring out at the wall Piper was hiding behind—I felt truly alone.

Lonely.

If Piper didn't want to see me, why had she come to the show tonight? And how had she gotten that all-access pass hanging from her neck? A pass that still shouldn't have gotten her into my dressing room.

Kicking my feet out across from me, I sipped slowly from my glass. There was a light bluish glow coming from the window of the apartment two doors down from Piper's, the TV probably. Piper's windows were dark, and I could picture her undressing in her bedroom, slipping between cool sheets that would have already been a messy tangle if I was inside.

But I wasn't.

Piper had kicked me out. Told me to leave.

With a muttered curse, I tipped the last of the liquor into

my mouth and bit out the name of the hotel I was staying in, cradling the empty glass in my hand. My stomach was still churning as we arrived at the entrance, and I pulled a couple of Benjamins from my back pocket and pressed them into the driver's palm with a half-assed smile. The guy looked at the bills in his hand, his face lighting up. He was still thanking me when the automatic doors swooshed closed behind me.

At least I made someone's night.

I jabbed at the elevator call button with a knuckle, my hands curled into fists.

Was Piper still alone? Or had that fucker been biding his time, knocking on her door the second I pulled away?

No way I'd get any sleep tonight. Not when my mind was still in Piper's apartment, in her bedroom, my veins thrumming with the need touch her, taste her.

Fuck her senseless.

I'd been the only one of the four of us to stay in the hotel last night, but everyone was crashing here tonight after the show rather than driving back to L.A. Between the high of performing and the after-parties, it was always easier to crash at a hotel even when we were playing in our hometown.

I wasn't in the mood to party, but I didn't want to be alone. And I didn't feel like hanging with the roadies and groupies that were undoubtedly jammed in the bar, either.

Shane was locked up with Delaney, and Jett was probably in the middle of a baker's dozen of chicks that would be content with any scrap he tossed their way. Dax though, he was the loner of our insular fucked-up family. The one who always listened more than he talked. He got his share of action, but only when he wanted it, which was rare. And never with the girls who followed the band.

I rapped on the door across from mine, the faint strains of a guitar riff coming from behind it abruptly stopping. "Busy. Go away."

I snorted. "Yeah? You fuckin' your guitar these days?"

A minute later the door was yanked open, just enough for Dax to shove his head through it. His eyes widened when he saw I was alone, and he opened it the rest of the way, stepping aside for me to pass through. "Your dick finally quit on you, huh?"

I made a show of adjusting my junk. "You intimidated by the competition?"

"Yeah," Dax joked, slumping in a chair and dragging his guitar against his bare chest like a lover, idly strumming a chord.

"Seriously, man," I asked, falling back into the sofa and kicking my legs onto the arm, "I need to know. Why don't you dick around as much as the rest us?"

Dax's thick black brows waggled over a soulful brown gaze that could have gotten him as much pussy as he could eat, even without the guitar. "Doesn't look like you're doing much with your dick right now, either."

I snorted. "Exactly. And it doesn't feel right—like I'm disappointing half the population."

Dax just shook his head. "Don't know how you do it."

"Do what?"

"Fuck anything that moves."

My lips twitched. "Depends on how they move, I guess." The way Piper had moved—she'd set the standard so high no one had ever been able to compete. Holding the weight of her body in my arms tonight, it had felt as if she was finally back where she belonged.

Another few chords covered the silence. "Why don't you?" I asked, genuinely curious.

"Besides the fact that I have higher standards than any of you fuckers?"

"Ha. Yeah, besides that."

Dax shrugged, his expression turning serious. "Nothing worth having comes easy."

Piper

Delaney managed to unglue herself from Shane's side long enough to meet me for coffee at my apartment the next morning, although her stubble-abraded cheeks and sex-mussed hair were glaringly obvious proof they hadn't done a lot of sleeping.

Not that I had, either. My sexually frustrated body had tossed and turned all night, imagining all the things Landon would have been doing to me if we hadn't been interrupted. That cocky grin wiped away by determined desire. His callus-roughened hands chafing my smooth skin, stoking a fire so hot it should have singed my veins. His mouth on mine, his tongue licking, his teeth biting. Sharp, intense spears of pleasure pricking.

And as for what I wanted to do to Landon…well, what *didn't* I want to do to him?

Anything. Everything.

Whatever he wanted.

Even now, riding the chemical edge of caffeine the next morning, my body was still thrumming with unspent lust as I filled Delaney in on recent events. From walking into Adam's apartment and overhearing his conversation with his college roommate, to breaking up with Adam, to nearly sleeping with Landon, and then kicking them both out of my apartment before going to bed alone.

Once I spilled the whole sordid tale, there was a moment of quiet as Delaney attempted to absorb it. She finally exhaled, eyes wide as she leaned forward. "Okay, I think I need some help taking this all in."

I let my head fall back on the couch cushion and groaned. "How do you think *I* feel?"

"Honestly, I can't even imagine." Delaney sighed, not saying anything else until I raised my head and looked at her. "Can I ask a few questions?"

"Fire away."

"Okay, first: did you really hear both sides of Adam's conversation with the roommate who was apparently more than just a roommate? And are you absolutely sure that Adam ..." The end of Delaney's unspoken question hovered in the air.

...cheated on you with another man?

Unspoken, the words still blared jarringly inside my ears. I winced. "Yes, I heard everything."

As I was leaving for work, I realized I'd forgotten my birth control pills in Adam's bathroom, so I let myself in. "He was in his spare room, on the treadmill, and his phone was on speaker."

I swallowed thickly, remembering how I'd crept quietly through the hall, intending to grab my pills from his medicine cabinet without interrupting his conversation. "Brian was angry. Accusing Adam of hiding from the truth. I didn't get it, not until Brian asked—'Then what was that kiss about?'"

In his bathroom, pills in hand, I froze.

As their argument escalated, it was clear that my boyfriend—who'd never even hinted at being bisexual—had been in a relationship with Brian in college.

It took me a few minutes to realize that "that kiss" meant

their kiss...last week. "Adam told Brian that it didn't mean anything. That it was a mistake, and he had a girlfriend now."

"Brian said Adam was lying to himself and that he was using me." I paused, my throat tightening. "Adam stopped the treadmill. He responded, 'I know.'"

Even now, the echo of those words was enough to break my heart. The pain in Adam's voice had been deeply visceral, impossible to ignore.

I knew how it felt to put on a front to the world. To be outwardly confident and cavalier when in reality you were just a painted Easter egg, one careless mistake away from being a cracked shell.

I grabbed more tissues and blew my nose. "I must have made a noise, or maybe I walked out of the bathroom, because the next thing I knew, I was standing in the hallway and Adam had turned around. He retreated behind this mask of, of...," I sputtered, looking for the right word, "fakeness, I guess. It just made me so angry, I threw my pills at his head and stormed out."

"Jesus."

"You called a minute later, as I got into my car."

"Oh crap, I'm so sorry." Delaney's tone was heavy with remorse. "And I was all, 'I'm coming to L.A., let's go to the Nothing but Trouble show together.' Ugh. I can't believe I was so oblivious."

I hurried to reassure her. "You weren't! You knew something was wrong, tried pressing me on it, too."

Delaney gave a shallow nod. "Right. So...Why didn't you want to tell me?"

"Honestly, I think I just needed some time to process it myself."

"And now you have?"

"Yes. No." I grabbed a pillow and held it over my face, muffling a scream of frustration. "Seeing Landon last night kind of put the whole Adam thing on the back burner."

"Ah, so that's how it is."

I glanced at her warily, sensing she was about to tell me something I already knew but didn't really want to hear. "What?"

"Do you remember the conversation we had the night Shane was arrested?" I offered a cautious nod. While we were waiting to hear when, or if, Shane would be released, Delaney had asked me if I'd ever been in love. I'd reluctantly admitted that I had, but that it didn't end well. An understatement.

Delaney continued. "Landon was the musician you were talking about, right? The one who took off without a word of explanation?"

I sighed. "Yeah. That was him."

She pulled at an invisible piece of lint on her leg, taking her time. "Piper, do you think maybe you were using Adam, too? That, in your own way, you'd hoped Adam would be the guy to get you over Landon?"

I choked on an inhale, sputtering as I reached for the mug of tea in front of me.

Delaney waited until I'd sipped, then added quietly, "But clearly he didn't."

Cradling the porcelain mug between my palms, I stared into the amber liquid, recalling the intensity that had shot through me in Landon's presence. The way every cell in my body had thrilled at his touch, as if awakening from a long slumber and swearing fealty to the man who'd freed them. "No," I said eventually. "No one's ever taken Landon's place."

"That good, huh?" Delaney released a quiet laugh, lightening the moment. "I guess the legend really does live up to his hype."

"Are you trying to remind me what a manwhore he is?" I snorted. "Because it's working."

"From what I've heard, Shane was just as bad before we got together. And I have to admit, there are some benefits to his…," she quirked a grin, "experience."

I blinked. There were times when Delaney didn't bear a shred of resemblance to the shy, awkward girl I'd known in Bronxville. She continued, "Either way, you're not going to figure out what Landon is *to you* until you see him again."

"No way. That's the last thing I need." I shook my head so violently, some of my tea spilled onto my lap. I set the mug back on the cocktail table and blotted at my thighs with a crumpled up tissue.

Pulling her legs beneath her, Delaney waited until I was finished. "Describe your sex life with Adam in one word."

"What? Absolutely not."

"Trust me. One word, the first one that comes to mind."

I pressed my lips together, opening them on an irate sigh. "Fine, okay. My sex life with Adam is—was," I corrected myself, "fine."

"Now describe sex with Landon in one word."

I squirmed on the couch. "I can't. It was so long ago. We were just kids."

Delaney put a hand on top of mine. "Come on. Close your eyes and try to remember what it was like with him."

"But I don't—"

"Humor me."

I squeezed my eyes closed. Before my eyelashes met, I was hit with a surge of lust that sent my internal temperature skyrocketing. "Hot, okay. Sex with Landon was hot."

She gave an impudent grin. "Why would you give up *hot* with a freaking rock star for *fine* with a CPA? It makes no sense."

It made perfect sense. "Because sex with Landon is all I'll ever get. It's all he's capable of. And I want—" Swallowing the heavy knot of longing clogging my throat, I took a breath before continuing. "I want so much more."

I wiped at my stinging eyes. "When Landon left me behind all those years ago, it hurt. A lot. If he had come back, or even called, I would've forgiven him. And if he'd asked me to go with him, I would have done that, too. He was worth it, Delaney. And what we had…" I sniffled. "It was magic. I thought we'd have a fairy-tale ending, you know."

"But Landon didn't do any of those things. And just because he's this big superstar now, I'm not going to let him treat me like I'm some kind of groupie. He owes me more than that, Delaney."

A minute passed, but I sensed Delaney still wasn't through. "Can I be blunt?" she finally ventured.

"Because you were soft-pedaling earlier?"

She ignored my sarcasm. "You guys obviously have unresolved issues. And until they're sorted, you'll never be able to have a healthy relationship with anyone else."

"Thanks, Dr. Phil."

"And, beyond that, you've been having sex with a closeted gay man for the past year—you deserve all the orgasms Landon Cox can give you."

Good thing I wasn't holding my tea, I would have been drenched. "Jesus, Delaney!"

"You know I'm right," she taunted.

"Even if you are, and I'm not saying you are, what do you expect me to do, knock on Landon's door and ask for a round of pity sex?"

"Of course not."

I breathed a sigh of relief.

"Landon's going to take one look at you tonight and—"

"I'm not seeing Landon tonight, or any other."

"Yes, you are. Or have you forgotten about Travis's party?"

I glared at her. "Of course not, but Landon never goes to Travis's parties."

"He'll be there tonight; all the guys will."

"Says who?"

"Shane."

I gnawed on my lower lip. It was hard to argue with that.

She cocked her head to the side, staring me down. "Don't you deserve a chance to see what you've been missing? Or at least figure out why you were willing to settle for *fine*? You're not the same naïve college kid you were six years ago. You are smart and successful in your own right, building a career you love. If you want to have a fling with Landon, you know exactly what you're getting into. He can't take anything from you that you're not willing to give."

I wanted to argue, to tell Delaney she was wrong. Because my heart had given things to Landon he hadn't asked for and clearly didn't reciprocate.

But I thought about what Delaney was saying for a minute. Why was I so quick to deny myself a night or two with Landon?

Earlier, calling my sex life with Adam *fine* was being kind. Our sex life had been boring. Perfunctory. And infrequent.

Maybe a fling with Landon, for old time's sake, was *exactly* what I needed.

Chapter Five

Landon

I hadn't been to one of Travis's parties in ages. But tonight, Travis insisted.

He was hosting an invite-only open-mic night and wanted us to check out a few of the acts as potential openers for our next tour.

At this point in my life, I preferred my scene less Beverly Hills glitz and more dive bar gloom. I wasn't interested in courting Hollywood's latest "It" girl. Why bother? Only one girl had ever been *it* for me.

Tonight, however, I was sick of my own company and eager for a distraction from thoughts that kept running back to Piper. Blonde hair, bronze eyelashes, skin that glowed like the palest gold. Long legs, full lips, and a fathomless blue stare that could cut to the quick or warm to the bone. My balls still felt like they were clenched in her fist.

Annoyed with myself, I looked up at the platform that was set up over the pool. In the hour I'd been here, a few acts had taken to the makeshift stage, although most intriguing was the pop princess currently killing it covering an early Gwen Stefani hit. But not even the fiery redhead holding the microphone could keep my attention tonight.

Fuck it.

I finally gave up. I might as well drive around L.A. until I found Piper's place again. If she wasn't home, I'd sit my ass on her stoop until she got back.

Taking my first deep breath since opening the door to my dressing room the other night, I spun on my heel and started pushing my way through the crowd.

Travis wouldn't notice I'd left, and I didn't give a fuck if he did.

A flash of sunshine glowing beneath the moonlight caught my eye, and I instinctively changed course. Knowing it couldn't be *her*, but drawn in just the same.

Blonde hair swung my way. I stopped short, rocked by the impact of her electric-blue gaze. "Piper?" Her name left my lips as a question, not sure she was real.

"Hey, Landon."

I shifted from one foot to the other, caught completely off guard. "I was actually just—" I looked around, spotting the men and women dressed in black wearing earpieces and shoulder mics. Security. How had Piper gotten in? "You were backstage the other night, and today you're here…"

Her lips twitched. "You think I'm stalking you?"

"No, of course not." Had it been anyone else, my answer would have been an emphatic yes. But I needed to understand the connection.

"Mmm-hmm," she murmured dismissively. "Well, to put your mind at ease, I'm here because I work for Travis."

"You work for Travis?" I repeated needlessly. The music was loud, but I knew I'd heard her correctly.

"Yes. And you shouldn't look so surprised we haven't run into each other. There're over fifty people on his payroll. I doubt you've even met half of them."

"How long have you worked for him?"

"Nearly three years now."

I clenched my jaw, the implication of her answer slapping me in the face. Hard.

Piper had been close to me for the past three years—and she'd intentionally avoided me for all of them.

Can you really blame her?

Cupping my palm around her elbow, I steered Piper toward the house. There were too many people outside, too much noise. Off the main room, there was a library with a fully stocked bar. I'd retreated there on more than one occasion, back when I'd believed every one of Travis's invitations was a command performance. "Want a drink?"

She looked uncertain for a minute, then shrugged. "Sure. Whatever you're having is fine."

I bit back a laugh and extended my glass in her direction. "You sure about that?"

Piper reached for it, the leaded crystal making it halfway to her mouth before she wrinkled her nose and thrust it back at me. "What *is* that?"

I laughed. If Piper drank the obnoxious blend of liquor I was having, she'd be unconscious within an hour. I uncorked a bottle of white wine and poured her a glass. "Not meant for sweet little girls like you."

She shuddered and took a sip of the chardonnay instead, then lifted her face to mine. "I don't want to be sweet. At least, not tonight."

My dick thumped the inside of my jeans. "Yeah? Why is that?"

"Does it really matter?" She lifted a tentative hand to my shirt, her palm seeking skin. "I just know that I want to be *not* sweet with you."

I studied the emotions sliding across Piper's face like a highlight reel. Hope. Fear. Desire. I could feel her nervous energy, see the skittishness of her jerky movements. "Who was that guy?"

Piper blinked in surprise, not anticipating the question. "Adam?"

I nodded.

"My boyfriend." At my raised eyebrow, she quickly corrected herself. "Ex-boyfriend."

I'd installed a revolving door on my zipper a long time ago, and didn't care one way or the other about the romantic entanglements of the women I fucked. Whether they had a husband or a boyfriend, that had been their problem, not mine. But the idea of Piper cheating didn't sit well with me, and I didn't want to be a part of it, no matter how badly I wanted her.

"I share the stage with three other guys. Shared plenty of women with them over the years, too." Piper winced at my crudeness. "But you, Piper..." I traced her jaw with the tip of my finger, brushing over those sweet, sweet lips. "Not gonna share you with anyone."

Her lower lip trembled beneath my touch, warm breath ghosting over my skin. "What I had with Adam, it wasn't—" She broke off with a slight flinch. "We were never meant to be more than friends."

I studied her expression, trying to read between the lines. There was something Piper was holding back, but I didn't sense any regret over the breakup itself.

I shoved one hand in my pocket and wrapped the other around my drink. "So tonight is a work event for you?"

"Yes. No." Piper faltered, clearing her throat. "I mean—yes, I'm on the list because I work for Travis. But I don't work on your account anymore, so tonight isn't—"

"Anymore." I repeated the word, rolling it around my tongue like an ice cube. "So, just how many times have we been in the same place, at the same party? How many times have you avoided me?"

"I—I…Not as often as you might think. I was mostly working with Delaney and—"

"You've seen me, been close to me, and yet you never—" My mouth snapped shut as I wondered *what* she had seen. Probably a whole lot of me trying to erase her memory with any woman—every woman—within reach.

Fuck. Frustration was a gnarled, toxic knot deep in my gut. Frustration at Piper, at myself, at this whole fucked-up situation. "Why?" I finally managed, the single word a harsh rasp. A desperate question. A damning indictment.

She took a shaky sip of her wine, setting the glass down with a slight tremble. "Because *you* left *me*. Because I didn't take a job with Travis just so I could be close to you. And because," her voice softened slightly, "until tonight, I decided not to waste my time pursuing someone who didn't want me back. Even if that someone was you."

I let her words seep into my brain, trying to make sense of them. "You think I don't want you?"

She hesitated. "Do you?"

I stepped closer, lowering my mouth so that it grazed the rim of her ear. "I'm going to make something real clear. When it comes to you, Pippa, want is all I've ever known. And I've never wanted anyone the way I wanted—*want*—you."

As Piper absorbed my words, I studied the rapid flutter at the base of her throat. Framed by the delicate bones of her clavicle, I had a sudden and almost irresistible urge to lick the shallow indent. Feel her heartbeat pulsing against my tongue. Taste her sweet skin.

I set my drink on the bar before I shattered the glass in my hand. "Wanna get out of here?"

Her breathless "Okay" sounded better than anything sung into the microphone outside.

We were just a few steps away from the front door when I heard my name called.

Travis's questioning stare landed on me first, then narrowed as it slid to Piper, his lips pressing into a disapproving line. *Fuck.* He probably had some rule against employees mixing with clients.

In a blink, I slumped against her. "Hey there, Trav," I fake slurred. "Your girl here was jess tellin' me I need to go home. But I don't wanna. Tell her who I am. Tell her I can stay." I punctuated the last word by appearing to trip over my own feet. Reflexively, Piper reached up to catch my weight.

Travis cursed, rushing across the marble tiles and grabbing my other arm. I shrugged him off. "Hey, get off. I don't do dudes."

Travis backed away, rolling his eyes and rubbing his bald head. "I can have security take him home."

Piper tugged at my elbow. "It's fine, they're short-staffed tonight and I was planning to leave anyway. He'll probably pass out once I get him in the car and I'll drop him off at his place on the way to my own. We'll be fine."

Travis eyed me again and I let my eyes droop. "All right. Thanks, Piper. I didn't realize…" He sighed, glancing back at his guests outside. "If he gives you any trouble, you call me right away, okay?"

Piper nodded and hustled me out the door. I continued my act, lurching diagonally across the driveway, changing directions every few steps, until the music was little more than a buzzing in the air.

Certain no one was following us, I transitioned into a normal gait and slanted a grin at Piper as I retrieved my keys from my pocket. "Maybe I deserve an Oscar to babysit my Grammys?"

She rolled her eyes, the childish gesture reminding me of the college girl who had set my heart on fire. "Don't get greedy. You play drunk well enough to fool Travis, but I don't think you're ready for Spielberg yet."

I laughed. "You drive here?"

"Yeah, my car is right there." She pointed at a Mini Cooper not much bigger than a golf cart. What it lacked in size it made up for in color—a bright teal.

"Jesus. Drive that on a highway and you're just begging to get run over."

She stiffened, yanking her arm from my hold. "Only by jerks who don't know the difference between actual driving and bumper cars."

I raised my hands, chuckling. "Relax, I happen to be great at both." Pulling my key fob out of my pocket, I pointed it at my truck. A black F-450 that could have driven over Piper's car with room to spare. "We'll leave yours here and I'll bring you back for it tomorrow."

"No way," she said with a quick shake of her head. "And besides, Travis knows I wouldn't let you drive anywhere in your state."

Hearing a pair of footsteps coming down the driveway, I decided we needed to get out of there. With a groan, I pushed my keys back in my pocket and held my hand out for Piper's. "Fine. But I'm driving."

She didn't budge. "How many drinks did you have?"

Damn she was cute. How had I forgotten how cute she was? "One and a half."

"I'm driving."

Throwing my hands in the air, I stalked toward her glorified go-cart. "Fine."

Piper

Fine.

A shudder ran through me at the single word Landon had huffed. He clearly didn't realize that, as far as I was concerned, tonight would be anything but *fine*.

I was putting *fine* in my rearview mirror.

And it was terrifying.

Uncertainty whispered through my veins, sending goose bumps rising to the surface of my skin.

I wished Landon had kissed me. I was craving a taste of the potent blend of insolence and intention that brewed within his soul. Just one would have quelled my hesitation instantly.

Because now, watching Landon squeeze into my tiny car, scrounging for the lever to push back the seat so his knees weren't at his throat...now I wasn't feeling very brave.

Silently, I cursed Delaney for making me think a night with Landon was some kind of stepping-stone to figuring out why I'd been so willing to settle for *fine* with Adam. To settle for *fine*, period.

"Piper," Landon called. "If I have to get out of this car to come get you, I'm not getting back in."

His teasing threat finally propelled my feet forward, and I slipped behind the wheel.

Christ. The overhead light transformed the hardened collection of planes and angles that made up Landon's face into a breathtaking work of art. A face that tempted me as much now as six years ago. Me and thousands of other women. "You'll have to give me directions," I choked out.

My heart was pounding, the effort making my ribs vibrate. I gulped a breath, but it only made things worse. The air inside the small car was heavy with Landon's scent—malt liquor and masculinity. Intoxicating.

Landon nodded, lifting an arm corded with ropes of muscle to push his hand between my neck and the headrest, his strong fingers digging into my tense shoulders. I released a soft moan and shifted into gear, every nerve in my body attuned to Landon's slightest movements.

For the next half hour, Landon assumed the role of navigator. I was thankful I'd stuck to my guns and insisted on driving. I had no idea where tonight would lead, but it was reassuring to be in control of the physical act of getting there. The steering wheel was solid beneath my fingers, the road signs comforting in their familiarity. The world hadn't changed overnight, and it wasn't going to change tonight, no matter what happened between Landon and me.

"Almost there," he said, shifting in his seat again, trying to find a position where his long legs could stretch a little farther before giving up with a muttered curse. I'd had only a few sips of wine but I felt drunk, buzzing from proximity to the sexiest man I'd ever known. Knowing I was about to get into bed with the sexiest man I'd ever known. Again.

How many women had Landon slept with since the last time we were together? My "number" was a whopping *one*. Adam— my gay ex-boyfriend.

Suddenly I wasn't just nervous about getting into bed with Landon, I was worried about being *good* in bed.

My throat was dry, my skin itchy. Maybe a sudden case of hives wouldn't be a bad thing. I could claim an immediate need for Benadryl and calamine lotion and get the hell out of here.

"This is it." Landon's voice pulled me out of my reverie. We were deep in the Hollywood Hills, a luxe enclave favored by celebrities and wealthy elites.

I pulled into a driveway practically hidden by jacaranda and birch trees, the gate already opening as he pointed his phone toward the window and keyed in a code.

It was impossible not to compare Landon's current setup with my lowbrow apartment complex. He'd come so far in just six years. In all the hours Landon and I lay in my twin bed, our skin sticky from the inefficient air conditioner, our sides practically glued together, talking about our future selves—Landon had never even hinted at wanting his own place. In fact, he said he'd rather spend his life on the road, on the stage. A traveling musician. A nomad. I had a feeling it was because he never expected to achieve the level of success he so obviously had. Back then he had kept his expectations low, not making any promises. To me, or himself.

That had been fine with me. The last thing I ever wanted was to be financially dependent on a man. I'd seen how that kind of relationship looked up close, and it wasn't pretty.

I wanted a marriage of equals. A partnership built on an even playing field.

Maybe now Landon had realized he could live in the moment and yet still plan for the future. That they weren't mutually exclusive ideals.

A heady mix of pride and admiration swept aside my anxiety, and I turned to him. "The day you bought this place, how did you feel?"

He flashed a proud grin. "Nearly as good as I feel right now."

I returned it, wondering what else had changed with him.

The second I parked, Landon grabbed my keys and launched himself out of my car with a relieved groan. "Jesus, your car is a freakin' torture device."

He came around to my side and opened the door. "Race ya to the pool."

I could only stare as Landon headed for a narrow path around the house. Grasping the back of his T-shirt, his muscles rippled as he pulled it off, tattoos gleaming beneath artfully placed exterior spotlights.

A rush of heat invaded my senses, racing through my veins before pulsing between my thighs. With one last squeeze of the steering wheel, I forced myself to get out of the car.

My four-inch wedge sandals felt unsteady on the gravel driveway, and not much better when I stepped onto the stone walkway Landon had taken.

Or maybe it was my composure that was wobbling.

A soft breeze ghosted over my skin, the night air cool and heady with the scent of lilac and lavender. I was wearing jeans and a frilly blouse that left my shoulders and arms exposed, but my shiver had nothing to do with the temperature.

Landon stood beside an infinity pool that went right to the edge of his property, the sprawl of Los Angeles rolling out behind him like a carpet woven through with twinkling Christmas lights. It was a gorgeous view…And by view, I meant Landon.

All six feet, two inches of him. Naked.

The glow of the interior pool lights danced over his ripped muscles, the ink covering his arms and chest coming to life. My fingertips tingled, remembering the feel of those arms. So many of Landon's tattoos had covered the visible scars of his childhood, the legacy of crackhead parents who thought the end of a lit cigarette was an appropriate punishment.

I stood still, unable to move a single muscle.

"Come on in," Landon called, as if skinny-dipping in the middle of the night was just a normal, everyday occurrence. Maybe for him, it was.

I tried to recall the last time I skinny-dipped.

Precisely the twenty-seventh of Never.

Landon executed a graceful dive off the edge, the silhouette of his body like a dark missile shooting through the water. Not until he'd reached the other end did he come up for air, standing in the shallow end and slicking his hair back like a wet Adonis. His eyes locked on to mine. I hadn't moved, still standing closer to my car than the pool.

"Do I need to come out there and get you?"

Yes. "No. I—I'm fine."

"You'd be a hell of a lot better if you came closer. Preferably in the water. With me."

The intensity of his stare pulled me forward until I was standing at the edge of the pool, not knowing how I got there.

Landon's lip curled as he glided through the water. "You gonna jump in?"

I looked down at my clothes, my shoes. "I'm not really dressed for swimming."

"So get undressed. For me."

I took a step back, but Landon was too fast for me. One of his hands wrapped around my ankle and held tight. As if he'd done it a million times before, he unclasped the buckle of my wedge sandal and pulled it off my foot, setting it down on the stone tiles. "Other one," he ordered.

Maybe it was the pleasure of his cool wet hand sliding against my overheated skin, or maybe relief at having the choice made for me, but I obediently shifted onto my now bare foot and let him remove my other shoe. Once it was standing next to its pair, Landon covered my toes with his palms and looked up at me, flashing a smile.

A smile that was both arrogant and achingly tender. A smile that shined from his eyes, too, making them crinkle at the corners. A smile I'd only seen him give to me.

That was the Landon I remembered. The one without the mega-mansion and infinity pool. The loner who practically hid behind his drum set. The lover who could keep me in bed for days at a time.

"I know you know how to swim," he taunted in a throaty growl.

That was true. Six years ago, Landon had known everything about me. Well, everything I'd been willing to tell him. Now, what did he know? Where I lived, that I had broken up with my boyfriend, and I could swim. Pretty scrawny list.

So, let him get to know you—even better this time.

But, did I really want that? Did I want to feel like complete shit when he walked away from me again? Would it hurt any less this time around?

I'd spent the first eighteen years of my life with a front-row seat to my mother practically begging my father to love her, unsuccessfully. I'd have to be crazy to doom myself to the same fate.

And besides, what did I really know about Landon anymore? Where he lived, what awards he'd won, and that he liked to skinny-dip at night.

Maybe we were on even footing, after all.

"Do I need to come get you?" Landon asked, with that delectable mouth of his.

Jesus, I think I want to bite that bottom lip.

I stepped back from the pool, holding Landon's gaze as I shimmied out of my jeans, then pulled my shirt over my head. Telling myself a bra and panty set was the same thing as a bikini.

Knowing it wasn't at all the same thing.

I shivered again, wishing I'd worn underwear that was more conservative, and with more coverage, than the pale pink lace set that blended with my skin tone and showed everything underneath.

But when I spared another shy glance at Landon's face, that trepidation disappeared. His eyes shined with reverence, gleamed with desire. A switch deep inside me flipped, and I allowed myself to feel like the woman mirrored in his gaze. Beautiful. Desirable. Valued.

Landon Cox could have any woman in the world. And, right now, he wanted *me*.

Chapter Six

Landon

Piper's pink lips were parted and glistening, needy breaths making her chest rise and fall. The hollow at the base of her neck fluttered as her hands moved from her sides to the band of her jeans, working the button. Lust curled around the base of my spine, the heat of my desire making the cool water feel like a bathtub.

Her hips swayed, inch after inch of flawless skin exposed as she smoothed the denim down her legs. Long and lean, my hands itched to touch.

I groaned as her fingers lifted the edge of her shirt and drew it over her head, exposing a tight stomach and full breasts barely contained by a whisper of pink lace. Letting the shirt fall to the ground, she shook her head, her blonde mane cascading down her back and shoulders like a silken veil.

Never one to be at a loss for words, my breath caught in the back of my throat, afraid to speak, afraid to breathe in case I unknowingly spooked her. In case I did anything to fuck this up.

And then she turned.

My heart pounded, gut twisting.

Piper was walking away.

Fuck. Fuck, fuck, fuck.

When I realized she was only walking to the shallow end of the pool, to the stairs, my knees sagged. I went from standing to crouching, my shoulders barely above the waterline.

Standing on the first pool step, her feet hidden by the water, legs together, Piper looked like a mermaid. Precious and ethereal. The stuff of myths and legends.

My gaze returned to her face as she took one tentative step, then another, my mouth going dry as the water rose higher, covering her knees, her thighs, her hips. I waited until she was at the very last tier before standing up and moving forward. The night was lushly quiet, the air layered with the sound of the pool jets and chirping cicadas, energized by our rapid breathing.

With Piper on the lowest step, we were closer in height than usual, her pupils dilated so widely I could see myself reflected in their dark depths. I lifted wet hands just above her shoulders, sending droplets of water to slide down her skin. They jumped over the ridge of her collarbone and raced along the curve of her breasts, dampening the lace of her bra.

I shuddered a breath and dipped my head low, sweeping my tongue over the tight buds of her nipples straining against the flimsy fabric.

Piper shivered, biting down on her full lower lip and letting her head fall back. Giving herself to me.

With the edge of my pinkie, I pulled the lacy edge down, exposing her breasts to the moonlight. A hungry growl rose up my throat from the pit of my stomach. "So fucking beautiful," I marveled, taking first one into my mouth, then the other. Piper arched her spine, a soft whimper trickling from her open mouth as she grabbed hold of my shoulders.

Fisting her hair in my hands, I licked my way up her breasts, my tongue dancing along her collarbone and throat, finally landing on her sweet, sweet mouth. I sucked on her bottom lip, savoring the taste of her.

I was like a fat kid in a candy shop—I couldn't get enough.

Piper melted into my embrace, her knees bucking. Needy hands slid from my shoulders to my neck, hopping off that step to lock her ankles just above my ass. Deepening our kiss. Demanding more from me.

If she only knew how badly I wanted to make one slight adjustment, one long thrust. I groaned my restraint into her mouth, releasing her hair to wrap my hands around her tiny waist.

With Piper in my arms, I backed up, moving farther into the pool, water climbing to the base of my neck. Slanting my mouth over hers, I kissed this girl with everything I had, everything I couldn't say, every ounce of wanting I'd stored up over the past six years. From the intensity of her response, she was doing the same.

Felt so fucking good.

My bare cock was pressed tight against her belly, pulsing to a beat all its own. Impatient to be deep inside the woman trembling in my arms.

I meandered in circles around the pool as we kissed, finally bumping up against a ledge and turning around to pin Piper's back to it. I pulled away from her mouth, trailing kisses along her jaw until I came to her delicate shell of an ear. Sucking the tiny lobe into my mouth, I licked along the baby-soft skin tucked close to her skull.

Every inch of this girl was delicious.

And I wanted every inch to be *mine*.

Piper was making stuttering noises, gulping at air between low moans and whispered pleas. In my head, they converted to beats, and I could feel music taking shape, rising and falling. I rarely came up with the words to my own songs, but I could feel them loitering at the edge of my conscience, almost twittering.

I found the back strap of her bra through the wet tangle of her hair, unclasping it easily and pulling the straps from her shoulders. Palming the perfect mounds in my hands, I flicked her nipples with my thumbs, my cock jerking at her throaty yelp. Her hips swiveled, her pelvis grinding against me.

Only my strong sense of self-preservation saved me from sliding my cock between her thighs and fucking her senseless in the pool. I'd never wanted anyone this bad, not even Piper herself.

Six years ago, I hadn't realized she was unique. A firefly among mosquitos.

I groaned, deepening our kiss, tightening my hold. Fighting against the memories, the sentimentality, the intrusive emotions.

Whatever this was, it wouldn't last. It *couldn't* last. Piper deserved a great guy—and that wasn't me. I could give her a great night, maybe more than one. I could give her kick-ass orgasms, plural. But I couldn't give her a future. Not the kind that ended well.

I needed a condom. Now.

With one last taste of her breasts, I walked us back to the steps and carried her straight out of the water, silencing what might have been the start of a protest with another kiss. Keying a code into the panel at the side door, I stepped inside, heading straight for my bedroom.

Depositing Piper gently in the middle of the mattress, I stepped back to admire the way the moonlight slanted through the windows and lit her porcelain skin like a statue carved by one of the masters. Rodin, maybe. Someone who knew his way around the female form. A man that saw beauty in their curves and hollows.

Piper lifted onto her elbows, looking at me with questions shining from her eyes. "What?"

"Can't a man look at a gift before unwrapping it?"

Her soft laugh hung in the air like mist. "I'm not quite unwrapped yet."

My eyes fell to the lace triangle that sat between her thighs. The most ineffective barrier I'd ever seen. Damp from the pool, it was entirely see-through.

I reached down, curving my fingers around the edge to stroke gently between her folds. Her eyes widened when she realized what I was doing, then fluttered shut as she practically bowed off the bed, a gasp rushing into her open mouth.

Piper wasn't just damp from the pool. Inside she was hot and wet. I pushed a little farther. She was so, so fucking tight. Her muscles clenched around me, pulling me deeper.

With a flick of my wrist, her panties snapped apart and I rubbed a thumb over her clit. Again and again, I slowly fucked her with my fingers. As I watched, Piper's breaths became pants, her hips lifting off the bed to meet my thrusts, her breasts shaking as tremors rocked her lithe frame.

I was completely enraptured. There was no other word for it.

My cock was a goddamn arrow, pointing straight toward Piper. Pulsing in frustration. My chest squeezed, tightening around my lungs as I absorbed the beauty and bliss that was Piper Hastings at the edge of an orgasm.

She was close, so close. I was tempted to pull back. To slide a condom on and finish the job myself. But I couldn't do that to her. And I wanted to watch her come apart without being distracted by my own release.

"Landon," she breathed my name. Cried it out again. The third time it was more like a shriek. My hand slowed as I watched her writhe and shake, her wet hair strewn around her head like brushstrokes on canvas. All the while her inner muscles were seizing, pulsing with aftershocks.

Her eyes opened at the same time as her thighs closed. One trapping my heart, the other trapping my hand. And then she grinned. Soft and sweet. Full of sinful temptation.

It fucking slayed me.

"I forgot what that felt like," she said, not a single trace of calculation in her voice.

I quirked a brow. "Getting off?"

Piper blushed, looking away. I pulled my hand from between her thighs, sliding my fingers across the tender skin above her hip bone. "Tell me."

She shook her head. "It's nothing."

I sat down on the bed beside her. "It's not nothing."

She huffed a sigh. "Maybe I'll tell you later. If you can do that again."

I leaned over her to pull open the drawer of my nightstand, retrieving a foil square, shaking it over her head. "Oh, I can do *that* again. After you tell me what's on your mind."

The minx swiped the condom from my hand and opened it with her teeth, sliding off the bed and crouching down in front of me. "I'm your guest. I get to choose."

And for a moment I was right back in her college dorm

room, hiding from her resident adviser and praying her roommate would stay out all night.

Her soft curse brought me back to the present. "This isn't—
Oh. Wrong way." Piper's tongue was poking out from between
her pressed lips. Her face a mask of concentration as she turned
it over and slid the plastic sheath down.

I sucked in a quick breath, her hands tight over me. Normally,
I would have grabbed a fresh one, but that would have meant delaying ecstasy. Couldn't do that.

I grabbed Piper, lifting her up and sliding her beneath me in
one smooth movement. "You drive a hard bargain."

Piper

On stage, Landon was laser-focused, rigid in his precision. Cre-
ating perfectly timed explosions of power and energy. The undeniable backbone of Nothing but Trouble.

In bed, he wasn't much different. If I took the condom from
him, it was because he let me. Because he wanted me as badly as
I wanted him. And that power imbued me with an unexpectedly
erotic confidence.

Even lying beneath Landon, caged between his powerful
thighs, his muscular forearms on either side of my head, I didn't
feel weak. I felt strong and desirable.

"What I did before, that was just a starter."

"A starter?" My legs were still quivering from the bonfire
Landon had ignited, and the flames were already rising again,
dancing and licking at my skin.

A smile slanted across his face as he nodded. "Just you watch,
Pippa. My skills have improved with time."

That last sentence both broke my heart and mended it at the same time. How many women had he practiced on over the years? Had any of them meant more to him than just a physical release?

Did I?

Yet Landon was here with me now, not anyone else. Even after I admitted to purposely avoiding him for the past few years. Even after I made it clear I wasn't going to chase him like all the others vying for his attention.

And tonight, those *skills* were mine.

My vision blurred for a moment, tears threatening. I blinked them away, digging my fingers into the heavy muscles curving above Landon's shoulder blades, breathing in air saturated with the scent of our mutual desire.

He edged my legs wider, and I complied. My hips lifting automatically, desperate to be filled by him. But even knowing what was coming, I was still taken aback by the weight of the broad head of his cock pushing against me. Nerves tangled in my stomach, afraid of the unknown.

Because this new, older rock *legend* was not the same Landon I'd laid with in my freshman dorm. What if I wasn't good enough? Landon had dated Hollywood stars and Victoria's Secret models. Rock chick groupies that probably had better skills than high-priced escorts.

"Hey," Landon said, running his finger along the curve of my jaw. I focused my attention back on him. "You still with me?"

I nodded my head, clearing the groupies and ghosts of Landon's past from it. The only woman with Landon right now was *me*. And I was damn well going to make the most of every minute.

I didn't expect to have very many.

Lifting my hands, I cupped Landon's face and brought it down to mine, hooking my legs over his hips and clasping my ankles at his back. "You've got a lot to prove, rock star. Better get started."

His gruff chuckle vibrated against my lips, his tongue entering my mouth at the same time as his cock drove through my slit.

Landon was bigger than I remembered. He kept sinking farther and farther, deeper and deeper, until I was so filled I started to squirm within his arms. "So tight," he whispered. "Fuck, Pippa." The raw need in his voice was achingly familiar.

Once upon a time, I thought Landon needed me.

Thought we were the stuff of fairy tales.

We'd been all too real. A love story cut short. No happily ever after ending for us.

But we had tonight.

This was Landon. My first love. My finest lover. The man who was a legend in my own mind before his fans had anything to say about it.

Tonight wasn't about making sense of this, of him, of us. It didn't have to make sense at all. Whatever *this* was—I deserved it.

The broken shards of my bleeding heart deserved it.

And so did the pitiful state of my current sex life.

Landon bottomed out inside me, dragging his pelvis against the slippery cluster of nerve endings just above where we were joined. I shuddered as he worked himself over me, the whole universe a brilliant show playing behind my lids—planets and comets and shooting stars. And when I thought I would die from the overwhelming enormity of it all—electric rays of color burning bright, light eviscerating dark—I opened my eyes and saw only Landon.

And the beauty of his face was even more overwhelming. There was a nobility to his sharp features, hinting at ancestors that had gone to war for love and country...and won. Conquered.

If Landon wanted my heart back, he was going to have one hell of a fight on his hands. I would not surrender it so easily this time. But my body...the look on his face told me he knew I was entrusting it to him tonight—no battle required.

With a cocky wink, he ground into me, his breath hot against my lips.

Then he stopped, and for a second I thought I'd done something wrong, said something to make him realize we were making a mistake.

But no, Landon merely picked me up like I weighed nothing, scooting to the edge of the bed so that I was on top of his lap, my legs still crossed behind him. Holding me by my upper arms, he arched me away from his chest, practically growling as he bent his head and swept a straining nipple into his mouth. I gasped as he rolled his tongue over the needy peak, my hips jackknifing into his.

"Ah, Pippa. You don't know what you do to me." His voice was gravel mixed with honey. Decadently abrasive.

Ink colored much of Landon's skin, but the marks he'd left on me were just as bright, just as symbolic. Some beautiful, some ugly. Most painful. They had been etched deep below the surface of my skin, invisible to the naked eye.

As if to remind me of them, a cruel whisper unfurled from inside my mind, taunting me.

What do you think you're doing—asking for one night of pleasure? Willing to pay for it with a lifetime of pain. Haven't you had enough? Hasn't this man—the same one doling out delicious swells of ecstasy—hurt you enough?

How much hurt can one person take?

Oblivious to the war raging within my body, Landon moved from one breast to the other, my nipples becoming impossibly tight, desperate for his attention. He swirled his tongue over one, licking and sucking as he palmed the other, pinching and squeezing. The pull of a climax tugged at me from deep within my core.

My hips undulated with each flick of Landon's tongue, waves of bliss crashing over me. I was drowning in ecstasy, my breaths reduced to sharp, broken gasps that didn't fill me with nearly enough oxygen.

"I can't, I can't—" I stuttered, frantic.

"You can, Pippa. You can with me. Always with me. Only with me," Landon growled, just before swallowing my escalating panic with a kiss. Giving me his confidence, his conviction that we were on the right path. Shifting me so that my chest was pressed to his, I could feel Landon's heartbeat thudding through my skin. My pulse found his rhythm, matching it.

And somehow that pure panic turned into something else. The pleasure came back. Rather than attempt to outrun it, I raced it instead. Going faster and faster, higher and higher.

Until I was floating within the circle of Landon's arms.

Airborne and cradled.

Softly swaying.

Wild.

Safe.

I came back to earth just in time to hear Landon's hoarse, breathy grunt as he found his own release, a sound that made my toes curl and heart shudder. A mix of vulnerability and strength, it was such an intimate, unguarded noise that I savored it, pressing tiny kisses to the pulsing artery of his neck.

I might have sought Landon out tonight, intending to take what I wanted from him. A night of pleasure. A litany of orgasms. The thrill of walking away from him this time.

But I wasn't prepared for the sudden rush of fear that what I really wanted wasn't merely the temporary high of a night well spent.

What if what I really wanted was *him*?

Chapter Seven

Landon

I woke up to an empty bed.

That wasn't unusual, not in my own house. I didn't bring women back here, ever.

And yet, I hadn't blinked an eye at inviting Piper over. Bringing her into *my* bed even though I had plenty of others to choose from. The condoms in my nightstand—they were there out of habit, not convenience.

When Piper cried out my name, why had it meant so much more than when it was screamed by a crowd of thousands? Was it because she hadn't hesitated to kick me out of her apartment when so many others would have done anything to lure me into theirs? Was it because she had haunted my dreams for years?

Maybe. Or maybe it was just the sense I had that Piper knew *me*, wanted *me*. Not the rock star or the manwhore or the fucking legend. She knew the lonely soul who was most comfortable hiding behind his drum kit, who loved making music and fought for every gig. Six years ago, I'd been no one with nothing. A guy with no home, no family, no cash, no cachet. The drummer of a band no one outside the gritty West Coast music scene had ever heard of. And yet, every night, Piper had looked at me as if I hung the moon.

She didn't look at me that same way anymore. Not quite. There was a wariness to her gaze that hadn't been there before. A wariness I'd put there.

We had sex three more times during the night. Our bodies restless and needy, resisting the pull of sleep. How could I sleep with Piper's soft breaths ghosting across my skin, her warm hand resting on my chest, her small, smooth calf tucked between my legs? In the semi-dark room, I could barely close my eyes. They were too busy memorizing Piper's curves, studying all her delicious hollows, staring at the sweep of her eyelashes across sculpted cheekbones, the hair cascading over my arm like a blonde waterfall.

And I'd gotten an answer to my question.

I forgot what that felt like.

"Getting off," as I'd so crudely put it, wasn't what Piper had meant. No, she'd clarified her offhand statement somewhere between round two and three. *Knowing something couldn't possibly be any better. That it was perfect, as is.*

I could have said the same about last night—all of it. Every minute we'd spent together had been fucking perfect.

Goddamn it. Had she left me already?

I sat up, automatically counting the condom wrappers on the floor just to be sure we'd played it safe. Four.

I heaved a sigh and roughed agitated fingers through my hair.

"Piper," I called, loudly. Only silence answered me back.

Dread and disappointment swirled within in my gut as I got up and stalked to the bathroom, splashing water on my face. For the first time in a long while, I actually met my own eyes in the mirror. Had I done something to make her leave? I didn't drink anything after leaving the bar. Didn't take any drugs. Physically, I felt great. No gaping holes in my memory, no chemically induced nausea.

Throwing on a pair of track pants—my housekeeper would show up soon and I didn't want to lose her by parading my nutsack out in the open—I headed for the stairs, spotting something unexpected as I passed a window. A bright blue something. Piper's car.

My spirits lifted as if they'd been shoved onto a high-speed elevator. "Pippa," I called again.

"In here." Her voice floated down the hall. Familiar and welcoming.

Rounding the corner, I saw Piper standing in my kitchen, wearing my shirt and, from what I could tell, nothing underneath. Might be time to add another condom wrapper to the collection littering my bedroom floor.

"Thought you'd run away," I said, coming up behind her and fitting her against me, Piper's sweet ass the perfect cushion for my dick that, despite his hardworking night, felt fresh as a damn daisy.

"That's your specialty, not mine," she mumbled.

Ouch. My arms dropped for a second, until I caught a whiff of her scent, a natural sweetness liberally mixed with sex. Then I wrapped my arms around her even tighter. "That was a long time ago."

Piper cleared her throat, trying to push away from me. I didn't let her, instead lifting the heavy curtain of hair obstructing access to her neck and dropping a kiss on the glimpse of bare skin just above the collar of my shirt, giving her neck a swipe with my tongue. She released a soft puff of air, the tension draining away from her frame as she relaxed in my arms. "Again?" she asked.

I nudged her ass, nipping at the spot I just licked. "Best way to start the day."

"But I was going to make you breakfast," she demurred.

For the first time I noticed the mess scattered on the granite countertop—eggs, bread, milk, fruit.

"Later," I said, turning Piper in my arms and pushing my hands through her hair, tugging a little to get her at the perfect angle for my mouth. My body was craving a different kind of nourishment.

My eyes swept over Piper's face as I leaned down to kiss her. The girl's skin was flawless. Creamy with golden undertones. And scattered across the bridge of her ski-jump nose was just the tiniest smattering of freckles, so light you could only see them up close.

With my tongue, I traced the plush softness of Piper's lower lip. Tasting the orange juice she must have had. Sweet and tart. Delicious. I growled, slanting my lips over hers, deepening our kiss. Wanting to devour her whole.

Piper slid grasping hands against my sides, flattening her palms against my back, pushing her body against mine. I unwrapped my fists from her hair, dragging them down her spine to squeeze her ass cheeks as I ground against her flat belly. Why didn't I keep condoms in the kitchen?

"Oh." Ana's surprised gasp sent Piper and I flying apart from each other like guilty teenagers.

My housekeeper recovered faster than we did, beaming a wide grin from me to Piper and back again. To Ana's credit, it barely even slipped when she caught sight of the mess cluttering the countertops she prided herself on keeping spotless. "Sit, sit." She shooed us to the planked kitchen table overlooking the backyard. Piper's shirt, the one she'd been wearing at Travis's party, must have blown into the pool during the night because it was now drifting in the deep end like a fallen cloud.

Piper tossed an embarrassed glance my way, so I grabbed her hand and brought her to the table with me. My shirt went practically to her knees, but unlike me, she'd actually buttoned it. "Piper, this is Ana. Ana, Piper is an old friend of mine."

I was met with a pair of equally dubious expressions. Ana probably wondering why she'd never seen or heard of her in the eighteen months she'd been working for me. And Piper, for too many reasons to think about right now.

Smothering her laugh with a cough, Ana turned back to the provisions laid out on the countertop. "So, frittatas?"

"Actually, I should probably—" The beginning of Piper's softly spoken excuse turned my stomach in a way I couldn't remember feeling. I didn't want her to go, and it wasn't because I was trying to figure out a way to get her back to my bedroom. I just wasn't ready for her to leave yet.

"Sounds perfect," I said, interrupting her.

Between the whir of the Vitamix, Piper and I managed to chat about inconsequential things. And by the time we were halfway done with Ana's amazing kale and berry smoothies, she had placed steaming plates in front of us. Digging into the frittata and toast with butter and strawberry jam, I couldn't tamp down the smile that had crept onto my face. This was *nice*.

Sitting in the kitchen of a house I loved but had never shared with any woman besides Ana. Sharing my home, my breakfast, my morning with Piper…it felt so goddamn *nice*.

A welcome change from dragging my hungover ass out of bed to force down whatever Ana wanted to feed me, not because I was hungry but because I knew I needed to eat if I wanted to start feeling like a human being again.

Was this how most people felt in the morning? Like they could conquer the day after some eggs and juice?

Or was it the warmth of Piper's presence that was making me feel this way?

I put my fork down, realizing I shouldn't be enjoying this so much. Sure Shane and Delaney were making it work, but they were the exception to the rule. Rockers weren't rocks. We were tumbleweeds, blowing with the wind. Subject to the whims of the industry. Our manager, tour schedule, award season, recording timetable, release dates. I was blown by those forces. And when it all got to be too much, when I needed to escape into my own world, that was when drinking and drugging and fucking came in so handy.

Except that right now, my kitchen felt pretty damn self-contained. Like its own world.

And it was leading me to think…maybe I could make things work with Piper.

Hope surged—a tempting lure for the unwary and undeserving.

So goddamn tempting.

I should know better than to give in to it.

If I was being honest with myself, I'd admit the odds were slim to none. At best.

How could I take the risk of hurting her again?

The thing I did even better than drinking and drugging and fucking?

Destroying.

Piper

I noticed the second Landon went from being relaxed and easy-going, shoveling eggs in around his smile, to the brooding, intense stranger I saw on stage. The change in energy was obvious. One minute the air in the kitchen was light and buoyant, and the next it was sharp and acrid.

I swallowed the food in my mouth, taking a sip of coffee to get it past the tightness in my throat. Telling myself I was wrong, or at least oversensitive, I spared a sideways glance at Landon.

I wasn't wrong. He was scowling at his plate like a cockroach had crawled inside his breakfast and died.

Setting down my fork, I wiped at my mouth with my napkin. "This has been lovely," I mumbled, forcing an appreciative smile onto my face for Ana.

She beamed back at me, and I wondered if the women Landon brought home didn't stay for breakfast.

What difference did that make?

Landon probably brought different women back to his bed every night. How could I have thought, even for one second, that I was enough for him?

I hadn't been six years ago, and I certainly wasn't now.

What Landon and I had done in my dorm room was great—he'd had the stamina and enthusiasm of a college quarterback. But last night…

Last night I discovered that the college kid had turned pro. The stamina and enthusiasm had still been there, in spades, but they were tempered—no, that was the wrong word. They were *enhanced* by skill and patience. There had been tenderness, too. And a reverence that had softened the intensity of it all.

It had been intense.

The press of Landon's mouth on mine, the scrape and bite of his teeth on my skin, the flex and pull of his muscles beneath my hungry hands, the grind of his hips punctuating each deep stroke.

Gasps of pleasure. So. Much. Pleasure.

Maybe his change in mood was because I'd overstayed my welcome.

Was there protocol to follow? A way to do this right, whatever *this* was?

After my conversation with Delaney, I'd thought of last night as some kind of game. A way to even the score between Landon and I, maybe even tilt the board in my favor.

There were probably rules to the game. Rules I wasn't aware of. Like checking my messy emotions at the door and leaving before first light.

The real problem, of course, was that this wasn't a game for *me*. I thought it could be. Had fooled myself into thinking that a casual fling with my ex didn't have to mean anything. But it did. He did.

And now I felt lost, and emotionally exhausted. Vulnerable in a way I didn't like, as if the seam guarding my emotions had come undone, Landon ripping a stitch with every kiss and bite and thrust.

I didn't know who I was supposed to be in this moment. And I didn't belong with this new person Landon had become. Maybe I hadn't belonged with the old Landon, either. Although I would always belong *to* him. New, old, it didn't matter. A part of my soul would always be his. Which was why I had to leave, before Landon used it against me.

"You hardly ate," Ana said, glancing at my plate.

It might have looked that way, considering how much food

she'd heaped on it. But I did eat, a lot. And every bite was now churning in the pit of my stomach, threatening revolt. "It was delicious," I insisted, sliding off the bench and picking up my plate and coffee mug, making an attempt to grab the mason jar with the remains of my smoothie before deciding to come back for it. With my luck the lot would wind up in Landon's lap.

Well, maybe I could lick—

Piper, focus.

Ana tsked as I set my plate on the counter, and I spun around to go back for the smoothie.

Landon looked up from his plate just as I was reaching out to grab the glass. The raw emotion in his eyes hit my chest like a flash of lightning. I don't know whether it was a spasm from the current, or just a self-fulfilling prophecy, but I overshot the mark and swatted his glass instead of grasping it. Right. Into. Landon's. Lap.

"Oh my god, I'm so, so sorry!" I screeched, clapping a hand—the offending one that had spilled my drink—over my mouth. Wishing I could just bite it off.

Thick purple sludge that had been delicious to drink, but actually looked like a slaughtered eggplant, was strewn all over Landon's plate and bare chest, pooling between his thighs and dripping onto the floor.

Landon pushed back his chair and stood up, staring at the massacre as if he didn't know how it had gotten there.

"Not to worry, not to worry," Ana said, brushing by me with a damp cloth.

Landon started to walk away from the table, probably to change out of his smoothie-drenched pants.

"Mr. Landon, you're dripping. You take those pants off right now."

Landon stopped in his tracks, sin and sarcasm written across his face. "Now Ana, if I didn't know better I would think you put Piper up to that to get me naked."

With one hand on her hip, Ana didn't look flustered in the slightest. "I raised three boys and still have a husband to care for. If you think I'm interested in any other man's cojones, your ego is bigger than your brain." As if realizing she'd overstepped some invisible boss-employee line, Ana finished with, "Mr. Landon."

Landon didn't look offended at all, pulling his pants off in one smooth movement and handing them to her. Ana kept her face averted, but I could have sworn I saw her glance at Landon's ass as he sauntered away.

Damn that man had a fine ass.

I sighed. Not that I would be seeing it again.

Landon

Well, so much for thinking Ana would be flustered by the sight of me in my birthday suit. She didn't even peek at my cojones. Although Piper did, with a flash of longing that made me want to grab her by the hair and bring her back to my bed like the caveman beating his fists inside my chest.

But I didn't.

And not just because Ana would probably have slapped my hand away and out-cavemanned me. Having Piper around wasn't supposed to feel so homey and natural. She wasn't the kind of girl who belonged in my life. I deserved groupies who didn't care which member of the band they fucked, as long as it gave them bragging rights. Piper deserved...

I yanked the lever in the shower, not bothering to adjust the cold spray, the better to calm my chaotic thoughts. I didn't want to think about the kind of man Piper deserved. I didn't want to think about her with another man, period.

Fuck.

By the time I got back downstairs, my hair still wet, I didn't have to worry about it anymore. Piper was gone.

Ana looked at me with a raised eyebrow as I sauntered into the kitchen. "Your *friend* said she would send your shirt back to you." There was a distinct air of disapproval in her voice.

I glanced out the window. Piper's shirt was no longer floating in the pool, her shoes and jeans also gone. "Did she—"

"Leave? Yes."

Guilt gripped me by the throat.

I've woken up in places I didn't remember going, with women I didn't remember meeting, much less fucking. I've woken up hungover and with bruises from bar fights I didn't remember.

I've woken up feeling like shit on a stick more mornings than not, for an impressive variety of reasons.

But this morning had started off great until I realized Piper wasn't in bed with me. Then I'd discovered her downstairs and felt great again. Better than great—happy. For once, I'd felt comfortable in my own skin.

Until I hadn't.

And now I didn't know how to feel. I had whiplash and the sun was barely up.

I wasn't happy Piper had left. Her absence wasn't a relief. It was an itch I wanted to scratch until it bled.

I walked to the foyer, standing beside the window where I'd seen the obnoxiously cheerful blue of Piper's car looking so out of place among the elaborately elegant landscape of trees and plants and flowers meticulously tended by Ana's husband. The gravel driveway had already been raked over, leaving no sign that she'd been here at all.

My chest tightened and I blinked away from the view, walking around the main floor like a guest in my own home.

Eventually, I ended up at the bar tucked into a corner of my oversized living room. A room that could easily have accommodated a party of a hundred people.

I poured myself my favorite drink: one-third bourbon, one-third whiskey, one-third scotch. It was my version of a Long Island iced tea, and existed for one reason and one reason only, to obliterate the thoughts cluttering my brain with a tsunami of alcohol.

I dropped onto a chair by a window, one of a dozen I could have chosen, and kicked my feet onto the nearby ottoman.

Staring at the sumptuously appointed space, I let my eyes jump from one piece of furniture to another, realizing that few had ever felt the imprint of a human ass.

There was no TV in the room, and I didn't have my phone near me to activate the sound system. Over the hum of air-conditioning, the sounds of Ana moving about in the kitchen were muffled. My thoughts were loud though. Frenzied and angry.

I took swallow after swallow from my glass, but they didn't calm down.

Once drained, I slammed my glass down on an end table that had been fashioned from birch and bronze, waiting to feel something.

Wanting to feel nothing.

Eventually, I made another drink and went in search of my

cell phone. What I was really looking for was Piper's number, which wasn't in my phone. I could get it from Travis, or from anyone in his office. But then I remembered how he'd looked at the two of us together, before I'd feigned drunkenness.

More importantly, how he'd looked at Piper. Like he was disgusted at the possibility that she'd fallen for a guy like me.

If I wasn't his client, he would have had me thrown out.

I could go to Piper's place, although even I wasn't stupid enough to get behind the wheel right now. My truck was still at Travis's place, anyway. I had another car, a ridiculously expensive Italian number I hated. Jett had taken it for a joyride last week and hadn't bothered returning it. He could keep it, for all I cared.

I scowled at the latest iPhone in my hands. Useless piece of shit. I tossed it on the ground, which was covered by a hand-knotted rug made in some former Eastern Bloc country I couldn't pronounce. We'd played a show there once.

Everything in this house, and of course the house itself, had been bought with the beat of a drum.

My success had given me so much. Money, trophies, fame, endless options for how to enjoy all three.

But there were times, like this morning, when I could only see how much that success had cost me.

I made another drink and retrieved my phone, unscathed from its padded landing. Maybe it was time to invite people into my life. Relax, open up.

I took another burning sip, hissing as the liquor scorched its way down my throat.

Piper and I probably traveled in the same circles and I'd never even known it. Maybe if I got out more, or threw a party every once in a while, our paths would cross again.

I glanced outside. Bright sun, nearly cloudless sky. Perfect day for a pool party.

Falling back into my chair, I pulled up my contacts and thumbed off a massive group text.

Maybe they could cross again this afternoon.

Chapter Eight

Piper

I drove home in a daze, my eyes on the road but my brain still trapped inside Landon's kitchen. What exactly had caused the shift in his mood? It was so sudden, so certain. With no obvious reason. At least, not one that I could see.

I shivered from the air-conditioning, then turned it off. My skin felt raw. I would have loved to take a long, hot shower, then retreat to my bed with a mug of hot tea and a bowl of ice cream, alternating from one to the other until even my taste buds had been neutralized.

Unfortunately, I'd barely unbuckled my seatbelt when I spotted Adam crossing the parking lot toward me.

For god's sake. I slammed my door in frustration. If I had to make the walk of shame, did it have to be in front of Adam?

And I was ashamed. The leaden emotion crept through my

veins like a toxin, turning my limbs heavy and stiff. Landon belonged in my past. What had I been thinking bringing him back into my present?

And now I had to deal with Adam, too. Life just wasn't fair.

At least, not mine.

I was still wearing Landon's shirt, although I'd pulled my jeans on before getting into my car. But going commando in denim, after last night's sexcapades, was its own kind of torture.

Adam's gaze roved from my head to my toes, taking in my appearance. "Nice shirt," he quipped.

I skirted around him and headed for my apartment, wanting to be left alone with my sore body and aching heart. "Adam," I said, pushing at my front door as if it were a ten-ton bank vault instead of flimsy particleboard, "now isn't a good time."

"But—"

"Go home." *Please.*

"Listen, I know things are awkward between us right now."

"Awkward?" A laugh I'd never heard before rumbled from my throat. A chortle, maybe. Or a cackle. I got distracted trying to categorize it.

Adam pursed his lips. "Fine. I'm sure she'll understand."

"Understand—" Out of the corner of my eye I saw the present, wrapped in bubble gum–pink paper, that I'd bought weeks ago. It had been sitting on a shelf of my bookcase for so long I'd stopped noticing it. "Devon's birthday party." The little girl was Adam's niece, but I adored her as if she was my own.

Adam stopped walking toward the door. "You still want to go?"

Whatever had happened between Adam and me, I'd promised Devon that I would be at her fourth birthday party. I couldn't miss it. "Gimme a few minutes." Jogging to my bathroom, I turned the water on high. The chlorine hadn't been kind to my hair, but I didn't have time to worry about it now. Twisting it into a bun, I pulled an old-fashioned shower cap over it and plugged in my hair straightener.

Fifteen minutes later I was dressed in a bright pink Lilly Pulitzer romper and a pair of gold gladiator sandals. The romper was a little loud for my taste, but I'd snagged it at a killer sale and it was Devon's favorite color. Not just pink—hot pink. The gladiator sandals were for me though—a reminder to woman up. Life went on, even if Landon Cox wasn't a part of it.

Adam raised his eyebrows when I came out. "Interesting choice."

How had I not realized the man was meant to be my gay best friend and not my boyfriend?

I bit my lip against a sharp retort that would make this uncomfortable moment even more so. Instead, I pointed at his madras pants and lime green shirt. "I hardly think you're one to criticize, Mr. Vineyard Vines."

He extended his elbow. "Touché, Lilly."

I took the joking insult, leaning automatically into Adam for a minute, wishing he could be The One as strongly as I knew he wasn't. At our contact, the anger I'd been holding on to suddenly fell away. We'd always been better friends than lovers. And after last night, I now knew I wasn't willing to sacrifice butterflies in my stomach and multiple orgasms on the altar of holy matrimony.

Landon had shown me at least that much.

Landon.

Even the thought of him sent a pang of longing shooting through my veins. Eventually, I hoped I would have the strength to appreciate Landon for what he was—my first love…not my last.

But right now, I wasn't there yet. Or even close.

Slipping the strap of my purse over my shoulder, I picked up Devon's gift and followed Adam to the parking lot, hesitating when he pointed his key fob at his own car. Did I really want to spend the next half hour trapped less than a foot away from him?

Then again, I didn't want to show up at his parents' house until we'd had a conversation. And, frankly, I didn't want be responsible for getting us there in one piece while having it.

"Want to stop for coffee?"

Gratitude softened the edges of my agitation. "I would love that, actually." I'd barely had a few sips from the mug Ana had given me earlier, and my veins were crying out for caffeine.

Ten minutes later, my fingers were wrapped around a cardboard sleeve and Adam was pulling back out into traffic. "So," we both began at the same time.

I bit down on a small smile, motioning for Adam to go first.

"I'm sorry for the other day," he began.

"You said that already. But are you sorry for what I overheard, or for keeping your previous relationship with Brian a secret?" I took a quick breath and decided to rephrase my question so it reflected what I really wanted to know. "Are you sorry for what you did…Or for lying to me about who you are?"

Adam coughed, one hand lifting from the wheel to rub at the back of his neck. "Is there an 'all of the above' option?"

I sighed. "Listen, I don't know if I'm up for a conversation about *us* right now. And I'm definitely not ready to be a sounding board for what you have going on with Brian or anyone else. At least, not just yet. But I'd really like to be on the same page before we show up at Devon's party. Can we at least figure that out?"

"Honestly, I'm still trying to figure things out on my end, Piper. Do you mind if we keep things status quo, just for today?"

"You want me to lie?"

"No. But do we really have to tell my family about us, about me, in the middle of Devon's birthday party? When should we do it—after pin the tail on the donkey and before she blows out her candles?"

Truthfully, *I* didn't want to do it at all. I adored Adam's family, but they were *his* family. Whatever he chose to tell them was his business, not mine. Not anymore.

I'd been to Adam's parents' home many times—practically every Sunday since we'd met. Except that this time, my cheeks burned with embarrassment walking through the door, thinking how disappointed they would be with me once they learned the truth. That Adam wasn't in love with me. That I hadn't been *enough*. Again.

The depressing thought was swept aside by a high-pitched shriek. "Auntie Piper!" Wearing a pink dress even brighter than mine, Devon launched herself at my legs, nearly knocking me down.

Stumbling slightly, I handed the present to Adam and lifted my favorite four-year-old, settling her on my hip. "Hey there, I'm here for the birthday party. Do you know who we're celebrating?" I asked, feigning ignorance of the pink crown with HAPPY BIRTHDAY spelled out in rhinestone letters.

"Me!" she yelled, a grin splitting her deliciously chubby cheeks.

"You? No way!"

She dissolved into giggles, and I laughed along with her.

"You came." Becca, Devon's mother, walked toward me with her arms already outstretched. An adult replica of her daughter.

I hugged her with one arm while my other remained curled around Devon's waist. "I wouldn't miss it for the world," I answered, feeling awful that I'd nearly forgotten about the party entirely. Yet another reason to be angry at Landon. The damn man had me so scattered I could barely remember my own name.

"You have to see the puppies, Auntie Piper!" Devon yelled, even though her face was only a few inches from my ear.

I looked at Becca. "Puppies?" The woman was allergic to just about everything with fur.

"Same concept as a petting zoo," Becca said, "although the dogs are all available for adoption. Unfortunately we can't take one, but between the fee and the possibility of finding forever homes, it's kind of a win-win for everyone."

The little girl between us squirmed to be let down. I relaxed my hold and followed her outside. Several large pens had been set up, each staffed by someone wearing a bright yellow T-shirt, red letters proclaiming HARMONY'S PETTING PUPS, and containing a few puppies big enough to hold their own with the enthusiastic pre-school set.

There was also a bounce house at the far end of the property and a slime-making station with a couple of teenagers supervising.

It was a perfect little girl's birthday party, and Devon looked happier than I'd ever seen her before, which was saying a lot.

One of the yellow T-shirted women came over to me as I watched Devon rolling on the grass with the puppies, squealing with delight at their wagging tails and licking tongues. "It's a shame her mother's allergic. She's so good with animals."

I nodded wistfully. "I know."

"How about you? Any room for a dog in your life?"

The question would have felt intrusive if the woman's tone

hadn't been so light. Floating a hypothetical rather than pushing an obligation.

"I wish," I said, honestly. Growing up, I'd always wanted a pet. Dog, cat, hamster, anything. But my father had flat out refused, and in our home, his word was law.

The woman's graying hair looked nearly white in the bright sunlight, though her cocoa-colored skin wasn't marred by a single wrinkle. She gave a small shrug of her shoulders. "Maybe someday."

"Yeah. Maybe." At that moment, a golden-haired puppy made a dash for my legs, chasing after the plastic ball Devon had thrown.

I was one of the few adults outside, and I didn't mind one bit.

Becca, I knew, would stay inside for most of the party, hyped up on antiallergy meds and drinking mimosas with the other mothers. Rather than feel excluded no one had made an effort to coax me inside, I was grateful to be spared the "So, when are you and Adam going to finally tie the knot?" questions.

Despite knowing for sure the answer was precisely, "Never," it wasn't my place to give it. Let Adam be the one to share the news, and deal with the inevitable questions to follow…another day.

Adam was the youngest in his family, and Becca had said she was done after Devon, so the spotlight was on him to add to the family tree.

I was an only child to two parents who probably shouldn't have had children at all—at least, not with each other. And while Adam's parents kept hinting that they were ready to be grandparents again, my mother and I only discussed the most benign subjects.

My father and I rarely spoke at all.

I didn't want a child of my own and right now the only bright side about not becoming a part of Adam's family was not disappointing them when I didn't produce any babies to add to the mix. Though I thoroughly enjoyed borrowing someone else's—especially when they were as adorable as Devon.

It was clear to me now that what I'd loved most about being with Adam was his family and his friendship. Not the romance between us. The thought of losing them made my heart heavy. Would I still be invited to Devon's birthday party next year, or the year after that?

Later, as I watched Devon blow out the candles of her birthday cake, cheered on by her parents, cousins, aunts, uncles, and her pint-sized friends, I was nearly brought to my knees by a wave of fierce longing. Had I ever been surrounded by as much love as this little girl?

Landon

I woke up to some new-age, shit-ass orchestra. Beeping, buzzing, blaring. Someone needed to turn that crap off before I ripped them a new one.

It went on and on and on. More irritating by the second. And as much as I tried, I couldn't open my goddamn eyes. My eyelids had turned into thousand-pound shutters. Or…was something holding them down? Trying to figure it out, trying to tune out that damn noise that didn't have the faintest relation to music was impossible with the sledgehammer pounding into my skull.

Noise. Pain. Darkness.

The beeping speed up, becoming an alarm. Jesus fucking Christ. Who the fuck set off the alarm?

I heard movement, felt a change in light. Brighter, I thought.

"Mr. Cox, glad you're joining us."

"Who the fuck are you?" But the question didn't make it from my brain to my mouth. What emerged instead sounded more like a seal's bark than a human voice.

My eyelid was lifted, and I jerked away from the brightness, only to have it repeated on the other side.

"Fuck off, asshole," said the seal.

"Pupils are reactive. He can have some water." There was the low hum of a vibration as the bed began moving, the pressure in my head increasing exponentially with every inch. Something was put to my lips.

"Drink this. Slowly," came a soft voice I didn't recognize.

I swallowed, although not nearly as much as I wanted to before it was taken away.

Suddenly the god-awful noises were turned off, and I breathed a sigh of relief, tentatively opening my eyes before promptly closing them again. Too much, too bright. A wave of nausea rocked into me.

"Mr. Cox, I'd like to go through a few basic questions. Are you okay with that?"

I grunted, tentatively moving my jaw and mouth. Wondering what would come out.

"Can you tell us your full name?"

"Water," was all I managed. After a few more sips, still not enough, I croaked out an answer. "Landon Cox."

"Can you tell us your address and birthdate?"

I did.

"Do you know where you are?"

I risked a glance. "Hospital." The word came out before I had time to process it. *I was in a hospital?*

"Correct. You were brought here, to Cedars-Sinai hospital, in an ambulance about an hour ago. Do you know why you're here?"

I thought back, trying to remember. The image that popped up was Piper's face. Piercing blue eyes that saw right through me. The palest suggestion of freckles trekking across her nose. And that hair. A sleek golden river that smelled like honey and ran through my hands like silk.

Fuck. I'd been such a dick. I let all the fears inside my brain ruin the first morning we'd spent together in years.

Piper wasn't stupid. She'd obviously picked up on my discomfort and thought I wanted her to leave.

Had I?

My skull felt like it was cracking apart. "My head," I groaned. If I was in a hospital, they had to have kick-ass drugs for the pain.

The man in the white coat, a doctor, I assumed, gave a condescending grunt. "Exactly. Drugs and alcohol don't mix well with parties and pools."

Spare me the after-school special morality lesson. I just wanted something to stop the—

Oh, shit.

Memories pricked at my brain like shards of broken glass, sharp but fragile. Liquor splashing into a crystal tumbler. The burn running down my throat. Drinking alone. Holding my phone in my hands, wanting to call Piper. A text about a party.

A party. *My party?*

I didn't remember a party.

The doctor had been pretty specific. *Drugs and alcohol don't mix well with parties and pools.*

The last time I'd been in my pool, I hadn't been alone. I'd been with Piper.

Confused, I tuned back into what the doctor was saying. "…drugs for the pain in a moment, but I'd like you to do something for me first." He put a notepad across the sheet covering my legs and held out a pencil. "Can you write your name for me?"

I lifted my right arm, feeling a deep twinge. "Sure."

Except that when I went to grasp the pencil, my fingers didn't close. The pencil dropped to the floor. I stared down at it in silence, panic driving nails through my already cracking skull. What. The. Fuck.

The nurse retrieved it and came around to the other side of my bed. "How about with your left?"

This time, my fingers pinched together, but my grip was like a toddler holding a crayon. I looked at the doctor, fear escalating. "What the fuck is happening? Why can't I use my hands?"

A monitor began wailing again, and both doctor and nurse swiveled to read the blinking red numbers racing across the screen.

"What's wrong with my hands?" I yelled again, feeling frantic and sluggish at the same time. It didn't matter. No one was listening to me.

A syringe glinted as the nurse injected it into the IV bag hanging near my head. I repeated my question again, but it never made it past my lips. I closed my eyes, and gave in to the darkness rushing up to swallow me.

Piper

Adam tossed a grateful smile my way as he pointed his key fob at his BMW. "Thanks for coming," he said.

"You don't have to thank me. I didn't do it for you." Sliding into the smooth leather seat, I leaned back against the headrest and toed off my shoes. It had been a long day. The other children and their parents left after cake, but Adam's family had stayed for hours afterward.

He had offered to take me home early, but I declined, not in any rush to leave the warm embrace of the Williams family. They came from a place of love, and even though I couldn't be honest with them about the state of my relationship with Adam, putting on a happy face while lying through my teeth came easily to me.

It was how I'd been raised.

That perfect facade I'd created in high school—prom queen, captain of the cheerleading squad, senior body vice president—had adhered to my skin like a permanent tattoo. Because when people saw something pretty and perfect, only the most cruel wanted to stomp on it, destroy it. Everyone else just enjoyed the view, or were too intimidated to get very close.

It didn't always work, of course. If someone wanted to find fault, there was nothing you could really do. Perfection would always be just out of reach, no matter how hard you tried.

But each failure, those countless attempts and misses, they left their mark. At first, each one hurt, like a bruise or a cut. But eventually, they piled up, one after the other, weaving together to form a dazzling costume.

I learned to settle for fooling most people, most of the time.

Except for my own father.

And so I was constantly on my guard. Hiding behind a disguise, feeling like an imposter.

A maid pretending to be a princess.

One tick from midnight.

Halfway home, my chaotic thoughts were interrupted by the buzz of my phone.

Travis: Get to Cedars Sinai. Now.

I stifled a groan. Travis's clients were always in the hospital.

Face-lifts, surgical implants of the breast, butt, and penis variety, organ failure brought on by extreme dieting, injuries from stunts gone wrong, and of course, an overabundance of overdoses.

There were unnecessary hospital stays, too. A client claiming exhaustion while Travis smoothed over ruffled feathers and renegotiated contracts. Incentives increased, schedules adjusted. The younger, sexier ingénue replaced with someone less threatening.

I turned to Adam. "Would you mind dropping me off at Cedars-Sinai instead?" I lifted my phone. "Work."

"Sure. Who is it this time?"

"Travis didn't say, and even if he did, you know I couldn't tell you."

I was curious though, and so I texted Travis, wanting to know who I was there to deal with. His answer was like a kick to the solar plexus. But I couldn't reveal my feelings. Adam glanced over at me. "You okay?"

I cleared my throat, shoving my phone in my purse as I flipped down the visor and checked myself in the mirror. Spending the day outdoors, surrounded by exuberant puppies and sugar-high four-year-olds, had left me with smudged makeup and a faint sunburn. Sighing, I rubbed at the liner beneath my eyes and applied a fresh coat of lipstick.

And then I plastered an efficient smile on my face and turned to Adam. "Of course. Everything's fine."

Chapter Nine

Landon

When I swam back into consciousness again, the room was quiet, save for a relentless tap, tap, tapping. My eyelids weren't quite as heavy as they'd been earlier, and I looked up to find Travis pacing the floor, his dress shoes slapping the tiles with relentless precision.

I wanted to tell him to knock it off, to just leave me alone and let me sleep, escape my throbbing head and aching body. But as if he was attuned to the slightest change in my condition, Travis stopped his pacing. "Finally, you're awake."

I closed my eyes again, hoping he would get the hint.

He didn't. "Landon, I know you can hear me. We need to talk."

I didn't want to talk. I wanted to sleep.

It wasn't Travis that kept me from doing just that. The doctor came back with his white coat and clipboard and shitty diagnosis. "As a result of your fall, it appears that you've herniated a cervical disk in your spine, and the swelling of the C8 nerve root is causing weakness with your handgrip. If we took you off the heavy doses of narcotics, you would feel numbness, tingling, and pain radiating down your arm."

My tongue felt thick and heavy in my mouth, weighed down by fear. "It's just temporary, right?"

The doctor paused to flip through the pages attached to his clipboard, a pause that seemed to last forever. I heard the scrape of his nails on paper, the bleating of voices outside the door, the rush of blood in my ears. Finally, he released them all at once to look at me. They made a ruffling noise as they fanned through the air, returning to a neat stack. "I don't see anything in your MRI that would lead me to believe this is a permanent situation."

I expelled a huge sigh of relief, then nearly choked on it when he amended his comment. "But the human body is a mysterious instrument. I can't make any guarantees on the length of time your recovery will take, nor your degree of utilization once the spine has healed."

I blinked, several times. "When will you know? I'm a goddamn drummer. My hands are pretty fucking important to me."

"Landon—" Travis stepped forward, trying to ratchet down my spiraling anxiety. As if that were possible.

The doctor held up a hand, his expression unfazed. "It's all right. Mr. Cox's fear is completely understandable. Right now, the most important thing is to reduce the swelling. To that end, I have you on a cocktail of intravenous anti-inflammatory medications. I'm going to recommend that you stay here for the next few days, at least. For right now, the less you move your spine, the better."

"Meds and staying still. What else?"

"Rest. And in a few days, once the swelling has subsided, physical therapy. There is a center not far from here. I'll get you the name—"

"Restorative Health Center," I said. I knew the place well, although I'd never been there as a patient myself.

The doctor nodded anyway. "Yes. They are the best on the West Coast, if not the entire country. You will be in expert hands."

I didn't give a fuck whose hands I would be in, as long as I got back full use of my own.

I was still absorbing the news when the door opened again. This time, I figured I was hallucinating. Because it sure looked like Piper Hastings was in my hospital room.

"You're finally here." Travis's tone was impatient.

Piper let the door close behind her, but didn't come any farther. She looked flushed...and worried. Worried about me.

Travis rubbed his hands together, looking back and forth between the two of us. "I called Piper because she had the good sense to get you out of my house last night before you got into trouble and there's no one I trust more to contain the fallout from a high-profile fuck-up. If Piper can handle the shitstorm Shane weathered last year, I suppose she can handle you, too."

Piper inched forward, wearing a sexy as fuck pink outfit that showed off her long legs to perfection.

My dick pulsed to life and it was a relief to know that not every part of me was broken. I attempted a wink, although I couldn't actually feel my face so I didn't know if it worked. Either way, she pulled up short and turned her attention back to Travis.

I tried to listen, but Piper's legs were too much of a distraction, and it took me a few minutes to tune in. "…insurance negotiations are at a critical point. If necessary, we'll spin this as just a minor backyard accident. No big deal, just taking all possible precautions."

Piper had pulled a small notebook out of her purse and began taking notes as Travis resumed his pacing. "I can't have anyone finding out that Landon is in a hospital, or the details of his injury."

She stopped him. "What injury?"

"The doctors will know more tomorrow." I caught the look he gave her, one that shut down further questions. "In the meantime, Landon will stay here, because if the press gets a photo of him with so much a Band-Aid on his knee, I won't be able to get Nothing but Trouble insured for their next tour."

Travis wasn't talking about health insurance, he was talking about the multimillion–dollar policy required by venues to reserve concert dates.

As if he felt the rancor rising from my skin, he turned to glare at me. "After last year, companies aren't exactly breaking down our door to cover the band. No insurance policy, no tour. No tour, no happy fans buying your music. No happy fans…well, everything goes away. Awards, magazine covers, hit songs, and most of all, money."

All hail the mighty fucking dollar. Of course Travis would put things in perspective. But as much as I didn't give a shit about money—I needed a shit ton of it for someone else. Someone for whom I'd sacrifice everything. Someone for whom I *had* sacrificed everything.

Even knowing it would never be enough.

Piper

Eventually, a nurse shooed us out of Landon's room and Travis offered to drive me home. The man had a sports car for every day of the week, and today it was a bright yellow Maserati. Shifting into gear, he wasted no time getting down to business, which was the real reason he'd offered me a ride. A place to talk without the possibility of being overheard. "Once Landon's discharged, I need you to stay with him."

My head swiveled so fast I gave myself whiplash. "Stay with him?" I rubbed at the throbbing tendons at the side of my throat. The idea was ridiculous. This wasn't the first time we'd dealt with a celebrity-gone-wild situation, and as far as I knew, babysitting services weren't a typical item on the Travis Taggert & Associates menu.

"You saw him at my place. He was a mess. And to attempt a drunken back dive into his pool today—it wasn't even noon, for fuck's sake."

Noon? I left Landon just two hours before and he was fine. Well, maybe not *fine*, but definitely sober. Had I made him so angry he needed to bust out the liquor at ten a.m.?

Travis was still talking. "Thank god his housekeeper was there to call 911. I don't know what's going on with Landon right now, but I don't trust him on his own. I want you with him at all times until I figure out what else he needs." I remained speechless, struggling to absorb the information coming my way. What Travis was saying made sense, but moving in with Landon, even temporarily…Not a good idea.

The awkwardness of this morning was still fresh in my mind.

And so was the imprint he'd left on my skin.

I didn't regret what we'd done. Not exactly.

I just wasn't sure I could bear to repeat it.

The chemistry, the closeness, the multiple climaxes. Last night had been incredible. But once Landon's mood had changed, the air between us turning heavy, it had felt illicit, even tawdry. Like a beautiful painting with a tear in the canvas.

In the moment, that's exactly what last night had been—beautiful.

And now the memory of it was ruined.

I slammed my hand against the car door, looking for a button that would lower my window. I needed air. I needed—

"Why can't his housekeeper watch over him?" I wheezed. Air, damn it. Did Maseratis not have working ventilation systems?

Finally, I found it, angling my head through the window like a golden retriever. I sucked in lungful after lungful of Los Angeles's finest, until the buzzing in my brain eased.

"What the hell is wrong with you?" Travis asked, when I finally settled back into my seat and closed the window.

"Sorry, just a little car sickness. All better now." I'd driven with him many times, and never had I experienced the slightest queasiness. Travis didn't have a chance to push the issue though.

Snatching his chirping phone from the console, he pressed it to his ear. I knew for a fact Travis had paid thousands in fines for using a handheld while driving, but he didn't care.

I couldn't hear the other side of the conversation, although it didn't last long. Travis ended the call with a guttural "Fuck!" Dropping the phone to his lap, he wrapped his hands so tightly around the wheel his knuckles turned bright white.

I shifted in my seat, waiting for more bad news.

"The police were called to a disturbance at Landon's house. They had to shut down a massive party—two to three hundred people on site. Graffiti on the walls, furniture destroyed, god knows what in the pool."

"What?" Landon hadn't mentioned a party this morning. Was that why he'd been so anxious to—

"The police questioned most of them. Apparently, Landon sent a group text, inviting half his contact list to his house for a pool party. Which was then shared god-only-knows how many times. When the lot arrived, the gate was wide open—probably from the ambulance—and no one was home."

"Ana…"

"The housekeeper and her husband followed the ambulance to the hospital, and must have forgotten to close the gate. Instead of going back to Landon's after they were assured he wasn't going to die, they went to see their kids. Meanwhile, the party raged on."

I glanced out my window, realizing we weren't headed in the direction of my apartment anymore. I didn't need to ask where we were going. Landon's house.

"I hope things aren't as bad as they say, because I can't risk filing a claim for him until I lock down the damn insurance policy for the band." Travis's expression rarely veered far from neutral, but when he was stressed, he swept a hand over his shaved head. Right now, he was polishing it like a cue ball. "The biggest problem is that Landon is having issues with his grip."

"His grip?"

"His hand grip. Seeing as the guy makes a living by beating the crap out of his drums, he needs to be able to hold the fucking sticks."

Suddenly the damage to Landon's house didn't seem all that important. "He can't play?"

"In his current state, no." Travis rubbed his head faster, holding the wheel with one hand. "Hopefully it's just temporary, but I can't have him worrying about anything besides getting better. He'll stay at Cedars until the doctors can't do anything else for him, or until he goes stir crazy, whichever comes first. In the meantime, you are going to track down any photos and videos before they make it online. I don't care what we have to pay—just buy them before TMZ or Radar Online does."

I pulled my notebook back out of my bag. "Got it. I'll follow up with our LAPD contacts, too, see if I can keep this off the police blotter."

"Reassign any other projects you're working on. I want you full time on Landon Cox."

Fuck. Me.

Chapter Ten

Landon

W hy the fuck can't I go back to my own house?" I glared at Piper as she propelled me into her apartment, trying to figure out what she was hiding. Because she was hiding something.

But when she met my eyes, hers were swirling with more than just annoyance. I took a step, then another. Enough for her to close and lock the door, then turn back around with one arched brow as if to say, *Take that.*

Like Piper's flimsy excuse for a door, with its one lone bolt, could stop me from leaving. I moved back into her personal space, trying to fight the urge to touch her. Because if I touched her, I didn't know if I could stop.

It was her voice, stern and clear, that stopped me. "Don't blame me. This is all your fault."

She was right, of course. Piper hadn't been anywhere near me when I decided to do a drunken backflip off the side of the pool. "I didn't say that. But you don't need to play nursemaid—"

"Yes, that's exactly what I need to do. Because *someone*," she glowered at me, "decided to use me as an excuse for leaving together from my boss's house. And now my boss has appointed me official nursemaid to one high-maintenance, self-centered, pain-in-the-ass rock star."

My mouth twitched. God this woman was extraordinary. I wanted to spank her nearly as much as I wanted to sooth all that prickly aggravation right out of her body. One heated glance told me she wouldn't be a fan of either right now. So I opted for a tease. "That's rock *legend* to you. And, if I recall, it was your skill at dealing with shitstorms that sealed your fate."

The noise she made sounded caught between a grunt and a snort, but she pushed off the door and walked away from me. "Carbon monoxide is nothing to mess with."

According to Piper, the carbon monoxide alarm had gone off earlier today and my house was swarming with people trying to find and contain the gas leak. How long could it take to make the repair and then air out the house? I rubbed at the back of my neck, wincing slightly.

Piper softened, patting the couch. "Come sit down."

I'd been stuck in the hospital for days, lying in bed like an invalid. Of course, if staying still would give me back the full use of my hands, I was perfectly willing to do it. Except that it hadn't. My grip had improved slightly, but it was far from one hundred percent.

I'd had a third MRI, and a bunch of other tests with acronyms I couldn't remember. Was poked and prodded by doctors who had flown in from all over the county just to examine me. And every single one of them said it was *most likely* a matter of time until I recovered fully.

Most likely.

In other words, there were no guarantees.

But they all agreed that it was safe for me to be discharged, and to begin physical therapy. My first appointment was tomorrow.

Despite nearly a week in bed, I was exhausted. I lowered myself stiffly onto Piper's couch. "Think you could bring me—"

"Your pills?" She jumped up, looking relieved to have something to do. "Of course."

Piper returned in a minute, holding out the prescription bottles I'd been discharged with and a glass of water.

"Thanks," I took them with my left hand, unscrewed the top with my teeth, and shook out a pill from each. Not exactly graceful, but it got the job done.

"Are you supposed to take them at the same time?" I looked up to see Piper sitting at her desk, a pen in her hand and a notebook open in front of her.

"What are you doing?"

"I'm keeping track of your medications. I think one can only be taken every twelve hours, the other—"

"Don't do that." I put the pills on my tongue, chasing them with water.

"Do what?"

"Track my meds like I'm a ten-year-old who just got his tonsils out." I recapped the bottles and set them on the end table. "I'm a grown-ass man, Piper. You want to play nursemaid, you can start with a sponge bath."

Capping her pen, Piper closed the notebook and rose rigidly from the chair. I swore I saw the faintest trail of smoke coming from her ears as she picked up the remote control from the coffee table and dropped it in my lap. "I'm going to do some work in the next room. You can just relax in here and pretend I'm putting together an aromatherapy plan for you."

I tossed the remote and blanket to the side. "If you're not here to watch me, I might just get bored and leave."

"I guess that shouldn't surprise me."

Beneath the acidity of Piper's tone was a wound I'd inflicted. I sighed. "I deserve that, but I'm not sitting in here watching TV while you're off in the next room. If you need to get work done," I stood, ignoring the knives slicing through my brain at the sudden movement, "I can go home and wait outside until my house is cleared."

"You can't."

I threw up my arms. "Why the fuck not? If you don't say anything to Travis, I won't either. He'll never be the wiser."

She pursed her lips, irritation rolling off her flushed skin. "Work can wait. We'll hang out together."

I grinned and sat back down, rearranging the blanket across my lap and lifting an edge before looking pointedly at Piper. "Do you have HBO? I'm running behind on *Game of Thrones*."

Piper

Travis owned real estate around the city for when he needed to stash his celebrity clients somewhere private to heal from surgery, hide from a stalker, or evade the media.

Unfortunately two of those homes had just been added to a fire evacuation zone, including the one I'd been planning to bring Landon to. While Travis secured a new place, I had agreed to bring Landon back to my apartment.

Not quite agreed, exactly. More like lost the argument. Because countering *I'm not going to risk dragging Landon Cox, one of the most recognizable men in the world, in and out of a hotel lobby,* with *Well, I'd rather not risk dragging Landon Cox, the sexiest and most infuriating man I'd ever known, anywhere near my bedroom* wasn't a bright idea.

Which was why Landon and I were spending the afternoon on my couch, watching hours of sorcery and gore. I'd binge-watched television with Adam, too. Usually HGTV shows like *House Hunters International* or *Property Brothers.* But Adam never held my hand as we watched, or wedged his palm beneath my leg, his thumb sweeping casually over my thigh in an unconscious motion. A motion that had every cell in my body buzzing.

It was like Landon couldn't bear to be near me and *not* touch me.

Landon's hands might not be able to grip a pair of drumsticks at the moment, but they had no problem making me break out in goosebumps.

And every so often, he would run the tip of his nose through my hair, breathing deeply as he planted light kisses along my scalp. It was more arousing than if he'd ripped my panties off, spread my thighs and plunged his tongue inside me.

Of course, that would be pretty damn great, too.

Under the guise of ordering takeout, I excused myself to the kitchen. Given the long list of inflammatory food Landon had to avoid, there weren't many options. I ordered from a vegan café, then placed a furtive call to Travis. "I'm just checking in. Your assistant hasn't sent me the details of where I'm taking Landon tonight."

"My place in the Valley."

I exhaled a relieved sigh. I knew the house well. There was plenty of room and it was relatively close to the rehabilitation center. "Great. We'll head over there soon."

"Don't. I'm having my security company install a pool alarm and it's not ready yet."

"A pool alarm, really?"

"I'm not taking any chances, and I don't want Landon there while the work is done."

"They need twenty-four hours for that?" I heard the desperation creeping into my voice.

"Well, while they're out there, I'm having the system upgraded and the whole place rewired. It will be done by tomorrow at noon."

I snuck a glance around the wall. "What am I supposed to tell Landon? He wants to go home. I ordered dinner and should be able to keep him here for another hour or two."

"Don't tell him anything yet. Can't you just let him sleep at your place for a night? Avoid the conversation as much as possible, give Landon his medication after dinner, and let him fall asleep while watching TV. The insurance policy is all taken care of, but the doctors said that stress could adversely affect his recovery." I imagined Travis rubbing his head again. "Landon may seem like he doesn't give a shit about anything, but it's just an act. He loved that damn house, and I'd rather he get a good night's sleep before he sees it."

"Landon's not stupid. And he wants to go home. I'm stalling but it's not going to work forever."

Travis acted like I had already agreed. "When he wakes up tomorrow, just take your time bringing him to his house. He won't be able to stay there for a while yet. I'll text you the new entry code to the house in the Valley as soon as I have it, and you can expect a big bonus in your next paycheck."

"Piper, you coming back?" Landon's voice came through the open kitchen.

I whispered a hurried goodbye to Travis, not caring at all about the money, and threw my phone in the back of a drawer. "Yep. Dinner should be here soon."

"Good," he said, eying me as if I were his next meal. "I'm starved."

* * *

Landon came up behind me as I was unloading our dinner. Standing so close, the warm pulse of his muscles sent a prickle of awareness across my skin. "I think maybe now is a good time to clear the air, talk about what happened with us."

My breath stuttered, and I nearly dropped the kabocha stew. Somehow I managed to right it before it hit the table, setting it down beside containers of kale salad, kimchi quesadilla, quinoa stir-fry, and fresh pressed juices. Panic thrummed within my veins. Landon wanted to talk now? On a night when I couldn't let him out of my sight?

No way. I wasn't ready for that conversation, and if I didn't like what I heard, I had no escape. We weren't back in my dorm room. Right now, Landon was my *job*. I couldn't exactly berate him over what a shitty boyfriend he'd turned out to be six years ago. Calling a client a douchebag, even when it was the truth, was a terrible career move.

I shook my head and pretended to be unaffected by the desire clenching my stomach. "I think I'd rather take a rain check."

Landon lifted his hands to my shoulders, and I swear they burned me through my shirt. "You sure? I thought girls were all about clear pathways of communication."

He reminded me of Delaney. "Um, have you been watching

Dr. Phil?" I stepped aside and looked at Landon once I'd put a few feet between us. His cheeks were flushed, and I laughed. "Oh my god, you have!"

He crooked a smile. "I balance it out with *Judge Judy* though. That woman has enough balls for the both of them."

"*Game of Thrones, Dr. Phil,* and *Judge Judy.* Your viewing habits are pretty indiscriminate."

He peered at the takeout containers while I arranged plates and utensils. "Makes up for yours. Every show on your DVR was from the same network."

"Adam and I watched them together."

He lifted an eyebrow. "I've been meaning to ask, since when did you start getting turned on by metro types?"

Had I ever been turned on by Adam? "My feelings for Adam are none of your business."

"Someone's a little sensitive about their boyfriend," he teased.

"If you're so interested in my ex-boyfriend, maybe I should invite him over." I gestured at the crowded table. "I mean, we have all this food."

He scowled at me, then at the scattered takeout containers. "Not sure this qualifies as food."

"Don't blame me. The list of what you *can't* eat is longer than what you can." Not entirely sure how well Landon could serve himself, I spooned out generous portions of each dish and set them in front of him. Trying not to appear as if I was paying close attention, I served myself and then held my breath as I waited for Landon to pick up a utensil.

Like most drummers, Landon was ambidextrous, although he had previously favored his right for eating and writing. Now he picked up a fork with his left hand, and I breathed a sigh of relief as he successfully attempted a few bites. For a few minutes, there was only the sound of forks scraping plates, and the sound of eating. "You know, I don't think you ever told me—what made you want to be a drummer?"

Landon tensed, shoving another mouthful of food past his lips and chewing slowly. "Why do you want to know?"

I shrugged, feeling his reluctance from across the table. "I don't know. Of all the options to pick up, drums seem the most intimidating to me." I'd only been trying to make small talk, and was surprised that this one question seemed to have touched a nerve.

For a long moment, Landon stared at his plate as if the answer was written somewhere in his vegetables. His brow was furrowed, a vein pulsing at his temple. Finally, he sighed and looked up again. "Drums were the only instruments you weren't expected to buy or rent in order to play. You could just use the kit they had at school. The Coxes had just taken me into their home and I wanted to play something, but I wasn't about to ask them for money." He paused. "I didn't want to give them a reason to send me away."

I swallowed the food that had turned to dirt in my mouth. I was looking at one of the sexiest men in the world, but it was an orphaned boy looking back at me.

My heart broke open for the foster kid that only wanted to be loved.

He blinked, and the boy disappeared back inside pupils so dark they were like mirrors. "You never played an instrument, right?"

I had to find my voice. "I wanted to, but my dad didn't like noise, so our house had to stay pretty quiet. I wouldn't have been allowed to practice at home, so I'd never be any good." I pushed my plate away. "What would have been the point, right?"

"The point?"

"The point of trying something I'd never be good at." I shrugged, picking up my fork and pushing at what remained on my plate. "Besides, I was already busy enough." French club, student council, cheerleading. Activities that kept me busy, and out of the house. Distractions were good; distractions that kept me away from home were better.

Before I could lob another question his way, I blurted out something I'd never admitted before. Not even to Landon. "I didn't like being home because my father hated me."

He glanced up sharply, his fork stopping halfway to his mouth.

The words kept coming. "Maybe it should have made me feel better that he hated my mother, too. But"—I shrugged—"It didn't."

He put the fork down, leaning back in his chair. "He told you that?"

"No, not explicitly. But it was pretty obvious."

That crease between his eyebrows deepened. "He hit her?"

"No, never. Although sometimes I wish he would have. Just once, so she would have had a reason to leave him. Because what my father did was worse. He just…ignored her. Can you imagine living with someone, year after year, who barely acknowledged your existence?"

"And you? How did he treat you?"

"The same, really. I spent my entire childhood trying to be perfect, but there was one thing I could never fix." Blinking back tears I refused to waste on that man, I pushed my half-empty plate away and met Landon's sympathetic gaze. "I was my mother's daughter."

Landon

All this time, I thought I'd been the one keeping secrets from Piper, holding back the kinds of details that would turn a conversation into a confession.

Seems Piper had withheld her share of secrets, too.

"He was a fool, Pippa," I ground out, knowing all too well how the feeling of being unwanted crept into your soul, corroding from the inside out. Knowing there wasn't anything I could say that would make it better. For most of my childhood, all I'd wanted was to be ignored, to be left alone. Piper and I had grown up on opposite ends of a shitty spectrum, and both had left permanent marks.

"Maybe. I used to wish I had a brother or sister, but I felt guilty enough leaving my mom there. I'm not sure I would have been able to leave a sibling in that house." She gave a small shiver.

"I used to wish for a brother," I admitted. "At least, until I was put into the system. There aren't resources to keep siblings together, so we'd have been separated."

Piper's gaze softened, and she stretched out her hand to cover my own. "That would have been awful."

I stared down at her smooth skin, the white half-moons of her nails at the ends of her fingertips. "Yeah, well. Be careful what you wish for, I guess." The second the words left my mouth, I wanted to sprint after them, swallow the whole damn sentence with a wheatgrass chaser.

Of course, Piper latched right on to it. "You got your wish? You have a brother?"

Her expression was so sweet, so open. So oblivious. I speared a piece of broccoli, but my stomach turned at the sight of it. I dropped it, along with my fork, grumbling, "It's complicated."

Piper huffed a small sigh, a look of resignation on her face as she started closing half eaten containers. "Yeah, I know all about that."

I stood up to help, too quickly. I swayed on my feet, the room tilting. Piper jumped to my side, pushing me back into my chair before I could fall over.

I closed my eyes, breathing in through my nose and out through my mouth like the nurses had told me to. When I opened them again, Piper was staring at me nervously. "What can I do?"

"Nothing, just give me my pills and I'll be fine."

"But you only took them—"

"Piper." Her name came out much harsher than I intended. Before I could attempt an apology, she'd crossed the room, gathered my pill bottles, and set them in front of me without another word.

I felt like a jackass, not just for barking at her, but for sitting at Piper's table while she cleaned up around me.

Then again, I didn't want to pass out on her floor either.

On one of her trips back to the table, I pulled her down onto my lap, wrapping my arms around her waist, kissing her the second she opened her mouth in protest. The only damn woman who could make kimchi taste sweet. I ended it with a groan. "My house is probably aired out by now. I should head home."

She shook her head. "I think you should spend the night."

Even with my head spinning, it felt like I took the first deep breath in six years. Just knowing I was going to spend my night with my arms wrapped around Piper made me believe my upside down world had righted itself. And this time, I sure as hell wasn't going to fuck it up again. "I thought you'd never ask."

She put her palms flat on my chest and pushed. "Um, no thank you." Surprise made me loosen my arms and she squirmed away.

I frowned. "Why not?"

"Because I'd rather you not pass out on top of me."

"That won't happen."

"Oh really?" She put a hand on her hip. "And how can you be sure?"

"Because you'll be on top." It was a tease, but I'd happily turn it true.

Piper's lips twitched and she held out a hand. "You think you can make it to my bedroom?"

I did, and I quickly stretched out on the mattress, pulling her down with me. Cutting off the protest that was on the tip of her tongue with a whispered, "Just until I fall asleep."

With the meds swimming through my veins and Piper secure within my arms, I was unconscious in minutes.

* * *

Piper must have fallen asleep, too. With the soft light of dawn coming through her shades, my chest to her back, her sweet ass nestled between my thighs, my dick rose with the sun.

Regardless of my ability to play drums, the day I couldn't give my woman an orgasm was the day I needed to find myself a pine box and take a long goddamn nap.

A subtle shift of my hips had Piper's legs inching open and I slid my left hand along the curve of her hip, the flat plane of her belly, working my way beneath her sundress.

Tentacles of pain clutched at my spine with each small movement, but the endorphin rush from waking up beside Piper was prying them loose.

Piper moaned a soft, breathy sound that had me impossibly hard and pulsing in an instant. But this moment, this morning, wasn't about me. I had so much to make up for when it came to Piper. If I were better with words, I'd craft a heartfelt apology. A plea both elegant and precise. Words designed to get me what I wanted. Forgiveness. I wanted more than that though. I just wasn't quite sure what, or how much.

But this—mastering Piper's body. Reading all her delicious cues. Giving her what she needed, when she needed it. Soft. Hard. Rough. Gentle. Fast. Slow. A little bit dirty. Here, at least, I could give Piper everything she wanted.

When it came to playing Piper's body, I was a fucking maestro.

For a moment I cupped my hand over her plump mound, pride of ownership racing through my veins as I bit down on her shoulder. My fingers delved into Piper's slick heat, and I caught a whiff of apples from her hair. Sucking the fleshy lobe of her ear into my mouth, I licked the tender skin beneath it. God, she smelled and tasted like the sweetest orchard.

Piper's limbs loosened in a drowsy stretch, my name leaving her mouth on a sleepy sigh. I loved this. Loved how Piper's body awakened beneath my touch, opening up for me like a rose at dawn.

Her tight muscles yielded for me, welcoming me into her body. And this time, the noise I heard was mine. A groan so guttural, so needy, it had Piper tensing in my arms, an ancient instinct for self-preservation sensing danger. And that instinct was right.

When it came to Piper, I was a lethal weapon with no kill switch. I wanted everything she had to give.

And then I'd demand more.

"Nah, baby. Don't fight this." My whisper was a gritty rasp, my lips hovering over her ear.

"Landon." She repeated my name, and it wasn't a sleepy sigh. It was a warning. A question. Questions. *Should we? Should I? Is this a bad idea? Will I regret this?*

Yes. Yes. Yes. Probably.

And I didn't care.

Because the girl in my arms was soft and warm and sweet and sexy.

She was everything I'd ever wanted.

She was exactly what I'd never deserve.

And I still didn't care.

When my thumb swept over that plump berry in the orchard that was Piper Hastings, she ceased to care, too. A shudder vibrated through her bones, and she melted once again.

Mine.

For now.

Chapter Eleven

Piper

I was furious with myself for giving in to Landon this morning. Furious in a blissed-out, post-orgasmic kind of way.

The air was laced with Landon's scent. Sex and seduction and sin. I wanted to drown in it.

"You need to take a shower," I blurted.

He grinned, leaning into me and running his nose along the curve of my neck, planting soft kisses on my shoulder. "You gonna join me?"

Goose bumps prickled my skin. Damn that sounded good. Although Landon would barely fit in my tiny shower as it was. If the two of us attempted it, we'd likely flood the apartment. I stepped back, shaking my head, my mouth dry from desire.

"You have anything in there that won't leave me smelling like an apple orchard?"

Reluctantly meeting his eyes, I nearly swooned at the tender smile tugging at his full lips. I hated that Landon was making it next to impossible to stay mad at him. "Your masculine pride is afraid of fruit?"

"Yeah," he teased. "My *pride* is terrified."

I turned away before he could see the blush rising on my cheeks. "Just don't use all the hot water." His throaty chuckle ringing in my ears, I spent the next ten minutes standing with my face inside the freezer door, trying to cool my flaming skin.

The walls in my apartment were thin. I heard his clothes drop to the floor and the metallic slide of my shower curtain across the bar. The sound of the spray hitting tile, then Landon's broad shoulders. His groan as the warm water pelted his back.

I imagined it gliding over Landon's ripped abs, his hands rubbing soap across inked muscles.

I was burning up from the inside, my freezer not nearly strong enough to cool my skin. Or my overheated imagination.

Finally, the water turned off with a tired shudder and the image in my head switched to Landon chasing droplets of water with a thick terrycloth towel, each one—

"Piper?"

I slammed the freezer door shut, jumping away from the appliance as if it had tried to swallow me. "Yes," I squeaked, my eyes darting to the hall in case Landon was standing there, half naked.

No such luck.

"Uh, do you have any towels?"

"Of course. Under the sink."

There was a pause. Then, "Nope. No towels."

Confusion battled the heat of my lust, with much more success than my freezer. It had been a crazy couple of days—how behind was I on laundry? Had I used my last clean towel yesterday? Darting to the closet in my bedroom, a plush bath towel was draped over my full hamper like an accusation. I didn't have to rifle through it to know there were three others beneath.

Cringing, I turned back toward the open door of my bedroom. Too much of a coward to actually step into the hall. "Are there any hand towels in there? Or washcloths?" *I have reached a new low.*

To Landon's credit, he didn't complain. "I have a washcloth!"

Like a man the size of Landon could dry himself with *one* washcloth. I spun away from my hamper before I was tempted to throw a dirty towel at him, and sprinted into my kitchen.

I had two dish towels. They weren't as absorbent as regular towels, but at least they were bigger than washcloths.

Knowing my face was probably as red as it felt, I shoved the towels into the bathroom and averted my gaze.

Except that instead of taking them from me and shutting the door…nothing happened. "Landon, here," I said, my face still turned.

Nothing.

Did the man pull a Houdini?

The sound of silence was deafening, I couldn't even hear Landon breathing. I turned my head, my eyes snapping open. No, Landon hadn't disappeared.

Standing two feet away from me, the door completely open, Landon filled the doorway. Naked and dripping wet.

I'd seen Landon naked before, recently. But the impact of every impressive inch of him slammed into me anew. Miles of tanned skin. Muscles earned from hours of drumming and the punishing workouts I knew he used as a hangover cure.

Who does that?

Not me. When I had even a glass too much I could barely manage not to puke during downward dog.

My eyes traveled up and down the entire length of him—twice—before coming to my senses and finding his face. The second I did, I felt his hand wrap around my wrist and pull me into his hard, wet body. "That was quite a sightseeing trip you just took. Any place you'd like to visit?"

I blinked at him, reading deeper meaning into the innocuous question, and wondering—*Where?* Whatever we were, wherever we had been—it wasn't a destination worth returning to. We were nothing. He was an ex-boyfriend I hadn't quite gotten over. A recent one-night stand that hadn't had the good sense to end there. And now my temporary assignment.

None of which meant much at all. At least, not to him.

I swallowed the knot of intrigue, of lust, though it didn't go down easily. It lodged itself in my chest, pulsing like a second heartbeat. "We've got a full day ahead of us."

"Good. We've got a lot of years to make up for." The husky growl of Landon's voice was an invitation for make-up sex—mind-blowing make-up sex.

But that was all.

I pushed away from Landon, knowing that what he was offering—casual sex, on his terms—and what I wanted—a committed relationship with a man who genuinely cared for me—weren't nearly the same things. Knowing we'd both be disappointed.

I'd had enough disappointment.

Any more and I'd lose hope that things would ever change for the better.

And hope was all I had left. I wasn't going to let Landon snuff it out. Used up for his benefit, then thrown away. Forgotten.

Again.

"No, we don't." My voice came out steady, almost indifferent. Going with it, I walked stiffly back into my bedroom and glanced through the few things of Adam's that had made their way into my closet. He wasn't as tall or broad as Landon, but the only other option was staying in my apartment for the next hour while I washed and dried the scrubs he'd worn home from the hospital.

I grabbed the only things he would fit into and shoved them into his chest. The cocky smile slid off his face. "What the hell are these?"

"Spare clothes you can borrow."

"I'm not borrowing your boyfriend's clothes."

"Ex-boyfriend. And beggars can't be choosers."

He leveled an intense stare my way. "I'm a lot of things, Piper. But I'm no beggar."

No. Landon Cox was a Greek god. "Fine. Would the rock star prefer to wait while I do a load of laundry?" I lifted my short pink bathrobe off the hook on the back of my bedroom door. "You can wear this."

Landon blinked, his mouth pressed into a thin slash below his flaring nostrils. Then he took a step back and closed the door. "Boyfriend's not going to want these back after I stretch them out."

Landon

I'm not sure what was worse, having my balls crushed in a pair of too small bike shorts or having to wear the spandex contraption at all. The shirt wasn't much better, leaving two inches between where it ended and the damn shorts began, although at least it was made of cotton.

Neither situation compared to actually having to squish myself into Piper's doll-sized front seat. I tried, and it was like having my nuts squeezed by pincers. "Fuck this." I jerked the lever beneath the seat and pushed it as far forward as possible, then climbed in the backseat. That was tiny, too. But at least I could spread my knees.

I glowered at Piper as she looked at me through the rearview mirror. "You all set back there?" Her mouth wasn't visible in the small piece of glass, but shards of her unreleased laughter poked at me.

"Yeah. Just didn't want to cut off my circulation. A certain critical piece of anatomy depends on it."

Piper's laughter spilled out, filling the car like the sweetest music, wrapping around me even tighter than the ridiculous bike shorts. "Your anatomy looks—"

"Enormous, I know," I interrupted.

Her lips twitched as she looked away from me to focus on the road. "Mmm-hmm."

Sitting in the backseat put me at the perfect angle to study the silken curve of Piper's neck, the golden sweep of her hair as it caressed her skin, the elegance of her fingers as they gripped the gearshift.

Piper's car was an automatic, there was nothing to shift. And yet still her hand curved over it, her soft palm on the hard knob, fingers tapping against the leather.

Pure lust bubbled up from deep within my gut. A steady stream that should have been crushed into a stupor by the unforgiving material.

But apparently lust was the only thing not held at bay by the tight spandex. I shifted in the backseat, again. My eyes jumping from Piper's skin to her hair to her hand as my dick tried to jackhammer its way to freedom.

And when I finally tore my gaze away and looked out the window, my brain filled in the visual gap by assaulting me with Piper's scent. So fresh and sweet.

Just when I thought I was going to jump out of my skin, we finally pulled through the open gates at the edge of my property.

What the fuck?

Even Piper's tiny car could barely find a place among the brigade of vehicles crammed into my driveway.

I read the logos etched onto the sides of the vans frantically.

Advanced Plumbing, LLC. Enterprise Electric. J & J Contractors. Fine Woodworking. Custom Windows, Doors, & Glass. Perfect Pools. Diamond Cleaning Company. Carmine's Custom Closets. Angel's Roofing.

Uh, this didn't look like "a tiny carbon monoxide scare."

Piper made a little hiccupping sound in her throat as she pushed open her door. I crawled out after her, barely noticing the ball-crushing capability of my shorts as I struggled to take in the hive of activity.

"Mr. Landon!" I followed the top of Ana's dark head through the Tetris maze of commercial vehicles arranged around us. She yanked me into an embrace that had my neck throbbing, but I wrapped my arms around her warm bulk. The woman had saved my life. "Thank you, Ana. I owe you...everything. And for the millionth time...can you drop the 'mister' already?"

She released me, and I looked down at my housekeeper with a smile as she wagged a finger at me. "No. Not while you're still signing my checks. But if I have to save your life again, I'm quitting, do you hear me?"

"Got it," I answered seriously. "Next time I'm on my own."

"No. Next time I will kill you myself." Before I could laugh, she'd wrapped her arms around me and hugged me again. My eyes met Piper's over Ana's head, and she was wearing the sweetest smile.

When Ana finally disengaged, I glanced over at my house. The door was open, various workers coming in and out. "Tell me. How bad is it inside?"

Ana shook her head, her chin quivering beneath a frown. "I'm so sorry, Mr. Landon. This is all my fault. I forgot to close the gate after the ambulance and—"

"Stop. If it wasn't for you, I'd be in a pine box right now." It was true. No matter what I found inside, the fact that I was here at all was a gift. A second chance.

Ana was having none of it. "You should take him away from here," she said to Piper. "Mr. Landon shouldn't see his home like this."

"It can't be as bad as it looks. And besides," I gestured at my Lance Armstrong getup and began walking toward the front door, "I need some clothes."

Inside, scaffolding had been set up in the middle of my foyer. I edged around it, my gaze drawn toward the one-of-a-kind blown-glass chandelier I'd had shipped back from Italy on our first European tour. It had hung in the lobby of our hotel, and I'd known immediately I wanted to be reminded of the rush of success I'd felt walking beneath it once I returned home.

It hung crookedly now, as if someone had jumped from the second floor landing and decided to swing from it, taking handfuls of crystal with them on their descent. The floor was covered with a canvas tarp, and from the rough feel of it beneath my feet, much of the glass that had belonged to the chandelier had shattered on the wood.

Continuing on, I trudged up the stairs, wondering what I would find in my bedroom.

A minute later, I had my answer.

People wielding measuring tapes and brooms.

Cardboard boxes and garbage bins lining the walls.

Air that stank of cigarettes and liquor. Acrid notes of perfume and piss and vomit.

In a daze, I wandered into my closet, expecting to find an assortment of clothes stocked by a personal stylist.

Being the most fuckable rock star on the planet meant I had to dress the part.

Except that there was nothing in my closet.

Nothing.

Not even a cardboard box.

"The people that came for your party—they took everything."

I spun around at the sound of Ana's voice. But my eyes landed on Piper. The woman whose absence had made me desperate to fill the void she had left. So desperate I'd needed to surround myself with the noise of people and partying.

And now, standing inside my broken shell of a house, I realized that nothing, and no one, could ever replace the woman I'd spent years trying to forget.

My home could be repaired. But righting the wrongs I'd done to Piper, becoming a man worthy of her—and proving it—was a task of Herculean proportions. I looked down at my hands, wondering if they could be fixed, too. But if I couldn't hold my stix again, I was worried I wouldn't be worth a damn to Piper. To anyone.

Chapter Twelve

Piper

Landon's mood took a nosedive while walking through his house, and I couldn't blame him. He was silent as I backed out of his driveway, but once I pulled onto the street, Landon's throaty growl filled the car. "You knew my house had been trashed, didn't you?"

I didn't bother lying. "Yes."

"Travis told you not to tell me?"

"To be fair, the doctors said stress could impede your recovery."

I was met with silence. "Landon…" He'd been so distracted that he was sitting in the front seat again, and offered only a resigned sigh, his head tilted back against the headrest. I drove into Beverly Hills, and we spent the next couple of hours at Blue Cocoon, getting Landon a new wardrobe, including half a dozen pairs of designer sweatpants that had no zippers or buttons for Landon to struggle with. All of our exchanges went through Jude, who was responsible for making Nothing but Trouble look like actual rock stars instead of overgrown boys.

Which apparently included dressing them in six-hundred-dollar sweatpants.

Once my tiny trunk had been stuffed full of garment bags, I headed out to the Valley, toward one of the houses Travis owned. I'd been there before, to work with an actress whose fiancé had implanted cameras and microphones in every corner of her home, uploading the feed to a website he'd set up on the dark net and earning thousands off the video stream.

Celebrities lived a life of glitz and glamour, but they were also easy marks, and often targeted by those closest to them.

"You've got to let me buy you a car."

I gave Landon the side eye. Case in point—they had a tendency to dole out outrageous gifts, opening themselves up to people treating them like human ATMs. "You're not buying me a car."

"Someone needs to. You're driving around in a shoe box, it's unsafe."

I snorted. "Because you're the poster boy for safety first? How's your neck feeling? Want to try another drunken back flip?"

I was saved the pleasure of a response when my phone rang through the car's Bluetooth speakers, MOM flashing across the display screen. *Crap.* Not a call I wanted to take with an audience. I was reaching out my finger, ready to swipe IGNORE when Landon, clearly eager for the distraction, tapped ANSWER instead.

I mouthed "asshole," before forcing an upbeat tone to my voice. "Hi, Mom."

"Hello, sweetheart. I'm sure you're busy, but you haven't

called in a while—" She broke off, interrupting herself before launching into an apology. "I'm sorry, I didn't mean to bother—"

"Mom, stop. It's fine, I'm glad you called. How are you?"

"Oh." She sounded startled, like she didn't know how to respond to someone being happy to hear from her. "Well, I'm okay, I guess. I'm taking a cooking class these days. You know how your father loves French food."

My heart sank. My mother could earn a Michelin star and my father would still find something to criticize about whatever she put in front of him. "That's great, Mom."

"And how about you? Is Adam taking good care of my baby girl?"

Tears came to my eyes. She rarely asked me about work or friends. As long as she thought I was being treated well by whomever I was dating, my mom was happy. Deciding to postpone telling her about our breakup, I gave her my standard line. "Like a princess, as always."

"Oh good, good. If he doesn't, you be sure to tell him your daddy won't hesitate to get on a plane and set him right."

I gripped the steering wheel so hard, my knuckles turned white. "Will do, Mom. I love you." I choked the words out, hating myself for ending the call before she had a chance to respond. There was only so much of the charade I could take.

I didn't realize I was crying until I felt Landon's finger sliding along the curve of my cheek. "Pull over."

I shook my head, gripping the wheel even tighter and pushing down on the pedal. If I stopped driving, I was going to completely lose it. The emotions choking me—rage, fear, sorrow, helplessness—they would settle down in a minute. They always did. "I'm fine, Landon."

He shook his head slowly. "No, you're not. And neither am

I." My foot eased off the gas, and Landon pointed out the windshield. "Up ahead there's a turnoff. Take it, and you'll see a cabin a few miles down."

"A cabin?"

"Trust me. I think we both need this."

I wanted to know what *this* was, but decided to trust Landon. Given our past, it probably made me a fool.

I navigated the turn off, driving down the secluded road in silence. As Landon said, a ramshackle cabin came into sight, and as we got closer, I was able to read the wooden sign posted in front. I read it out loud. "Harmony's Dog Sanctuary."

"It's a place I try to help at when I can."

Landon Cox volunteered for a nonprofit? I made an effort to disguise my surprise.

Most celebrities publicized their philanthropic efforts. One of my jobs in PR was to find causes for scandal-plagued stars to associate with—often televised fund-raisers or concerts to benefit the victims of the latest mega-storm or earthquake. For a celebrity to volunteer their time or money without benefitting from good press was rare. *Extremely* rare.

An RV was parked to the side of the cabin, and I read the letters painted on the side. HARMONY'S PETTING PUPS. "Do they do birthday parties?"

"Yeah, it's one of the ways they earn money to fund their rescue efforts."

The door opened and the woman I'd met at Devon's birthday party came out, a broad grin appearing on her face when she spotted Landon. They exchanged a warm hug as I stood awkwardly to the side for a moment before he motioned toward me. "Piper, this is Harmony. Otherwise known as the patron saint of abused dogs."

"Nice to meet you, Piper." She paused, studying my face thoughtfully. "I feel like I've seen you before though."

"Yes, at my boyf— At a birthday party about a week ago." The last person I wanted to think about right now was Adam.

"Ah. That's it." Now that she'd placed me, Harmony seemed content to let the matter drop. "You picked a good day to come. Shania had her puppies and she's just starting to get comfortable showing them off."

Landon's smile was brighter than the sun as he turned back to me. "Harmony names her dogs after country music stars. I keep telling her she needs to branch out of the genre."

The older woman rolled her eyes. "Just found out we're getting a few more, too. Rottweilers and pits that survived a dog-fighting operation up north. I'll be sure to name one of them after you."

I could understand Harmony's logic. Landon had the dark, guarded eyes and powerfully muscled body of a Rottweiler, the aggression and tenacity of a pit bull.

But there were glimmers of softness within him. Hints of a tenderness he kept carefully hidden. It was what made the man so damned hard to resist.

Landon rocked back on his heels. "Can't believe people still do that."

"You've spent enough time here, Landon. You should know by now what's done to the most vulnerable among us." Harmony broke the heaviness of the moment by giving Landon's arm a squeeze and taking a step back. "Now, take Piper back to the barn. Shania doesn't like to be kept waiting."

Landon

I filled Piper in on Harmony as we walked.

"And she also works the kiddie party circuit in her spare time?"

The tightness in my chest began to ease as we got closer to the back of the property, the sound of barking growing louder with each step. "She doesn't take any puppies that aren't old enough to be adopted, charges a thousand bucks for an hour and a half, and usually winds up finding a family to adopt at least one pup. I thought she was crazy when she first told me about it, but I have to say, it's brilliant."

As we neared the barn, I noticed Piper walking closer to me. By the time we were a few feet from the entrance, her shoulder was rubbing against my arm. I stopped. "Uh, do you like dogs?"

She bit her lip. "I like puppies and small dogs. Big dogs have always made me a little nervous though." She swept a curtain of blonde behind her ear, angling the side of her neck toward me and pointing at a small raised scar. "I was practicing cheerleading in a friend's backyard and out of nowhere, one of her neighbor's dogs came at me. He only managed the one bite, but if it had been just an inch lower…"

Her voice trailed off and I followed the movement of her finger to the pulsing artery below her skin. So close.

Was life just a series of near fatal accidents?

One inch lower.

One second later.

The finest of lines between life and death.

So fucking fragile.

Before I realized what I was doing, I'd drawn Piper into my

arms, covering that patch of skin with my mouth, my tongue sweeping over the tiny abrasion. Why did she have to taste so sweet?

I felt the vibration as she moaned, although the sound was overridden by the cacophony of excited animals. I pulled away reluctantly. "The only one biting you today is me."

Piper's eyes had darkened and I reached for her hand, tugging her into the barn that had been converted into a kennel. I would have kissed her again but if I did, I didn't know that I'd be able to stop.

Most of the dogs were out playing in the fenced paddocks that were now used as dog runs. Shania and her pups were in one of the larger stalls. Resembling a German shepherd, with some Labrador thrown in, she had been found on the side of the highway and brought to Harmony's by a good Samaritan, abused and near starved, and already pregnant. She was understandably wary of strangers.

The puppies were a mix of colors, as if Shania had decided to dole out a different shade to each. White, gray, brown, black, and tan were either nestled up beside their mom, or exploring the stall, pouncing on scattered toys.

At our footsteps, even the sleeping puppies lifted heads that seemed too big for their bodies before jumping to their paws and trotting over, sniffing at the small gap between the ground and the closed door.

Shania gave a low growl, looking pointedly at me. "Are you sure she likes you?" Piper asked, sounding doubtful.

"Everyone likes me," I declared. "Shania's just mad I haven't been around lately."

Piper's expression didn't waver as she looked from me to Shania and back again. I cleared my throat and opened my mouth.

"Come on over, come on in. Pull up a seat, take a load off your feet." I didn't sing nearly as well as I played the drums, but I could hold a tune reasonably well.

I paused, trying to remember the words, but Piper nudged me with her elbow. "Keep singing."

Luckily, the lyrics came to me. "Come on over, come on in. You can unwind, take a load off your mind." I got halfway through the song before Shania Twain's namesake rose to a sitting position and gave something resembling a dignified nod.

Piper was quiet at my side as Shania walked slowly to the door.

I crooned the next few lines, only stopping when the dog rose on her hind legs and stuck her head over the door, which only went four feet high

I lifted my hand, holding it out flat for Shania to sniff, and when she was finished with mine, I looked at Piper. "She just needs to check you out first." Piper offered her hand reluctantly and Shania gave her a cautious sniff before swiping her tongue across her palm.

My breath caught in the back of my throat. Goddamn it. I was jealous of a dog.

Piper tensed, but didn't jump away, and Shania pulled her paws off the door and backed up a few steps. "Does she want us to go in?"

I looked at Shania. "No, not yet. But I think she just told us we could come back."

I led Piper through the barn and out back toward the paddock area, explaining how Harmony separated the dogs by personality, not necessarily by size. I'd been volunteering here for a few years and I'd learned that the social norms of abused animals were subverted, so it was often necessary to keep them in small groups.

I reached for a stray tennis ball with my right hand before remembering that my left was the stronger of the two—for now, at least. Lobbing the ball over the nearest fence, I leaned against the wood and watched the dogs give chase.

Piper joined me, sighing. "You have a real gift, Landon."

"Nah. I can carry a tune, but Shane definitely deserves to hold the microphone."

She shook her head. "I wasn't talking about your voice—although I don't think anyone would boo you off the stage. I meant with animals. Shania likes you."

I shrugged. "Of course she does. What's not to like?"

She tilted her head to the side, but with the sunglasses covering her eyes, I couldn't read her expression. "Why do you do that?"

"Do what?"

"Deflect anything that isn't some sort of sexual come-on."

"Why shouldn't everything with a beautiful girl *be* a sexual come-on?"

Not even a tiny twitch of those delicious lips. "There's more to you than what's behind your zipper, and I'm not talking about what you do on stage."

This wasn't a conversation I wanted to have. "Nah." I stepped back from the fence, putting my hands in my pockets. "I'm not that deep. Want to see the dogs that Harmony is training as therapy animals? They're over—"

Piper grabbed my arm and I swear a bolt of electricity slammed through my bones. "Just answer one question for me and I'll let you off the hook."

I widened my stance, planting my hands firmly on Piper's hips. "What hook is that, baby?" Holding her captive, I closed the distance between us, fitting her perfectly against me. "Maybe I don't want to be let off. Maybe I want to be firmly entrenched."

This time, there was at least a glimmer of a smile on Piper's face. "See, you like how I tease you. I know you do."

"Yeah," she answered softly. "I do. But I also appreciate a kick-ass Shania Twain impersonation for a canine audience."

"Don't forget the blonde who was standing right next to me."

To my surprise, the beginnings of her smile slid right off her face. "I see you, you know. You can drop the act with me."

I raised my hands to cradle her face between my palms, staring into her eyes. "There's no act, Piper. With me, what you see is what you get."

"Oh yeah? Want to know what I see?"

No, not if I wasn't going to like the answer.

But she spoke up before I had a chance. "I see a guy that's trying too hard. Killing it on stage, slaying every woman that crosses his path, getting into trouble just to earn that bad boy reputation he wears so well. Landon, the part of you I actually like is the one you're trying to hide. You're not as big of a douche as you want everyone to think you are. And you're about to tell me *exactly* why you disappeared on me years ago. Over lunch. Your treat."

Chapter Thirteen

Piper

"We're here."

Landon looked around, making no move to open his door. "Where's here?"

I pointed to the food truck that was parked fifty yards away. "The corn tortillas are made fresh, and everything else is organic and local. I'm pretty sure your nutritionist would approve, and they're the best tacos you'll ever have."

He slanted me a dubious look. "I think your standards are lower than mine."

Rolling my eyes at his arrogance, I pushed at the door. "I highly doubt that."

Waving at the woman behind the counter, I sat at the farthest picnic table, my spine prickling in awareness as Landon's shadow fell over me. He sighed. "What do you want?"

I looked up at him. "For you to stop hovering and sit down."

"Your tacos aren't going to order themselves," he replied.

"Actually, they are."

Just then, the woman I had waved at came to our table carrying a tray laden with food. "Piper, it's been too long."

I jumped back to my feet as she set the tray on the table, sliding into an embrace that smelled of salt water and fresh cilantro. "I know, I'm sorry." I took a deep breath, feeling my shoulders relax. "Lupe, this is Landon."

Lupe grinned at him. "I love when you bring your friends here," she said, giving me a last squeeze and hurrying back to her customers.

Landon finally sat down, looking at me curiously. "First, eat," I said, helping myself to one of the small tortillas stuffed with guacamole, vegetables, and fresh fish. Each one was only a few bites, but they were heaven.

He picked up a taco, devouring it. "I stand corrected," he said, reaching for another one. "How did you discover this place?"

"Lupe's husband is one of the scrappiest paparazzos you'll ever meet. He always shops around his worst photos to celebs' agents before taking them to the tabloids. Not only do we pay just as well, then we owe him."

He grimaced. "It's like buying your belongings back from the thief who stole them."

"You got it. There's definitely a dark underbelly to fame."

His dark eyes appraised me quietly, roving over my face and delving deep. "Oh believe me, I know." I squirmed on the hard bench, taking a sip from my drink.

Lupe came out with another tray before we had finished the food in front of us. This time, Landon turned his charm on her, and in minutes she was giggling like a teenager, demanding that we get married and make lots of beautiful babies.

"Lupe." I flushed. "He's a client."

She put her hands on her hips, a dismissive expression on her face. "I thought you said he was a friend."

"No, *you* said he was a friend," I pointed out.

"And I'm always right," she pronounced, then flounced back to the truck where her nephew was struggling to keep up with demand.

"I take it you haven't brought Andrew here."

"*Adam*," I corrected. "And no. He's more of a white table-cloth kind of guy."

"Maybe you should. Lupe could have told him to put a ring on it."

"What makes you think I'm in a rush to get married?"

"You aren't?"

"In a rush? No. And before you ask, I don't want kids either."

He snorted. "Chicks are biologically programmed to want to reproduce."

"The only biological programming I'm feeling right now is an intense aversion to being compared to poultry. Just because I have ovaries doesn't mean I intend to use them." I wiped my mouth with a napkin. "For god's sake, I'd probably make a worse parent that you."

Landon looked offended. "I'll have you know, there are a lot of women who consider me baby daddy material."

I nearly spit out my mouthful, chewing furiously to get it down my throat. "No way. You?"

Landon frowned. "You don't think so?"

"No, I don't. No offense."

"To be honest, I don't understand it either." A smile stole

onto his face as he leaned his forearms against the table. "So tell me—what has you bucking the pull of genetics?"

My gaze drifted to a family of five sitting at one of the tables. Mom, Dad, two kids, and a baby. No electronic devices to be seen. Just people sharing a meal, engaging with each other. I inclined my head their way. "That's why," I said. "Some people are meant to have families that look like that. Some just…aren't."

Landon studied them unobtrusively for a moment, a look of longing passing over his face. "That's an observation, not a reason. Why aren't you one of those people?" He waited for my response for a moment, and when I stayed silent, stood up and took the tray with the remnants of our lunch to the garbage bin before going over to the tip jar. Lupe swatted his hand away, but from the look on her face, he managed.

The line in front of her truck had grown even longer, so I blew Lupe a kiss and waved rather than interrupt. Falling into stride beside Landon, we walked in silence to my car. Instead of getting in, I took a seat on the hood, sliding out of my sandals and putting my bare feet on the bumper.

"My father was in love with my aunt, my mother's sister, when they were young. My mom and aunt were twins. Anyway, my aunt was seeing some guy behind my dad's back, and she told my mom, who apparently had a crush on my dad, to cover for her. To go out with my dad while she went on a date with the other guy."

I glanced up at Landon, looking for judgment. His face was impassive though, and he motioned for me to continue. "Of course, immediately afterward, my aunt realized that my father was the love of her life, and swore my mother to secrecy about trading places. Which would have worked, I guess, until my mom found out she was pregnant."

"Shit."

"Yeah. My mother and aunt had to come clean about the trick they pulled, and my father married my mother to do *the right thing*." I added air quotes. "But he never forgave her."

"Your father didn't realize he slept with the wrong sister, and he's blaming someone besides himself?"

I looked up sharply. I'd never thought of it from that perspective. "I—I guess."

"How about your mom? How did she take it?"

"Well, she had a quickie wedding to a man who hated her and basically lost her sister over it."

"You found out about all of this from your aunt?"

"No. I've never even met her," I admitted. "My grandmother had Alzheimer's, and she lived with us for a while. She thought I was my mother toward the end, scolding me for bringing shame to our family and costing her a daughter. It got to the point where I could barely go home because my grandmother would fly into a rage every time she saw me."

"I'm sorry, Pippa."

My throat was tight, but I kept talking, unable to stop the flow of words now that they'd started. "Don't be. At least then I understood why my mother had always foisted me on my dad like some kind of consolation prize. Proof that what she did had been worth it in the end. He never bought it though, no matter how hard I tried to be the perfect daughter." I didn't realize I was crying until Landon swept his thumbs below my eyes. "I've spent my whole life trying to prove that I'm good enough. That I belong. I don't need to bring a kid into my particular brand of crazy. It would be cruel."

Landon

I pulled Piper into my arms, overwhelmed by her honesty. Looking back, neither of us had shared many details of our upbringing. But now I understood exactly why she'd been so reluctant to share them with me. With anyone. It was hard to talk about things you didn't want to think about.

I'd spent the first few years of my life with crack addicts, then nearly a decade bouncing between group homes and foster families. Beneath my tattoos were the scars of my upbringing. Knife wounds and cigarette burns. I'd felt the sting of abuse more times than I wanted to admit.

But Piper's story was different. It wasn't about inherently evil people. Just a crazy confluence of events that came together to destroy an entire family.

Piper's perfect facade made sense now. Never a hair out of place, her apartment spotless, always on time. She had coped by taking control of every possible detail.

I'd coped by losing control. Beyond the drinking and drugs, I barely glanced at a watch, left my house in Ana's hands. Walked away from my family.

Piper and I were so much alike that we were exact opposites. Mirror images.

But looking at her now, I saw the cracks. Tiny fissures where I just might be able to slip through.

If she let me.

If I wanted to.

Would she?

Did I?

Fuck, yeah. More than anything.

And I was also beginning to realize I didn't know Piper as well as I'd thought. Some things hadn't changed. Her favorite color was still blue, she still moaned at the first bite of a meal—especially when she was hungry—and she still couldn't sleep with her feet under the covers.

But now I also knew that she'd held so much of herself back. Just like I had.

Maybe the truth was that neither of us was ready to commit to each other back then. That our timing had been off.

Looking at Piper now, I saw a beautifully complicated woman. A shifting kaleidoscope of past and present, darkness hiding within light, and bold, vibrant colors.

The urge to spend forever staring through the lens she'd finally given me was like a kick in the gut. It took my breath away.

Piper's breath ghosted across the skin at the base of my throat, my dick jerking to attention. I slid my hands forward, resting my thumb against Piper's pulse. Feeling it accelerate. The comforting embrace I'd meant to give became something different, something deeper.

Piper lifted her chin, her silken hair sliding against my forearms. I bit down on a groan as her eyes met mine. This girl was just…too much. Too much for me to deserve. But damn, I wanted to take her places she'd never been, show her the dark corners of my soul I'd been hiding for a lifetime.

I drew in a deep breath, feeling it stutter in my throat. "Piper," I murmured on an exhale, the syllables vibrating with want and warning.

Her knees edged open and I slipped between them, scooping my hands beneath her ass and bringing her closer. "You feel me?" I asked, meaning more than just the bulge in my jeans.

Piper gave a shaky nod, pulling back slightly and staring

me straight in the face. "I feel you, Landon. But...I want to know you, too." Her expression tightened. "What happened with us? What made you run off? I want—no, I *deserve*—an explanation."

* * *

Six years ago

>Jett, Dax, and I were all assembled in Travis's office, trying to look like we weren't terrified. Not knowing if he'd called this meeting to announce that he was dropping our band.

>But since it was just the three of us in the room, a new fear was gnawing at my belly—that our manager had managed to convince Shane to pursue a solo career and we'd all been screwed out of our lead singer.

>Then again, Shane was fucking up a lot lately. We all partied too much, but Shane had taken it to a new level. Maybe Travis wanted us to find a new front man.

>Either option was fucking bullshit and I sure as hell wasn't buying it. Shane and I had been together for years already and things had jelled once we'd linked up with Jett and Dax. Our bookings were getting bigger, our songs better.

>So why the hell had we been called into the principal's office?

>I was the first to bite the bullet. "Where's Shane?"

>"Actually, that's what I wanted to talk to you about."

>Sprawled in the uncomfortable chair facing Travis's desk, I steeled myself for bad news. Trying to lull my nerves into nonchalance. "We're here. Talk."

Travis dragged in a deep breath, exhaling loudly. "I had to bail Shane out of jail last—actually, very early this morning."

Whatever I'd been expecting, that wasn't it. "What the fuck for?"

"Shane's been doing more than just drinking himself into a stupor lately. He got caught in a drug bust, but it's been taken care of. And now Shane's on his way to where he needs to be."

"That all?" Jett piped up.

I swung my head his way. "That's not enough for you?" I growled.

Jett bristled. "Nah, man. I was just worried we were about to be fired or somethin'."

I crossed my arms over my chest, giving no sign that I'd been thinking the same thing. Years in foster care had taught me never to show weakness around sharks like Travis. It turned you into bait. "Travis is too smart to fire us. We're on the verge of breaking out and he knows it."

Travis was accustomed to egos even bigger than mine, and his chuckle skated across my skin. "You're half-right, Landon. Nothing but Trouble is one album—one phenomenal album, mind you—away from the big leagues. If you can focus on your music, to the exclusion of all else, you'll get there. No doubt."

That bitter, churning sensation in my gut ceased, receding in the face of Travis's prediction. Success. I needed it, craved it. For reasons that went well beyond my own ego.

"But," Travis held up a finger, his dark eyes looking from me to Jett to Dax and then back to me again. He pulled out three plane tickets from his desk drawer and held them up.

"I'm going to tell you the same thing I told Shane. This is it. Your last chance. Either get on a plane this afternoon, or get out of my office and never come back."

There was silence as the three of us looked at the tickets in Travis's hands, and he looked at us. Dax broke it first.

"Where are you sending us?"

"To a house in the mountains. A cabin, really. That's where Shane is right now, with medical professionals helping him detox. There's a recording studio and everything you need to work on your music. And when Shane is able, I want you to start laying down tracks."

"You want us to go to a fucking log cabin with our dicks in our hands, waiting for Shane to feel like jamming?" Jett's face was red. "Why can't we stay in L.A. and get up there when he—"

"Because, we're a fucking band, dickhead," I lashed out, angry at the situation we were facing.

Travis dropped the tickets on his desk and steepled his fingers together. "What Landon is trying to say is that you guys are straddling this place between has-beens-that-never-really-were and bona fide rock stars. I want you away from the L.A. scene—and everyone in it. Today."

I thought about Piper, the sweet girl I'd met not even two months ago and had barely spent more than a few hours apart from. "But I—"

Travis lifted his hand. "Save it. I don't care what girl you were planning to fuck tonight, or where you were going to party. Commit to me and to your band, and this time next year you'll be taking private planes to sold-out arenas. In a few years, if you don't like what I have to say, you'll have enough fuck-you money in the bank to actually say fuck you to me." He lifted his shoulders in a casual shrug. "But that day is not today."

I was committed to Nothing but Trouble, that wasn't even a question. But it was the promise of fuck-you money that pushed me over the edge. I'd said those two words countless times over the course of my life, but they always came at a cost. Career success was so goddamn close, but along with it came options. Better therapists, cutting-edge treatments. Maybe that fuck-you money could be used to say fuck you to a brain injury. The one I'd caused.

Maybe the day would come when Jake would smile again. Laugh again.

Not that I would be there to see it, hear it. I didn't deserve to breathe the same air as my brother. Not when it was my fault that he'd been deprived of it. Precious minutes without oxygen that resulted in a devastating diagnosis. Jake could have led a charmed life, but I had ruined it.

I stood, holding my hand out for one of the tickets. "I'm in."

Travis lifted a skeptical brow. "All in?"

"Yeah." I bit out the word, seething at having my loyalty questioned.

He extended the ticket with one hand, and an empty palm with the other. "Hand over your phone."

"My phone?"

"You're either all in or you're out. I want you focused on Shane's recovery and focused on your music. You four are going to bond like fucking Boy Scouts until you come up with an album worthy of your talent. That means no calling your dealer, or sexting with your flavor-of-the-month girlfriend. All in…" He paused. "Or out."

I envisioned Piper—the sleepy, blissful look on her face just this morning. And then I imagined Jake, his eyes half focused, a smile that trembled with confusion. I slapped my phone in Travis's hand. "I'll keep up my end. You better fucking keep yours."

Chapter Fourteen

Piper

There was a faraway look in Landon's eyes, as if my simple question had him deep in thought.

Of course, it hadn't been a *simple* question.

There must have been a reason Landon had disappeared back then, a reason he didn't want to share.

But, why?

Why, why, why?

It shouldn't bother me so much, not after all this time.

But damn it, it still did. Like an itch between my shoulder blades, one I couldn't reach.

There hadn't been any drama between us. For nearly two months, Landon and I had been practically inseparable. My freshman roommate had all but moved out by the end of the second semester. Landon spent nearly every night with me, our bodies fitted together in a twin-sized bed, not needing or wanting to be separated by even an inch. And then he was just...gone.

No note. No phone call. Gone.

I would have freaked out, believing he'd been kidnapped or murdered or worse, if I hadn't seen the press release announcing that Nothing but Trouble was going off to record a new album. For the next few months, there was a lot of buzz around their supposed seclusion to work on a top-secret new album. Rumors swirled around high-profile collaborations with some of the hottest musicians in the industry.

I can trace my interest in PR to that summer. I was so hungry for news about Landon that I followed every bit of information there was to find, all of it tracing back to Travis Taggert & Associates.

My bones aching with loneliness, the three-and-a-half-foot width of my mattress might as well have been a mile. At night, I imagined barging into Travis's office and demanding to be taken to wherever he was keeping Landon hostage.

Instead, I watched from the sidelines as Travis built up interest in Nothing but Trouble, taking them from a crowd favorite at gritty downtown L.A. clubs to a band capable of opening for a sold-out international tour.

By the time I was in my senior year, Nothing but Trouble was sitting at the top of every chart and headlining their own tours. Their photographs were in gossip magazines and on the bedroom walls of teenaged girls. When an opening for an internship at Taggert's agency was posted through UCLA's career office, I applied on a lark, never expecting that I'd actually get the job. But I did, and almost turned it down.

Then I thought, why give up the most sought-after opportunity among every communications major in the entire school?

Screw Landon Cox.

I'd given him my heart and he left it behind.

I'd worked my ass off in school and had ambition to spare—why should I turn down my dream job for a guy who didn't deserve a single sacrifice from me?

It was bad enough that I'd chosen my major because of a man—my father. And worse that four years of college had taught me nothing about how to effectively communicate with him. Our relationship was as pathetic the day I graduated as it had been the day I left home.

I took the job, figuring I would deal with Landon if and when necessary—not a minute sooner.

Nothing but Trouble was hardly Travis's only client, and I wasn't assigned anywhere near the band until last year, when I worked with Delaney. There had been a couple of close calls where I nearly ran into Landon backstage, but he was always so surrounded by an entourage of groupies that it was easy to avoid him, especially since he was usually drunk or high. Or both.

It might have hurt, being so close to him and yet still so far. But Landon Cox, rock star, wasn't anything like the sweet, struggling musician I'd fallen in love with. Like Landon said himself, he'd become a legend, with the fan club to match.

Landon the Legend was also an asshole.

Except when I saw glimpses of the man I used to know. The man I'd fallen head over heels for. The boyfriend who liked me best without an ounce of makeup on my face. Who didn't care what I wore, and preferred my hair wild from a night in bed…with him, of course.

The kind of guy who would croon a country song to a mutt.

Landon was the only person I'd ever dropped my guard for. I might not have told him all the sordid details about my parents back then, but I didn't have to be a perfect daughter, flawless cheerleader, popular prom queen with him. I could just be myself, Piper Hastings.

Not perfect.

Just Piper.

Pippa.

But I hadn't been enough for him.

No call. No note. No goodbye.

Just gone.

Like I'd meant nothing to him at all.

The pain of being left behind, completely disregarded... It was soul-crushing.

I'd never believed there was a person on earth that could make me feel worse about myself than my father, but Landon had.

If the damage he'd done had been external, no amount of makeup could have concealed the wound. But, lucky me, it was all beneath my skin. Where it had festered for the past six years.

I became Perfect Piper, 2.0. A college student with a straight-A average and cardboard cutout sorority friends, and later, an ambitious, organized PR associate who never met a client she couldn't handle or a scandal she couldn't spin.

Now, Landon's hand curled around the back of my neck, pulling me into the hard plane of his chest. He smelled like green grass and dried hay, as if the air from the converted barn at Harmony's Sanctuary had seeped into his pores.

But this man was not *my* sanctuary, no matter what I once thought. I'd been wrong. So damn wrong.

And I needed to remember how much it hurt to learn that lesson, so I wasn't tempted to repeat it. If I had to go through that again... I wouldn't just be hurt. Landon would break me.

To hell with him and the explanation he wasn't man enough to give.

Pushing at Landon's chest, I slid off the hood of my car. Retrieving my shoes, I tossed them in the back and got behind the wheel barefoot.

I turned the ignition and fumbled for the button to lower the windows, my fingers stiff with tension. "You coming?"

Even from inside the car, I heard Landon's sigh, could feel it vibrating through my chest. For the first time, I wished I'd taken him up on his offer to drive that enormous truck of his. The more space between us, the better.

Landon opened the door and dropped into the seat, sweatpants stretched tightly across muscular thighs as he folded his legs into the small space.

In my current mental state, I was torn between wanting to scream at him and wanting to have sex with him. Or maybe both.

Neither. I should do neither.

Landon wasn't just my ex. He was my client. I needed to remain professional.

No easy feat when I'd spent the morning with his hand between my thighs.

Landon

"So what is this place?" I dropped the bags from Blue Moon on a bench in the foyer and took in the sprawling one-story adobe house Piper had brought me to.

"One of Travis's stash houses."

I lifted an eyebrow. "Trav is running drugs these days?"

There was a brief twitch of her lips before Piper did something to a panel and the wall in front of us slid open to reveal a massive interior courtyard with freeform pool, outdoor kitchen, and lush landscaping. "Nope, he's found troublesome celebrities to be much more profitable."

I grunted. "I take it you've been here before."

She nodded. "This place is just half an hour away from the rehab center and I've arranged for a therapist to come here for your sessions, starting this afternoon."

Out of habit, I walked to the outdoor refrigerator and peered inside. Of the three shelves, one was filled with water, another with an enormous platter of fresh fruit, and the other with half a dozen glass bottles, each bursting with a different bright shade. I read the labels out loud. "Açaí, blueberry, coconut; kale, apple, spinach; mango, turmeric, carrot; pineapple protein—"

"Water is fine," Piper interrupted.

I grabbed two waters and handed one of them to her. "So, how long am I supposed to stay here?"

"Shouldn't be more than two to three weeks, give or take. The general contractor overseeing repairs to your home said he would come by tonight to review his progress so far, and to discuss your vision for the scope of the project." She uncapped her bottle and took a sip, and I was transfixed by the droplet of water that lingered on her upper lip for a second, until she chased it away with a swipe of her pink tongue.

When I realized Piper was looking at me strangely, I asked, "What?"

"Are you sure you're up to meeting with him after your physical therapy session?"

I bristled at the insinuation that I wasn't. "Of course."

"Great, I'm going to go set up my laptop in the office and—"

I laid my hand on top of hers, reaching for the smile that had captivated fans all over the globe. "No, stay."

For just a minute, I really thought it would work. Piper cocked her head to the side, fluttering long lashes that distracted me from noticing the tight smile that had settled on her lips. "Some of us have work to do," she said, not falling for my ploy.

I couldn't help reaching out to pull at a lock of her blonde hair, wrapping it around my finger and closing the distance between us. "There was a time that wouldn't have stopped you."

For a second, Piper's eyelids blinked closed, those bright blue beams shuttered. But they opened again quickly, blazing with anger. "There was a time you would have been worth it."

In surprise, I released my grip and let her go.

Earlier, Piper had demanded an explanation. And she was right, she deserved one.

Maybe I needed to finally tell Piper what I'd been holding back from her. Why I left six years ago. Why I hadn't come back.

Why I wasn't worthy of her. Then or now.

Fuck.

That familiar fury bubbled up from a place deep within my gut. A toxic, bitter brew, it churned its way throughout my abdomen.

But that wasn't what sent the wave of nausea rising up my throat. Shame did that.

Even though no drug in the world could lessen its impact, I swallowed down a couple of pills anyway. Just in case.

Leaving my water bottle sweating on the flagstone tile, I went inside and meandered around the unfamiliar house until I found Piper in an impersonal office, plugging her computer's power cord into an outlet. The hem of another one of her sundresses inching up to display toned thighs, but not enough to expose that delicious ass that had been driving me crazy all damned day. I cleared my throat. "Think I'm about ready to give you that explanation now."

She glanced over at me, then sat back down in the room's only chair. "How do you know I still want it?"

Piper was giving me an out. I could easily shrug and walk away.

But I didn't want to keep Piper at arm's length anymore.

Leaning against the door's molding, I scrubbed a palm over my face. "Can't say I'd blame you." I glanced back toward the courtyard, sunlight glinting off the surface of the pool. "I hope you still do though."

She rose from her chair, and we walked back to where we'd been sitting a few minutes ago, a few feet away from a lemon tree growing in an enormous pot. I gulped at air tinged with the scent of chlorine and citrus as Piper took a seat beside me, resting her hand on my knee. Her palm lingering just long enough to sear its imprint into my thigh.

Piper crossed her long legs, slipping her fingers between her thighs as if protecting them. I stared at her delicate wrists, wanting to bend down in front of her, spread her legs as I pulled her panties over her hips, dragging the material from her legs until I had unfettered access to the flawless stretch of skin she was covering up. Access to every hollow and crevice. I wanted to touch and taste and feel every fucking tremble. I wanted. God, how I wanted.

Realizing I was staring, I lifted my eyes to Piper's face, expecting to be met with the same anger she'd shown earlier. But instead I saw something else. There was a flicker of lust, as if she'd been reading my thoughts and had similar ones of her own. But more than anything else, just an open-eyed interest. I had her undivided attention. Piper wasn't fidgeting, or searching for distractions. No, she was entirely focused on me, and the overdue explanation I'd offered to give.

As if to underscore the point, she swept a tongue over her lips and shifted toward me in the chair. "I'm listening."

"I have a brother. His name is Jake."

* * *

My adoptive father, Mike, was sitting at the kitchen table, papers spread across the surface, his laptop in front of him. The TV was on in the background, some basketball game. And Jake was in his high chair, the remains of his dinner smeared across his tray, the floor around him littered with pasta and peas. Mike barely looked up from his screen. "You're home already?"

"Yeah. Thanks for letting me go." He had surprised me by coming home early so I could go over to my friend's house. Of course, he didn't know that my "friend" was my girlfriend, and her parents weren't home. "I've got Jake now, if you need to get back to work."

His only response was a quiet grunt that could have meant anything as he pecked at his keyboard, entering invoices for the auto body shop he managed.

I should have stayed home, after all. Since she wasn't expecting me, my now ex-girlfriend, had invited someone else over. Typical. I was easily replaceable. But my family—Mike, Sarah, and Jake—I couldn't afford to lose them, too. I'd been a jerk this past week, annoyed that I was going to miss out on getting laid to babysit. What an idiot.

Sex was great, but finally having a family… it was everything.

I walked into the kitchen, intending to take Jake out of his high chair and get him cleaned up and ready for bed so that when Sarah came home she could relax.

That was when I noticed the grapes on Jakes tray. Whole grapes. Horror curled a fist around my throat, squeezing tight. Jake wasn't smiling and reaching out his arms to me, like he usually did. In fact, he was looking kind of—

"No!" I screamed, nearly slipping on the greasy floor as I dove for him, sweeping inside his mouth with my pinkie like they'd taught us in the CPR portion of gym class every year. Sure enough, I felt the slippery skin of a fat grape lodged behind his tongue.

I yanked Jake out of his high chair, holding him against my chest as I gave a swift compression with the back of my fist into his soft stomach. Mike was already calling 911 as the grape finally shot across the room. I put Jake on the floor to check his pulse. He had one, thank god. But he wasn't breathing. The next seven minutes were the longest of my life, breathing air into my little brother's mouth, forcing his tiny chest to rise and fall. Praying, hoping, wishing, wanting.

Knowing this was all my fault.

Mike went into the ambulance with Jake while I waited for Sarah at home. She rarely kept her phone turned on, and certainly not at choir practice. And Mike didn't want her driving to the hospital alone. So I waited. Stacking up all of Mike's papers, closing his laptop, putting everything into the bag he brought from work. I cleaned the kitchen, wiping down Jake's tray and mopping the floor. Throwing away all the uneaten pasta and peas. And grapes.

When Sarah came home, I explained what had happened. Except for the part about me not actually being home. I told her I had fed Jake grapes with his dinner. The ones she'd told me a million times to cut into halves and sometimes quarters, because they were a choking hazard.

I didn't want her to blame Mike when I was the one who should have been home with Jake. Feeding him dinner and taking care of him. Cutting his damned grapes.

I had just gotten my license so I drove us to the hospital, each one of her shuddering breaths and broken sobs a nail through my heart.

We sat in the waiting room together. Lots of crying and praying, very little talking. I didn't stand when the doctor walked through the swinging doors, but I could hear every word he said. Oxygen deprivation. Limited brain function. Wait and see. We were allowed in Jake's room, and he looked just like he was sleeping. We were told he would wake up, but he would be "different."

Between science and health class, I knew what that meant—that my baby brother might just remain a baby his whole life.

And it was all my fault.

The baby brother who'd taught me what love was with the first squeeze of his tiny fingers around my pinkie.

That love transformed into toxic sludge as I walked out of the hospital in a daze, packed a few things into a duffel bag and hitched a ride to L.A. I met Shane within days, and eventually we hooked up with Jett, then Dax. After Travis signed us, I told him about the family I'd left behind. And that I wanted every penny I earned to go toward Jake's care.

Chapter Fifteen

Piper

Interior courtyards were open to the elements, save one. Wind. Protected on all sides, there was no breeze, no gusts of air to shield against. I was shaken to the core by Landon's confession, and yet not a single hair on my head had moved. It was unsettling. "Why didn't you tell me any of this before?"

Landon's handsome features twisted in an expression of anguish that ran deep, well below the ink peeking through the cuffs of his sleeves. My skin prickled, the hair at the back of my neck standing on end when his eyes met mine. Darker than I'd ever seen them, each one a whirling dervish of rage and regret. "You think admitting I'm responsible for my brother's brain damage is easy?"

"Landon, no." The denial scraped from my throat, each word leaving a sour aftertaste on my lips. "It wasn't your fault.

Your brother's…injury wasn't your fault. You weren't even there."

I was almost glad when he looked away from me; at least I could draw a breath when the weight of his stare wasn't pushing down on my chest, pressing against my lungs.

"Injury." He repeated the word I'd used, for lack of a better one. "I always thought an injury was something you'd recover from. You see a doctor, get a prescription or stitches or a cast. Maybe you have a scar, or walk with a limp, but you'd get *better*."

Landon tilted his head back, his strong profile like carved granite as he glared up at the sky, his stare so intense it wouldn't have surprised me if every cloud in sight chose to hide behind the sun. "I didn't want a brother. I didn't want Jake. Not at first anyway."

"That's normal. You were a teenager, you were used to having the Coxes all to yourself."

"No." He stretched out his arms, glaring at the textured skin beneath his tattoos. "This is what I was used to. The lit end of a cigarette, the slice of a razorblade. Pissing myself in a closet during one of my parents' benders, then being beaten for the mess." He pulled his shirt entirely off, his eyes now on mine as I studied the map of pain he'd hidden with ink but couldn't erase. "The metal end of a belt, the cut of a knife. Blood. Pain. Being scared to close my eyes at night. Feeling hungry all the fucking time."

Landon had always been reluctant to talk about his past, and I had never pushed for more than he willingly offered on his own. We were treading on delicate ground now, and I could feel it shifting and trembling beneath me. I was afraid to say anything, but I was desperate to envelop Landon in empathy, soothe the wounded boy inside of him.

A minute passed, then two. I didn't realize I was holding

my breath until Landon started speaking again. "I knew crack-head parents and the government system. Some fuckin' system—bouncing back and forth from what felt like kiddie jail to families looking for a benefit check. Figured I'd just bide my time, age out, or run away if things got unbearable." His cadence matched the uneven thud of my heart. Sentences pushed out, words tumbling over each other. Then a deep inhale before the next.

"I didn't expect to be adopted, ever. Thought I was just doing my time, like a prison sentence. But then I met the Coxes and everything changed. I had a home, was treated like a human being instead of a punching bag or a burden. Life was good, finally."

Landon's jaw was tight, a vein pulsing at his temple. I knew if I looked into his eyes I would see a maelstrom of torment and, selfishly, I was glad he didn't turn my way. My heart was breaking enough just from listening to him.

"So when I learned that things were going to change, that they were going to have the baby they'd always wanted, a kid of their own, I wasn't happy about it—at all. Not that I said anything. I was too worried I'd be sent back. But when Jake came home, he was just...my brother. I loved him. Loved him so damn much."

Landon's voice cracked and I reached out a hand to cover his knee, giving it a squeeze. He picked it up, running his fingers up and down my pinkie. "What the fuck was so important that I couldn't watch him while Sarah was singing in the choir and Mike was working? They had given me everything, and I couldn't give them a few hours of my time?"

I removed my hand, but only to crawl into Landon's lap, pressing my cheek to his chest and winding my arms around his waist. Offering comfort with my body, knowing words wouldn't be enough. "He's why I don't want kids of my own. I'm not even related to Jake by blood, but when I saw him turning blue, I'd have ripped my own lungs out of my chest if it would have helped. But there was nothing I could do for him, not that day."

"You did, Landon. You were the one who saved him, breathed for him when he couldn't. If you hadn't come home when you did, Jake would have died."

"If I had been home in the first place, he would be healthy." Landon's anger was directed inward, his chin digging into my shoulder as a sigh shuddered through him. "Piper, the one good thing that's come out of my career has been the means to pay for Jake's therapy. That's why I left. Why I disappeared that summer and didn't look back. I had a chance to try—not to make things right, that's never gonna happen—but to do *something* to ease the strain on the Coxes. I needed to earn money. Real money—the kind that came from signing with a big label and having an album make the charts. I needed to do whatever it took for that to happen. Make any sacrifice. Even if it meant sacrificing you."

I pushed at Landon's chest so I could meet his eyes. "But why couldn't you just be honest with me? Or at the very least, say goodbye?"

He blinked. "There was a meeting at Travis's office, right after Shane was collared for buying drugs downtown. Travis gave us an ultimatum—commit to our band, and only our band, or get lost. We all had to turn over our phones and get on a plane immediately. I missed you, Pippa. Missed you so fucking much"—his hands reached up to cup my cheeks—"but I owed it to Jake to give everything I had to music. And by the time I came back, I'd decided I didn't deserve to have a girl like you."

"Landon." His name was a breath that quivered from my lips. "You deserve to be happy, to be loved. Everyone does."

He shook his head, sadly. "If that were the truth, life would be fair. And you know damn well it's not."

There was no disputing that. No, life wasn't fair. I ran a hand through Landon's thick blond mop glinting like a crown in the sunlight. With his hard muscles and chiseled jaw, it's easy to pretend that the man in front of me was all hard angles and impenetrable emotions. In reality, Landon's heart was just as fragile as mine. Not that he'd ever admit it. "How about honesty, do I deserve that?"

"Yeah. Yeah, you do." He exhaled. "I'm sorry, Piper. I'm sorry for lying, and for all the times when I could have told you the truth about what I was thinking, feeling, doing—and instead said nothing at all. I was a complete dick. Can you forgive me?"

My hands curled in his hair, ready to give a tug if he tried to look away. "That depends. Are you done being a dick to me?"

But Landon didn't look away, his gaze remaining firmly affixed to mine. "One hundred percent. And, believe me, my dick is entirely at your disposal."

Our faces were barely an inch apart and there was a distinct shift in the mood between us. As if we'd stepped from a confessional into the dark of a sultry night. I felt a hardening against my thigh, the solid press and pulse of his desire.

I opened my mouth to speak, but Landon stopped me with a finger to my lips. A finger that traced the curve of my mouth, so softly it was like being kissed by a ghost. I held my breath, focusing entirely on the sensation. And when he pulled his hand away, I moaned in protest.

"Are we done talking?" he asked in a husky whisper that had me wet in an instant. "Because there are other things I'd like to do with my tongue right now. Other things I'd like to see your mouth doing."

Air caught in my throat and I gave a jerky nod. *So. Done. Talking.*

Big hands gripped my ass, adjusting my position so I straddled his lap, one knee on either side of his hips, the apex of my thighs flush against the bulge between his. The skirt of my sundress flared outward, offering false modesty. Beneath, only the lace of my panties and the cotton of Landon's new sweatpants prevented us from joining.

One hand pushed into my hair, making a loose fist, tugging just enough that my back arched, my breasts on display. My nipples tightened, pointing at Landon, silently begging for attention.

Blood thrummed beneath my veins, every cell brimming with lust and want and desire. A needy cocktail infused with emotions that had grown more potent with Landon's confession.

My eyelids fluttered closed as Landon cupped my shoulder with his free hand, drawing his fingertips down one arm than back up again, trekking across my collarbone, then repeating the movement with my other arm. Goose bumps trailed after his touch.

My hips rocked forward instinctively, craving friction.

The hiss of Landon's breath was a reward. Proof he wasn't immune to me, to this. To *us*.

My chest cracked open, the heated air coming off Landon's skin rushing in, invading every dark corner I had intended to keep from him.

I thought he was the sum of my assumptions, most of which had been wrong.

I thought he was the product of my low expectations, most of which had been undeserved.

How could I have been so wrong? I needed to *know* him. The rock star and the wounded boy.

The loner.

The legend.

Landon Cox was all of those things.

And then some.

Landon

I released the knot of Piper's hair to push at a strap of her sundress. The narrow strip of fabric was an insult, covering up way too much of her flawless skin. "Take it off," I muttered, my voice hoarse with pent up desire.

There was no objection to my rough demand. If anything, Piper's eyes smoldered with hunger, a tranquil sea roiling from an unexpected storm.

Her delicate hands plucked at the hem of her dress, lifting it slowly. Agonizingly slowly.

And in those suspended moments when Piper's dress had yet to pull free of her face, exposing a buffet of soft skin and lacy lingerie, I pushed away all that remained unsaid between us.

After I got back from that cabin—where I'd spent most days in the recording studio, working on what would become our breakout album—I didn't *want* to go back to Piper.

Just like Shane had purged his body of alcohol and drugs, those months stripped away the comfort I'd found in Piper's arms. At first, I'd craved her sweetness like a diabetic. But as the weeks wore on, I realized I was the better for it. I needed to be hungry, focused.

I had the chance to take over the financial burden of Jake's care. To help Mike and Sarah, who had given me everything. Maybe one day there would be a treatment that would cure Jake, some way of restoring function to the parts of his brain that had died from oxygen deprivation. And if there was a way, any way at all, I wanted to be in a position to afford the best doctors, the best therapies, the best everything.

So I'd buried the memory of Piper Hastings in the deepest, darkest recesses of my mind, drowning the lingering taste of her kisses with alcohol, diluting the memory of her touch with dozens, maybe hundreds, of other women. Nameless, faceless women whose laughs scratched at my eardrums, whose perfumes made me itch.

Piper's head poked free of the fabric, a smile playing on her lips and a fire blazing from her eyes. Creamy skin, petal pink lips, and long lashes that cast shadows on sculpted cheekbones. A mosaic of attractive pieces, exquisitely arranged. Piper Hasting was so damn gorgeous it nearly hurt to look at her.

And her body…breasts swelling above a navy blue strapless bra, the firm, flat plane of her belly leading to matching lace panties.

Fuck. Who knew navy blue could be so goddamn sexy?

In my head, there was one word playing on repeat. Like the relentless kick of a snare drum: mine.

Mine, mine, mine, mine.

Above, a cloud passed over the sun, sending my shadow across Piper's face like a mark of ownership.

And damn, I wanted to own everything about this woman.

Her joy and sorrow. Her tears and laughter.

I wanted to own it all, especially the painful bits—so I could crush them to dust. Send each sharp, shiny grain into the wind, never to abrade her sensitive soul again.

Piper's pulse was a steady thrum beneath my palms as I skimmed my hands over the curve of her waist, the creased plane of her ribs, the cushioned swell of her breasts. Our heads came together, foreheads meeting, mouths not quite touching, my inhale synchronized to her exhale, hungrily consuming her every breath.

I was so fucking hard.

I swept my tongue along the tread of her lips, sinking my teeth into the plump fullness of her lower one. A bite, just hard enough, deep enough, to leave a mark, a reminder. *Landon Cox was here.*

Piper gave a ragged groan, nails pushing into the skin at the back of my neck, impatient hips rocking into me.

I pushed down the flimsy cups of her bra, revealing the tight peaks of her nipples, their usual rosy color dusky with want. My mouth sought out her right breast, my left hand toying with the other as my always composed Piper came apart at the seams. Making a mewling sound, she reached behind her back to unclasp the band of her bra, letting it flutter to the ground like a useless candy wrapper.

My cock was desperate to poke through the material keeping it from sinking into Piper's clenching heat. Wrapping my arm around her waist like an iron bar, I hooked a thumb around the band of my pants and jerked them down just far enough for my dick to finally break free.

Piper glanced at my ridged shaft, the crown dark and swollen, a bead of precum glistening. Before I could stop her, she had pushed off my shoulders and slid to the ground, her knees between my feet.

"Piper," I choked out, wishing I had the strength of mind to pull her back up, to switch positions so that I was the one on my knees before her.

If there was ever a woman worthy of worship, it was Piper Hastings.

But right now, my mind was entirely at the mercy of my dick.

Piper's face moved closer, tongue trembling just beyond the white gate of her teeth, hair a silken sweep across my thighs, glinting gold in the sunlight. She gave a little puff of excitement, the warm air a caress.

"Jesus, Pippa," I groaned, my eyes closing, a shudder rippling down my spine. And as the syllables of her name fled through my clenched jaw, I felt her hands wrap around me, her soft palms slowly gliding along my shaft. An exploration that was too slow, too gentle for the ferocity building inside my chest, threading to break my ribs wide open.

I gripped the edges of my chair, vaguely noting that my hold was tighter than it had been just a few hours ago. Maybe this was all the physical therapy I needed.

The thought was chased away by Piper's mouth, by that glistening tongue that lapped at the wetness smearing my crown. Delicate licks to start, like a cat tasting cream for the first time. And then longer, firmer strokes, as if her appetite had been whetted but not satisfied.

I'd satisfy her, all right. Just, ah Christ—

Piper's lips wrapped around me, her tongue flattening as she sucked me into her mouth. Deep, then deeper. Pulling back up, swirling her tongue while the fingers of one hand closed around my shaft, her hold on me tight and wet as she nibbled and kissed.

There was a wild beast inside me that wanted to grab Piper by the hair and thrust upward, seize my pleasure from her mouth at my own pace, under my own power.

But that would be taking the easy way out, at the expense of Piper's trust.

When it came to this girl, I didn't have much restraint, but I had enough not to ruin this moment. And enough sense to know she'd already ruined me.

In the very best way.

I rolled my hips toward her, my cock sinking into the cavern of her mouth as she sucked me deep, the edges of her tongue curling over me.

It was almost painful, the way pleasure unfurled deep in the pit of my groin, closing over my balls, clutching at the muscles and tendons of my thighs, turning my stomach into a rigid plane. The pressure built in strong swells, rising higher and higher until it was a struggle even to swallow. My world shrunk to the wet heat of Piper's mouth, the tight grip of her throat, the determined clasp of her hands. The sun above our heads was unimportant, the ground beneath our feet nonexistent.

I felt the point of no return coming with the force of a tsunami and I pushed at her forehead. "Pippa. I'm gonna—"

But she only moaned, shaking her head slowly. The vibration, the friction, it had the bones of my pelvis shaking and then, in the next moment, shattering completely. "Ah, fuck," I howled, another wave pounding me hard, and I was pulsing, pulsing. All the while, Piper's hands gripped my thighs, her throat working to swallow as I unloaded inside her mouth.

Finally, she pulled off me, and I looked down with what had to be a stupid, dopey grin stretching wide over my cheeks, just in time to see her tongue flick once more over me, before she lay her head flat on my leg.

An emotion that felt dangerously close to love, not because of the blow job—although, fuck if that hadn't been the best one I'd ever received—but because of *her*. Of the noises she made without realizing it, of the expressions on her face when she didn't think I was looking. Of the comfort I found whenever she was near.

Just...her. Piper Hastings. My Pippa. The woman who meant more to me than I'd ever imagined possible.

I waited a few moments, until the urge to taste her, to feel the press of her thighs on my neck, the perfect globes of her ass in my hands, became too much to bear. Rising to my feet, I gathered Piper into my arms, despite her protests that I shouldn't. Fuck that. I'd carry her to the ends of the earth if she'd let me.

But I didn't have far to go, just to the chaise lounge a few feet to my right.

That gorgeous body of hers stretched out on the cushion, all smooth skin and creamy curves, two perfect peaked nipples, still wearing that tiny blue thong. I pushed the lace into her crease, a mangled gasp escaping her throat as my thumb rubbed damp fabric over the swollen nub between her folds.

"Damn," I rasped, my voice like gravel. "You like that, don't you?"

She made another noise that sounded like it had at least a passing acquaintance with "yes."

My eyes swept over her, intending to take my time, knowing I'd enjoy every single moment.

I'd just dipped my tongue into the shallow well of her belly button, tasting each sweet pleat, when I heard the chime of a bell. I looked up, straight into Piper's wide eyes. "What—"

Disappointment was written all over her face. "The door. Your physical therapy appointment."

"Stay right here." I gave Piper a stern warning. "Don't move, don't get dressed. Just, stay."

Jogging to the front door, I opened it just enough to fit my head through. A guy wearing a black golf shirt with the RHC logo stood in front of me. "Hey, I'm in the middle of something. Bill me whatever, but I need about an hour. You can come back, yeah?"

"Ah, yeah. Sure. I'll just—"

"Great. See ya in a bit." I slammed the door shut and headed back for the courtyard. Money and fame could be a double-edged sword, but they certainly had their privileges.

Chapter Sixteen

Piper

Days passed, filled with Landon's physical therapy sessions, visits from Travis, Shane, Jett, and Dax, meetings with the general contractor working on his house, visits to Harmony's, and long walks in the canyons near the house. At night we lounged in the interior courtyard, skinny-dipping in the pool, making love beneath the moonlight.

A personal chef delivered meals and snacks every morning from the approved list of foods for Landon so we didn't have to shop or cook. For the most part, our time was our own. And we spent much of it rediscovering each other's bodies, and talking about nothing and everything…except *us*.

I finally ventured back into the office after a week, leaving Landon with Jett and Dax, thinking I needed to put in some face time.

Wrong.

Travis took one look at me and nearly had a seizure. Within five minutes, I was back in the elevator, under strict instructions not to leave Landon's side until further notice.

It felt like we were naughty children, sent away for misbehaving. And maybe that was what we were.

For the first time in my life, it felt pretty damn good to be bad.

Maybe that was why I decided to make a quick stop to see Shania on my way back. Travis would have had a fit, but he was too busy with a movie star's latest crisis to actually check up on me. Had Landon been home alone, I would have rushed right back, but between Jett and Dax, I figured Landon would survive an extra half hour without my hovering.

The cottage was empty so I went straight to the barn. Harmony preferred to let Shania and her pups outside when the other dogs were napping or eating. Since I could see a dozen dogs running around the paddocks, I made a beeline for Shania's usual stall. She glanced up at me, rising to her hind legs in one smooth movement and stretching her front paws on the door. I held my hand out for her to inspect, and she rewarded me with a lick before backing away and sitting down, making a low noise in the back of her throat.

"Sounds like someone just got an invitation."

I jumped at Harmony's voice, glancing over my shoulder to find the older woman grinning at me. "I don't know about that."

"I do," she said, sliding the metal lock aside. "When I open the door, get in quick before they all escape."

A moment later, I was standing in the stall, puppies squirming all over my legs. I looked back at Harmony. "What should I do?" I'd never been here without Landon.

She clucked at me, already walking away. "Sit down and soak up the love."

My nerves fell away as I glanced back at Shania, who was now stretched out on her side, eyeing me with what looked like a smile pulling at her whiskered snout. I lowered myself to the straw covered floor, crossing my legs just in time for a smooth gray pup to tumble into my lap, quickly followed by a tan sibling. A light laugh spilled from my lips as I ran my hands over their wiggling bodies. "No wonder why you've been keeping these guys all to yourself, Shania—they're irresistible."

I spent the next twenty minutes doing exactly what Harmony had suggested, soaking up the unconditional love that filled the stall. I'd never had a pet myself, and I couldn't remember ever feeling so…content.

And when I went to glance up at Shania again, I didn't have to look far. She'd slowly inched her way toward me, her wet nose barely an inch from my knee. "Hey girl, am I doing okay?" I whispered.

In response, she patted my knee with her paw, just once, and then inched even closer, pressing her side against my leg.

I released a happy sigh, running a palm over her head and neck, scratching beneath her chin. "Thanks. I think you're doing pretty great, too."

* * *

Landon, Jett, and Dax were hanging out in the courtyard when I got back. Landon wouldn't say it, but I knew he felt as though he'd let the band down with his injury. The last time they had gone so long without playing together was when Shane was awaiting trial, and the fear that things might not swing in their favor again this time was palpable.

Shane had gone back to New York, but there was an ease to their banter tonight, and I was glad. Landon needed that from them.

I went to bed early, and Landon joined me sometime in the middle of the night. But the next morning, I woke up feeling unsettled.

Stopping at an enormous rock formation after an early morning walk, I stretched out on it and scowled up at the sky. The sun was low on the horizon but rising determinedly, the air still cool. Landon's hand reached out for mine, the heat of his body keeping me warm.

For as long as I could remember, all of my actions and gestures were controlled and targeted toward my audience. Right now, damp from exertion, my limbs loose and rubbery, looking over at Landon beside me, I didn't know what my role was. He was my ex-boyfriend, and my current...what was he? Fuckbuddy? Fling?

Of course, Landon was also one of my boss's biggest clients, which made him, by extension, *my* client.

I had my choice of hats to wear, but none of them seemed to fit. Or maybe there were just too many to choose from.

Would there ever come a time when he was just...*mine*?

"What are you thinking?" His hand curved around my neck, fingers pushing into my hair at the base of my skull, curious eyes bearing down on me.

I tilted my chin up, letting my lips part just a bit, sweeping my tongue through the crease between them. Landon's gaze dropped, following the tip of my tongue from one side of my mouth to the other. His lips met my own, the warmth of his breath surging into my lungs.

Then he pulled back, not far, just enough that I could see the whole of his gorgeous face, pinning me in place with nothing more than a stare. It shivered through my body, weighing me down.

"That I don't want to think at all. Not right now." I didn't. Not when all the questions crowding my mind were chasing nonexistent answers. Landon was the source of all my uncertainty, but right now, he was also a damned effective distraction.

The mouth I wanted so badly on mine slanted crookedly. "Well, your thoughts are so loud they're giving me a headache. You might as well spill 'em, because I don't think I can take hearing you scream my name right now. Might be too much for me."

I wanted to jump up and stalk off…but I knew it would only be delaying the inevitable. This was a conversation we needed to have, so we might as well have it this morning. "Fine. Is that all we are? Great sex while it's convenient, a distant memory when it's not?"

A throaty chuckle rumbled from his throat. "That's what has you walking around like a storm cloud this morning—you don't know what we are?"

"Do you?" I shot back.

His expression turned serious. "Fuck, yeah. Just because I had reasons for leaving you before doesn't mean that it wasn't a goddamn mistake. One I'm never making again, you hear me? I'm gonna get my grip back, and when my house is ready, I want you moving in with me. Wasted six years without you, I don't want to waste another hour."

And there it was—*nearly* everything I'd ever wanted to hear Landon say. I was still absorbing his words when his hand thrust into my hair, his fingers cradling my scalp, holding me steady as I trembled. Lust pulsed between us, the energy sparking and swirling. "Landon," I whispered, so much want in those two syllables.

He made a sound, low in his throat as he flicked a tongue across my lips. Tasting me. Teasing me.

Sliding my hands along the wall of his chest, Landon's muscles rippling beneath my touch, pressing my body to his. Needing to be closer.

One of Landon's hands followed the track of my spine, curving over my ass, fitting me against him so I could feel every inch of his desire.

My mouth, my body, my soul—they were all Landon's for the taking. And I wanted him to take *me*.

I moaned, pulling away just enough to grab the hem of my shirt and lift it over my head. It was the kind that had a built in shelf bra, so once it was off, I was bare from the waist up.

Landon's breath caught in his throat as his eyes swept over me, and I felt a spark of pride that I could give him pause. Could give him pleasure.

I could bask in the glow of his adoration forever.

"Jesus Christ, Pippa. Do you have any idea what you do to me? You've completely wrecked me. The mess I've made of my life, you make me want to fix it. You make me think I *can* fix it. But more than anything else—when I'm with you, I want to fucking live. Just take everything I can out of this one shot we're all given. And I want to rock the shit out of it. Not just on stage or in a music studio. But with you. Anywhere and everywhere…with you."

A part of me cleaved open, so filled with joy I couldn't contain it all. I threw my arms around Landon's neck, kissing him with wild abandon.

Joy. Pure joy.

Maybe all this time apart had brought us back together again. Maybe we had needed the time to come into our own, become people that were actually good to each other. Good for each other.

"Show me, Landon," I mumbled the plea against his lips. "Show me."

He dragged his shirt over his head as I grabbed at the waistband of his pants and tugged them down, then did the same to my own. We were so close, I could feel the heat of his body calling out to me. "Don't even know who I am anymore. I'm not the guy I was, and not sure I'll ever be the man you deserve." His tongue slipped inside my mouth, staking his claim. Leaving me dizzy, breathless. "But I'm damn sure going to spend every day trying. I swear."

And I believed him. With every atom of my existence, I believed him.

Our eyes met and held, the promise shining from them a visceral thing. Visible and sincere. "You deserve the world, Landon Cox."

He touched his forehead to mine, his breath ghosting across my lips. "You are my world, Piper Hastings."

I melted, sagging against him. Landon caught me, holding me tight as we slid down the boulder. I didn't care if he could ever grasp a drumstick again...As long as he held on to me for the rest of our lives.

I was trapped between the rock wall at my back and the hard wall of Landon's rippling abs, our feet on the ground, his brawny frame dwarfing my own. His cock pulsed with heat, throbbing against my belly. Everything about Landon was big, overwhelming. The force of his personality, the strength of his arms, the lust driving through his veins. Especially the size of his body—every part.

My hips made a slow swivel, pressing against one in particular. A knowing smirk pulled at one corner of Landon's mouth.

"Ah, Pips. You do know what you do to me, don't you?" He leaned down, his breath dancing into my eardrum, the rough husk of his voice like a gritty ballad written just for me. "You know…because I do the same thing to you."

Lust spiked, sharp and insistent. Love softening the edges of my fierce desire. I knew it in my soul—I loved Landon Cox. Passionately. Wholeheartedly. Desperately.

Rocked by the realization, I was only vaguely aware of Landon dropping to his knees until he looked up at me like a starving beggar at my feet. Pressing a palm between my hip bones, he held me steady even as he dragged a leg over his shoulder, groaning as I opened to him. "So fucking perfect," he growled in the second before his tongue dove between my folds, giving me a long lick, then circling that needy bundle of nerves, achingly swollen and wanting.

I was done pretending to be perfect. But right now, in Landon's arms, this moment was nothing short of perfection.

I grabbed hold of Landon's hair, holding on for dear life as pleasure surged between my thighs, moving up and out through every limb, every vein.

I was panting, adding a needy whine to the soundtrack of Landon's grunts and groans as he devoured me with enthusiasm, his skillful, swirling tongue sending coils of sensation to wrap around me, pulling tight, so tight. Landon's fingers entered my body, angled to reach a place only he had ever discovered.

I couldn't breathe, couldn't see, couldn't think. Just when I wanted to scream from the intensity, the pressure broke, snapping entirely. Bliss rained down in jagged blades, ripping me open. With all the tension gone, I sagged against Landon as he kissed the tender skin of my inner thighs.

His grin was smugly sexy as I blinked at him. Landon set my

foot down and rose to his full height, sweeping aside a tendril of hair that clung to my cheekbone. I wasn't prepared when he spun me, gasping as he placed my hands flat on the rock and then pulled me up by my waist. "Curve that back for me, baby," he groaned, dragging his fingers in a whisper soft caress along my spine. Goose bumps rose up to meet him, racing after the trail of his fingers.

I shivered, satisfied and yet wanting more. Wanting to feel Landon inside me. There was the rip of a wrapper and then the head of his cock dragging along my wet slit, leaving tingles. I thrust my hips at him, pushing my forehead against the inside of my arm. "Landon," I whimpered. "Please."

"You want me?"

I choked on a breath. "Yes, I want you. I want us."

"Ah, Pips," Landon exhaled, the press of his thumbs into the skin at my waist the only warning as he drove into me, filling me body and soul.

Hard and thick, he was the missing piece that made me feel complete. The fit was tight, leaving no room for anything else. Not doubt or hesitation. Not fear or shyness. Only Landon. All of Landon.

I ground my teeth together as he rocked into me, his hips like a piston on overdrive, snapping hard and fast.

There was a fever to our coupling, something hot and unrestrained. No pretense, no restraint. Just lust and want and need.

The slap of his skin on mine filled my ears, a desperate beat. One of his hands crept between my legs. I wanted to twist away from his fingers, the pleasure almost painful. "Oh, god." I moaned, knowing what was coming but not sure that I could take it. But the choice wasn't mine. My body belonged to Landon, and what didn't break me would—

I screamed as he flicked his thumb over my clit, that wet slide shattering me completely.

Landon's strokes turned wild, untamed. Dragging every last bit of rapture out of me, until an orgasm came for him too, and he roared like a hunter who'd finally caught his prey.

After a minute, his rapid breaths pulsing hot against my skin, Landon pressed a lingering kiss along my shoulder blade, and pulled out of me with a guttural groan. I straightened, twisting into his embrace and pushing my chin into the welcoming place between his shoulder and neck. I had no words. All I could offer was the beat of my heart.

Landon

The past three weeks with Piper had lulled me into a sense of complacency. Made me believe that my life was finally starting to come together... Until our damn label insisted on a preview of the new songs for our next album. I'd said things to Piper, implied things that went beyond words—how could I follow through on them if I didn't get my grip back? Not merely enough to cut a steak or sign my name, but a grip with the kind of strength and precision our fans expected from a Nothing but Trouble performance.

Watching my drumsticks fly from my hands at the first slap of the cymbal was a brutal reminder that, although my grip had shown improvement when it came to some everyday tasks, it still had a hell of a long way to go before I was capable of playing a show.

Travis and the guys said I didn't have to come, but there had never been a Nothing but Trouble performance without me, and even if I wasn't on the stage, I was damn sure going to show up.

Shane clapped a reassuring hand on my shoulder as he passed by on his way to the stage. If there was anyone who understood how I felt right now, it was him.

However, when his arrest had forced us to cancel our tour last year, the charge stemmed from a dark night in Shane's past. A tragedy. And when the charges were dropped, he'd been vindicated.

Sheer stupidity on my part had sidelined me tonight, a glaringly obvious difference that had me barely able to look Shane in the eyes.

I should have stayed home, I realized. I should have stayed in bed with Piper, buried myself in her body, filled my ears with her needy moans.

Because now I was watching someone else behind my drum kit. Someone else performing *my* songs, playing with *my* band, in front of *my* label.

It was just too much. Too. Fucking. Much.

Standing at the side of the stage, my hands curled into tight fists at my sides.

Actually, no. They didn't.

In my mind, I was squeezing them so damn tight I should have popped a goddamn tendon.

The reality was, my left hand was balled up, but my right resembled a loose lobster claw—and was trembling from the effort.

Fuck drumsticks. My right hand could barely hold my own dick.

Piper came up behind me, standing as close as she could without pressing her body to mine. I felt the whisper of her skin along my arm, the press of her thigh against the back of my hand. I wanted to feel comforted by her presence. Knew she was trying to offer it through sheer proximity.

But instead of comfort—I felt only panic. My heart pounded against my ribcage, breath trapped inside my lungs. What if I never got my grip back? Was this going to be my life—standing just beyond the spotlight, envy and rage consuming me?

If I couldn't perform behind my drum kit, who the fuck was I?

No one. I was no one.

What would Piper want with a miserable son of a bitch, too blinded by shame to even see straight?

Permanently losing the only thing I'd ever done well, the part of myself that had brought success beyond my wildest imagination, would be soul-crushing.

If I had to watch the light in Piper's eyes dim as she lost respect for me…I couldn't even imagine it. I'd rather be dead.

But right now, I was watching my band perform…without me. I'd been replaced. And it fucking sucked. I wanted it to be *me* on stage. Blood and oxygen pumping through my veins, exacting each rhythm with precision and power. A man worthy of adoration and accolades.

"How the fuck do you do this?" I barked, loudly enough to be heard over the music.

Piper looked at me in confusion. "Do what?"

Anger brewed, hot and thick. At myself. At fate. Spilling onto Piper, too. I pointed to the guy behind my kit, a talented drummer who would have sharpened his sticks and sliced me open for the chance to take my place permanently. Not that I could blame him. "Stand here, on the goddamn sidelines."

Compassion softened her frown, turning it into something

that felt a whole lot like pity. "Not everyone needs to live in the spotlight, Landon."

But I did. I needed it. The lights were transformative. Magical, even. Made me something more than Landon Cox, fuck-up extraordinaire. Ruiner of love and lives. Turned me into a legend.

I craved the spotlight on my skin more than I'd ever craved drugs or booze. It had brought me safety, security. Allowed me to take care of my brother, barricade myself behind iron gates. Kept my interactions on my terms. Kept people safe from my sins.

"I'm not everyone," I choked out, pivoting away from her, needing space. Needing to get away from the stage before I fucking bum-rushed it and tackled the guy who had taken my goddamn place.

The doctors had warned me that drinking alcohol would slow down my recovery. I might have sold a kidney for a swig of liquor…but I wasn't going to risk my chances of getting back behind my drum kit as soon as possible.

Instead I grabbed a water from the makeshift bar in one of the back rooms, avoiding eye contact with everyone in it, and shook out a few pills from the bottle in my pocket, then a few more.

I crushed them between my teeth, savoring the gritty, bitter taste like it was caviar. A few minutes later I felt the buzz I'd been craving, my limbs loosening as the tension drained from my muscles. I knew I needed to go back to Piper and apologize for taking out my piss-poor mood on her. She didn't deserve it. That girl was the best thing that ever happened to me.

"You didn't have to come tonight." Travis appeared at my side.

"I know. But I've never missed one of our shows." My lips felt thick and uncooperative, like they didn't want to form words. "Didn't want to start tonight."

He glanced down at my hands. "I could have gotten them to reschedule for when you're better."

"Yeah, Trav? When's that gonna be?" I asked angrily, vaguely noting that my voice sounded distorted, like there was an echo in the room.

Travis didn't back off an inch. "I bet on you guys a long time ago, and I've yet to pick a loser. Stick with your rehab and do everything the doctors tell you to do. You'll get back behind your drums, Landon. I have no doubt."

I ran a tongue over my teeth as I watched Travis walk away. If it was possible to get strength back in my hands just by sheer force of will, I'd be killing it in no time. Tossing my empty water bottle into a bin, I pushed off the wall and glanced around for Piper.

There was a flash of blonde hair by the bathrooms. Good. I had to take a fucking leak.

But when I got to the door, the blonde I saw was an obvious dye job. Not my Pippa.

She looked up as I brushed past her, her eyes widening in surprise. "Landon Cox," she breathed.

I forced a grin. "Hey there, doll."

"H—hi. Oh my god, I love you." Sure she did. They all did.

"Love you, too." It wasn't exactly a lie. I loved all my fans. Showed many of them just how much. A few months ago, I would have shown this one, too. But right now I just wanted to fall back into bed with Piper.

"Can we take a selfie?"

"Sure." Somehow I managed not to flinch when she wrapped an arm around my neck and planted a kiss on my cheek while she snapped a few pictures. Not because my neck was still sore, but because the girl wasn't Piper.

Afterward, I slipped into the bathroom and closed the door behind me, grabbing for the top of my sweat—

Fuck. I wasn't wearing sweatpants. I was wearing jeans for the first time since waking up in the hospital. Jeans Piper had closed for me and I couldn't unbutton myself. Fuck, fuck, fuck.

Hunching my shoulders, I pushed my thumbs behind the band, trying to press my fingers against the opposite side. Trying until my shoulders were shaking from the effort, sweat breaking out on my forehead and dripping into my eyes. "Fuck!" I yelled, slamming my back against the wall.

The bottle blonde poked her head through the door. "Hey, there."

I swiped my forearm across my face and dredged up a sheepish smile. It was bad enough I wasn't on stage, I didn't need some chick selling a story about me throwing a tantrum in the goddamn bathroom. "Hey."

"Want some company?" she asked, a hopeful look on her face.

Chapter Seventeen

Piper

I think our boy needs to go home."

I arched an eyebrow at Travis. "Landon's no boy."

"You're right. He's a client and it was a bad idea for him to come tonight."

"Is he okay? What happened?" Anxiety leached into my voice.

"He's fine. But I think seeing someone take his place on stage is messing with his head."

The pain radiating from Landon when we were standing side by side had been painfully obvious and knowing there was nothing I could do to ease it had been excruciating. He'd stormed off a few minutes ago and I purposely hadn't gone after him, thinking he needed space. Had I been wrong? "I'll go find him."

Travis's suspicious glance stopped me before I could turn

away. "Is there anything between you two I should know about?" he asked.

Nope. I schooled my face into a nonchalant mask. Inside, I was busting at the seams to tell Travis about Landon and I. But I didn't want to do it here, tonight. I had a lot on the line, and I didn't want to burn any bridges by not putting a lot of thought into my delivery. Besides, Landon was in an understandably foul mood tonight. I didn't have the bandwidth to face off with an irate Travis, too. "He's a client," I said, repeating the party line.

My boss gave a slow blink, his gaze penetrating. "See that you remember that."

Walking away on legs that were less than steady, I realized I was putting everything on the line for Landon. My heart. My job. The reputation I was just beginning to build. He was worth it, I knew that. But it didn't make the risk any less scary.

Landon wasn't in the main reception room, where some industry bigwigs were holding court. Or in any of the dressing rooms. I noticed a blonde slipping into the men's room and fought the urge to roll my eyes. "Have you seen Landon?" I asked one of the security guards.

He jerked a chin. "In there. But he might want privacy."

Privacy? My pulse sped up. What the hell?

Grabbing for the door handle, I poked my head through the opening.

"Hey!" The blonde spun around, eyes blazing with anger, a smear of lipstick on one of her front teeth. "We're busy!"

I felt Landon's eyes on me, a corner of my brain noting that the woman's hands had been clutching the band of his jeans.

What. The. Fuck.

I threw open the door completely, glancing back at the security guard. "I think someone needs help finding the ladies' room."

"I do not," she squeaked. "We were just about—"

The burly man stepped forward, silencing the woman with a glare.

With a last huff of outrage, she tottered off on a pair of Lucite heels. The bouncer followed, leaving Landon and I alone. I turned my attention back to him.

"Piper, I—"

I lifted my hand. "Save it."

"But I didn't—"

I could barely look at him. Had our conversation the other morning meant anything at all? "You didn't what? You didn't think I'd mind if you—"

"I just had to take a leak, okay," he blurted out, lifting his shirt to expose a flat strip of inked muscle and a still closed button. "But I can't even fucking do that!"

A stab of empathy cut right between my ribs, draining some of my wrath. I exhaled, my shoulders loosening slightly as I crossed the floor. I'd help Landon with his jeans and then we'd leave, put this night behind us. Tomorrow we could hash things out, discuss what we really wanted and expected from each other. Catching him behind closed doors with some groupie was not on my list.

Warm skin brushed the back of my knuckles and the familiar thrill of contact raced up my arms. I glanced up at Landon's face, and he stumbled just a bit, his back sliding against the wall. Instinctively, I caught him by his shoulders, scrutinizing his features. His eyes were darker than I'd ever seen them, and I realized his pupils were so dilated that only the thinnest rim of chocolate covered them—like candy-coated truffles.

I jerked away from him. "How many pills have you had?"

Landon's expression tightened and he gestured at the urinals. "You wanna watch?"

Disgusted, I left the bathroom. What the hell was wrong with him? The man had turned the act of self-sabotage into an art. Every cell in my body wanted to leave, head back to my own place and cool off. Reassess the situation once I put some distance between us.

But Landon wasn't my stoner boyfriend. Right now, I was working and Landon was my client. And my boss, who had assigned me to keep Landon out of trouble, was somewhere in the building. I didn't have the luxury of allowing our personal relationship to impact my professional reputation.

My stomach was churning, a relentless cycle of uncertainty that gnawed at my intestines and had me feeling nauseous. I closed my eyes, trying to breathe through it.

A heavy hand clamped down on my shoulder. "What's going on?"

I swear my boss had a sixth sense for trouble. Quickly straightening, I opened my eyes to find Travis peering at me intently. "Nothing. Just waiting for Landon to—"

The door opened and Landon lurched through it. "Oh, hey Trav."

Travis's stare became a scowl as he picked up on the slight slur to Landon's words, the almost imperceptible slackness of his expression. He turned to me. "You'll take him back to the house." It was a command, not a question.

I would have agreed, but the nausea I'd been fighting to hold at bay surged forward with a vengeance. I darted past Landon, making it to the toilet just in time.

When I was done, Travis was waiting for me by the row of sinks. "You okay?"

I turned on the tap, swooshing water in my mouth and washing my hands. "I'm fine."

He grunted. "I've sent Landon home with one of the security guys. Go back to your place and don't breathe on any of my clients until whatever bug you have is gone."

Landon

At the sound of the front door opening, I darted into the foyer, the mouthful of apologies and explanations pressing heavily on my tongue eager for escape.

But it wasn't Piper that came through the door.

"Don't look so happy to see me," Travis deadpanned, reading the disappointment written across my face.

My eyes flicked to the mirror on the wall. It didn't take a mind reader. I looked like someone had run over my puppy.

"I, uh—" I turned away, walking into the kitchen, Travis following. "I was expecting Piper."

"She's sick."

"Sick?" When Piper ran past me into the bathroom, I just figured it was because she didn't want to take me home. And I didn't blame her.

"Yeah. Puking sick. I sent her home." He glanced at the open pill bottle on the counter, his eyebrow lifting.

"They're prescription," I said defensively, swiping the bottle and putting the cap back on, but not before giving a quick glance inside. *Shit, there were only a few left.* I shoved it into my pocket and crossed my arms over my chest. "You're telling the truth about Piper?"

"Probably caught a stomach bug. She looked pretty green."

"You sure it wasn't because of m—"

Travis barked a laugh. "Don't give yourself so much credit."

I allowed myself a small sigh of relief. "Got it. I'll check on her tomorrow."

"You'll check on her?" Travis slapped his hands on the granite and shot me a skeptical glare. "Jesus. What the fuck's going on with the two of you?"

"Nothing. We're friends."

"Friends." He chewed on the word. "The kind with benefits?"

I held his stare but kept my face impassive.

He shook his head and groaned. "She's my goddamn employee, Landon. And a good one, too. I figured if anyone was smart enough not to spread 'em for you, it would be her."

My eyes narrowed at the crude comment. "It's not like that."

"Oh no? Then explain it to me, because right now all I see is a talented, hardworking kid I'm about to fire because you can't keep your dick in your pants."

"You can't fire her."

"Oh really? And why is that?"

"Piper and I, we know each other. We have history."

"Ah, let me guess. She was president of your fan club and couldn't resist your charm when she met you in person."

"Don't be an ass, Travis. It doesn't suit you."

He quirked an eyebrow, then sat on one of the barstools tucked beneath the counter. "I'll have you know, I'm an ass to most people and it suits me just fine."

"The day you treat me like *most people* is the day I'll have a new manager."

"Landon, you know damn well I treat you better than you do yourself. But I'm not going to employ a starstruck fame-chaser on your word."

"That's not who Piper is, and you know it."

"I thought I did. Now I'm having serious doubts."

I sighed. "If I'm about to rehash history, you might as well know that it's your fucking fault things ended badly between us."

"My fault?" He shrugged out of his jacket and draped it over the empty stool beside him. "Now this I have to hear. But first, it's been a long day, and I'm starving. You have anything decent here?"

I opened the fridge and took out a few pint-sized containers, pushing them across the counter toward Travis. "Decent is arguable, but everything in this house is anti-inflammatory, organic, and a whole bunch of other things they say are good for me."

He popped a slice of mango in his mouth. "All right, tell me. How is your romance gone wrong my fault?"

I reminded him of the day he called me, Jett, and Dax into his office, understanding slowly clicking into place as I painted the scene. "You were with Piper that long ago? Jesus, was she even legal?"

"She was a freshman in college, Trav."

He grabbed another container, and I slid a fork across the counter. "So, let me get this straight. You have a great couple of months, then went away for a bit and didn't look her up when you came back?"

I flinched at the truth, but Travis wasn't through. "I mean, you're not a guy who doesn't go after what he wants. How many other chicks have you fucked in the past six years? You really telling me it's my fault you didn't go after the one who actually meant something to you?"

He shook his head at my silence, a disbelieving look on his

face. "I've done some pretty questionable things in my life, Landon. But that one, that's all on you."

Piper

Leaving my Mini at the venue, I sprawled on the backseat of a waiting town car and gave the driver my address. Travis had told me to go back home, but even if he hadn't, I didn't want to see Landon. Or anyone else, for that matter. I felt weak and shaky, though not feverish. But exhausted, as if I hadn't slept in days.

I dozed the entire way, and once I got home, somehow managed to wash my face and brush my teeth before crawling into bed fully dressed.

The next thing I knew, my bedroom was bright and Adam was standing over me. I groaned. "Jesus, Adam. What are you doing here?"

"I was about to ask you the same question."

"Me? This is my apartment."

"I texted you last night, said I was going to swing by to grab the last of my things. Figured I would do it while you were out." He pointed at the clock on my nightstand. "You're usually at yoga right now."

I blinked at the neon-green numbers. My early Sunday Bikram class—my favorite one of the week. I flopped back in bed, groaning. What happened with Landon was a lead weight pressing on my chest.

"Late night?"

"No, actually," I said. I'd gotten home before ten. "I must be coming down with something." Like a bad case of heartbreak.

Adam perched on the side of my bed. "Can I get you something? Soup, or toast?" I shook my head, my stomach giving an uncomfortable lurch. "Oh, they have this new place around the corner that makes the best mocha cappuccinos—"

I bolted upright, needing to get to the bathroom, immediately. Except that my legs got stuck in the covers, and Adam was in my way. I would have tumbled out of bed, headfirst, except that Adam caught me by my shoulders, concern streaking across his face. "Got it, no mocha—"

That did it. I threw up all over him.

For a second, neither of us said anything, staring wide-eyed at the mess I'd made of his salmon-colored button-down shirt and flat-front khakis with tiny sailboats on them. "Oh my god, Adam. I'm *so* sorry." And I was, not to mention mortified.

To his credit, he merely sighed. "First things first: are you okay?"

I wiped my face on a sheet I'd be throwing in the wash in a minute. "I feel a little better now."

He stood. "Okay. Do you need help?"

"No, no." It was bad enough Adam was wearing my vomit; he didn't need to clean it up, too. "Go take a shower, I'll handle this."

Toeing off his shoes, Adam walked gingerly down the hall and into the bathroom. As soon as I heard the click of the door, I changed into a bathrobe and stripped the bed, stuffing the foul-smelling pile into the washing machine tucked into an alcove off my bedroom.

After scouring my hands with soap and rinsing my mouth out in the kitchen sink, I was sucking on a peppermint at the table, hoping it would settle my stomach, when the peal of the door-bell sounded, quickly followed by several sharp knocks.

I wasn't expecting anyone. Which meant…*no*.

I tiptoed across the floor and glanced through the peephole. Landon Fucking Cox.

Of course.

More knocks shook the thin door. Pushing the mint into the well of my cheek, I opened it a crack. "This is a really bad time. Can we talk later?" *When I didn't look like a chipmunk, smell like vomit, and my ex wasn't in my shower.*

Landon's face was pained, and completely oblivious. "About last night—seeing the guys on stage without me, I fucked up my medication and I couldn't get the damn button of my jeans un—"

I cut him off. "I believe you. I'll call you later, I promise."

His brows pushed together over the bridge of his nose, the wiry hairs a few shades darker than the messy locks flopped over his forehead. He put his hand on the door. "You're still upset, I can tell. Can I come in?"

"It's a bad time. I'll come over in an hour, okay?" My voice climbed to a high-pitched whine.

Dark eyes blazed with regret and confusion. "Pippa, please." His tone was rough and gritted, but somehow still soft, and my heart clenched at the vulnerability bleeding from those two words.

"Hey, are my clothes still—"

I jumped, the door swinging inward.

Looking over my shoulder, Landon's expression transitioned from naked yearning to shock to outright fury.

I sucked in a quick breath and the mint shot past my tonsils like a hockey puck, scraping a minty path down my esophagus. Swallowing it down, I glanced from Landon to Adam, clad only in a towel wrapped around his waist, standing in the space between my bathroom and bedroom, and then back again. Except for the vein throbbing at his temple, Landon's profile could have been carved from stone. "I swear, it's not what you're thinking."

He turned, leaning toward me. The full brunt of his anger was like a knife in my ribs. Straight through my heart.

I took an instinctive step back, banging into the wall.

"You have no idea what I'm thinking." Spinning on his heel, Landon stomped off down the sidewalk. I wanted to run after him, chase him down and tackle him until he believed me. But I was frozen, clutching my robe to my throat.

"Was that Landon Cox?" Adam asked. "I was too distracted to recognize him last time, but that was him, right? Drummer for that band that swept the Grammys last year?"

My answer was to slide down the wall, bury my face in my hands, and break into sobs. I heard Adam curse, felt his shadow and a gust of wind as he closed the door.

He kneeled down in front of me. "Landon Cox shows up at your door when you're sick and PMSing? I think I'd cry, too."

Slowly, Adam's words penetrated my heartsick daze. I pulled my hands away from my face, staring at him as if he were a ghost. "What did you just say?"

"Sorry," he replied, cringing. "That came out wrong. I just meant that when a rock star swings by, you probably—"

I waved him off. "No, before that."

"What, the PMS thing? I've only seen you weepy just before your…" Adam paused, looking uncomfortable. "Your *time*. It's got to suck being both sick and hormonal." He stood, extending his hand. "Come on. You need to shower and then I'll tuck you back in bed with a cup of tea."

I let Adam help me up, my ears ringing. PMS. Hormonal. PMS. Hormonal.

When was the last time I had my period?

Chapter Eighteen

Landon

What the fuck just happened?

Did Piper's ex really walk out of her bathroom wearing only a towel? Was Piper naked beneath that tiny pink robe she'd taunted me with a few weeks ago?

I know he did. I know she was.

I just didn't want to fucking believe it.

I slammed into my truck, the one I shouldn't have been driving yet, instinctively heading for the Hollywood Hills. Pulling up to my own home, one glance at the unfamiliar cars parked in my driveway reminded me that my floors were being refinished and stained this week.

I wanted to bang my head against the wheel in frustration, but self-harm hadn't worked out very well for me lately. Instead I turned the music up to an almost intolerable decibel and peeled away.

Outside my tinted windows, it was a perfect Californian day. The sun was bright, the humidity low. Half the cars on the road were convertibles with their tops down. A perfect fucking day.

I hated everything about it.

Breathe, I reminded myself. Just breathe.

I opened the windows, needing to push air in and out of my lungs that wasn't recycled through a machine first.

Arriving at my temporary home, I was still just as angry and unsettled as I'd been when I left Piper.

Nothing about my life felt steady, not even the ground beneath my feet.

Everything important to me—my career, my home, the girl I'd finally realized was as necessary to me as breathing—was covered in question marks.

The fingers of my right hand were twitching. It was an involuntary motion, something the doctors had told me was merely a side effect of my nervous system working to repair and reestablish the connection between my brain and my hands.

Useless. If I couldn't play the drums anymore, couldn't dominate a stage with my skills, my hands were fucking useless.

Music was my soul. My touchstone. Not just what I did but who I was.

And Piper…she was my heart.

A heart that I'd left, broken and bloody, just outside her front door.

I needed music and I needed Piper. Had I lost them both?

I fucked up last night, I know that. But had I fucked up badly enough to warrant getting back together with her ex?

I didn't think so.

And Piper wasn't the type to get in a dig at me by having revenge sex with her ex.

Which meant Piper got back together with him because she felt *nothing* for me. And that was worse. So much worse.

How could she feel nothing for me when I felt everything for her?

Piper was the reason I'd lost my mind weeks ago and tried to drink myself into oblivion. And the reason I *hadn't* lost my mind when I woke up, unable to hold a pair of drumsticks. I'd actually begun to believe that things would work out. For me. For us.

Maybe I wasn't a legend, after all. Maybe I was merely a court jester.

A fool.

Pain thrummed through my veins. It pulsed hot and thick, burning me up from the inside. I deserved it. I deserved to be swallowed up in agony.

Six years ago, I'd thrown Piper away. Left her behind without a word about where I was going or why I left. Or what she'd meant to me. Came back and didn't head straight for her doorstep, brandishing flowers and begging forgiveness.

I hadn't understood the chemistry between us back then. Had been scared by her hold on me. Felt almost trapped by it.

Maybe it was fitting that, right now, I was terrified that she'd finally realized I wasn't worth the baggage and bullshit that was part of my life. Although, if I couldn't get behind the drums…

But, no. I couldn't go there. Drumming was as much a part of me as breathing. It was my life, my career, my identity. And my sole source of income. Sure, I had millions in the bank, but could I rely on some bean-counting accountant's estimate that it would be enough—not just for my lifetime, but for Jake's?

There was so much that was wrong about this situation.

Everything, really.

Especially knowing I'd let the guys down. Shane, Jett, and Dax—we were fucking brothers. Had come up in this crazy business together.

Now I understood why Shane hadn't wanted us to visit him last year, when he was extradited back to his home state to await trial. Knowing you fucked up was one thing, but having it reflected in the pitying expressions of the people you cared about was much, much worse.

I didn't want anyone's pity.

Taking a deep breath, I put a lid on my exploding emotions and pulled my shit together.

Time to stop acting like a pussy.

If Piper was so quick to walk away, to find comfort in another guy's arms... Well, fuck her.

The heat of anger felt good. Motivating. But fake. A lie.

The only person I was angry with was myself.

And maybe the ass-wipe she'd chosen over me.

I wasn't angry at Piper.

I was fucking devastated by her.

Piper

I could count the number of men I'd had sex with in my entire life on one hand. Two boyfriends in high school. Landon. A one-night stand from a spring break trip to Mexico. Adam.

Age was a number, too. I was twenty-five. I wasn't ready to be a mother.

I let Adam lead me to the bathroom and turn the water on. "Can you take it from here?" he asked gently.

The noise I made must have sounded affirmative, because he

gave me a pat on the shoulder and left me alone. As soon as he shut the door, I opened the bathroom cabinet and reached for a lone box at the very back, behind the set of hair curlers I'd bought off an infomercial and used exactly once, with disastrous results.

A pregnancy test. I picked it up a long time ago, thinking it was something I should have on hand. Like a thermometer, or cough medicine.

But right now, I didn't feel smart or responsible. Horror. Terror. Pure panic. Those were the emotions streaking through my bloodstream, eating away at my veins like acid.

With shaking hands, I pushed my thumb beneath the cardboard flap and pulled at the plastic. Quickly scanning the instructions, I peed on the tip and left it on the bathroom counter while I stepped into the shower.

I couldn't be pregnant. I just…I just couldn't.

Life wasn't that cruel.

But it was.

It was to me.

When was the last time I'd had unprotected sex?

My mind flipped manically through the past weeks. Landon and I had used a condom every time we'd had sex. Every single time.

Adam and I had stopped using condoms six months ago, when I agreed to go on the pill.

Oh no.

Adam's apartment. His phone call with Brian.

You're lying to yourself. And you're using Piper to lie to everyone else.

I know.

My pills had been in my hand…until I threw them at Adam's

head. Conditioner still coating my hair, I turned off the water and stepped onto the bathmat soaking wet. Holding my breath, I peered at the stick.

A pink plus sign was waiting for me in the little porthole set into the side of the test. Plus. Positive. Pregnant.

Pregnant.

Adam knocked on the door. "You okay in there?"

My head jerked up, and I grabbed for a towel. "Fine. Be right out."

I shoved the applicator back into the box, and the box back into the cabinet.

Adam was already dressed in khakis and a golf shirt, holding a shopping bag. He hoisted the bag up a few inches. "I've got the rest of my stuff so I won't have to bother you again. And I put my spare key on the kitchen table."

"Oh." It hit me then—Adam wasn't coming back. He was ready to move on with his life. Without me.

"I'm sorry, Piper. But you were right. I was lying to you, to myself, to everyone. I'm gay, or at least bi, and I deserve to be happy. So do you, just not…"

I dredged up the ghost of a smile. "Just not with you."

He gave a solemn nod. "Take care of yourself, Piper."

"I—" My breath caught in the back of my throat and for a moment I thought I was going to be sick again. "I will. You, too."

I blinked, and Adam left.

On the one hand, I was so proud of him for finally deciding to come out of the closet. The pain in his voice when I overheard him talking to Brian…even the memory of it hurt my heart. No one should feel like they need to live a lie. And I wanted Adam to be happy, to love and be loved in return. The kind of love I'd felt with—

I wrenched my mind away from a path that would only end in another round of tears.

But on the other hand, I felt betrayed that Adam had used me as his... what? His beard? Was that even a term anymore?

Not that any of that mattered. Not anymore.

Because I was pregnant.

With Adam's baby. My ex-boyfriend. My *gay/bi* ex-boyfriend.

The only scenario worse would have been if Landon was the father.

Not because Landon would be a bad father or an unsupportive partner, despite what he thought of his own abilities. But because I knew for a fact he'd been on the receiving end of a baby-daddy scam more than once. It only took one glance for him to think I was sleeping with my ex—he would probably assume I was trying to trap him into fatherhood, too.

Landon. This time I couldn't force my thoughts away from him. My mind tripped over his name, stuttered on the memory of this morning. The look on his face when he saw Adam in my apartment.

The situation had been damning, and Landon obviously believed the story his eyes captured.

But it wasn't the truth. It was an optical illusion, and he should have adjusted the picture using what he knew in his head and his heart.

He didn't do that.

He didn't trust me enough to let me explain.

And if Landon and I didn't have trust, after everything we'd been through and after what I'd walked in on last night, then we had *nothing*.

Nothing worth building a life on, anyway.

Every time I thought I was getting close to a happily-ever-after, it got snatched away. The promise of it so vivid, so certain.

Just before it was ripped to shreds, right in front of me. Destroyed. Gone.

Tears gathered at the corners of my eyes and slid down my cheeks.

Pregnant. The word was like a heartbeat, steady and insistent. Drowning out everything else.

I'd let Landon convince me I didn't have to be perfect anymore. I was his *Pippa*. I was *his*.

But now I was something else.

Pregnant, pregnant, pregnant.

I had come three thousand miles to escape the shadow of my parents' mistake. Three thousand miles just to make the same one myself.

An unplanned pregnancy.

An unwanted child.

Unless…

Landon

Every square inch of my body itched, although the worst was my scalp. So bad, I wanted to rip out my hair and peel off the skin. I was sweating, too.

Except I was fucking freezing.

For the thousandth time, I glanced at the clock, willing the numbers to move faster.

After I left Piper yesterday, I'd finished the rest of my pills. Biting down on them one by one, the relief they offered bitter on my tongue.

But no pill could erase the image that had been permanently seared into my brain. Another guy in Piper's apartment, wearing only a towel.

Even worse were the images my mind invented on its own. The two of them together. In bed. On her couch. In her tiny shower. No robe. No towel. Just his hands on her smooth skin. His mouth covering her sweet, sweet lips. Him. Her. Together.

I had chomped one pill after another. A week's worth in a day.

And now they were gone.

I had an hour to kill until my appointment.

And the only thing I wanted to kill was myself.

Not because I wanted to die. But because the itch driving me insane went deeper than my skin. It started in my soul. And no amount of scratching was going to ease the pain.

Fuck it. Doctors' offices were staffed by receptionists and nurses. There had to be someone I could charm into getting seen early. I just needed another month's supply. Another month and a stronger dosage.

By then the pain would be gone.

My grip will have returned.

And I'd be over Piper Hastings.

I wouldn't need pills to get through the days and nights anymore.

I'd be fine.

More time. A stronger prescription.

That was all I needed.

As I gripped the wheel, almost normally with my left and still pathetically loosely with my right, I felt a grin start to break across my face.

I was Landon Fucking Cox.

Or at least, I would be. Another month. A little orange bottle filled with lots of little white pills.

I'd be fucking *fine*.

Chapter Nineteen

Piper

So, our test confirms the positive result of your home pregnancy test." Dr. Huang sat on the stool beside me, wearing a white lab coat over her Chanel suit. Beverly Hills doctor chic. "I reviewed your chart, and couldn't help noticing your prescription for birth control pills. Was there a problem with the medication?"

"Um, no," I stammered. "I—I lost them in the middle of my cycle."

"Well, that will do it. Sperm can live for up to five days, and unless you use another form of protection, like a condom, it's quite possible to conceive if you abruptly stop taking your pills."

I'd been seeing Dr. Huang for my annual check-up the past few years, and I'd always liked that she was young and pretty, her sleek black hair cut in a sophisticated bob that danced below her ears as she talked. But right now, I didn't want to be in Beverly Hills. I wanted to be back in Bronxville, with my mom holding my hand.

I gave a dejected nod. "I didn't realize that."

Dr. Huang would never have gotten herself in this mess, I was sure.

She hesitated, then asked, "Are you here alone, Piper?"

"It's…complicated," I said, the room quiet except for the rustle of my gown as I shivered in the cold room. "I haven't decided what I want to do."

As I choked out the admission, a part of me rebelled against the idea of…Even in my own mind I couldn't say the word. I was all for a woman's right to make choices about her own body. But until today, that right had been hypothetical, abstract. Sitting here, alone, the harsh reality of it was overwhelming.

Another body growing inside my body. Nothing felt *right* about this situation.

Dr. Huang gave an efficient nod as she checked over my chart. "I'd like to start out by confirming the age and health of the fetus and then we'll go from there, all right?" Without waiting for an answer, she added, "I'm going to send in a radiologist, you just sit tight."

At the buzz in my purse, I reached over and pulled out my phone.

Delaney: Hey, I hear you're playing hooky today. Are you really sick or can we meet for lunch?

Eager for the distraction I tapped out a reply.

Piper: You're back in town?

Delaney: Yes, just a quick trip.

"Hi, there."

I put down my phone as a woman wearing scrubs bounced through the door. "Hi."

She beamed as if my barely audible rasp was a cheer. "I'm Neeva, I'll be performing your sonogram today. Ever had one before?"

I shook my head and Neeva reached for something that looked like it could have been sold at a sex shop in Ventura. "This early in a pregnancy, we do a transvaginal sonogram." As I watched, she unwrapped a condom and rolled it over the tip. A ghost of a smile pulled at the corners of my mouth, remembering the time I'd done the same to Landon, and how I'd put it on the wrong way at first.

"Go ahead and lie back now, feet in the stirrups." While I got settled, she positioned a cart with a flat screen monitor near my head and sat between my legs. There was the slow slide of something inside me, and I scrunched my nose at the inanimate intrusion. But then the screen flickered to life, and I listened as Neeva cheerfully pointed out parts of my anatomy I'd never seen before.

"What's that flickering thing?" I asked, pointing to a part of the screen that looked like a firefly.

Neeva grinned. "That's the heart."

"The…heart?"

I swallowed thickly, unable to tear my eyes from the grainy black-and-white image. Neeva's fingers tapped on the keyboard, and she used a roller mouse to draw lines and circles on various parts of the image. "Would you like to hear the heartbeat?"

Yes. No. I don't know. I gurgled a response that could have meant any of the above, along with a hesitant nod. A moment later, the room was filled with a fast *swoosh-swoosh-swoosh* noise that was simultaneously foreign and achingly familiar. I turned away from the screen, pressing the palms of my hands against my eyes, tears leaking out anyway.

I barely noticed Neeva removing the probe from my body, or the click of the switch as she turned off the monitor and wheeled the cart to the side of the room. In a soft voice, she said, "Dr. Huang will review the data and be right back."

Somewhere, deep inside me, was the beginnings of a baby. I'd listened to its heart beating.

Instead of joy, all I felt was cold, hard terror. I wasn't ready to be a mother. And I didn't want to share a child with Adam. In that moment, I wished so badly for Landon to be the father. Whether or not he'd want any part of a child we created together, at least I would have a piece of the man I loved.

Maybe, just maybe, he would want our baby.

And maybe, just maybe, he would want me, too.

But of course, that was only a pipe dream. Landon and I had used condoms. The baby was Adam's.

They say that those who don't study history are bound to repeat it.

But that wasn't true.

I knew well the history of my own birth. That I was unplanned, an accident. Born to a man who didn't love the woman carrying me, and by extension, didn't love me, either.

What the hell have I done?

How could I keep this baby? How could I bring a child into the exact same situation I'd wanted to escape for my entire life. How?

The only sane answer was: I couldn't. I shouldn't.

Dr. Huang came in a few minutes later, and before I could ask her about…the procedure, she sat down in the stool and blinked at me. "There is cause for concern regarding the data."

"Concern?"

"Yes. The heartbeat, specifically. It's slower than it should be. Were you considering termination?"

She said it so matter-of-factly that I recoiled, looking down at my lap instead, focusing on a tiny thread that had come lose from the hem of my gown.

Dr. Huang took the movement as a nod. "I'd like to suggest that you go home and take it easy. At six weeks along, there's a good chance this situation will resolve itself on its own and you won't need to make that choice."

Landon

"Ana, was that FedEx?"

I knew damn well what it was. I'd been staring through the second-floor window, watching the driver bring a small cardboard box to the front door. It had taken all of my restraint not to slide down the banister at the first peal of the bell. But I had to stay cool. No need to act any different than normal. No one else knew what was in that box. No one needed to know.

One of the first things anyone does once they get famous, if they have half a brain or a decent manager, was to come up with an alias. An alternate identity to use when paying for things you didn't want traced back. Gossip rags have pages devoted to celebrities walking their dog, going for Starbucks, pumping gas. Stars—they're just like you!

Except that we don't want some guy in the accounting department of Frannie's Freaky Sex Shop selling a copy of our invoice to TMZ. Or a curious postman opening our order of hemorrhoid cream before we have a chance to wipe it on our own ass.

My housekeeper spun around as I walked slowly, achingly slowly, down the stairs. If she was curious why I received so much mail for a Luke Cooper, she hadn't said anything. "Yes. Should I—"

"Nah," I said with a deceptively casual smile, pulling the cardboard box from her grasp and heading right back upstairs. "I got it."

Two days ago, my doctor had refused to up the strength of my meds, writing a prescription for a measly ten pills, saying I didn't even need that much. Fuck, yeah I did. I had a plan. One month to get over Piper. One month to get my grip back. One month of pills to help me do both.

So I called a sound mixer I knew who kept a well-stocked pharmacy in his recording studio. A few minutes later, I had a step-by-step primer on how to get around the dispensing guidelines of a stingy doctor.

A few keystrokes on a computer, a charge on my credit card.

Drugs delivered to my door the very next day.

Drugs that weren't in my name.

I could have gotten them from any of the dealers I knew. Prescription meds were as popular, and easy to obtain, as illegal ones. But I'd been around enough to know dealers got greedy. Capsules could be diluted with bullshit fillers. Pills could be faked, mixed in with real ones. And I wanted the real shit.

Kicking my bedroom door closed, I pried the tape loose with my thumbs and spread my bounty across my bed.

Legal prescriptions.

From a doctor I'd never met.

No big deal.

My phone buzzed in my pocket and I pulled it out. Shane. Guilt gnawed at my conscious with hungry teeth as I sent it to voicemail and dropped it, face-down, on the mattress. I didn't know what to say to him. Not right now. Not yet.

If I could just hold off a little while longer, there wouldn't be anything to talk about. I'd be back behind my drum kit and my life would go back to normal. Shaking out a few tablets of oxy, I tucked them in the Altoids tin I now used to hold my immediate supply, and safely stowed the rest of my loot in a drawer. It took one month to break a bad habit, right? Made sense, given that most rehab programs were twenty-eight days. Piper was the bad habit I needed to break. Then my life would go back to the way it was. The way it should be. I didn't need her. The pills would smooth the way, they were just a substitute for the drinks that I couldn't have until my nerve had healed completely. Once that happened, I wouldn't need them, either. I'd have my band back. I was going to be fine.

Piper

Delaney was sitting on the stoop outside my door when I pulled into my parking space. She sprung up, holding a paper bag. "You look terrible."

I grunted. "Thanks."

"Sorry." She didn't look sorry in the least, gesturing at my leggings and tank—both among the oldest in my entire wardrobe—and grinning. "But it's reassuring for the rest of us mere mortals that Perfect Piper isn't always so perfect."

Perfect. I'd spent my entire life chasing that unattainable ideal. Trying to look perfect. Trying to *be* perfect. And where had it gotten me? I was a mess. I jabbed my key at the lock, my vision so blurred I couldn't see a damn thing.

On my third try, the entire set slipped from my grasp. A sob wrenched from my throat as I slammed a palm against the door in frustration.

"Hey." Delaney's voice was soft, soothing. She bent to retrieve my keys, unlocked my door, and ushered me inside my own home. I headed straight for my couch and fell into it, covering my face with a pillow.

Which was, of course, a mistake.

It still smelled like Landon. The man I'd loved and lost. Again.

Unless… *Unless my situation resolves itself on its own.*

A miscarriage.

My mother used to say bad things happen in threes. Adam. Landon. Now this pregnancy. Or would the third strike be *losing* this pregnancy?

If I miscarried, there would be no need to undergo a procedure to scrape the life from my womb. A scalpel to remove my mistake. My firefly.

Maybe then I could try to fix things with Landon. Explain that what he thought he saw was nowhere near reality.

Delaney called my name, but all I heard was the swoosh of a heartbeat. The sound filled my ears, pounding against my temples, vibrating through every cell in my body.

No. No, no, no.

I didn't want to be pregnant by anyone.

But I am. I am.

Unless…

Delaney's fingers curved around my shoulder as she sunk down on the couch beside me, placing the small paper bag she was carrying on the coffee table. She gestured to the bag. "I brought you a muffin and some soup. Are you hungry? Can I get you anything?"

I wiped at my face with the ends of my tank. I wouldn't have thought I could eat anything, but I was suddenly ravenous. "What kind?" I sniffled.

"Corn muffin and chicken noodle."

Little alarm signals went up at the idea of poultry, but the muffin sounded like heaven. I pulled it out and began pecking at the crusty browned top. "Thank you."

"Sure. You never texted me back so I figured I'd come prepared in case you had a fever." At my confused look, she shrugged. "Feed a fever, starve a cold, right? Or is it the other way around?"

"Beats me." After a few bites, Dr. Huang's words came back to chip away at my appetite, and I returned the muffin to the bag. "I was at the doctor's office, but what I have is going to stick around longer than a bout of flu." *Or not.*

I turned to her, blinking wet eyes, my pupils overly reactive to my surroundings. "I want to keep my baby," I whispered, feeling the truth harden inside the marrow of my bones.

Delaney's eyes traveled from my face to my nonexistent belly and then back again, her initial shock giving way to awe. "You're pregnant?"

I nodded, my chin quivering.

"Oh my god, Delaney." She grabbed my hand and squeezed. "Did you just find out?"

"No. I knew already. I did a test here, a few days ago."

A fresh wave of tears broke and Delaney gently pushed a box

of issues into my lap, rubbing my back in soothing circles. Eventually, she asked, "Who's the father?"

I blew my nose. "It might not matter." Because my firefly might never become a baby.

Had I already destroyed it with my negative thoughts?

Maybe that's why the heartbeat was weak. Who could thrive in an environment without love, a place devoid of welcome? That's what I'd created. What I'd offered. Nothing. Less than nothing. I was a human warning sign. KEEP OUT. NO TRESPASSING. VIOLATORS WILL BE REMOVED.

I looked up at Delaney's face, but I could barely see her through my tears. "The h—heart rate was low, and the doctor implied I'd probably miscarry."

She was quite for a minute, but when she spoke, there was a quiet confidence woven through her voice. "Probably doesn't mean definitely, Piper," she said.

Probably doesn't mean definitely. I repeated her words inside my head, clinging to them like a lifeline.

Maybe there was something I could do to knock those signs down. A way to roll out a welcome mat.

"You're right," I finally said, wiping at my eyes and retrieving my laptop from my desk. Just because I wasn't a rock star didn't mean I couldn't nourish my body with healthy foods. I pulled up the website of an organic market that offered delivery, scrolling through their offerings and adding orange juice, eggs, milk, bone broth, and half a dozen fruits and vegetables into my virtual cart.

Once I paid the exorbitant amount via PayPal, and scheduled the soonest available delivery window, I closed the top and sighed.

"You should probably get prenatal vitamins, too," Delaney added.

Shit. How had I forgotten that?

I ignored the obvious, that Dr. Huang hadn't felt the need to prescribe them for me. Picking up my phone, I called the store and spoke to the one of the owners, who happened to be pregnant, too. She told me she would throw in a couple of sample packs. When I hung up, Delaney was looking at me with a strange gleam in her eye. "What?"

"You're going to make a great mom, Piper."

Mom. Such a simple word for such an enormous undertaking.

I was too young. And completely unprepared.

Yet, in this moment, I wanted the job more than anything else in the world. Not *eventually*. Now.

Chapter Twenty

Piper

Just like last week, I was in a tearful daze as I left Dr. Huang's office. But this time, they were happy tears. My firefly's heart rate was right on target. The relief that broke over me was needle sharp, so intense it hurt. And once the initial shock faded, for a few precious moments, what remained was pure euphoria. It slid through my veins, danced along my skin, curled around my ribs in a warm embrace.

My firefly was still pulsing with light. With life.

It was nothing short of a miracle, given that my own heart was a leaden lump inside my chest, each beat a pulse of pain, a metronome reminder of the man I missed so desperately.

God, what I wouldn't have given to lay my head on Landon's chest, taking comfort from the steady beat beneath my cheek while his fingers idly stroked my hair. To end each day with our bodies joined, to wake each morning with his lips on mine.

But I'd lost that privilege. There was another man's child growing inside my body. A baby I already loved. A fierce, selfless love that wouldn't allow me to choose Landon.

Landon's absence was like a rash that grew beneath my skin, a prickly discomfort that never went away. Never, no matter how much I loved my firefly. And yet every day, I made a conscious decision to choose another life over Landon's. Another life over the bliss I'd felt in his arms.

I spent the week from my first doctor's appointment to the next at home, mostly in bed, stuffing myself full of prenatal vitamins and every organic, brightly colored vegetable that could be delivered to my door—wishing every mouthful was ice cream devoured straight from the carton.

Since nearly throwing up on Travis's shoes, he'd repeated his directive to stay far away from him and anyone else I could possibly contaminate with my germs. I was able to accomplish almost everything I needed to from my laptop or phone, at least this week, and I had a few months before I needed to tell him that this particular germ would be sticking around for quite some time.

After leaving Dr. Huang's office, I intended to drive straight home, but my mind had wandered, and by the time I snapped out of auto-pilot mode, I was pulling into Harmony's sanctuary. Staring at her sign, I tried to convince myself to turn around. I wasn't in the right state of mind to be at a place with so many memories of Landon.

I still missed him so damn much. And I hated the way things had ended between us. Messy and misguided. Unfinished.

I was a patchwork quilt of hormones and heartache. If I got

out of my car now, the chances of me leaving without a furry companion beside me were slim to none.

I had the next seven months or so to prepare myself for becoming a mother…did I really need to start today by bringing home a fur baby?

But I needed the quiet comfort I'd found here, especially with Shania. Needed it desperately.

As if she heard my silent debate, Harmony came out of the ramshackle cottage, wiping her hands on her worn jeans. "Hey, there."

Shit. I pushed open my door. "Hi, Harmony."

"I was beginning to wonder if you were going to come back. The dogs have missed you." Her comment was said without reproach, more like a gentle nudge.

"I know, I'm sorry about that. Things have been a little crazy lately." Crazy wasn't the best explanation, but it was the simplest and most accurate. "How have things been here?"

"Good. Busy. We've had a bunch of adoptions lately."

"Oh." That was good news. Great news. But my heart still gave a lurch. "How about Shania?"

Harmony grinned. "No. Most of her pups, but not her. I think she's holding out for you. She barely comes out of her stall to meet anyone new."

Guilt merged with my second dose of relief for the day. I shouldn't take any comfort in Shania avoiding potential adoptive families. She was great dog, and she deserved a loving home.

Harmony was patiently watching the play of emotions on my face as if she had nothing better to do, which I knew wasn't the case. I wanted to duck away from the perception in her gaze. It made me feel too vulnerable, too exposed. She must have sensed my discomfort, because she looked away first. "I still have some paperwork to do, would you mind going back, releasing the dogs into the paddocks?"

They spent mornings and afternoons outside, but midday was for napping in the barn.

After spending so much time around them, I'd lost my fear of big dogs entirely. I took an eager step in that direction. "No, not at all." My pace was quick, and by the time I got to the barn, I was practically running. Frantic barking greeting my entrance. Every dog except Shania.

Now that Shania's puppies were older, all the dogs were on the same schedule. I went to the matriarch first, bending my knees and wrapping my hands around her neck. She gave me a long, slow lick on my cheek, making a sound low in her throat that could have come from a kitten. I smiled. "I missed you, too, Shania."

Straightening, I tapped my thigh, encouraging her to come with me as I unlocked the remaining doors. She did, staying by my side until we finished the last one. Shania had become more social in the time that I'd known her, and eventually she sprinted ahead with the rest of her friends, including her two remaining puppies, looking back at me every once in a while to make sure I was still there.

My mother would have been happy to have a family pet, but my father's refusal was adamant. "I will not have one more thing in this house that I didn't intend to be here."

Yeah. He was real subtle, my dad.

And he was also three thousand miles away.

Just remembering that fact had my shoulders loosening, a heavy breath expelled on a sigh.

I grabbed a bucket of tennis balls and started throwing them, one at a time, in different directions. The dogs, different colors, different sizes, different ages, ran full tilt, their mouths open, diving for whichever ball caught their eye. Five balls. Ten. Fifteen. Some of the dogs brought them back to drop at my feet. Covered in dirt and drool, a month ago I would have been horrified. But now, I didn't care at all. It was a joy just to watch them run and play.

A joy...and also more than a little lonely, too. Because I wanted Landon by my side. Throwing these balls had become part of his physical therapy, and he could spend hours doing nothing but alternating between his left and right hand, aiming sexy grins my way with heart-wrenching accuracy.

"You taking over for Landon today?" Lost in thought, I startled at Harmony's voice.

"Landon." My lips eagerly gave shape to the sound of his name. It had been too long since I said it aloud. "He's been here?"

"Of course. Was just here this morning, actually." She glanced at the now empty ball bucket. "He can do that for hours."

I smiled half-heartedly, feeling both relieved and disappointed that Landon had come and gone already. "I know."

Shania came trotting up, sitting down on my left foot and sniffing my knee. I reached down to pat her soft head, scratching just behind her ears.

"She likes you," Harmony said.

"The feeling is mutual. I wish I could take her home with me."

"That dog would jump straight in your car given the chance."

I knew she would. But how could I let her? My life was an absolute mess. Pregnant by a man I didn't love, who didn't love me. In love with a man who thought I'd cheated on him.

Even if I told Landon the truth, he would never want me now, with a baby in tow. My father put up with me, barely, because I was biologically his. What man—who didn't want kids at all—would tie himself to a child that wasn't his own?

I needed to keep my life simple. Focus on what was important. And my job was at the top of the list. If I was going to be a single mother, I needed a reliable paycheck. A raise wouldn't hurt, either. For that to happen, I needed make myself so indispensable to Travis that he wouldn't mommy-track me once I told him about my pregnancy.

"I don't think I can handle much more on my plate at the moment, I'm afraid." As if Shania understood what I was saying, she whined and lowered herself to the ground, her front paws and head on my other foot.

Harmony laughed and gave my shoulder a light squeeze. "Good luck with that plan. I thought I was going to turn this land into a substance abuse rehab facility. Tons of money in it, and no shortage of clients. The night I was driving out here to meet with an architect, I passed something that looked like garbage on the side of the road. Discovered it was a couple of dogs that had been left to die by an asshole running a dog-fighting operation." A look of disgust passed over her features, but then she shrugged. "I never did meet with that architect."

I turned my head, my feet held in place my Shania. "So that was it, you gave up on your dream?"

She made a tsking sound with her tongue. "No, not at all. I just realized that I was following the wrong dream. I've always liked animals more than most people—spending my days and nights dealing with entitled celebrities would undoubtedly have driven *me* to self-medicate."

I laughed. My job was dealing with entitled celebrities. But I liked it, and I was good at it. I could never do what Harmony did, become a Mother Teresa to abused dogs.

But maybe I could handle one in particular.

"You really think Shania would want to come home with me?"

She glanced down at the dog, then shook her head. "Honey, I dare you to try and leave without her."

* * *

"Well, at least you fit better in my car than Landon ever did."

Shania was perched on my front seat, her tongue lolling out, panting softly. Looking just about as happy as it was possible for anyone—dog *or* human—to look.

On our way back to my apartment, we stopped at a pet store. I held on to the leash and collar I'd borrowed from Harmony as we strolled up and down the aisles, picking out food and water dishes, an enormous bag of kibble, a doggie bed, and a leash and collar of her own.

Shania still wasn't keen on strangers, so I tried to be quick—but I couldn't resist the name-tag engraving machine.

I typed "Shania" into the keypad, then my address and phone number. Together we watched through the Plexiglas as a machine engraved a bone-shaped metal tag, and then dropped it into a slot with a sharp *clink*. Kneeling, I affixed it to her new collar. "Okay, girl. Just promise me you'll last longer than the houseplants I've brought home." I wasn't kidding. I could have filled a graveyard with the number of ferns and philodendrons I'd tried to keep alive.

On a whim, I took a picture of us together and sent it to Delaney.

Her response was immediate. A long line of hearts, clapping hands, and emoji smiles.

I considered sending the picture to my mother, too, but decided against it. She would probably call me the second it popped up on her phone. I wasn't ready to tell her about my pregnancy, or to face the onslaught of questions about the baby's father. Better to avoid talking at all, for now.

I was feeling confident that my little firefly would stick around, but I wasn't ready to tempt fate by telling anyone other than Delaney.

It was times like these that I wished we'd been friends in high school. Not that Delaney would have wanted to be my friend. I'd been such a jerk back them. Selfish and self-centered. But most of all, scared. Scared that if anyone got to know me, the real me, they would feel the same way my father did.

For eighteen years, I bided my time, trying to be perfect, never wanting to rock the boat.

I didn't yet know that perfection was an illusion. Easy to fake, impossible to achieve.

When I came to L.A., I finally let loose. I went to art shows and music festivals. Fraternity parties and feminist sit-ins.

It was freeing. UCLA was huge, and I could be friends with *anyone*. No one was looking over my shoulder, judging me by my appearance or who I was standing next to.

On the night I met Landon, I'd been in a grungy downtown club with my roommate, who heard that the bouncer barely checked IDs. Nothing but Trouble was the biggest act that night, although that wasn't saying much at the time. I danced in a sea of girls, losing myself in the music and the pulse-pounding beat. When their set was over, Landon had gotten out from behind his drum kit, and instead of walking off stage, he'd jumped from it. One minute I was clapping, the next we were kissing.

And what a kiss it was. It had felt as if I were flying and falling at the same time. Soaring and sinking. In Landon's arms, I didn't know who I was or what I was doing. Just that I was exactly where I was supposed to be.

My roommate went home with the bartender that night and I snuck Landon into my dorm room. It was late spring by then and I was already planning to stay for summer school. The week I'd spent at home over Christmas had been more than enough. My dorm was coed, and when it emptied out for the summer, no one even realized Landon didn't belong there. For nearly two months we'd been practically inseparable.

His face and body every bit as familiar to me as my own.

And then, one day, Landon said he had a meeting with his manager and he never came home.

So it shouldn't surprise me that Landon had walked away from me so easily again. It was for the best, really.

And maybe if I kept telling myself that, I'd start to believe it.

"Come on, Shania," I gave a gentle tug on her leash and she kept pace with me through the door and into the parking lot as I pushed the overflowing cart, "time to go home."

Landon

Yelling a goodbye to Ana, I got in my truck and drove to Restorative Health Center. My physical therapist usually came to me, but he said he had to move a few things around this week and asked if I could come in instead.

I'd agreed, it wasn't like I had anything better to do. He explained that there was a back entrance so I wouldn't have to come and go through the main lobby, and that we could work in a private room.

Typical L.A. Everything in a fifty-mile radius of the city was geared toward dealing with celebrities. People like me who made their money off the masses but wanted to hide from their fans.

Hypocrites. We were all such fucking hypocrites.

I walked a few steps to the wheelchair accessible ramp, the *whoosh* of the automatic doors opening and sending a blast of air-conditioned air in my face. I wasn't worried about running into Jake. Today was Tuesday, and Jake's sessions were on Mondays, Wednesdays, and Fridays.

Just like Chris said, there was only one door along the short hallway, and it was open. Chris was already waiting for me, lining up various objects on a table. Balls, dice, pencils. "Hey." He stepped toward me, his right hand outstretched.

Out of habit, I extended mine.

His eyebrows arched upward. "Nice. You're really getting your grip back." I looked down, seeing my thumb and fingers pressing into his flesh.

Not tightly. But tightly enough that a surge of hope ballooned within my chest. Maybe this really was only temporary.

For the next hour I did everything Chris told me to do, tackling each exercise as if it would be the one to finally put drumsticks back in my hands. By the time he said our session was over, my hands and arms were shaking. "I just need to finish this," I gritted out, completely focused on the task at hand.

"You sure? You can take them home if you—"

"I'm sure," I interrupted, focusing on the thin pieces of wood that were strewn in front of me.

"Okay." Chris stood. "I'm going to get things set up for my next client."

I gave a grunt as my fingers closed around a stick, successfully picking it up and navigating it into a cardboard container.

I felt them before I saw them. The pull of a family I'd once known. The family I'd destroyed.

"Hey there, Jake." Chris's pleasant greeting sent ice through my veins.

Shit.

Pick-up sticks completely forgotten, I turned in my chair. The last time I'd been this close to Jake was over ten years ago.

Oxygen deprivation had robbed Jake of the energetic, bubbly personality he had as a toddler. The tween he'd become walked with a lurching, unsteady gait, and there was a flat affect to his face, no hint of the smiles he used to blind me with.

"Landon." The harsh whisper had me looking straight into Sarah's eyes. And then to the man beside her. That she and Mike had stayed together, stayed a family, meant my sacrifice had been worth it.

"Sorry, I—I didn't realize." I stood up so fast I nearly upended the chair.

Jake had walked straight to Chris, standing close even if he didn't make eye contact.

After one last look, I bolted from the room, out into the hall and through the door, swallowing a couple of pills dry. I was fumbling with my keys when I heard my name again. Shit. I needed to leave, to run fast and far. Just like I'd done before.

But I couldn't do it. I rounded slowly. "Hey."

Sarah was walking, coming so close that I stepped back, flattening myself against my truck. She still didn't hesitate, getting right into my personal space and cupping my face between her palms. "Landon," she said again, like she wanted confirmation it was really me.

I wrapped my hands lightly around her wrists but couldn't bring myself to push them away. Her face had changed, tiny lines—worry lines—now etched into the skin surrounding her eyes, radiating from the corners of her mouth. "I'm so sorry," I wheezed, guilt and shame leaching from my pores.

Sarah didn't move. "For what?"

I fought for words to express the enormity of my regret. "For everything."

She shook her head. "No, my sweet, sweet boy. If you're apologizing for running away, I'll take it. But that's all."

"Stop. Just stop." Mike had come outside, standing behind his wife, his face a mask of pain.

I cast a glance at the building. "Jake—"

"Is fine. He's with Chris."

I clamped my lips shut, not knowing what to say. I knew what I *should* do. But this time, they weren't letting me go.

"I've been waiting for this day. Hoping, praying. Not knowing if it would ever come. Do you know we tried to look for you? We called the police, filed a missing persons report." Sarah expression turned stricken, her memories still fresh after all these years. "But you had only been with us a few years, and were in high school, nearly eighteen. The officers, they didn't take us seriously. The said you had probably run away and would come home when—if—you were ready." Sarah's eyes were big and round, her voice breaking. She released a puff of air on an anguished moan, then continued. "But you never came home. And not long after your eighteenth birthday, we got a call from the police saying that they had confirmed you were alive and they were closing the file. They wouldn't give us any more information."

I winced, remembering the night I'd gotten into a bar fight and been taken to jail. When the processing officer entered my information into the system, she told me about the missing persons flag. But I was eighteen, all she could do was circle back with the cops who had filed it in the first place to let them know I was alive and had been informed. I think she felt bad for me, because I was released an hour later. I went back to wherever I was staying at the time, and forgot all about it.

Sarah continued. "We would have hired a private investigator, but we just couldn't afford it. And then, years later, that man, Travis, showed up on our door out of the blue." She wiped at her wet cheeks. "We never would have taken that money if we didn't need it for…"

Jake.

The second I started earning real money, I'd sent Travis to talk to Mike and Sarah. Offering to take over the payments for Jake's therapy, to pull strings and have him treated by the best doctors, and cover all his medical bills. With one caveat—not to contact me. Ever.

I was an asshole like that.

Shane and I, Jett and Dax, we had bonded over our shared similarities. We were all runaways. Not from the same circumstances. But we'd all left behind family and friends that we'd dragged under our dark cloud. Nothing but Trouble—it wasn't just the name of our band.

It was our fucking motto.

I looked from Sarah to Mike and back again. "I couldn't." I pushed out words that felt like shards of glass, shredding my throat before slicing at the air between us. "Not after what I did."

Mike came closer. "What *I* did."

"No. No." I was shaking with the strength of my denial. He couldn't ruin this. Not now, after all this time. I wouldn't let him. "It was me. I fed Jake dinner. I took my eyes off—"

"Sarah knows the truth, Landon. I told her what really happened."

Breath bottled up inside my lungs. Staring at him in horror, I couldn't inhale or exhale.

Sarah grasped me by my shoulders, forcing my attention back to her. Somehow I managed to suck in a little air, enough to keep me from passing out. "He did. In the hospital. We didn't know you had left yet, but Mike told me the truth as we sat by Jake's bedside. The second his condition stabilized, we drove back to the house to get you. To make sure you knew we were still a family—the four of us."

I'd only been a couple of inches taller than Sarah when I left, but I was lean and gangly then, and her hugs were like being nestled within a protective cocoon. Now I towered over Sarah, in height and breadth, and yet her arms still wrapped around me, drawing me close. Mike ambled over, looping his arms over our shoulders.

A family hug.

Ten-plus years ago, Jake would have been in the mix, too, his delighted chortle bouncing of the kitchen walls.

But his laughter had been silenced forever.

A pain that hadn't lessened with time sliced at my heart, ripping through my intestines.

I'd been given something precious and I killed it with my selfishness.

That little boy had been a gift I never thought I would have. A brother. And I'd destroyed him. Proof that I'd never deserved him in the first place.

I stepped sideways, out of their hold. "No. You asked me something so simple, so easy. Just to watch my baby brother for a few hours. And I couldn't do that for you?" I shook my head, a fresh wave of disgust and loathing splashing me in the face, drenching me in filth. "You took me out of a group home.

Showed me what family was. It makes no difference that I wasn't the one to feed him dinner. I should have been home, should have been watching Jake for you. Just like you asked."

"Landon, you were a teenager," Mike said. "You wanted to hang out with your friends. I could have put my foot down, but I wanted to be home. I figured I could watch Jake, and the game, and get some work done. Turns out, I couldn't. It was a mistake. A horrible, tragic mistake with irreversible consequences." Mike's eyes bore into me, full of remorse, but swirling with sympathy and compassion. I deserved neither.

"I was off getting high," I yelled, despising myself for not going home straight after walking in on my girlfriend hanging out with some other guy. "Instead of being the son you deserved, I pissed away time by smoking with some kid I barely remember. You needed me, Jake needed me. And I wasn't there."

"You're here, now." Sarah's voice was firm, and she pointed at the building behind us. "And Jake's in there, now. He'd love to get to know his big brother."

"He should be on a soccer field, or riding a bike. He's in that rehab center because of me."

Sarah wasn't buying my excuses, I could see it in her face. And when she opened her mouth, she proved me right. "You know what, you don't get to hoard all the blame. There's more than enough to go around. I wanted to sing with the choir, was proud to be given a solo. Your father was busy with work and not paying enough attention. And you were a typical teen, doing typical teen things. All of that is true. But so is this—if you hadn't come home when you did, Jake might not be here at all."

Mike jumped in. "Do you know Jake loves music? A few months ago, Jake discovered the unopened drum kit we bought you for Christmas the year you left. It's his favorite thing to do, and he's pretty good. Music gives him an outlet for the language that's trapped in his head."

I blinked. "He—he plays the drums?"

He nodded. "His beat's a little slower than yours, but he's taught himself a few Nothing but Trouble songs. You're his favorite band."

It shouldn't have meant so much to me, I didn't deserve a damn thing from that sweet boy except his hate. My head lung low, heavy on my neck. "I have to go."

"Oh no, you don't. You're not hiding behind lawyers and wrought-iron gates anymore. Jake's session is nearly over. You're going to come home with us. Get to know your brother, maybe even play drums with him."

A bitter cackle tripped from my throat as I held up my hands. "Of course. That's the one thing I can't give him right now." I pinched my fingers and thumb of my right hand together, showing them how weak my hold was. "The one thing you want from me, and I can't give it to you. It's a sign. Let me go."

Just then, the automatic doors opened and Jake appeared at Chris's side, walking past me to stand by Sarah. "He did great," Chris announced, looking between all of us, his posture changing as he picked up on the tension in the air.

"Thanks for fitting us in today, even for a shortened session," Mike said.

"Ah, sure." He backed up. "See you next week."

I was staring at Jake, my heart pounding against my ribcage. He made a strange sound, kind of like a bark. Sarah ruffled the hair on his head, then lightly squeezed the back of his neck. "You want to go see the doggies?"

Jake nodded, glancing quickly at me for half a second before looking down at the ground again. He made another noise, this one more garbled, and then began flailing his arms. Mike grinned. "Yes. That's Landon. The drummer. He's going to play with you, but not today. Today we're going to see the doggies. Together, would you like that?"

I swallowed heavily as Jake nodded again. Mike started to explain about the therapy dogs that came to the rehab facility, and that they were based not far from here. "Harmony's Dog Sanctuary," I said.

"You know it?"

"Yeah. Harmony's a friend."

"Great. We're going to get Jake his own dog soon, but for now we've been visiting her after Jake's sessions."

I didn't admit I already knew that. That I'd been keeping tabs on them but had purposely kept my distance.

"You'll come with us?"

No. But what came out instead was a mangled, "Sure."

Chapter Twenty-One

Landon

There was a quick upward twitch of Harmony's wiry eyebrows as I walked into the barn with Sarah and Mike, but her expression brightened when her gaze slid to Jake. As he had done with Chris, he didn't offer a greeting, merely walked up to Harmony, positioning himself at her side, leaning in but not actually touching. But when she casually draped her arms around his shoulders, he allowed her to lead him into the puppy pen.

"He can spend hours here," Sarah said, gratefulness weaved within her words.

"So can I," I responded, thinking of Piper and wishing she was here, too. But then I remembered why she wasn't, and was smacked with that same sense of betrayal and rejection I'd experienced when I showed up at her door.

Sarah glanced from my hands to my face, then at Jake. "Is this part of your therapy?"

"Not...officially. I've been volunteering here for a while." I felt uncomfortably transparent. Those two pills had barely taken the edge off my unease, and I shoved my hand in my pocket, sweeping a finger over the tin containing more pills like it was a security blanket.

"A while." Sarah repeated, her brows pulling together. "How long?"

I shifted on my feet. "A few years now."

"You've been keeping tabs on us, haven't you? You didn't forget about us."

There was a hopefulness to her tone that I didn't have the heart to bulldoze. It was the truth, after all. "I didn't forget."

As if she knew the toll my admission had taken on me, Sarah didn't comment on it. Instead she pointed toward the two puppies I recognized as Shania's, although I didn't see Shania herself. "Harmony said we could take home one of them in a month or so."

I nodded, glancing at Jake. He wasn't smiling, but there was a brightness to his expression that hadn't been there before. "That's great." I'd spoken to Harmony hundreds of times about Jake, but I'd never seen him up close, actually interacting with any of the dogs. They were crawling all over him, jumping on his legs, licking his hands, putting their paws on his back and chest and trying to sniff his neck.

Mike gave my shoulder a light squeeze as he walked past me, leaning his elbows against the rails of the enclosure and peering down at his son.

"So, how did you find out about this place?"

"Uh..." I shifted on my feet, not wanting to explain how I

accidentally discovered Harmony's because I'd been following them to and from RHC, just to get a glimpse of them walking from the parking lot into the building, and noticed that they would often stop at the sanctuary on their way home. "I met Harmony at the birthday party of a friend's kid." My mouth tasted sour as I pushed out the lie, substituting Piper's story for my own.

I was at least ten feet away from Harmony, maybe more, and my voice was quiet, but she turned around from where she stood beside Mike, frowning as if she'd heard me.

"I should go," I said, looking down and nudging a stray tennis ball with the tip of my boot.

Before I could follow through, Sarah grabbed my arm in a tight grip. "Landon, losing people you love doesn't hurt any less just because you leave them first."

Something inside me deflated, and I raised a reluctant gaze to meet her penetrating one. "It's for the best."

"The best for who?" she prodded. "I can see in your face that you're not happy. And as for me, there's a hole in my heart just your size that no one's ever been able to fill. Don't you dare leave us behind again and think you're doing us a favor."

Tears gathered in Sarah's eyes, one shaking loose as she blinked up at me. "Landon, you are our son, just as much as Jake. Please let us to be your family again."

My throat clamped shut, and I couldn't say a single word. But I managed to make some kind of sound, and gave Sarah a squeeze.

Instead of walking away, I took a step forward, then another. Together, we watched Jake play with the puppies.

Piper

I woke up this morning feeling...different. Laying in bed, I tried to figure out what it was, running a tentative hand over my belly. My waist had thickened, though it was still relatively flat. At least, when I was lying down.

It had been five weeks since I realized I was pregnant. Five weeks since Landon showed up at my front door and assumed the worst of me. At first, I didn't think I'd make it through one day without him. But then one day became two became three. The first week slipped by, then another. The truth was, I'd passed most of the time sleeping. Time moved faster when you were unconscious for twelve hours out of every twenty-four.

Even so, not a day went by that I hadn't picked up my phone, pulled up Landon in my contacts, and stared at his face on my screen until tears blurred my eyes.

Travis had signed a new client—Verity Moore, a disgraced pop princess who had the potential to become a huge star in her own right. If she didn't flame out first.

With Landon back in his own house, and staying out of trouble, I'd been reassigned to Verity.

There was no reason for me to talk to Landon, or see him at all, but it took every ounce of willpower I possessed not to drive by his house, or call his number.

Recently, instead of avoiding places we'd gone together, I found myself retracing our steps, as if I could step back in time. Shania and I walked every trail I'd walked with Landon, and we visited Harmony's on the weekends. I ate so many meals from Lupe's food truck that she'd started setting aside scraps for Shania, too. Lupe had only asked about Landon once, and she'd clucked like a mother hen when I broke down in tears. Of course, that only made me cry harder, remembering Landon calling me a chick.

That's exactly how I felt. Like I'd just poked my way out of a shell and had no clue about *anything*.

Not my past, or my future. I was merely marking time, trying to survive the day.

I was nearly at the three-month mark, and so far my first trimester had been a blur. Nausea and absolute exhaustion. Heartache over Landon. Joy at this new life growing inside me. Guilt for bringing a child into the mess I'd created.

I peered at the clock on my nightstand. A few months ago, I would have been at my favorite early morning yoga class. Since becoming pregnant, I tended to hit snooze instead. Four or five times. And even then, I could barely get out of bed until I needed to make a run for the toilet.

That was it. I was lying in bed, awake even though I didn't have to be at work for hours, and I didn't feel sick. In fact—I felt great. Physically, at least. Clearheaded and energetic. All the books I'd been reading told me the second trimester was the best part of pregnancy, but I hadn't believed them. I'd envisioned week after week stretching out as one long crawl through brain fogs and body aches.

I glanced back at the clock again. I still knew the studio's schedule by heart. If I hurried, I could make the prenatal yoga class that began in half an hour. Throwing the sheet back, I stood up gingerly, waiting for that light-headed rush I'd been feeling whenever I changed position too quickly. But there was none. No nausea, no dizziness. I felt like a new person, or maybe just the old me. The me I'd been before Landon came back into my life and turned my color-coded world into chaos.

With a determined smile, I pulled my favorite pair of yoga pants out of my dresser. When I put them on, they were a little tight at the waist, just like the rest of my wardrobe, but wearable. Next came a sports bra, which felt like it was cutting off my circulation with every breath. My boobs had definitely grown at a faster rate than my belly. Cursing, I managed to wriggle out of it and into an older one that had been stretched from too many bouts with my unreliable washer and dryer.

I made it to the yoga studio in twenty-five minutes. At the front desk, the receptionist brightened when she saw me walk through the door, scooting from behind it and rushing at me with open arms. "Piper," Katie squealed. "It's been ages, where have you been?"

I returned her hug. "Oh, just busy with work. I'm glad to be back."

She giggled. "You've been gone so long, you've forgotten the schedule. Your usual class is just wrapping up now. The next one is for mommies-to-be."

And all of a sudden, I realized I couldn't take the prenatal class after all. At least, not unless I was willing to admit that I was pregnant. This was one of the most popular yoga studios in L.A., I could easily run into someone from work here. Damn it.

I trilled a fake laugh, an embarrassed blush rising up my cheeks. "Oh jeez, I'm so ridiculous."

"No worries, I totally understand." Katie flashed a conspiratorial wink as she glanced at my chest. "It took me a few months to get back to working out after my surgery, too. Your boobs look fabulous, by the way."

Christ. She thought I had gotten implants. I pulled away. "Ah…thanks."

The studio door opened, sending warm, incense-infused air

wafting into the lobby, along with a stream of sweaty students, most of whom I recognized. Katie gave my shoulder a light squeeze and resumed her place behind the reception desk. I turned away, pretending to retie my sneaker.

"Piper?"

Shit. I pivoted, holding my yoga mat in front of me. "Adam, hi."

"Hi. How are you?"

"Good, good." I looked around, gesturing with my free hand. "What are you doing here?"

He chuckled. "I've decided to take up yoga."

"You?" The entire time we were together, I had tried to get Adam come to class with me. Now that we'd broken up he finally decided to start practicing...at *my* studio?

"Yeah. Funny how life works, huh?" He grinned, but his gaze was focused on something over my shoulder.

I turned slightly, following the trajectory. Not something. Someone. "You brought Brian here?"

"I started coming over a month ago, and this is the first time I'm seeing you. I didn't think it would be a problem."

Anger swelled inside of me. Anger at Adam, and Landon, and at my body. "I haven't been here because I'm pregnant, you jerk."

Adam's eyes widened, and he took a step back as if I were contagious. "What?" His chin dipped, trying to see behind the rolled-up yoga mat I was holding in front of me like a shield. "I don't...Are you...Is it..."

As quickly as my flare of anger had appeared, it was gone. No one deserved to be told they were about to become a parent as if it were an accusation. A punishment.

Not knowing what else to say, or how to fix what I'd already said, I started to back away from Adam, babbling an apology.

He caught up with me in the parking lot, just as I was fumbling for my keys. "Piper, please. You can't just leave without being straight with me. Am I…"

Tears stung my eyes, overflowing in an instant. Yesterday I had cried at a commercial for boil-in-a-bag rice. I sniffed, wiping at my face. "Yes. You are."

"But…" Adam's voice was breathless, confusion radiating from every syllable. Sounding much like mine had been. "I don't understand. You said you were on the pill."

"The pills you probably should have returned after I threw them at your head. Apparently they're not effective if you stop taking them in the middle of the month."

He raked a hand through his hair, which was not something I'd ever seen Adam do before, and exhaled loudly as he sagged against my car.

I pressed the heels of my hands to my eyes. "This isn't your problem, it's mine. I'll be fine."

After a minute, Adam wrapped his hands around my wrists, pulling them away from my face. I blinked at him. Blinked again. Why was he smiling? Not just any smile. No, he wore one that nearly split his face in two. "Adam? Why are you looking at me like that?"

In the next instant, I was airborne, and he was spinning me around the parking lot. I grabbed onto his shoulders for dear life. "Adam! What are you doing? Put me down," I shrieked.

He did. "Sorry, I just—" He broke off, looking as if he'd just swallowed a helium balloon. Beyond elated. "This is just so great."

"Great?" I said the word slowly, tasting it on my tongue like an exotic spice.

"Yes, don't you see? It's like the best of all possible worlds. I've finally come out of the closet, and now I get to have a baby with the only woman I've ever loved. The woman I still love, actually."

I swallowed. "Adam, you don't love me."

He nodded frantically. "I do, Piper. Of course I do. Just not...you know."

"Yeah, I know." He just didn't love me *that* way.

"But I love kids. And after things ended between us, I figured my chances of ever having one of my own were pretty slim. But now—"

This time, I interrupted. "But now you get to be with Brian and have a baby that doesn't involve adoption or a surrogate."

And I have to share my baby with a man who will never again share my bed. I didn't realize I started crying again until Adam was peering at me with concern. "Hey, what's wrong?"

This time I couldn't wave off my reaction with an *I'm fine.* Instead I answered honestly, before breaking into sobs. "Everything."

Chapter Twenty-Two

Landon

My self-imposed deadline for playing drums again, giving up painkillers, and getting over Piper had long since passed.

And only one of those things had come to true.

I was playing drums again, although my right-hand grip still wasn't as tight as I wanted it to be, and if I played longer than fifteen minutes, I invariably lost one of my sticks. But my progress had been steady.

My failure to accomplish the other two were related. I wasn't taking pills to ease my nerve pain anymore. I was taking them because every cell in my body still ached for Piper. And I didn't know how to fix that. Pills were the only thing that helped.

Pills, and spending time with Sarah, Mike, and Jake. Sarah and Mike had helped me see Jake's accident differently. I hadn't forgiven   myself   exactly—that   would   probably   never happen—but I'd realized I didn't have to carry the burden alone anymore.

And now that I was back in my house, I'd invited them over for an afternoon barbecue—the exact opposite of the kind I had in mind when I'd sent that drunken text all those weeks ago. And it was great. Giving Ana and her husband the day off, I grilled steak and corn, and spent hours playing in the pool with Jake. There were no backflips, this time. Just food, family, and a kind of contentment that was just shy of perfect.

Because it was missing something. *I* was missing something. Someone.

Piper.

Sarah must have picked up on it. "So, do you really like having this big house all to yourself?"

Mike and Jake were in the pool. I was slicing a watermelon and Sarah was arranging the triangles on a tray. "I have Ana and—"

"That's not what I mean, Landon." She gestured at the pool, the house, the lushly landscaped grounds. "Do you have anyone to share this with?"

I wished I'd been wearing sunglasses. Mirrored Ray-Bans that would have hidden my thoughts from Sarah's too perceptive gaze. "I'm sharing it with you guys now. Why, you want to move in? I have enough room." I said it jokingly, but it sounded pretty damn good.

"Not what I meant, either." She reached for the pieces I'd just cut. "Fine, if you don't want to tell me about your love life, I won't push."

I gave a rueful snort. "Not much of one to tell."

Sarah frowned. "You know, there are successful musicians that have regular lives, too. Families, friends. Maybe when you meet the right girl—"

I dropped the knife, and not just because my hand was trembling from the effort of cutting through the rind. I was cutting through it though, which was more than I would have been able to do just a couple of weeks ago. "I met the right girl, Sarah. The only girl."

She wiped her hands on a dishtowel and looked back up at me. "Why isn't she here?"

I could spend the next year trying to answer that question, but three words summed it up best. "I fucked up."

"Oh, Landon." Her expression softened. "Don't you know by now? Nothing worth having comes easy."

The night I met Piper again, Dax had said the same thing to me. I should have listened.

"What are you waiting for?" Sarah added. "Go win her back."

And she was right. So fucking right.

Why did it take Sarah's reminder for me to realize it?

Six years ago, I thought I couldn't have a career and Piper at the same time. And maybe, back then, I couldn't have balanced both to be successful at either. Six weeks ago, Piper had come back into my life, but by the time I got my head out of my ass and realized I'd be a fool to let her go a second time, uncertainty that I'd ever overcome my injury made me question everything all over again.

After spending time with Sarah and Mike, and getting reacquainted with Jake, my perspective had been flipped on its head. At first, all I'd seen were the obstacles and limitations to Jake's life. But *he* didn't. To Jake, life was an endless pursuit of joy. Sure, it might take him ten minutes to tie his sneakers—but then he could spend hours strolling through a farmers market, sampling ripe berries and fresh honey. When Jake fell down, he would roll over and stare at the clouds in the sky, enjoying the feel the sun on his face. His laugh might not sound the way it used to, but now that I knew what to listen for, I heard it all the time. Jake was happy, and he was loved.

Piper was my joy. And even if I never made it back on stage, it didn't mean that I couldn't find other ways to fill my life with music in a meaningful way.

My injury wasn't the insurmountable obstacle keeping Piper and I apart.

I was the asshole getting in my own damn way.

Nothing worth having comes easy.

But if I gave up, I'd got exactly what I deserved. *Nothing.*

I couldn't leave right away—I'd promised Jake a jam session after he'd had his fill of the pool—but I got in my truck as soon as Mike pulled out of my driveway.

It wasn't until I'd arrived at Piper's apartment complex that I realized I had so much to say—and not the first clue where to start. I was still trying to figure it out when her front door opened, the paper bag in her hand no doubt filled with plastic salad containers and empty Vitamin Water bottles. She was a creature of habit, always taking out her recycling before going to bed.

Piper Hastings. Would this woman ever stop wreaking havoc on every one of my senses?

I'd seen with my own eyes how quickly I'd been replaced, and yet I didn't care.

It should have been enough to destroy the ridiculous pipe dream I had of finding my own forever with Piper.

But it hadn't. I missed the fuck out of this girl. Felt like a hollow husk of myself without her. The womanizing asshole I'd been for the last few years—Landon Cox, a legend on stage and off—he'd disappeared, too.

Replaced by a pill-popping pussy.

I couldn't blame Piper for choosing someone else. Anyone else.

Didn't make me want her any less.

And tonight, I'd be damned if I couldn't get her back.

I got out of my truck. "Piper." Her head perked up, and beneath the lights in the parking lot, I watched as her expression slid from recognition to anguish.

Tension thickened the air between us as her shoulders tensed, her mouth pursing with the start of a protest. "What are you doing here, Landon?"

That Piper cared enough to react to me, at all, was a good sign. "Thought we should talk."

"It's been over a month, and I haven't heard from you. Not even once. What's there to talk about?"

How much I miss you.

What an ass I've been.

Us.

The words clogged in my throat and what came out instead was a frustrated, "Everything!" My voice was louder than I'd intended and I glanced around, expecting to see someone pointing a camera phone at me. But the night was quiet, no one in sight. "Please, can I come inside?"

She shook her head, then started to walk toward the little house that sat in a corner of the parking lot, housing the garbage and recycling bins for the residents. She tossed her bag into the chute and walked back toward me, her flip-flops lightly slapping the pavement with each step.

She came closer than she'd been before, but still out of reach. "It's not a good idea."

The thin strap of her tank top slid down one shoulder, and

my fingers twitched with the need to touch her. The shirt was too big on her, although it hugged her breasts in all the right places. Breasts that seemed bigger, fuller, than I remembered.

As I stared, Piper's nipples hardened into twin peaks, pushing against the thin fabric. *Jesus.* I wanted to bite them. Devour every last bit of her until she was a part of me.

"Don't look at me like that." Piper's voice was husky, as if she knew exactly what was going on inside my head.

"Like what?" I snapped back to her face, noting her flushed cheeks and glittering eyes.

She worried at her lower lip, the heat from her stare setting my blood on boil. "Like…" Taking a quick breath, she rubbed the frown pulling at her brows. There was a war going on inside her mind. Her lips pressed together, a last line of defense against whatever she wasn't sure she should say. A beat passed, then two. But finally her mouth opened, and she looked back at me. "Like I'm yours, Landon. Stop looking at me like I'm yours."

She may as well have aimed a Taser to my chest. My bones ached from the force of her stare. "Pippa, you'll always be mine." The words came out on their own, hitting my ears and brain at the same time. Probably the most honest sentence I'd ever spoken.

She looked stricken, her flawless face contorting with a mix of anger and grief. "Goddamn it. You don't get to say things like that to me."

"You want me to lie? Say we don't belong together? That we should be fucking friends? Is that what you want from me—lies?"

She remained silent, and I wanted to reach into her soul and pull out the answers I was so desperate to hear. Answers that would have us rushing toward each other, a two-bodied tangle of heads and hearts and limbs, fused at the center.

Wind gusted, and her sweet scent nearly made me groan with longing. I was flooded with memories, drowning in them. The smiles she saved only for me, the noises she made when I was buried deep inside her, the way the morning sun kissed her skin. I was burning up, sick from the loss of a woman standing just a few feet away from me.

Because I had lost her. I could see it in the tortured curl of her lips, in the downward cast of eyes reluctant to hold mine.

Panic clutched me by the throat, squeezing tightly. Suffocating.

She started backing up. Small steps of escape.

Two feet became three, then five. Another and she stepped onto the curb.

"I fucking miss you, Piper." My voice broke free, emerging scratchy. Like an old vinyl record. I covered the distance between us before she could even blink. With Piper up on the curb, and me still on asphalt, we were nearly eye to eye. And she was shaking.

I reached for her, needing to enfold her in my arms, when she jumped back. "Don't touch me." Even her voice was trembling.

Piper's fear was a sharp blade, slicing deep. Shredding my soul at her feet. "Christ, Pippa. I'd die before I ever hurt you."

She eyed me fearfully, regretfully. "What do you think you're doing right now?"

"What am I doing? I'm trying to get you back. I don't know what you think you saw, or why you felt the need to retaliate by getting back with your ex. I'd rip my fucking eyes out if it meant never having to see what I did that morning. But I don't care. I just want you back. You're mine, Pippa. And I'm yours." Frustration pinched my shoulder blades, and I tried to dredge up the confident guy who could strut across a stage—any stage—as if he owned it. "We belong together. You know we do."

"It's too late for us." Her throaty whisper was haunting in its certainty.

I slowly shook my head as I stood up on the curb, my boots toe-to-toe with Piper's flip-flops, drinking in her glistening eyes, swirling with emotion. Emotions, plural. Too many to count. Turning calm ocean blue into a riotous cobalt sea. I put my hands on either side of Piper's face, her tears sliding along my thumbs.

I was so lost. The walls I thought I'd built to keep me secure, separate, had been crushed to dust. My heart was pounding, blood rushing through my veins, everything in me surging with want for this woman in front of me.

"Pippa," I rasped, in the suspended moment before I pressed my lips to hers, tenderly at first. A tortured moan rose up Piper's throat, her lips softening, opening. Her tongue seeing mine. Touching, tasting, teasing. So goddamn sweet.

My hands slid around Piper's neck, pushing into her hair, cradling her skull in my hands. I caged her against the stucco wall of the building.

There was bliss…and then there was pain. I could feel it bleeding from every pore in her body, turning our kiss into something different. Something that felt a whole lot like goodbye.

Neither of us ended it, but it did end. My lips scraped raw by her absence.

Our foreheads touching, eyes squeezed tight, we breathed each other in. Both of us knowing. Both of us hurting.

No longer an *us*.

"I wish…" She choked on a quiet sob, the unfinished sentence barely audible and yet blaring in my ears.

"What do you wish, Piper? Just tell me and I'll do it. Anything." Desperation clung to every syllable.

"There's nothing. Things are just different now. The way they have to be."

My soul twisted, an angry and raging thing. "Why? Tell me why." I pulled away, gently pushing Piper's chin up when she tried to avoid my gaze. "Look at me. Tell me why. Tell me what's different. Let me fix it."

The look on her face was so sad, and so certain. "Some things…they can't be fixed. Either they're meant to be, or they're not. You and me, we're just not. Not then and not now." She slipped away, her fingertips trailing fire as they slid across my chest and then down my arm. "I'm sorry."

The sound of Piper's flip-flops echoed in the still air as she walked away from me. She opened her door and slipped behind it, disappearing from sight.

I was mute, immovable.

Ruined.

I'm not sure how long I stood there, a statue blinking against the harsh glow of the streetlights.

But when I looked down, I noticed my hands were clenched into fists. Both hands. Fists. My right just as tight as my left.

I waited for a feeling of happiness, or of relief.

But I was numb to it.

I glanced at Piper's closed door, wishing I could go to her. Show her.

Instead I reached into my pocket, tossed a couple of pills into my mouth and headed for my truck.

Piper

The tabloids were wrong about Verity Moore. She wasn't a train wreck.

She was a freight train.

I'd met a lot of Hollywood starlets, but Verity had the work ethic and ambition of someone much more seasoned. It was easy to see why Travis had signed her.

Lately, we'd been practically inseparable. I didn't mind at all. Throwing myself into work was the only thing that kept my mind off Landon for more than a few minutes at a time.

The only thing that pressed pause on the memory of my last moments with Landon—those painful, heartbreaking moments—that otherwise played in an endless loop within my mind. Elation at the first sight of him getting out of his truck, pinpricks of hope sinking into my skin for the briefest of moments before reality set in. Our kiss, equal parts delicious and devastating. Walking away. Closing the door. Crumpling to the floor.

Even now, I wanted to go to Landon and tell him *everything*. Let him decide for himself whether he wanted to be a part of my life, our lives. It was only the memories of my childhood that had prevented me from giving into the impulse. Landon didn't want a child, and I wasn't going to force mine on anyone. No one should grow up feeling like a burden.

Thank god for Verity Moore. She certainly kept me busy. Travis had wanted a complete image makeover. Gone was the cute, perky Disney princess. Same for the angsty wild child trying too hard to show the world that she'd grown up. The only thing that had stayed was Verity's trademark bright red hair.

So far, she'd been a dream to work with. Between highly planned interactions with the press and our strategy of scheduling sightings with only the most conscientious celebrities at daytime charity events, her name was slowly beginning to shed its tawdry undercurrent.

Today, however, was different. Verity had been a brat since the minute I picked her up this morning. Which was exactly what she looked like when she scrunched her nose at the cucumber the director just handed her.

He quickly fled the room, but not before sending me a pointed glance whose meaning was all too clear: *fix her.*

The door closed, and I plucked the cucumber out of Verity's hand before she could throw it at the door. "I'm not doing this," she said. "No freakin' way."

This PSA had been Travis's idea, and if Verity caused a scene or walked off set, he would be furious. Mostly with me. My official title was PR associate, but in practical terms, I was Verity's handler. Eventually I would be brokering deals and signing celebrities, but until then, I needed to keep the client I'd been assigned doing what Travis wanted her to do.

Travis hadn't said anything to me about Landon, but I could tell he knew our relationship had gone beyond professional. I needed a win in my column if I had any hope of a promotion before I took maternity leave.

"I know this might feel awkward to you," I began in my best soothing voice.

Verity was having none of it. "Awkward is running into your ex in the tampon aisle." She grabbed the box of condoms that sat on the table between us and shook it at me. "Putting a condom on a cucumber, that's not awkward. It's ridiculous!"

My mouth twitched, and I had to bite my lips. It was hard

to disagree with her. This PSA was focused on promoting safe sex to teenagers. Several other celebrities were involved, and it would be shown during movie trailers, commercials, and in high school health classes. Unfortunately, Verity's part involved demonstrating the correct way to put on a condom.

Condoms were the last thing on my mind these days. I still hadn't told anyone other than Adam and Delaney about my pregnancy, but after discovering that I couldn't wriggle into my favorite pencil skirt this morning, it was obvious that would have to change soon.

Needing to look away from Verity's outraged expression before I started laughing, I glanced down at the script in my lap. "Why don't we go through this before making any decisions."

"I've already gone through it. Basically, they want me to put the condom on wrong, and explain that you can't just turn it over."

"Really?" A vague sense of unease clutched at my belly. "Why not?" I flipped through the pages, looking for an explanation.

Verity grabbed it from me. "You're kidding, right? Trying to convince me that I'm not just giving the late-night comics more material to crucify me with?"

It took everything I had not to steal the script right back. "Sex ed was a long time ago. Refresh my memory."

She sighed, holding out her free hand. "Cucumber."

I gave it to her and she put one end between her knees, then grabbed the bottle of moisturizer that had been sitting on the ledge below the mirror. She squeezed a small drop on the tip of the cucumber, then plucked a condom from the box and tore at the wrapper. "Because if I put it on backward..." She held it against the vegetable for a second, demonstrating that it was the wrong way by trying to roll it down. It didn't work, of course, and when she lifted it, a dollop of white cream clung to the tip.

"So, as you can see, if there was anything there…" Verity's words faded as I watched her roll down the condom with ease, the blob of white lotion like a pimple at the tip. "You wouldn't be having protected sex, now would you?"

I stared at the plastic-wrapped vegetable in unblinking horror. *Holy shitballs.*

"Hey, Piper, you okay?"

I looked into Verity's clear-eyed gaze and attempted to pull myself together. "Yeah, I'm fine." I managed a tight smile. "Learn something new every day."

A brief frown passed over her face before she flashed her perfectly veneered smile at me. "Maybe this isn't such an awful idea after all."

* * *

Apparently my obvious ignorance of effective safe-sex protocol was the motivation Verity needed to walk on set with her box of condoms.

I followed her, staying out of the way but still visible in case anything went wrong, or Verity needed me for something. *Please let this go off without a hitch.* I could barely speak, let alone cajole a difficult celebrity. Was it really possible that this baby inside of me, my firefly, didn't belong to Adam? Could I be carrying Landon's baby?

As Verity ran through her blocking, then her lines, and finally the filming itself, I tried to picture Landon as a father. The crazy thing was, I actually could. Because beneath all that rock star swagger and seduction was a sweet, selfless man.

But that was Landon with his guard down, the side of himself he rarely showed to anyone. And, of course, there was the little matter of him openly admitting that he didn't want a baby. That fatherhood wasn't for him.

Could I saddle Landon with a child he didn't want?

How would he react if I showed up to his house and announced I was pregnant with his baby? He'd probably slam the door in my face and be on the phone with Travis in seconds. I would become a *situation-to-be-handled*. Just another celebrity schemer out for a payday.

I could kiss my job and my reputation goodbye, and I'd never work in this town again. Where would that leave me? Pregnant and unemployed, that's where.

I'd have to move back to Bronxville, maybe even live with my parents again. And then what? My mother would help me raise my baby. My father would make my child feel unwanted and worthless, just like he'd done to me.

No. I would sooner give my child up for adoption.

And I wasn't giving my little firefly away. Ever.

I rubbed a protective hand over my slightly rounded belly. I'd signed up for weekly e-mails to explain exactly what was happening with my pregnancy. Right now my firefly was about the size of a peach and just beginning to wriggle his or her tiny little toes.

I was already a mother.

But who was the father?

And how the hell had my life become such a mess?

A few months ago, I thought I had everything under control. I had a job I loved and a steady boyfriend. I had vision boards, a color-coded calendar, and a five-year plan. I knew where I was going, and how I was going to get there.

I'd gone from *that*, to cornering the market on questions and uncertainty.

How could I ask Adam to take a paternity test?

How could I admit—to anyone—that I didn't know who had fathered my child?

It was just so...*Jerry Springer*.

Of course, there was one option I hadn't yet considered.

What if I didn't do anything at all?

No paternity test.

Just forget about what I'd learned. Pretend I was still just as oblivious as I'd been when I put the condom on Landon wrong in the first place.

Adam would be my baby's father.

No one would be the wiser.

Except me.

"Okay people, it's a wrap," the director called. I forced a bright smile as Verity and I walked back to her dressing room together. "You did great," I said.

"Make sure you tell that to Travis. I'm still waiting for confirmation on what he promised me."

I knew exactly what he had promised her. And with any luck, I'd be on maternity leave while she was touring with Nothing but Trouble. If the band agreed, that is. From what I had heard through the office gossip grapevine, the guys were putting up quite a fight. They didn't want a fallen pop princess opening for their tour.

Verity's last album was several years ago, a companion to the hit show she'd starred in about a young girl entering an *American Idol*–style reality competition, losing to her frenemy, and then making it in the industry on her own. Not exactly the kind of show Landon and the guys programmed into their DVR.

But Travis believed that the best way to grow an audience was to pull in new fans. In his mind, both Verity Moore and Nothing but Trouble would benefit from a collaboration. By now, I knew better than to doubt his instincts.

"Travis always makes good on his promises, Verity. You just have to give him some time. And besides, the guys haven't even gotten into the studio to record new material. Nothing's been finalized for the tour yet."

Verity grabbed a bag of Skinnypop from a basket. "Maybe not, but we both know he's already talking to sponsors and working out the details now. Until I see a signed contract with my name on it, I'm going to feel uncomfortable."

Speaking of uncomfortable. "One sec."

Verity watched me scoot toward the bathroom. "Again? I think I'm going to buy you some Depends, just so you can make it through an entire conversation without having to pee."

Oh, I'd be buying diapers soon enough. They just wouldn't be for me.

Chapter Twenty-Three

Piper

I can do this. I can be a mother, a co-parent, with Adam. Walking through the doors of Baby Bluebell, flutters of excitement raised tentative wings to bat at the nervousness lining my stomach, the feeling of being an imposter. A babysitter pretending to be a mom.

As we entered the store, Adam took my hand and tossed a conspiratorial glance my way as we headed for a sales clerk folding a stack of tiny onesies. I squeezed his hand back, pushing out the breath I hadn't realized I'd been holding.

Yes, I could do this. We could do this. There was no need for a paternity test. Adam would be a great father, the kind my baby deserved.

"Hi, we're here to start a registry," Adam said, beaming at the woman.

She returned his smile, then peeked at my belly. I still hadn't made the shift to maternity clothes, but I was definitely wearing loose tops and elastic waistband pants. "Wonderful." She came out from behind the tiered table and led us to a desk in the middle of the store to retrieve a pamphlet. "This is what we recommend starting with, and of course we can add on as necessary."

I accepted the pamphlet and opening it to find detailed lists written in an impossibly small font and organized by categories. Safety. Gear. Feeding. Sleeping. Nursery. Playtime. I flipped the page. Hygiene. Furniture. Travel. Clothing. Mommy Care.

"My name's Gretchen, by the way. Do you know if you're having a baby boy or girl yet?"

While I was trying to stem the tide of anxiety rising with every typed line, Adam answered her question for both of us. "Not yet, we want to do some kind of reveal. We were thinking about getting a piñata, or a powder bomb."

We were?

I looked up just in time to see her face light up. "Oohh, I love those. One of our clients put a balloon on a bull's-eye, and when her husband threw a dart it exploded with blue confetti. And I just went to a gender reveal party where they gave guests water guns and we squirted the parents-to-be with bright pink."

Adam turned to me with a huge grin. "Did you hear that? A gender reveal *party*."

What I heard was that two people had knowingly let their friends pelt them with water guns to find out something a doctor could tell them during an office appointment.

For the next hour, Adam and I followed the woman around the store as she pointed out everything we would absolutely need before bringing home a baby. It became apparent that what

I *needed* was a bigger apartment. Did babies really require so much stuff?

We made it to the "Sleeping" section of the registry list when a bell chimed over the door. Adam turned. "Oh, you finally made it," he called out, then said in a lower voice, "I told you I invited Brian to join us, right?"

No. No, he hadn't. "Hi, Brian," I managed.

He gave me a peck on the cheek, then stepped between us to slide his arm around Adam's waist. I moved aside, not missing the slightly pitying look I was now getting from Gretchen. I could practically read the thought bubbles rising above her head, trying to decide if I was just the surrogate or if we were in a polyamorous relationship. Or maybe just stupid. She covered by getting back to the task at hand. "So, we were just deciding on a mobile."

I already knew the one I wanted and walked over to the swarm of adorable fireflies hanging over a crib. "This one," I said, fingering the elaborately stitched wings. "It's perfect." Gretchen came over and pressed a button on the base. A familiar lullaby started playing, and the fireflies' tails lit up. My heart gave a lurch. "I love—"

Brian cut me off with a derisive snort. "Why would you want insects hanging over your kid's head?"

Adam chuckled. "Don't worry. We'll pick out something else for our place."

Right. My baby would have two nurseries. One with me and one with Adam—no, Adam and Brian.

It made sense, of course. Adam was already talking about hiring a lawyer to draw up a custody agreement, split fifty-fifty he said.

I was barely halfway through my pregnancy and it already felt as though my baby would be sliced in two the moment I gave birth.

Unless… Unless Adam wasn't the father, after all.

"So I should add this to your registry," Gretchen prompted, her finger poised over the iPad she was using to keep track of everything.

My lips tightened. "Yes. Absolutely."

I wondered if the store sold paternity tests, too.

* * *

For the tenth time in as many minutes, I checked the clock on my phone and looked for an opening to wrap up Verity's conversation with the *Vanity Fair* staff writer.

I'd been pitching a feature on Verity's comeback for the past month. This wasn't the interview, or even a pre-interview. This was supposed to be just an introductory meeting, half an hour max, to give him enough material to get a commitment from his editor.

The half hour I'd budgeted had stretched into a full hour, and didn't appear to be wrapping up anytime soon.

Normally I would be thrilled. Verity had the writer eating out of her hand. She was the perfect blend of industry ingénue and insubordinate misfit. I could picture the spread in the iconic magazine—pages and pages of Verity dressed up in haute couture, doing ordinary and unexpected things. Eating French fries out of the back of a pickup in lingerie, wading into the ocean wearing a ball gown, gathering a bouquet from a field of wildflowers wearing nothing at all.

But I was meeting Harmony at my apartment in forty minutes because she'd agreed to look after Shania while I flew to New York with Verity and Travis to do the rounds of the major labels and hopefully ignite a bidding war for her next album. It was a stretch, given that she'd been publicly fired from her last one. But a commitment for a feature in *Vanity Fair* might tip the scales in our favor.

A minute ticked by, then another.

Finally, the writer reluctantly put his notepad away and slapped his knees with his palms. I jumped to my feet, ushering him out of the private room I'd reserved before returning to walk out with Verity.

"So, do you think it's going to happen?" she asked as we left the restaurant through a back door.

I knew better than to promise what wasn't mine to give, but it was obvious the story was as good as written. "My guess, I'll have an e-mail confirmation before we land."

Verity broke into a dazzling smile. "This is really going to happen, isn't it?"

She was referring to more than just the interview. "Looks that way."

Verity Moore was going to achieve the nearly impossible: a successful transition from child star to A-list adult. It hadn't been a smooth one, and until Travis had taken her on as a client, didn't look like it would happen at all. In industry circles, I'd get some of the credit, too. It might not be long before I was a junior agent myself.

I was looking forward to telling Travis about the Vanity Fair coup. He'd put a lot of faith in me, and after nearly risking everything for Landon, I wanted to knock this one out of the park, preferably before I told him about my pregnancy.

Verity slid into a white Range Rover while I ran to my Mini, racing the clock home. I'd already packed, but I had at least two hours of work waiting for me at the office before our flight to New York.

I was relieved not to see Harmony's van in the parking lot yet, but that feeling evaporated when I realized my front door was slightly ajar. *Had I forgotten to lock up when I left this morning?*

Before I shifted into full-on panic mode, Shania nosed open the door, her entire body wagging as she pushed herself against my legs. "Oh thank god," I exhaled. We hadn't been together long, but I would never forgive myself if Shania had been lost or hurt because of my carelessness.

But how— I peered inside nervously. "Hello…"

"Piper?" Adam whirled around, looking guilty.

"Jesus. You scared the crap out of me," I said, my hand over my still-racing heart. "What are you doing here?" I'd returned his key to my apartment, mostly so I wouldn't have to get up off the couch to answer the door when he came over to check on me. But he'd never let himself in my apartment when I wasn't there before.

He held up his hands. "I'm just checking your calendar. Pretend I was never here."

Shania followed me as I walked inside, sniffing my legs for signs that I'd cheated on her with another animal. I patted her head, scratching behind her ears. "Why are you checking my calendar?"

He shifted on his feet, then sighed. "Piper, you're taking all the fun out of the surprise."

"Adam, I hate surprises."

"Well, you won't hate this one. It will be very tasteful, I promise."

I groaned. "I don't have time for this right now, just tell me—"

"I can see I'm going to be the fun parent," he said, pouting slightly. "Brian and I are planning a gender reveal party."

"Seriously, you're still thinking about that? I did some research, and it's not exactly a popular concept with the gay community, you know."

"You're telling me how to be gay now?" Adam quirked a brow, his voice teasing. "C'mon Piper, boy or girl, it's just an excuse to have a party with a fun theme. I promise, it will be a blast."

For who? I imagined an entire room full of people looking at me like the salesperson from Baby Bluebell and shuddered.

Distracted, I didn't notice that Adam had turned back around to peer at my desk with its neat stack of mail and the oversized calendar I kept meticulously updated with color-coded markers.

My way of framing my life the way I wanted it to appear—in neat, attractively arranged pieces.

Until I remembered, too late, what else was there.

I took a step forward. "Let me—"

My breath caught in my throat as he picked up the envelope that had just arrived yesterday. "Oh, looks like the results came in," he said. An envelope I hadn't the heart to open yet.

That thin, innocuous envelope was a bomb, capable of destroying my entire life.

A bomb Adam was about to detonate, using my Kate Spade letter opener. My mouth was dry, my heart racing. I licked at my lips, trying to force a sound out. But I was frozen, rendered mute.

A couple of weeks ago, I had told Adam that my doctor encouraged all her patients, even low-risk healthy couples, to buy a simple, at-home test as a way to determine if further genetic counseling was necessary.

A quick cheek swab, one from Adam, one from me, was all it required.

Except I didn't send those swabs to a facility that would evaluate our genetic compatibility.

Adam unfolded the letter, his expression going slack as he scanned the page. "This is a paternity test." His eyes latched onto mine. "You ordered a paternity test?"

I found my voice, but it was weak and thready, more of a squeak. "I—I thought we should be absolutely sure. Just in case."

He looked back down at the letter, his hand visibly shaking. "This looks pretty sure to me. According to the lab, I am excluded as the father with 99.9999 percent certainty."

At my feet, Shania let out a keening whine, rubbing her face against my leg. I walked on shaking legs to my couch, feeling sick. Worse than any of the times I'd spent on my knees puking my guts out in the bathroom. Adam wasn't my baby's father. Which meant...

"Who?" Adam said now, shaking the results at me. "Who is the father?"

I bent over, putting my head between my legs and sucking in deep breaths. Adam's voice sounded as if it were coming from another planet.

I heard him swear, then stomp into my kitchen. A minute later he was pressing a glass of cold water into my hand. I took it, sipping gratefully. The liquid splashed over my tongue, soothing my dry throat. I selfishly hoped Adam would walk out, leave me alone, but he was still standing in front of me when I set the empty glass down on the cocktail table. "You told me we made a baby together, Piper. Were you lying to me this whole time?"

"No, of course not. I thought—I thought it was yours."

"Really? Then why the paternity test?"

I didn't want to get into the whole condom and cucumber explanation. "Adam, please. I didn't have any doubts until recently. The test was only a precaution."

"A precaution," he scoffed. "Maybe you should have taken precautions with…" He threw up his hands. "Jesus Christ—was it Landon Cox?"

I gave a shaky nod, rubbing at my chest. The name was an icepick stabbing me in the heart.

Adam's nostrils flared. "Great. That's just great. You got knocked up by a fucking rock star. Good luck, I'm sure he'll make a great father."

The letter fell to the floor as Adam strode to the door and yanked it open, only to be met with Landon's upraised hand, as if he'd been about to knock.

Landon's entire body tensed, although it was Adam's cackle that kept him from saying anything. "Look who it is, the baby daddy himself. I'm sure you'll make a very happy family."

Landon

Piper's door was pulled open before I'd even knocked, and it took a few seconds for my brain to latch on to the words being thrown my way. I was too focused on the sight of Piper cowering on her sofa, her face tear-stained and terrified. Instinct had me reaching for the shoulders of the man in front of me, ready to smash his head into the sidewalk for whatever he'd done to my girl. But there was such devastation blazing from his eyes, I hesitated.

And that was when his words slammed into my chest, exploding like a flash-bang grenade in my ears.

Two of them even louder than the rest. *Baby. Daddy.*

What. The. Fuck.

As I stood there like a fool, Adam pushed past me. Shania came bounding over, but before I could lift a hand to touch her, she raced back to Piper and barked, staring at me impatiently.

The dog's orders were about the clearest thing I could focus on right now, so I stepped over the threshold and walked slowly across the room to stand in front of Piper.

"What's going on?"

She opened her mouth as if to speak, but then her eyes slid away from me, to the piece of paper lying on the floor at my feet. I picked it up, reading it line by line before turning my attention to Piper again.

"You're pregnant?"

She gave a weak nod.

"How far along?"

She took a long time to answer, and while I waited I thought back to the first time we got together. Three months ago.

Finally Piper cleared her throat and spoke in a hushed, trembling voice. "Almost four months."

I gave a sigh of relief. "It's not mine."

Piper stiffened. "Just how many men do you think I've slept with?"

I scraped a hand over my face, feeling combative and apologetic all at once. "I didn't mean that. It's just that we got together for the first time—"

"I hate to break it to you, but a woman's pregnancy is back-dated to the first day of her last cycle, which usually adds about two weeks to the date of conception. So that means—"

I blinked. "You're pregnant…with my baby?"

"Exactly." She slumped, her earlier pique evaporating. "I'm sorry, I would never have wanted you to find out this way."

Suspicion slipped through my veins, blending uneasily with shock. *This couldn't be happening.* I hung on to my composure by the thinnest of margins, trying to think, to rationalize.

Women had been trying to trick me into fatherhood for years, but Piper was the last person in the world who would run that kind of scam. If she said she was pregnant, and I was the father, I believed her. *Fuck.*

An ugly anger rose up in me as I backed toward the door. Not really at Piper. But at myself. And at fate—that dumb, vengeful bitch.

When Jake entered the picture, I thought he was a replacement for me, the teenaged adopted kid my parents must not have wanted anymore. But he was such a gift, making everything better, brighter. I had a brother.

Until I damn near killed him.

No kid deserved to have me as their father.

I should have had a vasectomy years ago, when that stalker chick had shredded the condoms in my nightstand drawer. "Please tell me you're not honestly considering going through with this."

The hurt that streaked across Piper's face—the hurt I'd put there—nearly split me in two. But it was gone in a moment, covered by a mask of icy reserve that was even more painful to witness. "*I* am." She stood up and wiped at her eyes, the better to glare at me with. "But *you're* not."

"What the hell does that mean?"

"Look at me. How many pills have you taken today?"

"They're prescription," I shot back.

"Yeah—from the doctor who treated you at Cedars? No way anyone at that hospital would still be prescribing you painkillers all these months out. You do everything in excess, Landon. It's who you are. It's not enough that you're a musician. No, you have to be a rock star. A legend. It's not enough that you nurse a beer or two, enjoy an aged liquor. No, you drink any bottle in sight until you can't function."

"I haven't drank a goddamn thing since I woke up in the hospital."

"And yet your eyes are glassy, unfocused. You're high right now, aren't you?"

"Jesus. I just had a couple of pills. You act like I'm—"

"High." She could have been announcing a verdict. And she was right. I was guilty as charged. I was the child of addicts. It was what I knew. "What are you doing here anyway?"

I blinked slowly, trying to remember. "I offered to pick up Shania for Harmony." Had jumped at the chance, actually.

Piper nodded, reaching for her purse and the suitcase that was positioned at the end of the couch. Halfway across the room, she turned back, her features softening slightly. "I'm sorry you found out this way, Landon."

"Really? Because it doesn't sound like you were planning to tell me at all. I came here last month, all but begging for another chance. You didn't say a damn thing."

She shook her head slowly, wide eyes huge in her face. "Oh no, you don't get to do this."

"*This?* I haven't done a fucking thing—you've kept me in the dark."

"And why do you think that is? For all of the spotlights shined your way, you stay in the shadows. Landon Cox, life of the party, legend of the rock scene—for just long enough to make an impression, grab a drink and a girl. Girls." She rolled her eyes. "You hide from everything, unless it's on your terms. Hell, you straight up told me you don't want to be a father. You think I'm going to put my kid in the same situation I ran from?"

I didn't say anything. What was there to say? Each sentence was an arrow, hitting its intended target with painful accuracy. But Piper wasn't through. "Your brother. Your adoptive parents. You left them behind, just like you did to me." She took a breath and kept going. "No family, no real friends except your band-mates. How's it working out for you?"

"Don't go there," I warned.

"Why? Because the truth hurts? Landon, you were a typical teen who wanted to hang out with his girlfriend. Something bad happened, but look at how you reacted. You took all the blame, every bit of it. And you isolated yourself from that day on."

I wasn't doing that anymore, but instead of explaining all the changes I'd made recently, I went on the offensive. "You want to talk about family?" A bitter laugh gurgled up from my throat. "Look in the mirror, Piper. You're not exactly a role model for healthy family dynamics."

"That's my point! I spent eighteen years stifled by my father's disappointment. He blamed my mother and hated me just for existing."

She stopped, breath heaving, tears spilling one by one down her cheeks. "Landon, *you* said you didn't want kids. Said women have been trying to trap you into fatherhood for years. Well, I'm not. Besides being an asshole, you're an addict—and I don't see you trying to change either. This baby wasn't planned, but I won't ever let my child feel unwanted. My baby will not be re-sented or blamed or feel like a mistake. He or she deserves better than you'll ever be capable of."

A baby.

Not just Piper's baby. My baby, too.

Our baby.

Two words was all it took for an abstract concept—an *it*—to become real. Our. Baby.

I could afford to give Piper more money than she'd ever need. And she was giving me an out. Saying she didn't want me. Didn't need me.

My eyes fell to her midsection, and I could detect just the slightest roundness there.

A wrecking ball of longing struck me dead center in my chest, and I had to put a hand on the wall to stay upright.

Pregnancies could be faked, lab results doctored. But Piper wasn't faking the swell of her belly. Or the test results I wasn't meant to see.

I was going to be a father, whether I was ready for it or not. Actually no. According to Piper, I was just the sperm donor. I would have to earn the right to be a father.

Jesus.

I needed distance. I needed to think. I needed another pill. Or a dozen.

Chapter Twenty-Four

Piper

So...you just left him there, in your apartment?" Delaney's voice was both incredulous and kind.

I covered my face with my hands and nodded. "Yes." The word was muffled but I had no doubt Delaney heard me just fine. I'd been curled up in a ball on her couch in New York for the past hour, and it had taken nearly that long to fill her in on everything that had happened.

The image of Landon as he stood there while I hurled painful truths at him with virtually no filter, his expression a mix of shock and hurt and raw fury, would be forever seared into my consciousness. I wasn't sure how I managed to drive myself to the airport. But somehow I did. I made small talk with Travis, Verity, and the crew during the flight, holding off my complete breakdown until I left them at the Soho Grand Hotel and took a cab to Delaney's.

Shane had bought a gorgeous downtown loft close to NYU that was designed to be a haven for celebrities looking to escape the limelight but still live in a city at the center of everything. Passing through three secure checkpoints before finally being escorted into the elevator and to their door, it felt like entering Fort Knox. Each layer stripped away another one of mine, and by the time Delaney enveloped me in a hug, I felt as vulnerable and exposed as a crab without its shell.

I wanted to gush over every gorgeous detail and hear all about her life with Shane. I wanted to be the kind of supportive friend Delaney deserved…but right now I was a useless puddle of hormones and tears.

She led me to an enormous sectional, then settled herself beside me, rubbing my back in a soothing motion. "God, Piper, that's—"

"Pathetic," I interjected.

"Stressful," she countered.

I heaved a deep sigh and pulled away, reaching for the tissues Delaney had put on the cocktail table and taking not just one, but the entire box.

Shaking my head, I listed my regrets. "I shouldn't have thrown my birth control pills at Adam in a fit of anger. I should have known how to put a condom on correctly. I shouldn't have lied to Adam about why I was doing the lab test. I should have given Landon a few seconds to absorb the news before ripping him to shreds." I blew my nose and wiped at my eyes, wallowing in abject misery.

Delaney made a comforting sound. "Hindsight is twenty-twenty. You can't go back, no one can. And it sounds to me like you and Landon are going to have to figure out a path forward, together."

A sob rose up from the deepest part of me. "I don't even know if I did the right thing. Adam was becoming so involved, it started to feel like I was just a surrogate he and Brian hired. I didn't get the paternity test out of spite…but a part of me wanted my baby back, you know. And now—now I can't help but feel like I went from Adam, the helicopter dad, to Landon, the absent dad. Did I destroy any chance of my baby having a father?"

Delaney waited a few minutes, until my tears slowed to a trickle. "You know what—none of that matters. DNA doesn't lie. And it doesn't matter why you got the test, either. Landon is your baby's father, period. Better to know the truth sooner rather than later. You and Landon have the next five months or so, right? Maybe after he adjusts to the idea, you can figure things out together."

I groaned my doubt. "With Landon, the highs are the highest I've ever felt. But the lows…they're so, so horrible. I will love that man until I'm six feet under. But I don't think we're meant to be together, at all."

"Like it or not, you're about to be co-parents together. You're going to have to figure out how you want to handle it."

"I don't even know what I want anymore." An uneasy silence descended, and Delaney didn't rush to fill it. "I keep replaying what Landon said to me. What he said about my own relationship with my parents. He wasn't wrong, I've definitely been avoiding them."

Delaney gave me a knowing glance. "Running away never works, does it?"

"Apparently not." I wiped at my swollen eyes. "Were you tight with your dad growing up?" Delaney's father had taken a prison sentence for his daughter. I didn't even know if mine would take my calls.

"Yeah. I was the very definition of Daddy's little girl. I guess I still am. I thought he would want to move away, but he's been working as an advocate for prison reform and using his experience to help others. Shane and I try to get together with him and Shane's brother, Gavin, as often as we can." She tucked a loose strand of dark hair behind her ear. "It's hard not to appreciate people when you've almost lost them."

When it came to the men in my life, all I'd known was loss. My father was emotionally distant, Adam physically disinterested, and Landon... The man had dumped me, not once but twice.

I just wanted to be *done*.

Landon

Shania whined anxiously at my feet as I watched Piper's car pull out of the parking lot. Neither of us moved as we stared out the open door, expecting her to reappear at any second.

She couldn't have just left like that. She was coming back. Any second now.

But seconds turned into minutes. When a car pulled in, a car that wasn't Piper's, I shut her door and reached for the Altoids tin tucked into my front pocket. I had two pills out and halfway to my mouth before I realized what I was doing.

Cursing, I put them back and shoved the tin deep in my jeans, feeling beads of sweat break out at my temples. "Come on, Shania," I grumbled, crossing the room and collapsing into the closest chair. Shania followed dutifully, putting her head on my knee and staring at me with a pair of sad, soulful eyes.

"You look how I feel," I said to the dog, patting her head and scratching behind her ears.

How had my life gone so completely off the rails? A few months ago I was living the dream.

Wasn't I?

Fuck. Who was I kidding?

No, I wasn't.

I hadn't been happy living the rock star life, banging and boozing and basically avoiding anything that required more than just my physical presence or skills with sticks.

I was a kid that had been taken away from my own parents by Child Protective Services. They could have fought for me, wanted me back enough to get off the crack and meth that eventually killed them. But they didn't.

So maybe I was meant only for the stage. Pounding out a beat that filled my soul, sharing the only good thing I had with the world.

Maybe it was all I had. All I'd ever have.

The Coxes had been the first people to ever give a shit about me. They gave me their love, gave me their name, gave me a brother. And I fucked that up, big time, for all of us.

Piper had given me her love, too. And I'd screwed that up. Twice.

And I'd given her something—my child.

It was the worst thing I could have done.

My entire history read like a "what not to do" manual on raising a kid. I knew nothing—less than nothing—about being a parent.

What if I hurt another kid? Put Piper through what Sarah and Mike have had to deal with? What if I really was an addict like my parents? What made me think I'd be better at raising a kid than them?

Could I live with myself if I destroyed one more life?

No. I had to protect Piper *and* our child. Even if I was protecting them from me.

Especially if I was protecting them from me.

I shook my head like Shania did when a fly came too close to her ear. This whole situation was crazy. A few months ago, Piper said she didn't want kids, wasn't cut out for motherhood.

Her opinion had obviously changed. And I had to wonder, if I didn't walk in when I did—would she have told me at all?

Maybe that would have been for the best.

Because Piper was right.

I'd been hiding my entire life. Hell, I still had the scars to remind me what happened when I'd emerged from the closet and interrupted one of my parents drug-fueled "parties." The scars were covered by tattoos now, but I'd learned how to hide at a very early age.

I'd even learned how to hide in the spotlight. Using it as a goddamn shield to keep anyone from getting too close.

Somehow Piper had pulled me out. Not to steal the limelight, or even to share it. No, she wanted no part of fame or notoriety for herself. She had only wanted *me*.

And now Piper was going to have a piece of me forever.

They say that if you don't learn from history, you are doomed to repeat it.

That warning settled on me like black soot, the plain truth of it choking me. Coating my throat, searing my lungs, burning my skin, dimming my sight.

I should have tattooed a warning sign across my chest. I was a danger. A hazard. The best thing for Piper, for the baby we'd made together, was to leave them alone. For their own good.

I loved her too much to keep hurting her.

Chapter Twenty-Five

Landon

I wallowed in a fog of disgust that turned even Piper's perfectly ordered apartment into an ugly, messy blur until Shania let out a soft yelp, nudging my knee with her wet nose.

Groaning, I picked up Shania's leash from the coffee table and clipped it to her collar. "Let's go, girl."

I opened the door to my truck and Shania jumped right in while I tossed the pills I'd resisted earlier into my mouth.

Relief coated my agitated nerves at the first bitter crunch, soothing their fraying edges. If I couldn't have Piper, if I couldn't build a life with her and our child, at least I could make myself numb to what I was missing.

The problem was—they didn't work as well as they used to. I'd stopped keeping track of how many I took in a given day. But I knew it was taking more and more to bring me any sense of peace at all. The temporary high fading faster and faster.

Now that my grip was back, I'd started adding alcohol to the mix. Just a little bit, to broaden the high, quiet the relentless noise inside my mind. I hadn't brought any with me though, so I pulled into a liquor store a few blocks from my apartment, grabbing two handfuls of the mini bottles they kept by the register.

The chick behind the counter lit up as if she'd won the lottery. "Landon Cox!"

I couldn't even dredge up the ghost of a smile. "In the flesh," I gritted out.

She licked her lips, pushing her chest so far over the counter I thought she might topple over. I moved the pile of plastic bottles closer to the register. "Just these."

She covered up her streak of disappointment with a toss of her head, then made a show of opening up a paper bag and slowly—agonizingly slowly—scanning each bottle. "My boss doesn't usually get here for another hour…" she said, pausing halfway through.

"Sorry," I lied. "I've got somewhere to be."

"Oh." She added the last of the bottles to the bag and before I could shove cash at her, she dropped a business card into it. "My number's on the back—call me and we can party."

Party. I needed to party like I needed a hole in my head.

I slammed the door to my truck, chasing a shot of Jack Daniel's with Johnnie Walker. "Don't judge," I grumbled, spotting Shania giving me the side eye.

Although, maybe I was wrong. If I couldn't have Piper, I might as well reinstall that revolving door on my damn zipper. Now that I could actually work my zipper again.

But not even the taste of liquor could wash away the stench

rising up my throat when I thought about another woman. I wanted my Pippa. *Only* my Pippa.

Goddamn it. I chugged a mini-bottle of tequila on the highway, nearly gagging.

Was this it? Was this going to be my life?

Just as the question wrapped around my head like a vise, the alcohol hit my bloodstream and combined with the Vicodin, snapping the tension in two.

I took a deep breath, lowering the windows. Shania poked her head out, looking significantly happier now that she had access to fresh air that wasn't polluted by my unease. I kept my speed steady, my truck in one lane. It would take more than three shots to put me over the limit on a Breathalyzer, but with the pills in my system, I knew I shouldn't be driving.

Not wanting to be tempted by any more bottles, I tossed the paper bag in the backseat, driving the rest of the way coasting on the high I already had.

The only bright spot in this disaster of a day was pulling into Harmony's and noticing the Coxes' car in the parking lot. I'd nearly forgotten. Today was the day they were picking up the last of Shania's puppies. Jake was finally getting his dog.

Turning off the ignition, I decided to have another couple of pills. And another of the bottles. They were tiny, anyway. They probably didn't do anything at all. Might as well be drinking Kool-Aid.

Fuck. I hadn't had Kool-Aid in…I tried to remember, my mind bouncing over a bumpy road of memories. But they were elusive, and I couldn't pin them down.

I shrugged, reaching for Shania's leash as I hauled my body through the door. But my fingers felt uncoordinated, and the leash slipped away from me. My feet felt strange, too, like they'd fallen asleep on the way over. How many pills had I had today? Two since leaving Piper's apartment…or was it more? And before that— I stumbled getting out of my truck, my knees smashing into the gravel.

There was a blur of fur to my right, and Shania jumped over me.

Fuck. I struggled to my feet, turning toward the barn. She must have headed there, she would be fine.

But when I looked in that direction, I didn't see her.

Fuck. Fuck, fuck, fuck. I spun in a circle, ignoring the dizziness that pulled at my equilibrium. *There.* I spotted a brown blur running into a grove of trees bordering Harmony's property. I lurched toward it, finding myself surrounded on all sides by tall branches in minutes.

"Shania!" I screamed the dog's name, fighting back an image of Piper's face if I had to tell her I'd lost her dog. Or that she'd been run over by a passing car on my watch. Or killed by a wild animal. "Shania!" I screamed her name again. And again and again and again. Until I was hoarse. Until my vocal cords were nearly paralyzed with desperation.

Typical. So fucking typical. I couldn't even keep a damn dog safe. Any not just any damn dog. Piper's dog.

After what felt like hours, but I hoped to hell had only been minutes, I knew I needed reinforcements. Harmony and I would organize a search party, and maybe the other dogs could track Shania's scent.

But when I emerged from the trees, I realized I wouldn't need to. Jake was walking toward me, holding the end of a leash. Two leashes, actually. Mike and Sarah flanked him, and Harmony was striding just ahead.

"Hey, there," she called, lifting a hand. "Shania came tearing

into the barn and we figured you had to be around here somewhere." Unaware that I'd been on the verge of a mental breakdown less than a minute ago, she grinned at me. "What were you
doing in there—taking a leak or something?"

I coughed. "Uh, yeah."

Jake kept walking toward me, Shania and one of her offspring
looking like they were just out for their daily stroll. I figured Jake
would come to a stop by Harmony, like he usually did. Instead
he walked straight past her, planting himself solidly by my side
as the dogs wrapped their leashes around our legs.

I looked into the guileless face I'd always loved but had
avoided for too many years, then at Sarah and Mike, and finally
back at Harmony.

Grinning, I fought a wave of dizziness by clamping a hand
down on Jake's shoulder. Startled, he made a squealing noise and
tried to run back to Sarah and Mike. But the leashes were tangled around his legs, and he tripped. He fell and started to cry.

"I—I'm sorry." I backed up, not knowing what to do. But
then I tripped over a dog, falling on my ass.

And that's exactly what I felt like. An ass.

What the fuck was I doing—trying to numb myself? Doing
my damnedest to dim the brightness that had finally come back
into my life?

I was going to ruin everything. Again.

Mike went to comfort Jake, Harmony untangled the leashes,
and Sarah knelt down by my side. "Landon…"

She didn't have to say anything else. I felt the weight of her disappointment sitting on my chest, making each breath a struggle.

I cleared my throat, fighting against the greedy clutch of
booze and pills, my head hanging heavy on my neck. "I'm sorry."

She took my hand in hers and waited until I lifted my face to meet her concerned gaze. "You're better than this, Landon. All the apologies in the world won't change that."

"It's all I've got right now."

"That's not true. You've got us. And we've got you, too."

The sky was clear, but there was a buzzing in my brain, as if I'd been struck by lightning. I wasn't alone anymore. And I didn't want to be.

I turned to Harmony. "You work with rehab places, right? I mean, not just physical therapy centers. Places that treat substance abuse."

She nodded, her expression neutral. "Of course. I've brought therapy dogs to just about everywhere in a hundred miles."

"I think I need to go somewhere. And not just a glorified celebrity vacation spot." I swallowed heavily, glancing back at Jake when panic drenched my nerves. "I need help."

And more than one reason to get it.

I didn't want to be numb anymore, or hide in the spotlight.

The guys in the band were my family, and they always would be. But I wanted more. I wanted to be a son, and a brother.

A father.

And I was sure as fuck going to get Piper back, too.

Piper

Rather than call ahead, I decided to surprise my mother.

I timed my visit for late morning, expecting to find her outside in the backyard, gardening shears in hand. Instead, what I found was a FOR SALE sign out front and a real estate agent waiting at the door.

What the…?

My mother and I didn't speak often, but surely she would have told me if she was selling the house?

"Hi, I'm Piper. Piper Hastings."

"Ah, the daughter from California? How wonderful to meet you," she enthused.

"Yeah, same here," I stuttered, caught off guard. "Um," I chewed my lower lip, glancing around at the empty street, "are my parents at home?"

"Normally, I tell my clients not to attend their open houses, but your mother"—her slanted smile hinted at disapproval—"wasn't quite ready to leave. I think she's somewhere out in the garden."

I mumbled a "thanks," deciding against walking inside and through the back door. Something told me the real estate agent wouldn't have approved of that either.

Striding along the perimeter of the house, it appeared as well tended as always, but there was something different about it, too. How long had it been since I'd been back in Bronxville? Two years, maybe three?

When I came to New York for work, I sometimes extended my trip an extra day. My mother would meet me in the city for dinner and a Broadway show. My father rarely joined us, and I was always glad. The air was less burdened without the weight of his disappointment, my mother more comfortable beyond his watchful gaze. What he was watching for, I'd never known. For as long as I could remember, everything she did revolved around the man. His wants, his needs, his rules.

I'd run to California to get away from all that.

But I hadn't intended to run away from my mother. I loved her. And even though I didn't like my father very much, I loved him, too, in a way I couldn't quite understand.

In a matter of months, I was going to be a mother myself. It was crazy and terrifying and exciting, all wrapped up in a package I couldn't quite get my head around. Ready or not, it was happening.

And I wanted to share the news with my own mother.

My father, too.

Although maybe not quite yet.

The other day, when I yelled at Landon in my apartment, I'd been so certain I didn't want him to be a part of my baby's life.

But now that I'd had a little bit of time and space, I knew that wasn't true. Not exactly.

What I wanted was for Landon to *want* to be a part of our child's life. For the abandoned child in him to grow up and realize he didn't have to parent the way he'd been parented.

He'd had it rough, no question. And I probably didn't even know how rough. I'd been wounded by my father's resentment. But Landon…I'd felt the scars he'd inked over with tattoos, seen them when I looked closely. His scars were internal and external. Engraved on his body and his soul.

I honestly didn't know whether Landon could ever move past them. Or if I had any right to expect it of him.

He'd had crackhead biological parents, foster homes with people using him to get a government check, group homes ruled through terror and pain. And then the Coxes. What happened had been tragic—but it wasn't Landon's fault.

I placed a hand over my belly as I walked around the hedges and beneath the white lattice archway covered in climbing wisteria.

The gate squeaked.

I paused. The gate never squeaked.

My mom had wielded a can of WD-40 every week, making

sure that its hinges operated soundlessly. For my father, of course. The man hated any noise he didn't make himself.

"Mom?" I called out softly, wrapping my sweater around me. It wasn't unseasonably cold, but New York weather had a distinct chill compared to Los Angeles.

There was no answer, beyond the chirping of birds. I took a few tentative steps forward, noticing the birdfeeders handing from the trees. The last time I was here there had been just one. I spotted two more now. Beautiful miniature replicas of homes, suspended from tree branches, swaying slightly in the wind.

From the shed at the far end of the property, I thought I heard a noise. Bypassing the garden, I walked straight across the yard and tapped lightly on the door.

It swung open, and my mother blinked owlishly at me, holding a pair of wire clippers in her gloved hands. "Piper," she exclaimed. "Sweetheart, what are you doing here?"

"I was in the city for work and—" I stopped when I heard the chatter of a couple behind me. My mother motioned me into the shed and quickly shut the door.

Once my eyes adjusted to the dim light, I saw that she'd turned it into a craft corner. Gone were the lawnmower, leaf blower, and snow blower that had once been shoved into the small space. Instead, she had managed to fit a chair and a small workbench, the surface strewn with various tools and what looked like pieces of a birdhouse that hadn't yet been assembled. "What's all this?"

She sat down and pulled out a gardening stool from beneath the desk, patting it.

I sat, waiting for her to tell me what was going on. Why was our house for sale? And why was she hiding in the shed, building a birdhouse?

"Sweetheart, I don't know how to tell you this..." She brushed at a patch of dirt on her knee.

A sudden fear took hold and I covered her hand with my own. "Mom, are you sick? Is Dad?"

"No," she looked surprised. "Of course not. It's just, well, I've asked your father for a divorce. He moved out last month, and—"

"Last month?" I repeated dumbly. *What?* "Why didn't you tell me? I could have come home, helped you."

"Piper, don't be silly. You have a life out there, you don't have to come home to help your mother."

I'd been so wrapped up in my own world, I'd completely neglected the woman who raised me. *How could I be a good mother if I was a terrible daughter?* I gave her hand a squeeze. "I'm really sorry, Mom."

She nodded. "Don't be. It was time. Past time, actually. Once you were gone, and it was just the two of us...well, it took me a while, but I finally realized that there was never really much of an *us* between your father and me." She offered a flicker of a smile that was more relieved than anything else.

"And you're okay?"

"Yes. Of course I am. But I don't need that big house for just me. I'm selling it and moving into a condo closer to town. Some of my friends have downsized recently, too. I'll be fine."

"But, what about your garden?" I couldn't imagine my mother in a small condo, with no outdoor space of her own.

"I spent so much time out here, weeding and mulching and planting. Busywork, really." She gestured at her desk. "I started making these birdhouses after you left for college. Once I'd made more than I could hang, or gift to friends, I decided to start selling them. Several of the florists in town place regular orders, and now I have an Etsy shop online, too."

I looked at my mother in disbelief. "You have an Etsy shop?"

She trilled out a laugh. "Yes. I'm on Instagram and Pinterest, too," she said proudly.

I shook my head slowly, looking at my mother with new-found appreciation. "That's really great, Mom."

"It's still busywork, I guess. But I enjoy it, even more than gardening. And I'm actually making quite a bit of money. Now"—she patted my knee—"tell me what's going on with you?"

Looking at her expectant face, a confidence in her posture I'd never seen before, I was overwhelmed by all the changes we'd both experienced recently. And all the changes to come.

Before I could get out a single word, I burst into tears.

Chapter Twenty-Six

Landon

You came," I said, glancing around the room at the men surrounding me. Shane, Jett, and Dax. Travis, too.

They all nodded, looking at me as if there was no place else they would rather be. "Of course," Shane and Travis said in unison.

"Makin' sure you're really in rehab, that you didn't ditch us," Dax said, his lips twitching.

Jett cleared his throat. "Just so you know, I tried to smuggle in some good stuff, but it was all confiscated by Nurse Ratched at the door."

"Shut the fuck up." Shane sounded like he was only half-kidding.

Listening to their banter, I swallowed against the sudden tightness in my throat. I'd missed these guys. They had been the only family I'd allowed myself for over a decade.

I wasn't alone in rehab—there were forty other people here—but it was lonely. I hadn't been allowed any visitors for the first month, although the Coxes had come several times recently. Both for sessions with my assigned therapist and just to join me on hikes through the canyon paths we were encouraged to explore.

Harmony had suggested a rehab that was nearby, set into the foothills of the Mojave Desert. I'd seen her several times, too, when she brought therapy dogs to visit.

The low-key, no-frills place had been a good fit for me. If I'd asked Travis, he likely would have suggested what had worked for Shane. Hiring a team of medical professionals and renting a house with a recording studio. Making the guys drop everything so we could all be together, recommitting to music and each other.

But we weren't young punks struggling to make a name for ourselves anymore. We had lives now, and I didn't want Shane, Jett, and Dax to put theirs on hold for months just because I'd fucked up mine.

After coming so close to losing my ability to play drums, I'd realized that music couldn't be my sole focus anymore.

I needed to focus on me, too.

I'd been using sex and alcohol and drugs to numb myself.

Given my biological parents' addictions, I was genetically predisposed to become an addict myself.

But my head was just as fucked up as my gene pool. Maybe more.

Getting clean was only a small part of my recovery. The bigger one was…well, bigger. It was *everything*. How I approached life. How I avoided love, or any kind of attachment that wasn't directly tied to music.

I'd met people in rehab that were hanging on by a thread, barely able to go a minute without the overwhelming urge to use again. I'd been like that my first few weeks, which was why I'd opted to stay another month. Now, I was considering doing a full ninety days.

Because I had plans for when I got out. Plans that didn't include ever coming here again. Or any place like this. I wanted to get my life back.

Actually, I wanted to build a new life. A real one.

One that included more than just the guys in the room with me now.

I wanted to continue building a relationship with my parents, and with Jake.

I wanted to go to bed every night with my arms around Piper. And I wanted to hold my child every morning.

I thought I'd been living the dream. Platinum albums. Grammy Awards. Millions in the bank—even after setting up a trust fund for Jake's care. More fans than I could meet in a lifetime. More chicks than I could fuck in ten lifetimes.

But that was the dream of an insecure, immature teenager. Somewhere along the line I'd become an adult. A man.

I had different dreams now. Or maybe just one.

Family.

One word. So simple. Except that it felt so damn out of reach, I didn't know if I'd ever hold it within my grasp.

I looked at Shane. "Have you seen Piper lately?"

Silence fell, as heavy as a downed tree. "She's been in New York a couple of times since you've been in here, stayed over our place to hang out with Delaney."

I leaned forward, my elbows resting on my knees. "How is she?"

Shane's eyes slid away from me, glancing toward Travis. "She's fine."

I practically growled. "Don't pull that shit with me. I'm in here, working on all the fucked-up parts of me that weren't good enough for her. And I'm still working on them. Piper is the reason I checked myself in here, the reason I've stayed every fucking day. I'm not leaving this place until I deserve her. So dude, don't tell me she's fucking *fine*."

Shane blanched, taken aback by the vehemence in my tone, and probably by what I'd said, too. Hell, I was surprised by what I had said. Not that I'd said it, because every word was true. Just that I'd actually said it aloud to anyone but the asshole I saw in the mirror.

I turned to Travis. "She works for you, how is she?"

He steepled his hands, index fingers rubbing below his chin. "I don't get into Piper's personal life, Landon. She doing a great job working with Verity Moore, is all I can tell you. She's got her work cut out for her with that one."

Dax gave a snort. "And yet you want her to open for our next tour. A Miley fucking Cyrus knockoff."

Travis dropped his hands and leveled a stare at Dax. "She is one of the most talented musicians I've ever worked with. And she doesn't have half as much baggage as I had to deal with from you four when I decided Nothing but Trouble was worth my time. I launched your careers and I'll re-launch hers."

"And before you bitch too much about going on tour with her, let me remind you that I had to push back your next album and tour because a certain someone couldn't pick up a set of drumsticks for over a month, then decided to check himself into rehab for the past two. Verity happens to be under contract to your same label, and everyone, including Verity herself, has agreed to be patient when it comes to our timetable. You guys should be grateful."

An irate snort from Dax. "Grateful, my ass." But the edge to his words had dulled, and after roughing a hand through his hair, he retreated to a corner of the room and leaned up against a wall.

"Getting back to Piper," I prodded Shane again.

He sighed. "I'll be honest with you, Landy. Never realized how good life could be until I found the right person to share it with. Piper's a cool chick, and she and Delaney are tight. But she's got a lot on her plate right now, and if you're going to give her problems, you should leave her alone."

Sometimes the truth fucking hurt.

Shane was right.

The only thing I'd been able to do for Piper from here had been to ensure that she wasn't hurting for money. Beyond paying her medical bills, I told Travis to give her a raise and take it from my accounts. But he'd scoffed outright, saying that he'd already promoted her to junior agent, which came with a substantial raise—and that she'd more than earned both on her own.

Swallowing my temper, I said, "I don't disagree with you. But I'm in here to get Piper back. To become the father my kid deserves." I rolled my shoulders. "What the fuck do I know about family, right? I destroyed the only real family I ever had. Almost destroyed my ability to play with you guys."

I slowly cracked my knuckles, one by one, then continued. "Been numbing myself against everything for so long. Came here because I knew I couldn't get clean on my own. And I've stayed because I want to get my head on straight, too. I don't want to be numb anymore. I love that girl. More than I hate the wreck I've made of my life."

Shane squinted at me. "You want Piper to come here?"

I thought about it for a minute, as if I hadn't been asking myself that question every day for the past two months. Did I? But I shook my head. "Nah. I don't want some doc's psycho babble guilting her into letting me back into her life. I want the choice to be all hers." My lips twisted as an image of Piper filled my mind.

Not Perfect Piper, with her meticulously checked off to-do lists and color-coded calendar.

My Pippa. The girl only I got to see. Messy blonde hair and too-big tank tops. Short shorts and worn flip-flops. Miles of long, tanned legs and a smile that set my skin on fire. "That girl's going to choose me. Because I'm going to love her like I play the drums. Better than any other fucker on earth."

Jett grinned. "I missed your massive fuckin' ego, man."

"Not for much longer. I'll be out soon, pushin' you to keep up with my beat."

"My bass can keep up with your beat just fine." He thrust a chin at Shane. "You should tell him."

Shane regarded me thoughtfully with his amber stare. We hadn't spoken much in the past few months, though there was so much history between us, I knew he understood why. Now he gave a single nod. "Delaney's planning a party for Piper."

"A party…what kind of party?"

Dax gave a long suffering sigh. "A girlie party that Shane's insisting all of us have to go to. I think I'm feeling a stint in rehab coming on. Might not be able to make it."

"Of course it's a girlie party," Jett added. "That's the whole point of the thing, right?"

Shane pulled up something on his phone and handed it to me. "*Please join us as we shower Piper and her baby-to-be with love!*" I read the invitation out loud, my soul twisting tight. That baby in Piper's belly.

Our baby.

Holy fuck, this was really happening.

I glanced at the date. The party was in six weeks.

I had six weeks to get my head on straight.

Because I was going to that damn party. And I was going to get my girl back.

We would be a family.

Piper

I nearly choked when I saw the name flashing on my phone's screen. "Dad?"

"Piper. I just spoke with your mother."

Silence stretched out. It had been nearly two months since I'd shared the news of my pregnancy with my mother. I hadn't told her not to tell my father about it…but I'd assumed they weren't speaking. And even if they were, I couldn't remember the last time my father had actually called me.

"I, uh…" He cleared his throat. "I guess congratulations are in order."

Surprise and confusion streaked through my veins. My father was calling to congratulate his unmarried daughter for getting knocked up? It was as if I'd stepped into an alternate universe. "Thanks," I choked out.

Knowing I would have to tell my father about my pregnancy eventually, I'd warmed up to the idea by telling Travis a few weeks ago. He wasn't a father figure exactly, but as my boss and mentor, I figured the conversation would be good practice.

I'd been terrified. Sure, there were laws to protect pregnant women from workplace discrimination…but did they apply when said pregnancy was proof you'd slept with a client?

In the end, he'd been professional to a fault.

And when I got to the part about Landon being the father, he'd been a friend.

Travis Taggert might have a reputation, a well-deserved one, for being an industry shark—but beneath his sleek exterior and killer instincts, he had a kind soul.

I'd felt so good after our conversation, I hadn't wanted to ruin Travis's everything-will-be-okay vibe by subjecting myself to my father's brand of pessimism and condescension.

But the man on the other end of the line wasn't reacting like I'd expected him to. And he sure wasn't acting like the father I'd grown up with.

Congratulations?

I was still processing my surprise when he continued. "I was just thinking…I have a business trip to Palm Springs next week. It's at one of those big hotels with a spa I know you and your mom will like. I'm trying to convince her to come out with me, make it into a vacation. I'd like you to consider joining us."

And our conversation kept getting stranger.

"Mom told me she asked you for a divorce." It got quiet on his end again. After a minute, I prompted, "Dad?"

"Yeah. I'm still here." He sighed. "She did. And it was quite the wake-up call. I—I, well, I've made a lot of mistakes. With your mother, with you. With life. I think it's time I try to correct them. Do you think…" He paused again, his voice strained. "Is it too late?"

Was it? I took a moment, analyzing my conflicted emotions. Did I want to let my guard down with my father, try to build a relationship with him? The part of me that had put distance between us out of an instinct for self-preservation resisted the idea of knocking down the walls I'd spent a lifetime building. What was his angle? "Are you inviting me just so there's a better chance of Mom agreeing to go?"

"No. No, I'm not. But I understand why you'd think that." I listened closely, but his voice sounded genuinely contrite. "Even if your mom doesn't want to go, I'd love to see you."

Suddenly I wondered if my mother hadn't answered truthfully when I asked if she and my father were healthy. "Dad, are you okay? Is there something I should know?"

"What? No. Of course not. I'm fine. I just thought it might be nice, is all. A family vacation—"

I didn't have a chance to muffle the snort of derision that rose up from deep in my chest. "We've never taken a family vacation."

To his credit, he didn't hang up on me. Instead he said something that surprised me nearly as much as his congratulations. "Maybe we should start."

The air left my lungs in a rush. *Maybe we should.*

Chapter Twenty-Seven

Piper

Mom, what's your rush? The restaurant is open all day, I promise they're not going to run out of food."

She rolled her eyes at me, pushing me out the door. We were meeting Delaney for lunch. I didn't want a baby shower or a big party, but I knew they wanted to do something fun to celebrate. A casual ladies' lunch with my mom and best friend—I could handle that.

Things had changed a lot in the past few months, especially my expanding bump. My mother had sold the house I'd grown up in and moved into a condo like she'd planned, although her divorce from my father was on hold. She hadn't flown to Palm Springs for that long weekend, but I did meet up with my dad for dinner one night while he was there. He'd looked good, but sad, and a little lost. Lonely.

He'd looked how I felt.

Apparently, once he had to live without my mother, he'd finally realized what he had lost. He'd been trying to woo her back, and we were building our relationship, too. The kind we'd never had. It was nice having a father, and I was getting to know a side of them both that I'd never known existed.

The downside was realizing that my child might never know their own father. Landon had gone completely off the radar, and I hadn't heard from him for months—not since I left him in my apartment with Shania and the echoes of my angry accusations.

Office gossip was that he'd gone to rehab—but that could be code for *anything*. These days, rehab was mostly a generic, one-size-fits-all excuse, not an actual destination. I could probably find out the truth, but it would be like picking off a scab that had just begun to heal. I needed to move on, let Landon go. He was the one who had turned into a ghost, while I was right where he'd left me. Well, technically, I'd been the one to walk away last time. A distinction without a difference. If Landon wanted to find me, he knew exactly where I was.

As best I could figure, he'd brought Shania to Harmony, and then taken off. I had a feeling Harmony knew where he was though, and Landon had definitely been in touch with Travis, because my boss had made several overtures to ensure I had everything I needed, plus some, when it came to my pregnancy. He'd given me a raise and a promotion, too. At first, I'd been afraid those had come from Landon, but I had a friend in payroll look into it. She confirmed that my salary increase wasn't coming from Landon, and since I was working my ass off dealing with Verity Moore—a client everyone in Travis's firm was terrified of having to take over when I went on maternity leave—I wasn't about to turn it down.

I actually liked working with Verity. She was smart and ambitious. But she was also impulsive and unpredictable, and drawn to trouble like I was to pistachio ice cream.

Verity insisted she wanted to keep the drama in her life to a minimum, but every time I turned around I was putting out another fire she'd inadvertently started. Verity drove me absolutely crazy, but at least she kept me busy.

It was bad enough that I dreamed of Landon every night—awakening to an empty bed, feverish with need—but my mind ran to him every free minute, too.

I missed him so damn much.

If I could, I would have taken back every word I'd thrown at him. Not that they weren't true. Perhaps he would have responded better if they hadn't come in the form of an ambush.

Boom—I'm pregnant.

Boom—you're the father.

Boom—you're a useless addict.

Boom—I don't want you around.

How many men *wouldn't* have staggered away from the stench of my verbal vomit?

Not many. And not Landon.

But I wasn't going to think about the legendary Landon Cox today. No. Today I was going to have a nice ladies' lunch with my mom and Delaney. Tea and pasta and crème brûlée.

I'd been looking forward to it all week.

And by the time we left, I would know whether the baby swimming inside my belly was a boy or a girl. I'd finally asked Dr. Huang to send my mother the gender, so we would have something to celebrate today. Until recently, I'd been adamant about keeping it a surprise. Mostly because it felt wrong to find out without Landon by my side, and maybe because I had visions of him striding into the hospital when I went into labor, like a knight in shining armor.

Except that legends were just made up stories about people that didn't really exist.

Landon was merely a sperm donor, not a father.

He would never be *mine*.

And we would never be *his*.

The first sign today wouldn't be an intimate ladies' lunch with my mother and my best friend should have been the pack of paparazzi clustered around the entrance of the restaurant. I'd asked Delaney to pick someplace that wasn't known for being a celebrity hot spot, and she had.

They peered inside my car, quickly dismissing my Mini as unworthy of their interest. I parked, and if my mother hadn't practically leapt out of the passenger seat, I would have suggested we call Delaney and meet up elsewhere.

"Come on, sweetheart. I'm starving," she said, barely giving me time to put the key fob in my purse before locking her arm within mine and propelling me across the parking lot.

I heard a few camera clicks as we passed—insurance in case the paps found out later that we were worth the space on their memory cards.

"Hi, this is my daughter, Piper," my mother greeted the hostess, speaking so loudly I checked the woman's ears for a hearing aid. "We're here to meet her friend, Delaney, for a very special lunch."

I wriggled out of my mother's grasp, turning around just in time to see the exaggerated wink she attempted.

But the hostess took it in stride. "Right this way." I was about to point out that she hadn't grabbed any menus from the stack where she'd been standing, when I nearly peed my pants. Not that peeing my pants was an unusual occurrence these days. It happened nearly every time I sneezed. But having twenty people yell *Surprise!* did the trick, too.

Clutching my chest, I gaped at the crowd in front of me, realizing immediately why there were so many paparazzi outside. Verity Moore was grinning at me, nearly dwarfed by Jett and Dax on either side, and Delaney was wrapped in Shane's arms.

What happened to a ladies' lunch? My eyes skipped over the people in front of me. I noticed Travis and my father, too.

My heartbeat sped up, the saliva evaporating from my mouth as I looked for one other person. The hair that had risen up on the back of my neck meant he was here, even if I couldn't see him yet.

I spotted a couple I didn't recognize, and beside them—

Landon Cox.

A sudden ache in my chest clawed its way up my throat, squeezing tightly. But I couldn't take my eyes off him. Damn, the man was gorgeous. Painfully so.

But there was something different about him today. A substance behind the swagger. A seriousness behind his smile.

Like the legend had finally become more man than myth.

Landon

I'd had nothing but time these past few months.

Three and a half months.

Fourteen weeks.

Ninety-eight days.

2,352 hours.

141,120 minutes.

8,467, 200 seconds.

But at the sight of Piper Hastings…time stopped.

In a room full of people shouting, laughing, breathing—there was only her.

My Pippa.

Our eyes met and the energy in the room spiked, charging through me. If I looked down, I wouldn't have been surprised to see singe marks below my feet. But I wasn't looking anywhere but at the woman who stole my breath. The woman who made me feel *alive.*

My gaze dropped to her sweetly rounded belly.

Inside was a tiny human in the making, one half of each of us. A physical representation of the fact that we were, and always would be, connected.

Before I realized what I was doing, my feet were moving. One step after another, each one taking me closer to the love of my fucking life.

I stopped a few inches away from Piper, wanting so badly to touch her but feeling the weight of all that had been said the last time we spoke. And the weight of all that had gone unsaid for too long.

I could have sworn there was joy in her face, but the closer I got, the less sure I was. Mostly, I detected a guarded wariness. Like she was afraid of what my presence meant. Both for her and the baby she didn't yet trust me to know.

All those minutes and hours and days and weeks—I'd thought about what I wanted to say, practiced it in my mind and out loud. To mirrors and nothing but open air as I hiked in the desert.

But now, all my passionate declarations, my ardent apologies, they were gone. Erased so completely it was as if they'd never been there at all.

I had no words.

What I did have was a heart bursting with emotions. Love. Passion. Fear. Want. Joy. Desire.

What *didn't* I feel for this girl?

The older woman standing beside Piper gave her shoulder a squeeze and pushed her toward me. "Go talk for a few minutes. I'll get everyone settled and we'll wait for you."

I gave her a grateful smile and extended my hand toward Piper, pulling her to the other side of an enormous fish tank.

She yanked it away the second we were hidden from view, her face flushed, fury radiating from her eyes like blue flames. "How dare you just show up here after three months. Did you do this?" She gestured to the other side of the restaurant. "Did you have Delaney turn what was supposed to be simple lunch into some kind of welcome home party for you?"

I could only shake my head. "No, the party was Delaney's idea, I think. And she told me I wasn't allowed to come. I showed up on your mom's doorstep last week to beg for an invite."

"You went to see my mom—"

I dropped to my knees, pressing my forehead to the swell of her belly. "'Course I did. I want the world to know what I've finally fucking realized. Been waiting my whole life for one person, Piper. You. I love you, and I'm not letting you go, ever again."

My voice vibrated with longing as I looked up at the woman who had rocked my world—for the better. "I'm clean, Pippa. Ninety-eight days without a single pill or drink. You were right, I didn't need them. I was abusing them. I'll tell you everything you want to know, later. But I'm here now, and I'm not leaving. Ever. My world is on your axis, babe." The doubt clouding her beautiful blue eyes killed me. "Piper, I went away so I could come back. It nearly killed me, but I had to leave you. I had to leave…so I could learn how to *stay*."

She made a hiccupping noise in the back of her throat. "I don't know what to say. This feels like an ambush."

"Don't send me away yet. Give me a chance to prove that I've changed. Let me introduce you to the Coxes. And Jake, too."

"Your family—they're out there?"

I stood up, wrapping my hands around Piper's waist and pulling her into me. "Yeah. But my family starts right here." I gave her a squeeze, feeling a distinctive tap just below my belt buckle.

I looked down. "Was that…?"

Piper pressed her lips together, trying to stifle a laugh. "The baby?" Her brows arched upward, two shades darker than the thick waterfall of gold cascading down her shoulders. "Yes."

"Our baby." Another wave of adoration rocked into me. "I've never stopped loving you, Pippa, even when I couldn't admit it. Six years ago, I didn't realize—I don't think either of us realized—how little we really knew about each other. But I swear, you seeped into the marrow of my bones the very first time I held you in my arms. It's taken me longer than it should have to figure out that's exactly where you are, exactly where you'll always be. Inside me. A part of me." My hand curved around her belly. "Just like there's a part of me inside you right now."

Piper

My heart was beating wildly inside my chest, struggling to keep up with my frantic thoughts. Damn Landon for showing up when I least expected him...and for finally saying everything I'd ever wanted to hear.

Jesus, I was such a cliché.

The knocked-up pregnant girl who swooned the second her man came back around, making all kinds of empty promises.

Except...they didn't feel empty. Staring at Landon now, his face was full of regret. Full of hope, too. And he looked good, so damn good. Not just hot, but healthy. His gaze was clear and direct, searching mine for answers I didn't have.

Tears stung my eyes and I blinked them away. "I don't know, Landon."

One slipped down my cheek anyway and Landon lifted his other hand to my face, stepping close as he swept the tear away with his thumb. "Give me today, Pippa. I swear on my life I'll give you everything you've ever asked of me, everything you deserve. Honesty. Trust. Loyalty. Love."

I bit down on my lower lip, trying to fight the magnetic hold he had on me. "What if I'm not enough for you? I haven't been so far, what's changed?"

He winced, tiny worry lines spreading out from the corners of his eyes. "Not enough...That's what you think? You're more than enough. You're everything. What's changed is that I'm finally man enough to realize that I'm not a prisoner to my past. What's changed is that I've spent the last three and a half months—more than that—without you. And that's no life. It's nothing. Without you, *I'm* nothing."

His head dipped and he pressed his lips on mine as if sealing a promise. "Let me love you, Pippa. Let me love you today, and I swear on my life I'll earn every day that follows."

Terrified I was making the wrong choice, but believing in my soul I owed it to the baby inside of me to give Landon this chance, I took his hand and walked on trembling legs to the other side of the restaurant. This time, I barely noticed the small crowd of family and friends.

Because all I saw was a sea of pink balloons. One in particular caught my eye, its sparkling letters right in front.

it's a girl!

Epilogue

Piper

Worshipping a porcelain god is infinitely more preferable than invoking the names of everything holy while in stirrups.

"Jesus Fucking Christ, get her out of me!"

They've been trying. I know they've been trying—because so have I. For the past nineteen hours.

Nineteen hours.

Machines beeped and buzzed as the nurses cheered me on. The doctor was nowhere to be seen, because I still wasn't ready to push. Correction. *I* was ready to push. My little firefly-turned-watermelon, not so much.

I squeezed Landon's hand in a white-knuckled grip. "Please, reach up and grab your daughter. Pull her out. I can't do this, I can't."

The whites of Landon's eyes were showing as he leaned down

to kiss my forehead. I was scaring him. I was scaring myself. "You're almost there—"

"Fuck almost there. You do some of the heavy lifting. Get. Her. Out." Blood throbbed against my eardrums, pulsing hot within my veins. I felt like a parked car with a brick on the accelerator. Engine revving, going nowhere.

We were in Cedars-Sinai. And even though a part of me was worried being back here would set off memories of Landon's own hospital stay, along with it the urge to self-medicate with prescription drugs, I knew I was being irrational. He'd been my rock ever since showing up at my surprise baby shower. He wouldn't leave me now, not when I needed him the most.

I'd been in labor for so long that my parents had already arrived from New York and were both outside in the maternity ward's waiting room. Landon went out to see them not long ago and he said they were holding hands. My parents, holding hands? It almost made me want to see for myself.

Another contraction hit, a deep twist and pull from the depths of my engorged belly. They had turned down the epidural over an hour ago, saying that I would be pushing any minute. That it would all be over soon.

It. Wasn't. Over.

I nearly bowed off the bed in pain, shrieking as I squeezed Landon's hand tighter. If it didn't end soon, there was a good chance I'd inflict more damage to his grip than any drunken backflip.

The contraction had barely faded before there was another one, right on its heels. And another one after that. The room blurred, and even Landon's face—the most perfectly put-together collection of angles and planes and hollows—went vague.

The lock holding me to this room, to Landon, to the overwhelming, unrelenting pain simply unclasped. I was loose, untethered. Closing my eyes, I drifted away from the bright lights and sharp sounds, from the anxious tone of Landon's voice as he called my name.

I tried to resist the darkness that gathered at the very edge of my consciousness, remain connected to the man I loved more than life itself. Memories flashed, like shooting stars across an inky sky. Cutting the cake at our baby shower, so filled with love and hope and fear I couldn't even taste it.

The look on Landon's face as the crib he'd spent the entire day building, using a newly purchased drill and all of urban dictionary's foulest curses, fell apart just as he was proudly showing it off.

Landon and Jake drumming together, side-by-side in the music studio of his home. *Our* home.

Breakfasts and lunches and dinners. Long walks, longer hikes. With his parents, with Jake, with Delaney and Shane and Travis and Jett and Dax. With my parents, too.

The first time he said *I love you*, and all the times after. So many times, so often, I'd taken to saying *I know* back. Because he'd proved it to me every day, in a thousand different ways.

And I did—I loved Landon Cox with every atom of my being. I craved his touch every night, and woke up the next morning wanting more.

The last trimester of any pregnancy felt like forever, but in my case, forever wasn't long enough. Landon and I spent every moment rediscovering each other, rebuilding our own relationship and strengthening the bonds we shared with family and friends.

I held on to those memories, following their bright arcs as they broke apart above me. The last thing I saw, before I saw nothing at all, was the way Landon had looked at me when I felt the first twinge in my belly yesterday. Gone was the pain and reluctance that had filled his eyes less than a year ago. He didn't have to force a cocky, smug grin anymore. His confidence was quieter now, and one hundred percent real.

I'd given that to him. And now I was about to give him a daughter.

For Landon, I was *enough*.

More than enough.

I was his everything.

And he was mine.

Mine.

Landon

My house and grounds were once again overrun with people, my driveway bursting with cars. None of them had been invited by text, or were there to repair damage.

This crowd was definitely invite-only, and those invitations had been handwritten calligraphy drawn on heavy cardstock, delivered not by postman but by private messenger.

One had even been delivered to Adam. He and Piper had reconciled after Luci's birth, and I suppose if Piper wanted to stay friends with her ex-boyfriend, I couldn't complain much when he had a boyfriend of his own.

Besides, today I would become her husband.

Piper and I were tying the knot and I was never going to let her go.

Today was a day that almost didn't happen, for too many reasons to name. But the latest, and most devastating, was that I didn't think Piper would be alive to see it. Even now, as I stand at the end of a white satin aisle, the rolling carpet of Los Angeles falling away to my right, Shane, Jett, and Dax to my left, fear grips me by the throat when I recall the maelstrom of Luci's birth.

I've never known fear like the moment Piper slipped away from me. One second, she was right there with me, sarcastic and spirited and *alive*. And the next, the light that shone in her eyes was gone, extinguished. I was pushed from the room, feeling like my heart was being ripped out from my chest. And then the question that wasn't a question. *If we can only save one…*

How do you choose between your heart and your soul?

Just bring Piper back to me.

Before Luci was Luci, she was the reason Piper was rushed into surgery. The reason I might lose my Pippa.

Right then, before Luci was Luci, I hated her.

Hours later, the doctor returned. *You have a daughter. A healthy—*

Piper, how is she?

There was a tightening of his lips and I felt something inside me crack. A deep fissure no amount of time would ever heal. *Touch and go, but she's hanging on.*

Before Luci was Luci, I didn't even want to see her. At Piper's bedside, holding her limp hand, searching her sallow skin for signs of sunshine, I was torn apart by grief and rage. The nurses hovered, asking if I wanted to hold my daughter. If we'd chosen a name. *No* and *no*.

In the end, Piper's parents were the ones to hold and comfort Luci in the NICU. They fed Luci her first bottles and changed her diapers.

Piper didn't open her eyes for three days.

Three fucking days.

I didn't leave her side, I couldn't. Even unconscious, I felt her soul twisted up with my own, heard my name in every one of her breaths.

A rippling sigh of appreciation swept over the crowd and drew me out of the memory. Our flower girl, Devon, had just finished emptying her basket of rose petals and Piper appeared at the far end of the pool, her gorgeous blonde hair loose and flowing around her bare shoulders, dressed all in white. Instead of carrying flowers, she held our daughter. More beautiful than any bouquet.

Piper had moved in with me before Luci's birth, and after she was discharged from the hospital, her parents had stayed with us for a month. It was time that they needed to become the family they'd never been. And when they met her at the other side of the drawbridge that had been erected over the pool, its surface now strewn with flowers, I knew they had become my family, too.

My eyes dropped from Piper to Luci, and my heart, already so full, nearly broke through my chest. Once Piper had emerged from her coma, and I was assured she would be okay, I had finally trudged to the NICU where the most vulnerable infants were kept. Luci hadn't been premature, but her birth had been traumatic and she'd been born with a fever.

Piper's father had been in one of the chairs, holding her, when I walked into the room. He got to his feet slowly, passing my child into my arms. Shock and love had raced through my veins as I stared into her angelic face, a nearly paralyzing rush. I squeezed my eyes shut, not realizing he was still there until I felt his hand clamp down on my shoulder. "I've spent the past quarter century blind to the best parts of my life. Don't be like me, son. Even when it hurts, you've got to open your eyes."

I swallowed hard. He was right. I had two souls to keep safe now, two hearts that were as vital to me as my own. More, even. Unable to speak, I blinked my eyes open and managed a shallow nod, catching a whiff of my daughter's downy soft skin.

Reaching a tentative hand, I rested my palm against the swell of her back, the crook of her elbow, the plush padding of her tiny, tiny diaper. Planting lingering kisses on her head, the thinnest wisps of blonde hair—more platinum than gold—tickled my lips. I turned my face, rubbing my cheek against her scalp. Her newborn skin was like brushed velvet, and she weighed next to nothing on my chest.

"Firefly," I murmured, nuzzling my nose into the crook of her neck. The fissure that had cracked open when I thought I'd lost Piper broke open a little further, revealing a secret reservoir of love and contentment I'd never known existed. But it was there, full to overflowing. Pure and potent. "Our little firefly."

"What did you say?"

I startled at the quiet French-accented voice, glancing over at a nurse attending to a baby in an enclosed bassinette.

"Sorry, I didn't mean to interrupt. I thought maybe you had a name for your daughter."

My heart sank. No. Piper had only woken up briefly. I hadn't thought to ask her. "Not yet. Just the nickname we used for her. Firefly."

The woman's face registered surprise, and she pointed to a bassinette labeled COX—BABY GIRL. There was a Post-it note affixed to the side. "Luciole." I said the word hesitantly, unsure of the pronunciation.

She nodded. "Even with the dim lights, your daughter's hair practically glows. I sometimes give the babies names—just for me, so I have something to call them when I take care of them here. It means 'firefly.'"

I said the name again, this time shortening it. "Luci."

The next day, when Piper was well enough to visit her daughter for the first time, she spotted the note immediately. "Luci." The perfect name for the light of our lives.

Now Piper handed our daughter to her mother and I shook her father's hand. They sat in the front row, on the other side from Mike, Sarah, and Jake. I winked at Jake just before gathering my bride in my arms. "Fuck, I love you," I groaned against her lips, not caring that we were surrounded by people.

From the look in her eyes, Piper didn't care either. Her arms wound around my neck, lips pulling into a seductive smile. "I know."

Travis cleared his throat before she could say anything else. "You're supposed to kiss *after* your I do's." Rather than a preacher we'd never met, Piper had wanted Travis to marry us, so he'd gotten some online certification that sounded bogus but as long as Piper was happy, I was happy. I'd finally figured out that life was a hell of a lot brighter basking in the glow of Piper's smile than in any spotlight. Not that I didn't love my time on stage. I craved that, too. But, like I'd told Piper a few months ago—my world was on her axis.

I didn't want it any other way.

Author's Note

Piper represents an all too common problem in our society—women clinging to the idea that they have to be perfect to be worthy of love.

No one is perfect.

To everyone reading this note—it is our differences and imperfections that make us who we are. Please, embrace them.

Life would be painfully boring if we were all the same!

I would love to know your thoughts on *Rock Legend*! If you have a chance to leave a review, I would be incredibly grateful. Please send the link to me (tara@taraleighbooks.com)—I'd be honored to send you a personal thank-you note!

You can keep in touch at www.taraleighbooks.com, and you can also follow me on Amazon, Facebook, BookBub, Goodreads, Instagram, and Twitter.

Happy reading!
xoxo Tara

Don't miss Dax and Verity's story in *Rock Rebel*,
coming in fall 2018

Chapter One

Dax

Being back in New York City had me on edge.

These were my old stomping grounds. I'd been born and raised here, in the rarified air of the Upper East Side. Attending LaGuardia High School of the Performing Arts, then Juilliard.

I wasn't supposed to become a rock star. Until six years ago, I hadn't played anything but classical music.

Which was when wearing a suit became the exception rather than the norm.

My fingers fumbled with the knot of my tie as I swore softly at my reflection. I wasn't looking forward to the next few hours. Only within the snobby circles of classical musicians was a multi-platinum, Grammy Award–winning musician looked on with disdain, as if playing sold-out arenas filled with thousands of adoring fans was some sort of rebellious phase.

With a last tug at my collar, I left my hotel room. Heading down the hall, my phone buzzed in my hand.

Shane: Dude, you're in NYC!

Me: Yeah, just for a couple of days.

Shane: You free tomorrow night?

Me: Not sure yet.

Shane: K. If you are, come over.

Me: The new place, right?

Shane: Yes. Bring whatever chick you're not telling me about.

I smirked. Now that Shane was head over fucking balls in love, he wanted everyone else to be, too.

Me: I'll let you know.

The elevator doors slid open and I darted aside just in time to avoid the kid who burst from the car and streaked down the hall, someone I assumed to be his harried nanny chasing him. With a sigh, I shoved my phone in my pocket and jabbed the button for the lobby. It didn't change color. I pushed it again. Nope, still bright yellow. Realizing that every button was lit up, I swore softly. No wonder the kid had run, he must have pushed every damn button before he took off.

"Hold the elevator!"

My arm shot out instinctively, my years in Manhattan training me to hold the elevator for any and all who asked, because you never knew when you would need the favor returned. Karma was a bitch best left unprovoked.

Something that kid had yet to learn.

"Thanks." At first glance, the girl that burst breathlessly into the elevator car could have been seventeen or twenty-seven. Her hair was piled into a messy bun on top of her head, her bright green gaze clear-eyed and direct, and she was wearing running sneakers and a thick sweatshirt that would have been too big on me. It was also unzipped, revealing a tight tank top and tiny bike shorts.

Goddamn. Just looking at her had my pulse stutter for a few beats, then take off at a gallop.

Her body didn't belong to a teenager, that was for sure.

She pulled one of her earbuds out, wisps of red hair framing a heart-shaped face. Messy and disheveled. "Can you press the one for the gym?"

Sexy as fuck.

I jerked my chin at the lit-up display on my side of the elevator. "Apparently we're on a local tonight."

Her full lips, unadorned by even a swipe of gloss, twitched up at one corner, revealing a dimple etched into her left cheek. I felt a tug of desire deep in my stomach, and a ridiculous curiosity to know if it was part of a matched set. "Courtesy of the little boy who ran out of here like he'd just shotgunned a can of Coke?"

"That'd be my guess."

She broke into a full-fledged grin. I stared back, feeling like I'd won the lottery. Dimples, plural. "Knew it," she said as the doors closed and the elevator trundled down a flight.

I should have kept my mouth closed when she looked back

down at her phone, but I wanted to feel her eyes on me again. "Don't get too cocky, that one was obvious."

She raised her head, a look of surprise on her face. Her *familiar* face.

Did I know this girl?

The elevator doors opened and closed. Again. And again. And again. With each floor, the energy in the confined space shifted, becoming charged by something I didn't quite understand. The smile that had played on her lips disappeared, the bow of her mouth drawing tight. She crossed her arms, clearly piqued. "So any girl that dares to voice a correct assumption is cocky?"

The redhead was more spitfire than leprechaun.

Lust charged down my spine like the bolt of a Taser. "Only when it's too easy."

"Easy, huh? How about you give me a hard one then?"

Oh, I could give her something *hard* all right.

She arched a brow that was the same red as the hair on her head, which immediately begged another question…

"Whenever you get your mind out of my pants, of course."

I forced a gruff chuckle. What the fuck was wrong with me? Two hours in this city and I'd transformed into the horny kid I'd been when I left. "What kind of question are you looking for?"

She changed the subject. "I'll bet I can guess your sign."

"My what?"

"Your zodiac sign." I must have still looked confused, because some of her irritation smoothed away as she leaned against the dark mirrored glass at her back. "You don't read your horoscope?"

"Ah, no."

"You're not exactly making this a challenge." There was something tenacious about her stance, the sharp set of her jaw. Like she had something to prove to me.

Or maybe just to herself.

"That what you're into?"

She stared at me with one finger pressed against her lips, those emerald eyes of hers narrowed at the corners. I ground my teeth, trying to tamp down the want flooding my veins with heat. Unsuccessfully.

"I was torn between Aries and Taurus, but you settled it for me. Aries, definitely." Holding her phone with both hands, she attacked it with her thumbs. "Born between March twenty-first and April nineteenth, no?"

I frowned. "How—"

"Oh please, you're a Ram through and through." She flashed her screen at me. "Want to know your horoscope?"

"Not re—"

"Your love of the chase is your greatest weakness, but what you seek is already inside yourself. Today is a day to appreciate the road taken and go where you heart leads you."

I snorted, jabbing at the DOOR CLOSE button. "And that's supposed to mean something to me?"

She shrugged. "Up to you."

I was silent for a minute, watching our descent on the screen above the doors. The redhead stepped forward as the door opened on the third floor, the scent of vanilla and cloves rising off her fair skin. My mouth watered.

She was close enough to touch, and my fingers twitched with the temptation of freeing her hair from the band holding it captive. She glanced up, meeting my eyes. "This is me." Her voice was soft, almost breathless, even though she'd long since recovered from her sprint down the hall.

The doors opened. "So, if I'm a Ram, what are you?"

She crossed the elevator's threshold, and turned back to face me, her elegantly sculpted features embellished by a mischievous half-smile. "Wouldn't you like to know."

The elevator doors closed before I could pull my balls from my mouth and say anything else.

But she was right. I *would* like to know.

It was a fucking problem.

Verity

What's gotten into me?

Was I flirting...with Dax Hughes? Granted, in a dark suit, tugging at his collar, pulling at his sleeves, his normally tousled hair slicked back, he'd been more approachable than the rocker I'd seen on stage and in magazines. That Dax, with his bedroom eyes and shredded jeans, his inked skin and aloof expression, was every inch the cocky celebrity I made every effort to avoid. But today, the prick of desire had stung my skin with every glance, as sharp and distinct as the snap of a rubber band.

Clearly, he hadn't recognized me. Not that I could blame him. Without so much as a swipe of lip gloss, dressed in workout gear, I wasn't exactly looking my best.

Replaying the exchange my head, I scanned my key card at the door and groaned. *Wouldn't you like to know?*

So embarrassing. The man was Dax Hughes, for Christ's sake. He could have any girl he wanted—what would he want with me?

Verity Moore, disgraced pop princess.

The description followed my name so often, if I died tomorrow it would probably be carved into my headstone.

Why not? It was true enough.

At least the gym was empty, and I could wallow in my mortification alone.

I pumped up the incline on the treadmill, setting the speed faster than I normally ran. I welcomed the sweat breaking out on my forehead, the shortness of my breaths, the strain in my muscles. There was an emptiness to the exertion that I craved, a zone where my body detached from my mind.

It took a couple of miles to get there, but when I did, I felt invincible, unstoppable. Exactly the headspace I needed to be in to win over the cynical industry execs tomorrow morning.

Otherwise my head would be buzzing with worried thoughts. I could only imagine what they'd heard about me. Or worse—what they'd seen.

I ran and ran and ran.

And when finally the burn in my legs and my chest were too painful to ignore, I pumped up the speed and ran another mile.

At least, I would have, if MOM didn't suddenly appear on my phone, cutting off the music coming through my ear buds. "Damn it."

I slammed the emergency stop button and accepted her Face-Time call, wiping my sweaty skin with a towel. "Hi—"

"Where are you?"

"I'm working out. What's up?" I would have preferred to ignore her, but I'd learned that the only way to keep physical distance between us was to be reachable by phone.

"I can see that, but I asked where you were."

"I'm in New York."

The image wobbled, as if she'd grabbed her device, and then my screen was filled with a close-up of my mother's face, an age-progressed replica of my own. "What are you doing in New York?"

"I told you, just a few meetings to see what's out there right now." I uncapped my S'well bottle and took a long drink.

"You're going to see Jack, I hope."

Jack Lester. I nearly spit out my water. "No, I'm not."

"Well, I don't understand why you wouldn't. Millie called me the other day, she—"

"Millie called you?" I clutched my stomach, the water I'd barely managed to swallow transforming into curdled milk.

"Yes. Such a sweet girl. She said Jack is developing another show and that you would be perfect for it."

"Absolutely not."

Her features hardened. "Verity, I have been more than patient with you, but I am not only your mother, I am your manager. It's time for you to get back to work."

"That's exactly what I'm doing," I interjected, then immediately regretted it. I hadn't told my mother that I signed with Travis Taggert. And I wasn't going to—until I had a contract in my hands and money in a bank account without her name on it. My mother couldn't know I was taking control of my own career, of my own life. Yet.

I had planned my escape as meticulously as an abused wife fleeing her monster of a husband.

"That's it, I'm getting on the next plane. You can't make important decisions without me."

I already have. "Mom, that's ridiculous. I'm not making decisions, I just want to show my face around, let people know I'm ready to get back to work. I'll let you know how it goes, and we can strategize next steps." I'd already warned Travis that those next steps might involve sending my mother a cease-and-desist letter when she found out she'd been fired.

She squinted at me. "Well, if you run into Jack and Millie, be nice. They've been so good to you, Verity, and I think Millie feels like you've taken them for granted."

"Once day I'll be sure to let them know just how grateful I am, don't worry." I nearly choked over the words. "But I don't think I'll run into them here."

"Why not? They're in New York right now, too."

Blood rushed to my head and I flung out a hand to grip the treadmill's sidebar. "What?"

"They're showing a new script to the networks, I think. Or maybe they're trying to lock down a record label first." She shook her head and sighed. "One or the other, I can't remember which."

The urge to reach through my phone and choke her was almost overwhelming. "I—I really have to take a shower now. I'll let you know how things go."

"You do that," she said.

Anxiety spiraled through my nerves as I sat down on the floor and leaned against the side of the treadmill. I opened my browser window, my trembling fingers managing to get Jack's name right after several tries. On the second page of my Google search, I found what I was looking for. An article about his new project—another music-driven show-within-a-show concept. Just like his last—the one I'd starred in a few years ago.

I'd move into a homeless shelter before I accepted a role in one of Jack's productions ever again.

I hauled myself to my feet and left the gym, bypassing the elevator in favor of the stairs even though my sneakers felt like they'd been made of lead. I was a sweaty mess, and the thought of someone's eyes scraping my skin was painful.

My mind was untethered, bouncing from Dax to Jack and the ghosts of boyfriends past that called Manhattan home, painful memories twisting my stomach into knots. With each step, I felt pulled backward through time, felt the touch and press of unwanted hands, the harsh male cackle of intimidation assaulting my ears. My lungs tightened, each of my short, shallow breaths echoing against the cement.

Needing a distraction, I pulled my phone back out of my pocket and opened the app I had used with Dax. I might as well admit that I hadn't actually guessed his sign. The fact was, ever since Travis had floated the idea of me opening for Nothing But Trouble's next tour, I had done my homework. Dax was born on April first. April Fool's Day. It had stuck in my memory. But the man I met in the elevator was no fool, even if he didn't know anything about the zodiac.

You have a lot on your mind and the secrets you keep are preventing you from thinking clearly. To move forward, you must learn to let go of the past.

I read my own horoscope three times before shoving my phone back in my pocket. Maybe it really was nothing but a crock. True, I had a lot on my mind, and plenty of secrets to keep, but I was definitely moving forward.

Because there was no way in hell I was going back.

About the Author

TARA LEIGH attended Washington University in St. Louis and Columbia Business School in New York, and worked on Wall Street and Main Street before "retiring" to become a wife and mother. When the people in her head became just as real as the people in her life, she decided to put their stories on paper. Tara currently lives in Fairfield County, Connecticut, with her husband, children, and fur-baby, Pixie. She is represented by Jessica Alvarez of BookEnds.

Learn more at:

www.taraleighbooks.com
Twitter @TaraLeighBooks
Facebook.com/TaraLeighAuthor

You Might Also Like...

What to expect when you're royally expecting

In five years of marriage to Dylan Hale—the hottest (not to mention most deliciously insatiable) duke in England—I've learned one cardinal rule: *Never* say "no" to the Queen. Her orders? I'm to be the matron of honor at the royal wedding of the century...which is, coincidentally, my due date. Dylan's plan is to seduce me into an early labor to avoid this royal ruckus. So now I'm caught between the Queen's command...and my sexy duke's desire.

No celebrity secret stays buried for long in *USA Today* bestselling author Leslie A. Kelly's sexy and suspenseful Hollywood Heat series.

A cold case is suddenly too hot to handle

Police officer Rowan Winchester wants nothing to do with his family's A-list Hollywood legacy. Working with the LAPD is his way of atoning for the Winchesters' dark and secretive past. And, right now, the last thing Rowan needs is true-crime novelist Evie Fleming nosing around the most notorious deaths in Los Angeles—including the ones that haunt his own family.

To make things worse, he's torn between wanting the wickedly smart writer out of his city...and just plain *wanting* her.

While researching her latest book, Evie suspects that a dangerous new killer is prowling the City of Angels. Now she just has to convince the devastatingly handsome cop that she's *right*. Soon Evie and Rowan are working together to try to find the killer, even as their attraction ignites.

But when the killer hones in on Evie, she and Rowan realize they'll have to solve this case fast if they want to stay alive.

Fans of *New York Times* bestselling authors Samantha Young, Sylvia Day, and E. L. James won't want to miss this modern—and deliciously wicked—take on a classic fairy tale...*She never should have come here.* Twice a week, Lily Moore comes to work for me, stealing my breath with her light and beauty and sweetness. She doesn't know the dangerous path she's on. All she knows is that I am a reclusive artist living on a crumbling estate. That I am scarred, broken by life. *A beast...*

Lily ignites a hunger unlike anything I've known, one that could shatter the isolated world I live in. Even as I see the same longing for me in her oh-so-blue eyes, I know she belongs to another—one who does not deserve her. But it's just a matter of time before the tension between us breaks. For this beast will have what he desires. To hell with the consequences. This is *my* world...and I will claim my beauty.

CPSIA information can be obtained
at www.ICGtesting.com
Printed in the USA
LVHW09s2327270718
585090LV00001B/41/P